THE
WOMAN
IN OUR
HOUSE

OTHER BOOKS BY ANDREW HART

Lies That Bind Us

Other books written as A.J. Hartley

The Mask Of Atreus

On The Fifth Day

What Time Devours

Tears Of The Jaguar

Steeplejack

Firebrand (Steeplejack 2)

Guardian (Steeplejack 3)

Cold Bath Street

Act Of Will

Will Power

Cathedrals Of Glass: Planet Of Blood And Ice

Cathedrals Of Glass: Valkrys Wakes

Darwen Arkwright And The Peregrine Pact

Darwen Arkwright And The Insidious Bleck

Darwen Arkwright And The School Of Shadows

With David Hewson

Macbeth, A Novel

Hamlet, Prince Of Denmark, A Novel

With Tom DeLonge

Sekret Machines: Chasing Shadows

Sekret Machines: A Fire Within

THE
WOMAN
IN OUR
HOUSE

A NOVEL

ANDREW HART

LAKE UNION
PUBLISHING

Published by Lake Union Publishing, Seattle

www.apub.com

Amazon, the Amazon logo, and Lake Union Publishing are trademarks of Amazon.com, Inc., or its affiliates.

ISBN-13: 9781542092777 (hardcover)
ISBN-10: 1542092779 (hardcover)
ISBN-13: 9781503905443 (paperback)
ISBN-10: 1503905446 (paperback)

Cover design by Faceout Studio, Jeff Miller

Printed in the United States of America

First edition

For my family. Always.

Hell is empty and all the devils are here.

—William Shakespeare, The Tempest

Chapter One

ANNA

I always thought of happiness as something yet to come, a goal or target I might reach, or that might reach me, when all the wrinkles of the present were smoothed out, the loops of absence closed, so that contentment would blossom through my life like spring in a cold place. Till then, happiness was always just around the next corner, out of reach, and endlessly deferred as a necessary condition of ordinary life.

Which is not to say I was unhappy. Just that I was still waiting for real happiness, looking for it, like a woman standing by the shore of a wide, gray sea, waiting for a glimpse of distant sails on the horizon.

Stupid, perhaps. But it felt real, wet and cold as that great sea, though I knew it was also just a habit of thought, familiar as the crib where my daughter sleeps, its sugar-maple rail smooth beneath my fingers. I waited for happiness like I waited for dawn on the long, restless nights after Grace was born, knowing that before it came, she would wake, hungry and crying, and I would have to get up to feed her in the dark.

Then came the solar eclipse: August 21, 2017. And it changed my life.

I didn't know it at the time, of course. I had dutifully purchased the eclipse-watching glasses—making sure they were rated ISO 12312-2, as advised in the *Charlotte Observer*—and had tried to make it feel like an event for Veronica, our eldest, but I had begun to find the country's swelling obsession with the thing a bit baffling. When I learned that even with something close to 98 percent of what the radio announcers were calling "totality," it still wouldn't actually get dark where I was, my enthusiasm took another hit.

The day of the event, I almost forgot about it. Veronica, who had been sulking over how much of my attention Grace had been getting, lay on her bed and fell asleep, a few feet from her finally silent sister. I stood in the doorway watching them sleep, wondering how to use this unexpected break in the middle of the day, and was suddenly struck by how dim the room had gotten. Curiously, the sky beyond the curtains still looked bright and blue, but indoors, it felt like evening. I went downstairs, absently picking up the flimsy cardboard glasses with the black lenses for which I had paid an outrageous twenty dollars each, and stepped outside.

Only then did the full strangeness of the thing hit me. There was a constant, excited chirping of crickets and cicadas, but the birds had fallen completely, uncannily silent. The light was . . . hard to describe, flat and tinted somehow. The leaves of the dogwood in the front yard cast odd semicircular shadows and left ghostly afterimages on the concrete driveway. The sun itself seemed distorted, and when I looked up in my absurd glasses, I saw how it had squeezed down to a mere sicklelike sliver, golden bright around the upper edge of the dark sphere that was the moon. I actually gasped, feeling the ancient and alarming bewilderment of the thing, the unnaturalness that had generated all those myths they had been talking about on the radio, the dragons and other monsters that people had thought were trying to devour the sun.

This, I thought, was an event, after all, and I knew I should get Veronica up to show her. The impulse soured in my head. She would be grumpy at being woken, and would be as likely to shrug the thing off as unworthy of her attention as she was to celebrate it or share my awed and watchful silence. Guiltily, I realized that I didn't want to risk it. That I would rather experience the moment by myself, relishing the rare stillness for what it was, and keeping it as a private treasure. I got so few of those these days. I had been a professional, even a rising star. Now, I was a wife and mother. I had been pushed to the side of my own life, my star eclipsed. That produced another gasp—not awe this time—but a startled, even horrified, realization.

Perhaps happiness was not something I was moving toward, something coming very slowly but inexorably closer day by day. Perhaps it was both distant and locked into a separate orbit of its own, forever apart, never drawing nearer but moving as I did. Always on the other side of the moon.

Eclipsed.

I have thought back to that moment many times since, wishing it had been different. Perhaps if I had taken Veronica out with me, or stayed indoors in the first place, things would have been different.

But then again, maybe not.

The eclipse was, after all, only a metaphor. My brain would have found another eventually.

In any case, the following morning, it came out. I hadn't planned it. It just slid out when I wasn't looking and rolled out into view like a dropped ball.

"I want to go back to work."

The thought that I had been pushed aside—*eclipsed*—had been steeping in my head all night, soaking into my consciousness as if waiting for the moment when its truth would drive out the guilt that came with it. I'm not sure that moment ever came, but it became at least familiar.

Josh looked up from his cereal, his spoon hovering two inches from his chin. His brow wrinkled as it always did when he was choosing between things to say, gauging what I was hoping to hear.

"OK," he said. "Great. You can go part-time, work from home, right? You need more help around the house?"

It was almost the right answer, but he hadn't fully grasped what I was saying. I spelled it out.

"I mean, I want to go full-time again. I can still work from home, but I'll have to go back to New York from time to time, and we'll need real help here. A nanny."

Again, the hovering cereal spoon, the wrinkled brow.

"You've been thinking about this for a while," he said. It was almost a question, but not one I needed to answer. "Anna, you really think . . . I mean, the girls? You'd be OK with someone else looking after them?"

Our daughters, Grace and Veronica, are nine months and three and a half, respectively. I have been home alone with them since they were born.

I love my kids. I would walk through fire for them. But in the last two months, I have become convinced that I would be a better and more attentive mother if I was not with them all the time.

Does that sound self-serving?

Perhaps, but I still think it's true. I'm a capable woman. Not a genius or a prodigy by any means, but capable. I did well in school, got an English degree from Dartmouth and an MBA from Boston University. I interned with Ramkins and Deale, literary agents in New York, and became a junior agent five years ago. My husband, Josh, is in finance. For the first two years of our marriage, he worked in New York. Not on Wall Street but close enough, and I thought that was where we were going to stay, working our way from a small Queens apartment to something a little grander on the Upper West Side.

But my husband is good at his job, and one of the consequences of competence is promotion. It had never occurred to me that that might mean moving to an entirely different part of the country at a moment's notice, but that was what happened. Four years ago, he came home with a choice: stay where we were, doing the same jobs for the same money for at least two more years, or take a leadership position in Charlotte, North Carolina—where your money goes a lot further—for a significantly increased salary.

It was tempting, but we were settled and liked being so. Still, we forced ourselves to take the full week he had been given to make his decision, and on that Wednesday, we were ambushed by something unforeseen.

I was pregnant.

Suddenly, we weren't looking at being settled either way, and the move to Charlotte became not simply a job but a massive shift in lifestyle, in our sense of who and what we were. When people—Josh included—had asked before if I wanted kids, my answer was always the same: not yet. But confronted by my unexpected and unplanned pregnancy, it changed. I wanted a family, and for reasons I couldn't explain, I wanted it now.

Charlotte seemed as good a place as any to begin.

I didn't leave Ramkins and Deale, but I went on hiatus, passing my fledgling client list on to my colleagues and asking that I be taken off the website and the internal LISTSERV. After years of working my way toward my dream job, I put it aside without so much as a second thought, sure in my bones that the tiny life beginning inside me was all I would ever need.

I continued to feel that once Veronica was born. We moved into a sprawling mansion of a house in the swanky Myers Park region of Charlotte, a neighborhood where we were surrounded by bankers, traders, lawyers, doctors, and their largely stay-at-home wives. For a while, it was good. Veronica was perfect, a portion of myself and not myself, of Josh and not Josh, who fit into our lives like she had been destined to be there. I had worried that I might not feel connected to her, the way parents should, but those fears had evaporated the moment I held her. To be with her felt right in ways nothing else ever had.

So when I learned I was pregnant again two years after she was born, I was delighted. I knew the logistics of raising two children at once would be challenging, but I felt more than ready. I felt euphoric. But though I reveled in my second pregnancy, I'd be lying if I said it was as easy. The mystery and excitement I had felt the first time was replaced by anxiety about all the things that could go wrong, and when the doctors put me on bed rest for the final two months before delivery, I grew increasingly bored, uncomfortable, and restless. When I realized that even Veronica had stopped being a comfort, my low-grade apprehension spiked, becoming something urgent and frightened, like a trapped animal. Despite everything I had been through, I was going to be a bad mother, after all.

I wasn't. Not really. But I felt the constant tug of exasperation, of exhaustion, and it didn't stop with Grace's birth. Quite the opposite, in fact. While Veronica had been a quiet, easy baby, Grace wouldn't sleep through the night for months and settled into a routine that was fussy, prone to tears and to not eating, so that for a time when she was four months old, she was briefly hospitalized for failing to thrive.

It felt like failure. My failure.

Josh did his part, particularly when asked, traveling as little as possible, keeping the late-night drinks meetings to a minimum, and taking his turn walking the babies in their two-seater buggy. But there was only so much he could do, and after a month of him gamely getting up to keep me company while I nursed Grace, I told him—less kindly than I meant—that it was a waste of time and wasn't achieving anything. The next day, seeing the hurt in his tired eyes, I apologized, but the point had been made. I couldn't do this well by myself, but no one could do it with me.

When Josh suggested I get help, I thought he meant psychiatric. I reacted badly and then, embarrassed by how quickly my mind had gone to my well-being rather than Grace's, continued to sulk and bicker with him as he tried to clarify that he had meant someone to cook or mind the children for a couple of hours each day. We had, like everyone else in the neighborhood, a cleaning team who came in once every couple of weeks. Having grown up doing the cleaning myself, I couldn't turn the job entirely over to professionals, though most of the wives who lived close by did, even though hardly any of them worked. But I resisted. I knew I was doing a lousy job, but knowing that didn't help.

It was no wonder Josh responded so cautiously to my sudden desire for a nanny.

"Is this entirely about the girls?" he asked.

"As opposed to?"

"I don't know." He ate a mouthful of Cheerios to buy himself time. "I mean, do you want to work, or do you just not want to be responsible for the girls all the time by yourself?"

I felt my back arch and my face set, though I knew it was a fair question. There was just no way to ask it without sounding dissatisfied with my performance as Mommy.

"I think," I said, my voice hard enough that I decided to take a breath and start over. "I think I need to be something other than . . ."

"A wet nurse," he completed for me, when the words dried up.

"No!" I said. "Yes. Maybe. I don't know. I miss work. I miss reading and being around adults, even if it's only in my head. There's only so much Bob the Builder, Caillou, and Thomas the fucking Tank Engine I can stand, Josh. Sorry," I said, realizing with a shock how raw that had sounded, then realizing—worse—that as my voice had gone up a notch and threatened to break, tears had started to form in my eyes.

"Thomas the fucking Tank Engine?" he said. And then he was laughing, and I tried to be mad at him but couldn't be. I started laughing, and then he said we'd talk about it all when he got home from work, and I felt like a bridge had been crossed or a weight had been shifted off my shoulders. Something. I felt better. Better than I had for weeks or, God help me, months even.

It was a glorious day. Grace slept between feedings while Veronica colored and ran around in the garden. It was breezy and the sun was bright, but not as relentlessly hot and humid as it had been. The crepe myrtle at the front was in full bloom, vermillion flowers improbably vivid against the rich waxy green of the leaves. Everyone talked about the magnolias in the South, but I had been dazzled by the crepe myrtles, the full-on tropical intensity of those blooms. I gazed at them now, Grace's tiny form cradled to my breast as Veronica ran around the tree, laughing at her increasing dizziness, and felt the kind of privileged joy I hadn't known for months.

But I remembered the semicircular shadows of the dogwood leaves as they had been during the eclipse, and I felt the truth of the private message they had sent me.

Eclipsed.

Happiness wouldn't just arrive like dawn. I had to go to meet it.

I spoke to my neighbor Tammy Ward about hiring a nanny, and she gave me a doe-eyed stare and asked if I was serious. I told her I was, and she pointed me toward a local service for au pairs, then asked me lots of questions that I hadn't thought about: how many hours a day we'd want her, what skills or experience we'd expect, and how much we were prepared to pay. I thought that if we were going to do this, we may as well do it right. What with Josh's travel schedule and my desire to really put some time into rebuilding my client list, I wanted someone who would be far more than a babysitter.

Tammy nodded thoughtfully. We were sitting in her vast, open-plan kitchen drinking coffee while her kids slept upstairs, and she was making a list in a round, childlike hand on a pad with clothed rabbits in the corner. Her scrawny terrier, Angus, came in periodically to yip at me, till she shooed it from the room in a voice so molasses sweet that it was impossible not to picture my other, and rather more acerbic neighbor, Mary Beth, miming throwing up.

"How many hours a day?" Tammy asked.

"I don't know. Five? Six?"

"Morning or afternoon?"

"Well, it will probably vary. When Josh is out of town . . . I don't know. Let's come back to that."

"Skills and experience. You want her to have any special training?"

"Like what?" I asked.

"A relevant degree, something in education, perhaps. First-aid training."

I bit my lip. This was all sounding suddenly quite daunting.

"I guess so," I said. "I hadn't really thought about it."

"And how much are you prepared to pay?"

She looked embarrassed by the question, but I shook it off.

"Whatever it costs."

She looked vaguely impressed.

"If money is no object . . ."

"Well, I wouldn't say . . ."

"I mean, if you can afford it," she said, looking at me, then tapping the list with her pen, "you might want to consider someone full-time."

I thought about this and nodded, glad that it had been she who'd suggested it.

"And if you are thinking that this person will be spending a lot of time with your girls," she added, "I don't think you should confine yourself to local services. When we lived in Ballantine, I had two separate friends who got their nannies from a placement agency based out of Utah."

"Utah?"

"Yep. Apparently, it's a whole big thing out there. Mormons and all. A lot of them go into family-type employment. It's a traditional-gender-role-type deal."

I could hear the quotation marks she placed around the words, but she wasn't being snide. Tammy rarely was. I'd often suspected she was more politically conservative than I was, but in this case, that didn't bother me.

"Really?" I said.

"I guess the women grow up being trained to look after the house, the kids. Maybe that's a stereotype, but still. There must be some truth in it because there are a lot of Mormon nannies, at least till they have families of their own."

"Huh," I said. "And your friends were satisfied with them?"

"Over the moon. Best thing they ever did. Both of them said so. I can get you some agency names if you like."

"There's more than one?"

"Oh yes. But I'm sure they can help point you in the right direction."

"Right," I said, feeling a tiny thrill of excitement. I was actually going to do this. "Great. Thanks."

"One thing, though," Tammy cautioned. "They'll have to live in."

"What do you mean?"

"With you. In your house. These agencies send someone for six months, a year, or whatever, and they live with you."

"Oh, I don't know about that. We're pretty private people."

Tammy pursed her lips slightly, as if she knew as much and thought it a minor failing.

"Would give you the flexibility you want, and would save you money in the long term," she said. "Not paying an hourly rate, I mean."

"Right," I said, nodding vaguely. "I guess so. I'll have to think about it."

⁓

I relayed our conversation to Josh that evening.

"Live with us? Really?" he asked. He was cagey, gauging my response.

"I don't know," I said. "Is it a terrible idea?"

Josh blew a long breath out of the side of his mouth and stared off at nothing for a moment.

"I don't know," he said. "I hadn't really thought it through like this. Live-in? Wouldn't that feel . . . I don't know. Intrusive?"

"I thought so at first," I replied.

"But now?"

"I just don't know. Maybe we could try it for a while . . ."

"Then what? Send her back to Utah if we don't like the arrangement?"

"Probably doesn't work like that, huh?"

"Probably not."

"Then we shouldn't do it," I said. "We can't possibly know it will work out. A complete stranger in our house for a year . . ."

"Might be a bit much."

"Yeah. I mean, it would be great to have someone *on call*, as it were, around all the time, able to step in no matter what our jobs demanded, but I don't think we could handle it."

"Probably not," said Josh. "I mean, unless we really wanted to."

"I suppose."

"Where would she even sleep?"

"In the basement, I guess," I replied. "We're not using the space, and there's a bathroom down there."

"I suppose. Would give her some privacy. We'd have to have ground rules about where she could go and when."

"Absolutely."

"And we'd need some time completely to ourselves," he added.

"For sure."

There was a thoughtful silence, and Josh's frown shifted into a knowing half smile. It was a look he gave me whenever we made impulsive choices, and I returned it. This, crazy though it was, was very *us*. We waffle for ages on decisions—when and where to take holidays, whether or not we need a new car, even the discussion about moving to Charlotte. We circle the issue vaguely, noncommittally, and then all of a sudden, we reach a kind of critical mass and commit, just like that.

"Are we thinking about this?" he said.

I put my hands to my face, my fingers massaging my temples.

"I think," I said, then hesitated. "I think we might be."

⌒

I spent the next morning, while the girls were napping, searching online through a list of Salt Lake City agencies forwarded by Tammy's Ballantine friends. I was drawn to a particularly slick and professional-looking site for a company called Nurture, which sent nannies all over the country. I clicked through their listings and read their policies, including their payment schedules. That gave me pause, not because we didn't have the $600 to $1,000 a week that seemed to be the going rate—plus transportation costs from wherever the nanny was currently based—or the basement room that could be a self-contained apartment, but because the hard economics of it all raised key questions. What if we hired someone and didn't like her? We could terminate the contract and send her home, but while Josh made enough to cover the cost, at least part of the logic of my working was that it would bring in more disposable income. If the experiment wound up costing us money and failed, I might not have the heart to press for a second attempt.

Better get it right the first time, then, said the less flappable part of my brain.

I made coffee and began sifting through the women's profiles. They were all women, though I suppose that wasn't a surprise. Some of them would be better described as girls, and a lot of those who were old enough to have been to college hadn't been. They were also mainly white, and a good half of them were Mormon. I wasn't sure how I felt about that. Neither Josh nor I was religious—he having been raised by a fiercely Catholic grandmother whose beliefs had soured him against

12

the church, while I had grown up in a family where religion was simply a kind of hobby other people pursued. My immigrant parents kept their Japanese heritage largely to themselves, as if sharing too much of it with me might make me less American. When I was small, I would escort my father to the temple, where he would light incense and bow his head in a brief, loaded silence, but he never explained what he was doing or why. I learned the pattern of his devotion—if that was what it was—was keyed to certain dates, particularly the anniversaries of his own parents' deaths.

I wasn't opposed to God, religion, or ritual observance, but it all made me uneasy, something I hadn't really been aware of till we moved to Charlotte and had the bizarre experience of meeting neighbors who asked me what church I went to two minutes into our first conversation. I had no doubt that many religious people were good, caring members of society, but I also saw that a lot weren't—thinking, saying, and doing monstrous things in the name of the God they professed to worship. I had nothing against religious people, but I didn't assume that the fact that they went to church made them better suited to look after my children.

But when I looked at other websites, they seemed either more local or less professional. One had a typo on its (not *it's*) opening page, a stupid and irrelevant detail perhaps, but one that my literary eye could not ignore. One looked like it was aimed primarily at babysitters. Some were little more than help-wanted bulletin boards. None had the rigorous vetting process that Nurture's site detailed.

Within a half hour, I was back there, sorting through the smiling faces with their quirky Mormon names—I'd already seen a Tynslee, a Drakelle, a Kyzli, and an Alivian, which I thought sounded like a PMS drug. I skimmed their achievements, qualifications, and letters of reference, passing over the ones I thought of as au pairs, girls whom I guessed—based on nothing, really—were more likely to be nannying as a way of traveling and seeing the world. I wanted women who seemed more mature, women who had chosen nannying as a way of life because they loved it and were good at it. Some of them, even the older ones, were gorgeous in a fresh-faced midwestern kind of way. I tried not to hold that against them, but I found myself drawn more and more to the ones who seemed to have more substance, more strength in body and character, more experience. I imagined that the pretty ones didn't make it beyond their midtwenties before being snatched away by boyfriends or husbands who didn't want to share their beloveds with a strange family. That made sense. That the ones who interested me most were usually less pretty was unimportant.

Probably.

I checked in on the girls, still thinking about the strangeness of having an unfamiliar adult living in our house with us, and a conversation I had had with Mary Beth Wilson, who lived two doors down, popped into my head. She had been talking about the various small doings of the neighbors—the modifications to their kitchens, the Wards' new car, the new construction on Queens Road—when she had slid into her favorite eye-rolling gossip about Tommy Ward and the leggy, blonde college girl who had been babysitting for him and his "clueless" wife, Tammy.

"I mean," she had exclaimed, "who would let a girl like that in your house for hours at a time, and then have your famously rampant husband drive her home? Have you seen her? Oh my God. I'm straighter than the inside of a cannon, and I think *I* might do her."

I had laughed because it was Mary Beth, the most delightfully and self-consciously outrageous friend I had in our sedate corner of sleepy Myers Park, but the point had been clear. Tammy was out of her mind for allowing her kids to be babysat by a girl that cute. If her husband strayed, it was practically her fault.

It was an old and stupid argument, of course, a familiar device that somehow managed to blame women for what men did, but it came back to me now. I wondered if my prioritizing the frumpier candidates over the prettier ones suggested I was already enacting Mary Beth's warning. It wasn't necessary. I trusted Josh. I did.

Still. Why risk it?

I went back to the computer and pulled up three more profiles. The last was in her late thirties, with a warm, smiling face, slightly pink. Shoulder-length hair, prosaically styled. It generously might be called chestnut. Brown eyes. An ordinary face, a little fuller than the norm. But the smile was warm, spontaneous. It implied spirit.

I reread her references and qualifications. The latter were few beyond high school but included certificates in first aid and CPR. The letters made her sound like an angel: warm, caring, dedicated to children. A joy to be around. Honest. Hardworking. Generous.

I looked back at her picture and remembered how that last word had come to me simply by looking at her.

Her name was Oaklynn Durst.

"This one," I said.

Distantly, as if waking from a dream, I caught the climbing wail of Veronica starting to cry.

Chapter Two

Two months earlier

"Tell me I'm not crazy for doing this," said Oaklynn Durst, gazing at her friend with wide-eyed anticipation.

Friend was perhaps overstating the case a little, but only a little, Oaklynn would have insisted, and only because she had known Nadine for five short months. Also because technically, Nadine was her employee.

Her cleaner, to be precise.

But having spent most of her life since adolescence doing not only her own cleaning but everyone else's as well, Oaklynn still hadn't gotten used to the idea of being, as Decken said, "the lady of the house." In most respects, married life suited her, felt like the destiny she had been waiting for, and she often thought that she had strayed—guided surely by the hand of God—into a dream as close to heaven on earth as she could imagine. She knew that was in part the combination of honeymoon euphoria on top of their almost indecently brief engagement—six weeks! She had barely been able to keep her face straight when they had announced the news to her congregation. It inevitably would fade over time as they grew more accustomed to working together side by side, and Lord knew the world had trials enough to derail the lives of good Christian couples, but she didn't care. She was happy. The relief of finding a good and willing husband so late in life—she was about to turn thirty-eight—had swept away all other concerns. She knew Decken still felt the loss of his first wife keenly, but she would heal that wound with patience and kindness and hard work. She felt complete in ways she had not realized she was missing, and life had come sharply into clear and satisfying focus.

All that was missing were children, and that was only a matter of time.

Oaklynn smiled at Nadine, loving and pitying her at the same time. Nadine was smart and warm and loving, but there was a hollowness Oaklynn sometimes caught in her face when she thought Oaklynn wasn't watching. A loneliness.

Nadine had blown into Salt Lake City on a Greyhound bus nine months earlier. She said she had come from Louisiana, but she didn't like to talk about it, and Oaklynn knew there was a boyfriend in her past she didn't want to find her. Carl, his name was. Think of that! Traveling halfway across the country just to get away from someone you once loved. Oaklynn had never been so far in her life, which was why the next few weeks held such joy and terror for her.

"I think it's good," said Nadine. "A change of scenery, a chance to start your lives together doing what you love. It's good."

Oaklynn beamed, relieved. She could always tell when Nadine was holding something back and when she was being utterly and openly honest, and this was definitely the latter. She made a girlish squee of delighted excitement, waggling her hands at the wrists, then threw her arms around her friend and squeezed their ample bosoms together.

They were both biggish girls, both in their late thirties, and those were also reasons Oaklynn felt so fortunate in her sudden marriage, so blessed. She feared for Nadine, that for all her friend's gifts, the world would not see her potential for goodness and beauty behind that slightly frumpy and aging exterior.

"What still has to be done?" asked Nadine, ever the coolheaded organizer compared to Oaklynn, who was apt to get flustered by any of the pressures that didn't involve cooking and cleaning and looking after other people, particularly kids.

"Well, the movers come tomorrow," said Oaklynn. "They say they won't need help, but I'll have to be here just, you know, for peace of mind. The boxes that are going with us have already shipped. The stuff that goes to the church is all stacked in the living room, so everything else is supposed to be going into storage."

"How long is your storage unit leased?"

"Two years, to start. Paid up front. Then, I guess, we decide if we're coming back, or want stuff sent on or . . . I don't know."

She ended with that familiar flicker of apprehension and sipped her lemonade. Oaklynn made excellent lemonade. Nadine put her large hands on hers and gave her an encouraging smile.

"You can always come back if it doesn't work out," she said. "Or if you feel you've done all you can."

"Well," said Oaklynn, returning the smile but tipping her head from side to side noncommittally, "that will really be up to Decken."

"I know," said Nadine, "but he's a good man. He wouldn't make you do something you weren't happy with."

That was true, thought Oaklynn, nodding. Decken was a good man. She was immensely lucky to have him. She leaned in and gave her friend another hug, urgent this time. Grateful. She didn't know if she would have been able to go through all this without her.

"What about credit cards? Bank accounts?" said Nadine.

"I'm closing everything but the Mastercard," said Oaklynn. "New joint bank account as Mrs. Burgraff." The girlish glee bubbled over again.

"He's with Mountain America Credit Union?"

"That's right! How on earth did you know that?"

"I'm the cleaner, remember?" said Nadine, grinning. "I pick your mail up and separate it into piles according to whom is the designated recipient." She said it in a fancy voice, miming the action like she was some high-powered Madison Avenue secretary.

"And very good you are at it, too," said Oaklynn. "I wish I could bring you with me. Help me stay organized. Speaking of mail, you haven't seen my replacement driver's license, have you? I put it down a few days ago, and now . . ."

Nadine shook her head and frowned. "Any chance you packed it?"

"Not on purpose," said Oaklynn. "Which doesn't mean I didn't. I'm so tired today. I don't know why. Would you keep your eyes open for it?"

"Of course. I'll check in with the bishop when they have had the chance to go through what you donated. See if it turns up there."

"Thanks. I mean, it's not like I'm going to need it, but it might be useful to have if we come back in a few years."

There was that note of uncertainty again, hastily brushed away with a cheery smile. Though it cost her something, the smile managed to light her whole round face, burning off the uncharacteristic weariness for a moment.

"Tell me," said Nadine, taking her hands in hers and leaning closer, "about your kids."

That's clever of her, thought Oaklynn vaguely, *and sweet*. Because she did think of them as *her* kids, even though she had in fact only been their nanny. She felt her heart lift. If there was one thing guaranteed to raise her spirits, it was this.

"You don't want to hear about them," she said coyly, smiling that bashful sideways smile that Decken said he loved so much.

"I do!" Nadine insisted. "Get me your photo albums. And the packet."

The packet. Oaklynn's joy, her secret pride, which she confessed to no one in case someone thought her full of herself. She wasn't sure how Nadine had wormed it out of her, but she had one day about a month ago, shortly after Decken had announced his travel plans—their travel plans—and she had been down, lost in doubt, and suddenly missing the only true achievement she could call her own before her marriage.

She'd called it simply "the packet" to make it sound less grand, less prideful, though its official title was the Nurture Official Candidate Listing and Data Report, *Nurture* being the name of one of the state's preeminent suppliers of nanny services. There was a digital version, of course, but Oaklynn liked the physical copy, the heft of the slick binder, the homey professionalism of its crisp and curly lettering, the way her face—younger than she was now, but still recognizably the same—smiled out at the world from its cover. Before her marriage, and the journey she would soon be undertaking, the packet had represented her life, her achievements to date, laid out in proven black and white like testimony.

It *proved* her value as a person.

She cradled it now in her lap, as Nadine flipped through the photo album with its cartoon cats and crayoned love notes from little Janice and Arthur, the images of Ben hugging his puppy, Dot and Max in the bath, almost buried beneath mounds of soap bubbles. Oaklynn laughed indulgently at the pictures, but they tugged at her heart, and before she could stop them, tears ran down her cheeks. She really was very tired.

"Which are these?" asked Nadine, kindly ignoring her friend's weepy mood.

"The Cavendishes," said Oaklynn, blinking and opening the packet. "Dot and Max." She turned each page of the application binder ceremonially as ever, as if she had to prove her eligibility to be part of the lives she had put before her own. The first sheet presented her own information: name, address, phone and Social Security numbers laid out like qualifications. Then the photocopied driver's license. Then the drug tests—amphetamines, cocaine metabolites, marijuana, opiates, and phencyclidine—all negative. Then the driving record—clean. The identity report and criminal-record search—also clean. And then, the packet's true glories, the references: six glowing reports from the families she had worked for. Her families. The accolades about her work ethic, compassion, sensitivity, and playfulness with the children positively glowed on the pages. They filled her face with light like a reflecting panel, and for a brief, indulgent moment, Oaklynn basked in it as if it were sunshine.

I've never seen anyone better suited to being with children, said Jill Cavendish in one letter.

A pleasure to be around, said Charlynne Mayberry.

The family loved her instantly, said Clara Hubert. *I was worried it would wear off as they got used to her, but if anything, they just found more things about her to love . . .*

The last page was Oaklynn's own personal statement, which, if she were honest, the placement secretary at Nurture had coached her to say. It included all the things that looked best on an application—the wholesome interests, the Sunday school teaching report, the hospital reading circle. She hadn't needed the guidance. These were all things Oaklynn had actually done, though when she told the secretary as much, she wondered if the woman either didn't quite believe her, or did but thought it all a little silly. Naive. *Down-home hobbies*, the secretary had called them, in a way that Oaklynn would have called arch if the word was one with which she was comfortable.

That all seemed like a long time ago now. And in a matter of weeks, she would be going farther than she had ever been before and leaving all this behind, venturing into a world about which she knew next to nothing beyond the fact that she was needed. Tears that had been clinging to her thin lashes fell suddenly, and she gave a shuddering breath as she wiped them away.

"Hey!" said Nadine, taking her hands again. "I'm sorry. I thought this would make you feel better."

"It does," Oaklynn gasped, her voice cracking. "It's just . . . I'm just tired. And *scared*."

She hadn't said it before. Not aloud. She had pretended it wasn't true, that she was taking it all in stride, but in her heart, Oaklynn was terrified.

Japan.

It was a world away. She was glad to be a missionary, to stand with her husband doing the Lord's work in a foreign land. She just wished it wasn't quite so foreign.

"What can I do to help?" said Nadine.

Oaklynn shook her head, feeling foolish, but her friend wouldn't let her off the hook.

"Let me cancel those credit cards for you," she said.

"Don't I have to do that?"

"Is the balance paid off?"

"Of course," said Oaklynn wearily. She never carried charges on her credit cards, partly because she hated wasting money, partly because she felt guilty if she bought things and didn't pay for them right away.

"Then I can handle it," said Nadine. "Leave them with me. Take a nap."

"Me?" Oaklynn laughed, as if the idea were preposterous. "I don't take naps."

Nadine met her eyes, and the longing in them was so obvious that Oaklynn abandoned the pretense.

"I'm just exhausted," she confessed.

"It's stress," said Nadine. "You've run yourself ragged these last few days. Go take a nap for an hour or two, and I'll handle the credit cards." She lowered her voice conspiratorially, grinning. "And I won't tell Decken."

Oaklynn bit her lower lip, considering, then nodded.

"Good," said Nadine. "Get me those cards, missy."

Oaklynn blinked, then got up, trudged over to the counter, and rummaged through her purse, setting them down in a neat little stack.

"You sure you don't mind?" she asked. "I can do it later. I don't know why I'm so tired . . ."

"It's fine," said Nadine, smiling and extending a hand. "Give 'em up."

"Thanks," said Oaklynn, handing her the cards. "You're a real treasure. One day, some man will see that and . . ."

"Go to bed," said Nadine, grinning and waving her away.

"OK, OK. You need anything else?" Oaklynn asked.

"Leave the packet with me," said Nadine. "If I need any more information, it will be in there."

She smiled, and Oaklynn felt again a wave of gratitude for her friend's many kindnesses.

"I'm so lucky to know you," Oaklynn said. "I have barely slept all night through for two weeks! I don't want to say anything to Decken in case he thinks I'm not, you know, enthusiastic about the mission, but . . ."

"Go and lie down," said Nadine. "Here." She popped open her purse and produced a foil-backed packet of pills, smiling at Oaklynn's instant wariness. "It's just melatonin. Quite natural and not a narcotic. Take a couple."

Oaklynn's eyes fastened on the pills with something like hunger.

"I *could* use a nap," she said. "Are you sure you'll be OK if . . . ?"

"Go," said Nadine. "Sleep."

And, after one more lingering hug, she did, waddling to the foot of the stairs and giving a last, wan smile back at Nadine. Raising the sleeping tablets in a kind of wave, she headed up to the bedroom.

Nadine sat by herself, listening to the lady of the house moving around above her, to the closing of doors and the flush of the toilet, then nothing. Five minutes she waited, then ten, confident that the pills

23

would knock out her friend. She'd already crunched two into Oaklynn's lemonade and added an Ambien. That would certainly do it. Still, Nadine waited and listened because Nadine was nothing if not careful.

At last, she picked up Oaklynn's precious packet and began leafing through it again. Then she did the same with the photo album, snapping pictures of the images with the prepaid cell phone she had bought from the Gateway mall the day before. Finally, she turned back to the Nurture letterhead, keyed the numbers into her phone, and waited for the voice on the other end to direct her.

"Yes, hi," said Nadine, becoming suddenly guileless and apologetic. "My name is Oaklynn Durst, and I used to be in your listings. You've placed me in state four times before. But I've not been working for a little while. I'd like to reactivate my listing."

"Certainly, Miss Durst," said the woman, who had identified herself simply as Rachel. She spoke slowly, clearly keying in terms to her computer as she talked. "Oaklynn. Let me just. Pull. Up. Your. File. Yes, I see you. OK. So you want to be listed as hirable, yes?"

"That's right."

"Staying in state?"

"No, I'm ready for a change," said Nadine.

"Excellent. Anywhere you don't want to go?"

"Not overseas. Preferably East Coast, but not north of Washington, DC. I've had enough of winter."

Rachel laughed. "I'll make a note," she said, "though I assume that's not a deal breaker."

Nadine heard the note of warning and backtracked.

"Not at all. I was really only kidding. I'll go where I'm needed, if the family seems nice."

"And are you willing to make a long-term commitment? Six months? A year?"

"I can do a year," said Nadine.

"Excellent. And I see you have terrific references already, so we should get some interest quickly. Are those up-to-date, or are there more you'd like to add?"

"No, everything looks fine."

"Personal statement?"

"I'm OK with it as it is, unless you see anything you think I should tweak."

"Looks good to me," said Rachel. "Now, you've been off our books for a little while, so you will have to do a new round of drug tests. Is that OK?"

"Sure. No problem. I should update my profile picture, too."

"Great. I'll give you the address of our walk-in clinic partner in a second. We can take care of the profile pic then, too, OK?"

"Sure."

"You can include other pictures as well, but we want to have one that shows you exactly as you are now. It's good for the clients."

I'll bet, thought Nadine. The lonely single father who picks out a perky bombshell from a photo doesn't want her older, saggier incarnation showing up on his doorstep.

Rachel gave her the clinic address and led into her closing speech.

"Our terms are the same as they were when you were with us last," she said. "Since you are already on our books, you won't have to pay for the initial listing, and we'll just take the usual ten percent of your annual salary as a finder's fee. You can check on your profile at any time with the same log-in information you provided before, and we'll notify you by phone if you have interested families. Is the phone we have on record still current?"

"No," said Nadine. "Let me give you my new cell number."

She gave it and Rachel read it back, then wrapped things up.

Easy.

After she hung up, Nadine worked her way through the credit cards, calling each number in turn and requesting a change of billing address.

"Just for a few weeks," she explained to one. "I'll have to do it again soon. Moving."

"Anywhere nice?" asked the operator cheerfully.

"You know," said Nadine, "I haven't decided yet."

"Sounds like an adventure. Fun!"

"Yes," said Nadine. She had introduced herself as Oaklynn and had the address, phone, and Social Security numbers to back it up. "I think it will be."

When she was done, she left a note for Oaklynn, saying that she had cut up and burned the cards, though she had actually slipped them into her purse beside the driver's license she had put there the day before. She considered it now, thinking about colored contact lenses and a trip to the hairdresser. That would take care of most of it. They didn't look that similar, but attitude went a long way, and Nadine was good at simulation. Always had been. She smiled to herself. It was a smile that the woman sleeping upstairs—the woman whose name was on the cards and the driver's license, the woman stored away in Nurture's carefully vetted computer system who would soon be leaving the country for a minimum of two years—would not have recognized.

She moved into the living room, gazing up at the clear blue Utah sky through the high windows, and as she turned, she caught her own reflection in the glass.

"Oaklynn," she said aloud, trying the word for shape and taste in her mouth. "Oaklynn. My name is Oaklynn Durst. Hi." She paused, fixing her ghostly reflection in the window with a hard stare, then smiling cheerfully. "Hi, I'm Oaklynn. Oaklynn Durst."

Yes, she thought. *That would work.*

Chapter Three

August

Josh Klein pulled into his designated space in the parking garage under the Bank of America tower in uptown Charlotte, turned the engine off, and got out. He closed the driver's door and wiped a speck from the mirror on the silver LS 460, wondering vaguely if he would have to give up the car and get something more family friendly. The girls tended to travel in Anna's Camry, and he had deliberately not fitted child seats in the Lexus, saying he needed the space—and the professionally detailed spotless interior—for when he had to drive clients, but as the kids got older, they'd need something bigger. Was it possible they'd also have to drive around this new nanny? She looked like she'd need some room.

He scowled at the smudged finish, wondering, not for the first time, how it would be sharing their house—their life—with another adult. Anna had been down for a while, the kind of paralyzing surprise he hadn't seen coming. It had been painful to watch, doubly so because he'd felt so powerless to do anything about it. So when she had raised this new idea, he had grabbed on to it without a thought, like it was a rope holding her in one of those flash-flooded streets he'd seen on the news from Chile or Ecuador. And if the result meant trading in the Lexus, well, that was a price he was more than happy to pay.

Still, another woman living in our basement . . .

It wasn't the first time Anna had tried to go back to work. The first time had been a year after Veronica was born. He wasn't sure what the motivation had been because the boredom, the depression—postpartum or whatever—hadn't set in yet. She'd said it was about being connected to the industry, staying on editors' radars, building what she called her stable of authors, like they were thoroughbreds waiting for the Kentucky Derby. But with no help at home, it hadn't worked. She hadn't been able to travel and felt, she said, alienated from her work by her environment. She insisted that she didn't blame him, but it was impossible for Josh not to take it personally. It was, after all, his fault they were in Charlotte in the first place, and while they were infinitely more comfortable than they had been in New York—and the salary! My God, the salary!—the move had, at least in the short term, torpedoed her career. When she abandoned the attempt to work from home, he had sensed her frustration and disappointment, and she had sensed how responsible he felt. It was, she said, like an O. Henry story, a reference he just about understood. She smiled when she said it, but it was that knowing kind of smile that was just this side of sad.

Anna was a good person. A kind person. She was also as deep and still as a well, and somewhere down there was a spring that fed her creativity and imagination and generosity. Sometimes, beneath the surface, he wondered if there was something else stirring, something cold and slippery that whispered to her that she was not good enough. He sensed it when he caught her critical view of herself in the mirror, or when she lay in bed beside him, staring at the ceiling, and he did not know how to make the feeling go away or even how to ask her about it. He felt it, but he was ill equipped to talk about it, and the attempt would only embarrass them both.

Anna lacked his hardness and therefore, he thought, his talent for unvarnished honesty, the blunt assessment he could offer about someone's work, for instance, without fearing he might hurt feelings in the process. It was a mode he had, and because he used it without malice or in pursuit of any ulterior motive, it served him well at work, particularly since he knew how to turn it off—or turn it down—when he left the office. It was a skill that Anna—who was always sensitive to other people's feelings—did not have. While that had always been part of what he loved most about her, he knew it made her life a little harder. She did blame him for the move, for the turn her life had taken. She just didn't want to admit it for fear of making him feel bad. Hell, she probably didn't admit it to herself.

But his colleagues and clients valued his bluff, manly directness. He knew that instinctively. It was at least as much a part of his success as his talent for numbers or his ability to follow and guess at market trends. He was what they called a guy's guy. Someone to play golf with, drink a beer with. Someone who could talk sports but who, more important, never came across as a stats nerd or even a fan. He knew enough to offer opinions that felt informed, authoritative, but as soon as he reached the limits of his knowledge, he'd say so, and anyone who knew more would immediately feel slightly absurd, as if the range of Josh's insight demonstrated just how much a man should care about such things.

The car was a case in point. Josh had the ability to flaunt what he bought in a way that was assured—almost proud—but was also genuinely careless, as if the purchase of a particular high-end vehicle made perfect sense, but buying the next model up would be ridiculous. Other men at the firm tried to one-up each other on such things: cars, first and second homes, vacations, girlfriends, mistresses. Not Josh. When people tried to outshine him, only to get his slightly bewildered and absolutely genuine shrug, they immediately looked like they'd overstepped, exposing their shallowness.

Not being an intensely self-analytical person—another part of his easy, comfortable version of manliness—Josh was only dimly aware of this. He saw it in the faces of his coworkers, but he never tried to engineer the effect. He didn't have to. It seemed to him that his instincts, his tastes, were simply right. They didn't need strategy. Very little at work did. The judgment calls, the client meetings, the stock assessments: 90 percent of it was just instinct. Yes, Josh had training and experience, but most of the time he did his job, and did it well, on instinct. As he had once remarked to Anna in a rare confessional moment, it barely felt like work at all.

Anna was a different matter, not because he had to think about how to please her but because he really wanted to. Her opinion was—it had occurred to him with the kind of bemused shock he had once experienced when he woke up to his first earthquake in California—the only one in the world that actually mattered to him.

Josh had never been very good with women. They liked him, or had in college, because he was decent-looking, athletic, and unselfconscious, so it had been a while before he realized that serious dating was the one area of his life he really didn't understand at all. The stakes felt somehow thoroughly unimportant and impossibly high at the same time, and he never quite knew what he was supposed to offer. He wasn't good at intimacy. Desire, yes. Play, yes. Friendship, yes. But he found the kind of secret closeness women seemed to want from him baffling. He didn't know what it was they wanted or why. He tried, but not wanting anything similar from them, it felt like throwing darts in the dark: you had to turn the lights on to see if you had even hit the board.

Then he had met Anna, and it had been bizarrely easy. He didn't have to dig for the feelings other women had wanted him to articulate. He was still halting and tongue-tied compared to her, but at least he knew the emotions he couldn't quite speak were there, and after a surprisingly short period, so did she. There were times he wished he had more to offer, knowing that a part of her would like more, but he also knew she wouldn't want him to do it for her benefit, and she absolutely wouldn't want him to fake it. He told her he loved her, maybe not daily, but he said it when the thought occurred to him, and she smiled, sometimes patting his hand indulgently, and said she knew.

The only blot on their life that he didn't know how to fix was what he privately thought of as her depression, though he never called it that aloud, because he knew it couldn't be fixed with shrinks or pills. He was happy—in his family, in his love life, in his work—though that happiness was mostly a low, simmering contentment, not a laughing, manic joy. He was content. But contentment was not enough for Anna. She wanted the simmer turned up just a little higher, and however much she loved him and the kids, he knew that extra heat would have to come from work.

So it was no wonder he had agreed to this nanny business so quickly. He would make it work, he thought, his fine shoes ringing on the concrete as he walked to the employee elevator. She deserved that and more. He might not say it, but there was nothing in the world more important to him than Anna's happiness. Nothing. He wondered dimly if she knew that.

Josh's phone pinged. He pulled it out and glanced at it. A text from Vasquez, his division head. It read, My office. Soon as you get in. Bring the Doherty file.

Josh stopped midstride, his heart racing.

Chapter Four

Mary Beth Wilson looked out of the window to the quiet street and scowled at the blossom-heavy crepe myrtles. She had the landscapers coming in an hour and needed to get her run in before they arrived. The fucking pollen count would be off the charts.

Maybe she could skip the run and spend an extra hour in the gym tomorrow?

It felt like a dodge, and the last thing she needed now was to let herself go. She'd seen Tammy Ward walking her runty-looking terrier last night, and that was a woman who had abandoned all self-esteem. The transformation was amazing. Admittedly, she'd had twins, but the rug rats had to be a year old by now. Six months at least. Or maybe they just had their second birthday party? She wasn't sure and couldn't tell from looking at them. She had no intention of having kids of her own and had zero interest in anyone else's, though she'd learned not to advertise that fact—not to the neighbors, most of whom were veritable baby factories, and not to Kurt, her husband. He still liked the idea of being a dad, or claimed to. She couldn't see it personally and thought the interest would fade pretty quickly as soon as any son of theirs turned out not to be interested in baseball, earlier if they had a girl. She'd seen that kind of parenting before and knew what it led to: the husband sitting on the couch yelling at the Panthers offensive line while the wife drove the kids to soccer practice and sleepovers and God knew what else.

No, thanks.

Easier to let Kurt pretend he liked the idea for a little longer, then tell him she was too old to try safely. In the long term, he'd be relieved. They were, in their own ways, selfish people, and they didn't have room for kids. She knew that and had come to terms with it, shrugging off all the old bullshit that women were told about the destined joys of bringing life into the world, along with the sins and sorrows of living for yourself. Men did. They claimed not to, saying they were just doing what the world and their jobs demanded—the drinks meetings, sometimes at strip clubs; the endless hours of golf; the schmoozing and glad-handing at the country club. It was all part of the responsibilities of being a guy. Well, what's good for the goose was good for the gander. Or she supposed, thinking vaguely that the gander was the male, the other way around.

The street outside was quiet, but then the street was always quiet. Settle Road was one of those corners of Myers Park that had, until recently, gone unnoticed by the developers as areas elsewhere swelled in prestige. It wasn't what they called gentrification because Myers Park had always been swanky, but in the past, it had been old-money swank: great plantation-style houses with white-columned porticoes and sprawling, manicured lawns. Between these islands of wealth nestled the little ranch-style two bedrooms where ordinary people had lived. As these salt-of-the-earth types had died off, their loving kids had found it worth considerably more to bulldoze Grandma's place and erect a giant McMansion that pushed as close to the property line as local ordinances would allow. The result was that Settle Road was a permanent building site, vacant slabs awaiting developers' eyes, empty shoebox houses awaiting demolition, and then the sprawling miniature castles—all vast open plans downstairs, with hardwood floors and granite counters—that had elbowed their way in and lorded it over the neighborhood.

There were only three such houses on their street at the moment: Mary Beth and Kurt Wilson's, Tammy and Tommy Ward's (their names alone surely grounds for annulment), and then the most recent transplants from Yankeedom, Anna and Josh Klein. There were twice as many lots that were either vacant or under construction, so the neighborhood, which was well spaced and shaded by the massive trees characterizing this part of the city, felt oddly deserted, isolated. You could walk, cycle, or, in Mary Beth's case, run, without the usual Charlotte fear of cars mowing you down, but you couldn't actually go anywhere. You could walk around the neighborhood and into one or two more like it—more built up but otherwise similar—and if you felt like braving a few segments of road where the sidewalk gave up entirely, you might wander up to the local library, Queens University, and the Methodist church, which loomed over the intersection where Providence Road took a wacky hard turn to the south. But stores, restaurants, bars, and other lively spots were all too far to reach without a car from their little corner.

During the daylight hours, the area rang with god-awful Mexican music from the construction workers' radios and sometimes with the laughter of the neighborhood's kids, but it was mostly quiet, like now, and at night, it could feel weirdly woodsy. To the immediate north of the houses on Settle Road ran Briar Creek, a greenway with a dense line of trees along the bank that completely obscured the midtown skyscrapers, except in the middle of winter when the leafless branches showed the lights of Two Wells Fargo Center and the Bank of America tower. Two weeks ago, Mary Beth and Kurt had been woken by the howling of coyotes in that little strip of woods and had sat up in bed, transfixed by the eerie imminence of something that felt like it belonged in some mountain forest from a thousand years ago. Settle Road was in the city, but it didn't feel like it, and a less possessed woman might have found it frightening.

Mostly, Mary Beth found it tedious. But if life as the homemaker wife to a wealthy banker (and it seemed like every guy in the area was a banker) wasn't quite the dream of success she'd seen in the brochures, it wasn't going to be made better by stuffing her life full of lame people. Enter Anna and her new nanny.

What in the name of all that was holy was she thinking?

Turning their lives upside down—remodeling their damn house, no less—to make way for a woman whose picture made her look like a Soviet weight lifter and whose sole credential was her love for little people who couldn't speak?

Kill me now, thought Mary Beth. Was it not bad enough that her friends were all auditioning for Baby Factory of the Year without adding dollops of Mormon nanny into the mix?

Christ.

She needed a better class of friend; that was for damn sure. And the irony, of course, was that Anna had been the best of the bunch, and not just because she was originally a New Yorker. She had become a good deal less fun of late, but Mary Beth thought it was at least possible that, having the nanny to take on the feeding and burping of the little flesh blobs who had colonized her house, Anna would get more interesting again. The Kleins had been—cautiously, watchfully—a breath of fresh air when they'd moved in, before the pink parasites came along. Maybe they would be again.

It was just possible, of course, that Anna's desire to spend more time working was—bizarrely—real, and the nanny would make no difference. But surely, after all this time, the three years of constant pregnancy and nursing, it was time for her to kick back and open a bottle of chardonnay or two with her cool neighbor. Was that too much to ask?

Chapter Five

ANNA

With the vetting already completed by Nurture's rigorous hiring procedures, there wasn't much for me to do except phone Oaklynn's former employers just to make sure the references were solid. There were no surprises. In fact, in addition to singing her praises all over again, several of them seemed a little jealous, either that I was getting someone of her skills and temperament, or that I was living a period from which they had moved on only reluctantly. Mrs. Cavendish talked about her two girls as if they had grown up and moved away, but when I asked—part just making conversation and part checking that the dates lined up— she said, quite wistfully, "Twelve and thirteen now. How the time goes! I do miss Oaklynn."

I felt a little sad for her, and a little jealous. Whatever Jill Cavendish's relationship with her infant children had been, it was surely better than mine with Veronica and Grace. But then, that was why we were getting Oaklynn, and for all I knew, it was the nanny who had made the Cavendish home so joyous that they wished time had stopped in those first years.

I spoke to Oaklynn several times, both by phone and by Skype, calling from Josh's ground-floor office because the handset in the bedroom was always cutting out. We worked out the specifics of her responsibilities and payment. Josh and I didn't really want to mess with the nanny's taxes, so we agreed we would write up an annual report of her income, and she would take responsibility for paying the taxes herself, probably quarterly to avoid penalties. She might not, of course, but that was her decision, and we could not be held accountable for it, in the unlikely event that she was audited.

"That's absolutely fine, Mrs. Klein," said Oaklynn in that open, accepting way I had already come to associate with her.

"Please," I said. "Call me Anna."

The basement of the house had been only partly finished when we moved in, and one of our first priorities had been to make it a real living space with a self-contained guest bedroom and full bath. This now seemed prescient on our part, and as we geared up for Oaklynn's arrival, I focused on some swift and homey decoration, determined to make the lowest level of the house as welcoming and livable as the two stories above it. It was a good-size area, almost as large as the New York apartment we had left behind, and its rear windows looked out across the backyard to the creek and the dense trees of the greenway, which insulated us from the rest of the city. I found myself anxious that our guest—which was how I was determined to think of her, even though we were paying for her labor—would feel at home there. I was concerned that the open stairwell would afford her no privacy unless she was in the bedroom itself, so I had Josh reach out to one of the local builders and have a contractor drop by to see if some kind of partition wall and door could be added. He said it could but not before she was due to arrive.

"Does it matter?" asked Josh, reading my obvious deflation. "I don't really think it needs doing at all. It can certainly wait a couple of months."

"I just wanted everything to be perfect when she got here," I said.

"You know she is working for us, right?" said Josh, grinning over his laptop. "Not the other way around."

"I just want her to be happy," I said. "I don't want her leaving half-way through her term. It wouldn't be good for the girls."

He conceded that point, though it wasn't really why I was anxious. I think I had taken to heart an idea that had emerged from a couple of Oaklynn's Nurture references describing her as coming to feel like one of the family. They had made it sound like that was her achievement, and I got that, but it was also surely about the nature of the family itself. What if she didn't like us? What if she hated the house? What if she didn't *want* to become part of our family?

Josh picked up something in my tone and gave me one of his shrewd, considering looks.

"Is this really about the house?" he asked.

"What do you mean?"

"Are you worried she won't like the house, or are you worried she won't like us? The girls?"

I flushed and looked away, feeling transparent and guilty. Grace was still fussy and unpredictable, while Veronica, though a sweet, curious child, could be needy and insistent.

"They're great kids," said Josh. He met my eyes and held them, making sure I heard, but he spoke kindly. "We are a great family. And if *Oaklynn* decides she wants a little more privacy, we can install the partition wall and door in the basement." He still said her name as if it had quotation marks around it, sounding slightly ridiculous. "But maybe she won't, and we can save ourselves the three grand or whatever it will cost to do the work."

I thought, then nodded. He was right, and the last thing I needed to do was make this whole experiment even more costly.

So I went back to what Josh called my "cheap and cheerful" decorating: an accent mirror here, a noncontroversial piece of art there, and laid out the bathroom with color-coordinated hand towels and matching soaps. On impulse, one Saturday when Josh was watching the girls, I drove down to the Home Depot on Wendover and picked up a gallon of cornflower-blue paint with which, over the next three days, I completely repainted what I now thought of as Oaklynn's room.

"Pretty!" Veronica declared.

"It is," said Josh, snaking his arm around me. "Better on the walls than on your face, but yes. Pretty."

Veronica peered up at me, then pointed at the blue smears on my face and laughed with surprised delight.

"You think?" I said to Josh.

"Yeah," he said. "It looks great. Really nice, Anna."

"Nice?"

"Fresh. Inviting. Wholesome. Something like that. You're the word lady. I'm just the banker. If she doesn't like it, that's her problem."

He was trying to be supportive, but the remark bothered me all the same, and he read it in my face. He squeezed me playfully. "Come on," he said. "Let's get these windows open and go upstairs. I'm starving. What do you say I order us some *gyoza* and noodles from Yama?"

My favorite little Japanese restaurant.

"That would be perfect," I said, meaning it.

"It will be once I open a bottle of wine."

"Deal."

When I wasn't frantically tidying and decorating, I was on the phone to Ramkins and Deale, figuring out how best to use the new time

Oaklynn's presence was going to give me. I was secretly thrilled by the prospect of taking trips to New York for meetings, conventions, and author events, but the bulk of my work time would be spent in Charlotte. Since renting office space, however modest, in the city was utterly unjustifiable, I had to make sure that my current home office felt like somewhere I could work. I already had a kind of study—the smallest bedroom in the house—in the corner tucked away from the noise of goings-on downstairs, and now I set out to strip it of anything that wasn't work related. By the time I was done, apart from shelves groaning with books, there was only a desk, an office chair, a phone that worked better than the one in the bedroom, a table lamp, and a laptop. In one corner, hanging on the wall, I had a small tatami mat below a kanji scroll that had belonged to my grandfather. Everything else that might prove a distraction went, some of it migrating to the basement for Oaklynn's use. Josh approved, if only because the purge meant that we could now claim the room as a home office for tax purposes, though to me it felt a little stark. The prospect of spending hours in there every day with the door closed struck me suddenly as daunting.

"You OK?" asked Josh. "We can still cancel if you want. Pay her the part salary and punt."

"No," I said, not even considering it. "We said we'd try, so let's try."

"OK," he said. "But if at any point you decide it was a bad idea, for any reason at all, we call it quits and do whatever we have to do to put things back the way they were, whether the nanny likes it or not. It's our call, Anna. Me, you, and the girls. Mostly you. The nanny is an employee. If it's not working out, we stop. Yeah?"

I nodded but couldn't stop myself from adding, "Oaklynn. Don't call her *the nanny*."

"*Oaklynn*, then," said Josh, rolling his eyes.

"I mean it, Josh. She has to feel welcome. Her name is Oaklynn."

"Fine. Though we may need to repaint her bedroom."

"What?" I said, genuinely shocked.

"I mean, not sure the blue will go with the red carpet we're rolling out . . ."

I slapped him playfully on the shoulder.

"Not funny," I said.

"OK," he said. "Just remember: she . . . Oaklynn is welcome, but it's still our house. Our lives."

I nodded.

Oaklynn arrived two days later. Josh offered to go to the airport with me, but I said I wanted to be the one to greet her. I didn't take the girls in case the flight was delayed or Oaklynn needed more luggage space than I had anticipated, so it was just me at Charlotte Douglas baggage claim, holding a hand-lettered sign with her name on it. I didn't think I really needed that—I already felt like Oaklynn was someone I knew— but I thought it made me look more professional.

The flight from Salt Lake City was nonstop, but one of those typically southern "popcorn" thunderstorms so common in late summer had moved along I-85, bringing driving rain and the kind of lightning that stabbed down in sudden flickering branches. For an hour and ten minutes, the airport was effectively closed, nothing landing or taking off, and I had to sit on a plastic chair, my anxiety building. I asked someone in the blue uniform of American Airlines about her flight, but he shrugged.

"They can't circle forever," he said. "Fuel gets low. If the storm doesn't clear soon, they may have to reroute."

"Where to?"

Again, the shrug.

"Raleigh," he said. "Atlanta."

"Then how will they get here?" I said, worry making me stupid.

"Lady, I'm in baggage, not air traffic control. When they get here, you can come to me if they can't find their suitcases. Till then, chill a bit. They'll announce soon enough."

I did not chill. I paced, then went up the escalator to the check-in area and explored every area I could without showing a boarding pass, asking the same idiotic questions and getting the same noncommittal answers. At last, the storm slid northeast, and the airport came back to life, sending me scurrying back to baggage claim, convinced I would now miss her entirely. I was still studying the monitor in the arrivals hall, trying to figure out which carousel Oaklynn's luggage would come in on, when a voice beside me made me turn.

"Mrs. Klein? Anna?"

It was she. She looked exactly like her picture: late thirties, pink, a bit frumpy in a shapeless flower-print dress and a faintly absurd floppy felt hat, but a smile that was runway wide. Overcome with relief, I muttered, "Oh, thank God," and threw my arms around her. To her credit, she did not freak out, and as I started coming back to sanity and babbling my apologies and explanations, she smiled and said that it was fine and that she was so glad to finally meet me in person.

As if the hug hadn't happened, she extended her hand to shake but offered me only her top two fingers to hold. I took them and shook anyway, feeling the oddness of the gesture, and it was only then that I looked down and saw that, in addition to a plaid backpack at her feet, she had a blue plastic carrier. For a second, I wondered if she had somehow already recovered her suitcase from the carousel but then realized that the carrier had a heavy metal mesh gate on the front and a similar grill on the top. As I looked, something inside moved. Something with fur.

"Yes," said Oaklynn, abashed. "This is Mr. Quietly. My cat."

I dragged my eyes back to her face, but no words came.

"I say my cat, but he belonged to my friend Nadine," said Oaklynn, reading the bafflement in my face.

"Right," I said vaguely. "I'm sorry, I don't recall you saying . . . I mean, in the application . . ."

I spoke hesitantly, caught between real confusion and the awkwardness of asking what she was thinking. A cat? She hadn't mentioned a cat. She couldn't bring a cat into our house! And as the thought settled, all my previous panic and anxiety roared in my head. It was all going to go wrong because I hadn't noticed, or she hadn't mentioned, that she had a fucking cat. After all the preparation and worry, she was going to get back on the next plane and leave . . .

"I didn't mention it," said Oaklynn. Her smile was gone, and she looked miserable. "The agency doesn't like us to say we have pets. Employers don't want them. But this just happened, and I didn't know what to do and . . ."

We stood in the grayness of the airport, surrounded by distracted and irritated passengers and the equally distracted and irritable people who had come to collect them. I realized with a thrill of horror that there were tears in the woman's eyes.

"What do you mean this just happened?" I asked.

"Nadine, my friend. Mr. Quietly was hers, and she was driving across a railroad track near Park City, and the signal was out. It was dark, and I think she had some kind of engine problem, and . . ." She faltered, her eyes down, then looked suddenly up into my face. "She was hit by a train."

"Oh my God!" I gasped.

"She lived for a few hours, but the damage was just . . ." She shook her head. "And there was no one else, so Mr. Quietly was going to have to go into a shelter and probably . . . well, you know what happens to abandoned animals in those places. So I said I'd take him, but if it's a problem, I can take him to a shelter here or try to find a new owner. I'm really sorry. I should have said. I just didn't know what to do and . . ."

"It's fine," I said. "Really. Don't worry about it."

"Are you sure? I mean, if it doesn't work out, I won't keep him. He's super quiet. That's why he's called . . . you know. That's how he got his name. You probably won't know he's there. And if he's a nuisance, I can totally find him a home or take him to the Humane Society or . . ."

"It's fine," I said. "The girls will be delighted."

~

"She has a cat?" whispered Josh, wide-eyed. "When did she say anything about having a cat?"

"It was her friend's," I hissed back. Oaklynn was unloading her things from the car. "She was killed when her car was hit by a train."

"Jesus!"

"Right," I agreed. "So for now, Mr. Quietly stays with us. And if it doesn't work out . . ."

"Mr. Quietly?"

"The cat."

"Oh," said Josh. "Right." He stared at me, then opened his hands in bewildered resignation. "She was hit by a *train*? OK. OK. I guess we have a cat."

On cue, Oaklynn appeared in the front doorway, overwhelmed with luggage but beaming as she set down two huge pink suitcases. She looked bigger in the house, broad shouldered and not as much heavy as strong, centered. As she pushed past the cases, I had a fleeting image of her as a farmhand, shoving her way through unruly pigs.

"Let me help you with that," said Josh, quickly. "Hi, by the way. I'm Josh."

"Oaklynn," said Oaklynn, offering him the same two-fingered handshake she had given me.

I kicked myself for not warning him about it, but he shrugged and said, "OK" and shook.

She said, "Oaklynn Durst. So nice to meet you."

She sounded so genuinely pleased to be here that Josh hesitated, then nodded, returning the smile, the bizarre handshake and unwanted cat momentarily forgotten.

"Let me show you to your room," said Josh, picking up one of the piggy-pink suitcases and adjusting to its unexpected weight.

"Actually," said Oaklynn, making a face that was half apology and half delighted expectation, "before I do anything else, can I meet the girls?"

"Of course!" I said, charmed by her enthusiasm. "Veronica!" I called. "Oh, there you are!"

Veronica sidled out of the kitchen, looking wary and watchful, slightly uncomfortable in her new black skirt and patent leather shoes. She was holding Lamby, a plush sheep that was her constant companion.

"Well, hi there," said Oaklynn, dropping into a squat so she could meet my daughter's eyes on her level. "My name is Oaklynn, and we are going to be the best of friends. And who is this?"

Veronica, still cautious, uncertain, her eyes still lowered, spoke softly. "Lamby," she said. "She's a lamb."

"She is adorable!" said Oaklynn, apparently oblivious to Josh and me watching in careful silence, like this was a play or an interview. "What does she like to eat?"

The question seemed to catch Veronica off guard, and she looked up, her expression complicated, as if she thought she was being tested but found the process amusing.

"Grass," she said. "And gummy bears."

"Veronica!" I said, fractionally embarrassed. "You know she doesn't eat candy."

"Lambs love gummy bears," Oaklynn agreed, not looking at me. "Especially when they are really fresh, straight from the ground."

"From the ground?" echoed Veronica, intrigued.

"Oh yes," said Oaklynn with absolute certainty. "Gummy bears are best when they are just picked, before they get all wrapped up in the

45

factory. Luckily, I know a place under a waterfall where they grow best. Would you like that, Lamby?"

Veronica's eyes widened, and she held the plush toy up and made it nod enthusiastically.

"Would Lamby like to make a friend?" cooed Oaklynn. "This is Mr. Quietly."

Veronica stared, eyes like saucers, as the cat—a long-haired tabby with calculating yellow eyes—was presented to her, turning in delighted disbelief to Josh and me, hardly daring to believe it was true.

We had denied her a pet several times over the last year. Josh shrugged noncommittally, and I managed to nod, so that Veronica squealed and hugged the cat, oblivious to the way it fought to get away, and declared this the "greatest day ever."

And that was that. Veronica shrugged off her cautious apprehension and insisted on showing Oaklynn around, talking her through the mundane features of the house and its various workings. Josh and I trailed after, pleased, relieved, proud, and—for my part—very slightly jealous. Oaklynn gushed at her little suite downstairs, calling it gorgeous and—confidingly to Veronica—"just like a palace."

Then we showed her Grace, fussy after her nap, and Oaklynn begged to hold her. She sat in the rocker in which I used to nurse her and hummed vaguely. Grace stirred and considered her, eyes unfocused, then fell miraculously quiet in her arms. Josh and I glanced at each other, feeling once more like the audience at a special theatrical performance, the kind where the stage is bright and the audience sits in deep shadows, irrelevant and unnoticed. Oaklynn seemed to forget we were there, curling into and around the baby in her lap, her face a mask of contentment, Veronica settling at her feet and stroking Lamby with a dreamy abstraction I had never seen before. Josh and I might not have been there at all, and as he looked on admiringly and gave me the facial equivalent of a thumbs-up, I had to fight down the urge to say that this had all been a terrible mistake.

Chapter Six

Despite polite protestations from Josh and Anna, the woman they called Oaklynn made dinner. One of her suitcases had been partially stuffed with ingredients so they wouldn't have to go to the store and she could start cooking the moment she had settled in. Anna was nonplussed, since they had never discussed Oaklynn cooking for the family, but Josh pronounced it thoughtful of her, generous, in a way that asked Anna not to make a fuss or to take offense.

Nadine read the exchange perfectly but kept her bland smile in place.

"What are we having?" asked Anna, trying to enter into the spirit of the thing.

"Surprise," Nadine said with a grin. "But don't worry: no shrimp."

Anna wasn't great with seafood generally and shrimp in particular, her Japanese heritage notwithstanding. It was the texture. Still, she made a puzzled face.

"How did you know I didn't eat shrimp?" she asked.

"You said so," said Nadine. "Don't you remember?"

"No," said Anna, whose smile was a little fixed.

"When we were talking about the area," said Nadine, gesturing vaguely around her to indicate the city beyond the house, "you were telling me about all the restaurants close by, and you mentioned Napa, which had really good hanger steak, but you said you hadn't tried the shrimp because you didn't eat them."

Anna blinked.

"That was weeks ago," she said.

Nadine tapped the side of her head knowingly. *I remember things,* said the gesture. *I take notice.* Anna looked unnerved, so Nadine adjusted.

"Oh cripes. I'm sorry," she said, suddenly downcast. "I've over-reached a bit, haven't I? I just wanted to say thank you for the opportunity and . . . oh dear. Cripes. You're upset. Jiminy Christmas, I'm such a dunderhead. I don't have to cook. Really. I'm so sorry. It was just my way of . . . but I really don't . . ."

"It's fine," said Anna, rallying. "Sorry. I was just surprised. What a wonderful memory you must have! Of course you are welcome to cook. We'd be delighted."

"I thought you could spend some time with the girls," said Nadine, back to her former perky self. "I mean, my being here isn't just about your being able to work, right? It will get you some quality family time. If I get in the way, just say so. You won't hurt my feelings. But till then, take a break. You must have been working like crazy getting everything ready. That bedroom is beautiful, but the painting must have taken it out of you."

Again, Anna caught herself.

"It did a little," she admitted. Then she added, "How did you know I'd painted it specially?"

"You sent pictures of what would be my living quarters when we first connected online," said Nadine breezily. "It was beige then. The blue is much cheerier, if you don't mind my saying. It really is lovely. Thank you."

She didn't say that she could smell that the paint was fresh or that Anna still had a faint smear of cornflower blue on the inside of her left elbow. Instead, she reached out and offered a kind of side-and-shoulder hug, not overly intimate but sisterly, something the real Oaklynn had been fond of doing.

Anna softened at the half embrace, and her smile as they parted seemed real enough, but Nadine thought that her employer didn't like physical intimacy, not between strangers, anyway. Maybe it was an Asian thing: a firmer sense of personal space than Oaklynn—the real Oaklynn—would have assumed.

Good to know, thought Nadine, stirring her pot on the stove like a pro. She glanced up and gave Anna a look as if pleasantly surprised she was still there.

"I'll go check on the girls," said Anna.

"How about we eat in an hour?" asked Nadine.

Anna nodded vaguely, then said, "Great. Though the girls usually . . ."

"Eat at five," Nadine completed for her. "I know. I have some treats for them, too."

"Excellent," Anna managed, but Nadine could see that her employer, though she was doing her best to go along with it all, was a little stunned.

It wasn't a problem, though. This was exactly what Oaklynn would have done. Mrs. Klein would adjust soon enough. And if the truth were known, Nadine was a better cook than Oaklynn, whose tastes tended to the bland and starchy, more in keeping with the upper Midwest than the deserts of Utah. Nadine would have to at least occasionally dish out the mac and cheese with Spam, and the carrots in green Jell-O for a little Mormon verisimilitude, but she had more appetizing fare in her repertoire, and tonight would, as it were, set the table.

Before she got to work, however, there was the formal introduction of Mr. Quietly to baby Grace—who cooed and babbled with predictable delight—while Anna hovered, just managing to restrain herself from ripping the child away before the tabby slashed the infant's throat with his claws. Nadine hadn't had room for a litter box in her overstuffed luggage, so the cat was then whisked away and confined to her quarters, where she could take care of whatever mess he made. There was no point pushing her luck on the first day.

Then she cooked. Nadine preferred to work to music and plugged her iPhone into a portable speaker, which she kept turned low so as not to disturb the rest of the house. She had been afraid that her new identity would doom her to listening to nothing but the Osmonds and the Mormon Tabernacle Choir, but she had found some nice contemporary alternatives on a website dedicated to music with strong ties to the Church of Jesus Christ of Latter-day Saints. Her playlists now featured the Killers and Imagine Dragons. She even had memorized a little speech about Gladys Knight, who had converted later in life. Playing the music now, albeit softly, helped complete the impression that she was absolutely not eavesdropping on whatever furtive conversations were going on elsewhere in the house. Oaklynn would never do that.

Dinner was served exactly when she had promised and presented impeccably on the Kleins' best china. As soon as Veronica had wolfed down spaghetti with broccoli—a favorite Nadine had discovered from careful scrutiny of Anna's unselfconsciously public Facebook page—and Grace had been settled in her crib, the adults sat down to chicken breast, floured and fried till golden in olive oil, then braised till tender in marsala with mushroom caps and spinach, then tossed over angel-hair pasta. Tuscan chicken, she called it. Nadine had made the recipe exactly as she'd served it twice before, and it garnered the praise she had expected.

"This is amazing!" said Josh. "Oh my God, Anna, it's almost exactly like the first meal we had together. Remember?"

Anna did, though the memory was, Nadine thought, more complex for her. Again, Nadine wondered if she'd overplayed her hand, but Anna's sense of displacement seemed to relax as they ate. She didn't ask how Nadine—that is, Oaklynn—happened on so perfect a meal, one designed to trigger only the best and most comfortably nostalgic of feelings, and after a couple of mouthfuls, she was offering wine. Nadine, of course, declined, but the Kleins sipped their glasses of pinot noir and, for the first time since Nadine had arrived, seemed to release some of the caution with which they had been watching her.

"You never said you could cook!" Anna exclaimed. "We might need to add some kitchen duties to your workload."

She was kidding, but Nadine took it in stride.

"I'd love that," she said. "I mean, I don't want to get under your feet or take over or anything, but if you wouldn't mind me cooking once or twice a week . . ."

"That would be great," Josh said. "Yes, Anna? Give you a break from slaving over the stove. If this is anything to go by," he said, considering his empty plate, "I'd say we'd jump at the chance."

Anna's hesitation was only momentary, but Nadine saw it.

"Well, I'm sure you don't want to make a lot of decisions now," she inserted before Anna could say anything. "It must be quite an ordeal having a stranger move in with you, and the last thing I want is to get in the way. I'll leave it up to you," she added, addressing Anna directly. "If it would help for me to make the odd meal, just let me know. If not, no worries."

It was like releasing the guy rope on a tent. Anna didn't quite buckle, but a tension you wouldn't have known was there, slackened off, and she settled a little deeper in her seat, smiling with genuine pleasure and relief.

Perfect, thought Nadine.

They talked about the schedule for tomorrow, what Nadine would need to get done on her own, and whether it would be all right for her to use the car. It would. That was great, Nadine said, because in addition to swinging by the grocery store and a PetSmart where she could get supplies for Mr. Quietly, she'd really like to scope out the local parks, especially if there were places the girls particularly liked. Maybe they'd find time to all go for a walk together—Nadine, Anna, and the girls: get to know the immediate neighborhood. Sounded like a plan, said Josh, who was sitting back and watching everything with muted delight. Anna had some work to do in the morning, but maybe after lunch . . .

After dinner, Nadine loaded the fancy stainless-steel dishwasher and went over Anna's routine one more time, taking notes in an ostentatiously efficient ring binder and enthusiastically agreeing to everything Anna said. The cat—currently locked up in the basement bathroom—might still be an issue, but that could be finessed. The story of the imaginary friend and her tragic railway accident had done most of the work for her. Nadine had a gift for convincing other people that what she wanted was what they needed, but in this case, she would barely need to do that. Anna would never deprive Veronica of Mr. Quietly. The child had bonded with the cat at first sight.

Apart from being the one thing with whom she could be almost entirely and honestly herself, Mr. Quietly was also useful, she thought, as she sat in the basement, stroking him absently. He would act as a kind of barometer, a way of testing how well she was doing, how welcome she was, and what the Kleins would sacrifice to keep her around. It was important that she stay alert to all the signs. By the time she settled into her nauseatingly pretty room for the night, Nadine felt that some of the highest hurdles had been crossed. So far, in fact, it had been easy. But Nadine wasn't born yesterday, and she knew exactly how bad things could get.

Not born yesterday, she thought, considering the cliché and wishing, just for a moment, that she could have been, that she might walk into this house as a fully grown adult but one with no past, no guilt, nothing to hide. She sat quite still, lost in the thought, then blinked suddenly and glanced about her, anxious, as if someone might have taken this moment when her guard was down to flip open her head and peer inside. Nadine didn't like that. In truth, she had to admit, neither would they.

Chapter Seven

ANNA

"She's just so . . . *easy*!" Josh gasped as soon as he had put his toothbrush down.

It was true. Dinner had been a surprise and, like the cat, had put me slightly on the defensive, but that had passed quickly, and not just because Oaklynn had been so poised and professional, so good with the girls. She just seemed to fit in effortlessly. The niceness I had found slightly jarring in so many of the Nurture profiles, something that seemed either superficial or slightly holier-than-thou, seemed deep-rooted in her, stemming from something surprisingly genuine and ordinary. She didn't think she was a Disney princess slumming it in the woodland cottage, bandaging injured rabbits or whatever the hell she did while the dwarves were at work; she was a real person doing a job she was good at, a job she *liked*. No doubt the dinner was designed to be ingratiating, but I couldn't fault her for that, especially when the food had been so good.

"I could have cut that chicken with a fucking spoon," Josh mused, going back into the bedroom. "Was that fresh basil in there? That hint of pesto?"

"Yep. Brought a whole plant with her in her hand luggage," I said wonderingly as I brushed my hair. "Says she's going to plant it in the garden."

"My God, it's like moving in with Mary Poppins!"

"Right?" I said.

"I was a bit weirded out by that two-finger-handshake thing, but . . ."

"Oh my God, I was going to warn you!"

"I know! I was like, what the hell?"

We were both a little giggly after the wine. Alone upstairs and speaking in hushed voices, we felt like kids who'd pulled a fast one on their parents and couldn't believe they were getting away with it.

"But tomorrow," I said, "I get to read submissions. During the day! Do you know how long it's been since I got to sort through my in-box to see if there was anything decent in the slush pile? On a weekday? Before bedtime?"

"Let me see," Josh considered, grinning. "How old is Veronica now?"

"Exactly!" I said, climbing into bed and pulling the sheet around me. "God, Josh, I feel like I'm getting my old life back. Don't get me wrong: I love the girls. But it's like a door that has been locked for years just opened, and there are all these rooms down there full of great stuff—I'm talking *really* great stuff, and I'm, like, '*Oh yeah; I remember that . . .*'"

"And did you see Veronica's face when Oaklynn produced that spaghetti?"

"I know! How did she know that was the one thing Veronica would always eat?"

"Must be some nanny sixth-sense thing."

"Maybe it's Mormon magic," I whispered. We both got the giggles again and started shushing each other, which made it harder to stop laughing.

"You are so going to hell," said Josh.

"I'll save you a seat."

"Oh, I've got a first-class ticket to the other place."

"You wish. Strictly hellfire for you, my friend. Nonstop disco inferno."

"Well, since we're going, anyway," said Josh, switching gears and sliding over onto my side of the bed, "a little more sin can't hurt, can it?"

"Not unless you want it to," I replied in kind.

"Well, now, Mrs. Klein," he said, snuggling up and burying his face in my neck, "now that you have all this free time on your hands, what do you plan to do with it?"

"All the time when I could be cooking and cleaning and making sure Veronica doesn't take a Sharpie to the dining room walls, you mean?"

"That's the time I mean," said Josh, kissing his way up to my chin and cheek.

"I don't know," I said. "Needlepoint? Basket weaving? Crochet?"

"You thinking of becoming a live-in nanny?"

I shook my head vigorously.

"You can't trust the husbands," I said. "They get a bit handsy."

"Like this?" Josh tried.

"More like this," I said.

"Interesting."

"Very."

Afterward, when we lay on our backs, listening to the silence of the house and feeling the cold draft of the AC on our sweating bodies, Josh said, almost dreamily, "I know it's early and all, but I think this might be really good for us, Anna. You know, I was skeptical, but I think it was a good decision."

"And the cat?" I asked, grinning.

"The cat's interview will be rather longer," Josh said. "I'm going to reserve judgment."

"Veronica has wanted a pet for as long as she could say so."

"True," said Josh. He was drifting off now. I could always tell, though it had been, it suddenly seemed, months since I'd gotten to witness it. Maybe close to a year. Could it have been that long since we'd had sex? I started thinking back in stunned disbelief, counting the times since the kids had been born, and realizing that I could, all too easily. The thought brought me up short, but by the time I rolled over to ask him, he was snoring softly. Overcome with a quiet joy that he was right, that this business with Oaklynn may indeed have been the best decision we ever made, I closed my eyes.

I fell asleep quickly, body and mind relaxed in ways they hadn't been for a very long time indeed, sure of good things to come. I dreamed of a cornflower-blue sky and a meadow where gummy bears grew, Veronica as she had been when she first began to walk, stumbling through the grass and laughing so hard that at last she tumbled over and lay there, tears of hysterical delight streaming from her eyes. I woke chuckling, lay still for a while, breathing in the night, then slept again.

When I woke next, it was to a strange, disorienting sound that felt like I was still inside a dream: a nightmare, in fact. An unearthly howling was coming from outside, high and keening, like the wailing of small children, but also somehow booming and laced with an edge of menace. Not dogs. The sound brought me to a boiling panic, and I sat bolt upright, clutching the covers to my chest. My mind was slower than my body to respond, and I pushed the wrong word—*wolves?*— away before the right one settled in my head and set me to shaking Josh.

Coyotes.

It sounded like dozens of them, right outside the house. The unnerving, feral sound rose in pitch and volume as more voices joined the general cry, and then, as suddenly as it had started, it was gone.

"What?" murmured Josh, vague with sleep.

"Did you hear that?"

"Hear what?"

"That howling. There are coyotes in the yard, Josh."

I was hissing at him, breathless with fear and the sheer strangeness of it. I was a city girl. All my life. I'd never heard anything like it.

"Probably just dogs," Josh grumbled. He hadn't opened his eyes.

I snapped the bedside light on.

"I need you to look outside," I said. "See if they are in the garden. They sounded really close."

I was up now, pulling a light cotton kimono-style wrap—a *yukata*— around me and moving into the bathroom. I peered out through the window over the bathtub into the yard, but it was too dark outside to see anything. Josh made it worse by blundering in and turning the bathroom light on.

"Turn that off!" I said.

He mumbled something resentful and did so, but the darkness didn't really help. The ground fell away toward the creek at the back of the garden, so it was a long way down from the top floor. I fumbled in one of the drawers and pulled out a black flashlight with a bluish LED light. I had to cycle it through some weird flashing program before I settled on a good, solid beam, but though I swept it along the under-growth just visible by the side of the creek, I saw no telltale shapes moving in the dark, no eyes flashing.

"Are you sure you weren't dreaming?" said Josh, yawning.

"Positive," I said. "Mary Beth said she'd heard coyotes close by a month or so ago."

"She was imagining it," said Josh. "Kurt said he thought it was probably dogs."

"Kurt doesn't have a baby to worry about," I snapped back. My heart was racing, and I felt tense with anxiety.

"Neither does Mary Beth. And ours are asleep in the house. They are perfectly safe."

"We need to get some kind of protection," I said, not really thinking.

"Like what, a shotgun? You wouldn't have it in the house."

That was true. I was, Mary Beth said, *gun averse*, like it was a slightly comical condition you picked up from living in New York.

"Go to bed," I said.

Josh rallied. "Anna, if you really think you heard something, I believe you. I'm just saying . . ."

"Go to bed, Josh," I repeated, more kindly this time. "You have work tomorrow."

Chapter Eight

ANNA

In the morning, I went to check on the girls, only to find that Oaklynn had their breakfast already in hand. Veronica barely spoke to me, so enamored was she of Oaklynn's syrupy chocolate-chip pancakes, so I warned her that she was only being allowed to skip her usual fruit and Cheerios because this was Oaklynn's first day.

"Did Oaklynn do wrong, Mommy?" asked Veronica, trying to decide whom she should be criticizing.

"No, honey," I said, feeling Oaklynn's watchful nervousness. "Let's just say this is a special occasion."

"Sorry," mouthed Oaklynn, as soon as Veronica got up to put her plate away. "I should have asked."

"It's fine," I said. "But yes, we should chat about the girls' dietary restrictions."

"Do they have allergies?" asked Oaklynn, baffled. "I don't recall seeing anything in their . . ."

"No, just general health," I said. "We try to restrict their sugar intake, processed foods, things like that."

"Right. Of course. Oh cripes! Sorry. There's coffee made if you want some."

"Thanks," I said, getting a mug and splashing milk in the bottom. I felt churlishly ungrateful, like I was starting the day off on the wrong foot.

"If it's not how you like it, tell me. May take me a couple of tries, but I'll figure it out."

"I'm easy," I said. "However you take it is fine."

"Oh, I don't drink coffee," she said. "Or tea or Coke."

Right, I thought, feeling stupid. It was a Mormon thing. Which meant that the coffee that lent the kitchen a warm, homey aroma had been made exclusively for me.

"Sorry," I said. "I'm tired. I had a weird night."

"The coyotes woke you?" asked Oaklynn.

"Yes!" I said, delighted, pancakes forgotten. "You heard them, too?"

"Of course! Cripes! Who didn't?"

"Josh," I said, loading the delivery so that she rolled her eyes, grinning. I poured my coffee and sampled it. It was good and strong, just this side of bitter. The way I liked it.

"And he didn't believe you," said Oaklynn knowingly. "Jiminy Christmas."

"He *said* he did. Eventually. But that's what it was, right? Coyotes? Not dogs or . . . anything else."

"Definitely coyotes," said Oaklynn. "You hear them a lot in Utah."

"I knew it!" I said. "Man, they sounded so close. Freaked me out." I took my cup over to the window and gazed outside. "Why are they here now? They never used to be."

"The population is expanding all over the country. I heard a thing on NPR about it. It's like in Europe with foxes moving into cities, changing their diet and whatnot."

"Coyotes, though," I said vaguely with a shudder. "Where do they go during the day, you think?"

"Bed down somewhere safe," said Oaklynn. "You've got some serious greenery out there for a city."

"It's the creek," I said. "Designated greenway. Runs right through the city. No one can build on it. We saw a couple of deer there a few months ago, walking along it like it was a highway."

"Keeps them off the roads, I guess."

"Yeah. We've always loved it," I confided. "Makes the area quiet and peaceful, and when you look out there and it's just trees . . . It's like we're not really in the city at all, you know? There are turtles and herons. But *coyotes*? Not crazy about that. In fact," I added, turning back to her, "I'm going to look in the yard. See if there are paw prints."

"You want me to come?"

"No, you stay with the girls. I won't be a minute."

The fence at the back of the property was really just a guide, a warning to Veronica not to stray beyond it unless she was with me, three wire strands held up on uneven wooden posts. It was easy to climb over or through, and the little gate that gave access to the creek itself was often left open. That was the case now, and I was horrified to see the dirt bank from the trickle of mud-colored water covered in paw prints. A few of them—possums or raccoons, presumably—were like tiny hands with slim finger lines ending in little indentations from claws, but the vast majority were doglike, and they were all over the yard. I stared at them, remembering the unearthly horror of the howling, and felt suddenly unsafe, as if the pack might emerge from the bushes and attack me right now.

I shoved the gate closed and latched it, though I was doubtful that it would actually keep the coyotes out, then walked quickly back to the house, checking over my shoulder and wondering what kind of fence we could get built quickly that would be more functional. Oaklynn read my face as soon as I got back inside, by which time I was already hunting for my yard guy's number on my phone.

"You OK?" she asked.

"Not really," I admitted. "Not used to the idea that I may have to defend my family against wild animals."

"I think they are mostly harmless."

"Maybe, but there's a big gap between mostly and completely, and I don't want Veronica falling through it."

Even as I said it, I knew I was being melodramatic. *What are you doing?* I wondered. *Is this a performance of what a good mother you are because you're feeling guilty about hiring a nanny?*

I shook my head, and Oaklynn gave me a worried look.

"Can I do anything?" she asked.

"Look after the girls. Maybe take them for a walk. I'm going to call Eduardo, my yard guy, to see if he can do something about that fence. What do people do in Utah?" I added. "To keep the coyotes away, I mean."

"Everyone has guns out West." Oaklynn shrugged. "I bet a lot of your neighbors here . . ."

"Not in our house," I said, more forcefully than I meant to, so that Oaklynn looked chastened. "I'm just not comfortable with them. Especially with kids in the house."

"I get that."

"Is there an alternative?"

"Well, putting poison down is probably against city ordinances . . ."

I shook my head vehemently.

"I'm not looking to wipe them out," I said. "I just want something that would be helpful if I felt the need. Put my mind at ease."

Oaklynn shrugged again. "Bows are hard to use," she said. "A crossbow?"

"Aren't they dangerous, too?"

"To whatever you point them at, yeah," said Oaklynn. "But they take a lot of strength to cock, and you wouldn't leave one lying around loaded."

I couldn't help but be impressed.

"Cooking and crossbows," I remarked, smiling for the first time since I'd come downstairs. "If I'd known you would be this versatile, I would have hired you years ago."

Oaklynn grinned bashfully.

"You pick a lot of things up in the country," she said.

It was a slightly odd remark, layered somehow, as if I'd cast a stone into a pool whose ripples somehow concealed its depth, but then she was smiling and cleaning up breakfast, all ordinary efficiency, and I put it down to my uneven night.

"You need a nap?" asked Oaklynn.

I made a scoffing noise.

"Yes, but no," I said, giving her an appreciative look. "That's not what you are here for. I need to do some work. Can I leave you with the girls till lunchtime, and then maybe we could go to the park together?"

"Perfect," said Oaklynn. "I thought we'd take a walk. Veronica says she has things to show me."

"I'll bet she does," I said.

And I went upstairs. It wasn't even nine in the morning, and I went up to my little book-crammed office and closed the door, ready to work. It felt . . . OK. There was the smallest tug of guilt as I climbed the stairs, a twinge of regret like the one I experienced when Grace turned six months old and I decided to stop nursing. But then I was at my computer and working through my email, and I felt the rush of being my own person again.

In my first few years at Ramkins and Deale, I had begun to cultivate a stable of writers in various genres, particularly in the slightly more literary end of the mystery and thriller market and, in nonfiction, in history and biography. When I went on hiatus, however, most of my writers were switched over to Bob Greene and Rachel Martinez, who had joined the company around the same time I had. Some of my writers had stayed in touch, and it was easy for me to check on their progress through my colleagues, but it had been made clear to me that when I came back full-time, I would not be getting them back.

"It's been nearly three years," said Theresa Ramkins when we'd first started to wrangle weeks ago with the specifics of my return. "Your clients have been with their present representation longer than they were with you. It's not fair to ask them to come back. We'll keep the door open, of course, for those who really want to make the move, but I'm not comfortable putting them on the spot."

She was right, of course, and it wasn't surprising, but it was still hard to hear, and not just because I was the one who had gotten them their first publishing deals. It was daunting to feel that, despite my years of experience, I was effectively starting from scratch. It felt like a demotion, like the detective who gets busted down to traffic in a seventies cop show. Everything I had achieved so far felt oddly irrelevant, like I was a newcomer, some intern hired straight from school to sift through the slush looking for the impossibly rare gold nugget. Worse, I had to do it not from the heart of a bustling community where agents discussed their submissions with each other and met with acquisitions editors over lunch at Manhattan sidewalk cafés, but from the wilds of North Carolina. The coyotes prowling my yard might have been symptoms of my professional isolation. It was demoralizing.

Or rather, it had been, and there had been days when the whole idea of going back to work had seemed more trouble than it was worth. But now the nanny was here—efficient, likable, and oozing competence—and, coyotes notwithstanding, the landscape suddenly looked quite different. I felt the old excitement, the eagerness to get started, to find some remarkable writer and share his or her work with the reading public. That was the real thrill: not the commission, not having clients hitting bestseller lists or coming home from awards shows with little statuettes. It was the electricity of finding magical, compelling words, stories, and ideas, all entrusted to me to put them where they could be seen. I sat down at my laptop and powered it on, licking my lips and flexing my neck and shoulders like a sprinter in the blocks. As the computer came to life, I felt ready, as I had been four years ago, to take on the world.

Doing so with what was in my in-box, however, was going to prove tricky. I had reactivated my portion of the R&D site a week ago and had been pleased to see that twelve submissions had come in since, but my optimism stalled quickly. Two were offering vague story ideas that their authors would like to sell to "one of your other writers." Three were projects I had no experience with and no interest in representing (an "in the tradition of" Louis L'Amour Western, some hilariously awkward BDSM erotica, and a Native American cookbook). One was a picture book about a cantankerous rabbit that promised that the author's spouse would provide the illustrations, and one consisted of a seven-page query letter expounding the writer's Ayn Rand–derived philosophy structured as a self-help book. Of the remaining five, one had a decent query but an impenetrably self-absorbed writing sample; another could turn a sentence but had no story to speak of; and a third was almost a carbon copy of Gillian Flynn's *Gone Girl*, a subgenre whose day in the sun was long past its expiration date. That left two. One was a solid if not especially original police procedural set in New Orleans featuring a heavy-drinking divorced cop and the murder of a Realtor who may have been connected to shady dealings at city hall. As I shaped a boilerplate "thanks but no thanks" to the other writers, I opted to put that one aside and mull on it a little, turning in the meantime to the last submission, sent only this morning.

It was called *Hell Is Empty*, not an original title—a quick Amazon search showed it had been used several times before, though that wasn't why I recognized it. I punched the words into Google and got the rest of the half-remembered quotation. It was from Shakespeare's *The Tempest*.

"Hell is empty and all the devils are here."

A resonant phrase. The author, Ben Lodging, described himself as a writing instructor at a community college in Pennsylvania. He had a few short stories in minor journals and had self-published another novel two years earlier, the sales of which he was brutally—endearingly—candid about. The current novel was a thriller told from the perspective of an absolutely average man called Joseph Carried, an accountant who found himself increasingly drawn to murder to relieve the tedium of his loveless existence. The query came with two chapters totaling thirty pages. The story's bleakness was countered by a dry, self-deprecating wit, and by the query's tantalizing promise that the final sections had not yet been written, so whether Mr. Carried actually committed murder had not been decided yet.

It was an unconventional tease, and though I found myself immediately skeptical about whether anyone could write a thriller in which—perhaps—no one actually died, I could see the power of the premise in marketing. Anyone who studies bestseller lists and reads a lot knows that the innate quality of a book is only one of the factors that shape its success or failure in the marketplace. Lots of other things can propel a mediocre novel into the spotlight. Sometimes details of the author's own experience made a better story than his or her book. Sometimes a cultural coincidence, an accident of timing, made an ordinary book seem strangely prescient or compellingly relevant. Any number of things could be the lead for articles and interviews that might be the difference between massive bestseller status, sequels, international fame, and movie deals, and—on the other hand—utter oblivion, the book vanishing without a trace in a matter of weeks, never earning out its meager advance and actually harming the chance of the author ever selling a second book.

Would a backstory about a novelist not knowing whether his character was a killer till the very end be nothing more than noise, or the hook that would draw real attention to what promised to be an intriguing and at least competently written novel?

"Taking the girls out!" called Oaklynn from the downstairs hall.

"Great," I shouted back. "Have fun! Call me if you get lost."

"Will do."

I heard the snap as the front door opened, the smatter of conversation between Oaklynn and Veronica, the latter babbling cheerfully and relentlessly about where birds went to sleep. Then it shut with a *thunk*, and I was alone in the house for the first time in what felt like years.

Unnerved by the stillness, I got up, went to the window, and watched Oaklynn maneuver the baby buggy down the steps and into the driveway, feeling a pang of guilt that I wasn't helping, though it was clear she didn't need it. She was strong and resourceful. I could almost sense her concentration from here, though her face was shaded by the wide brim of the navy blue floppy hat she had been wearing when she'd arrived. I watched her check the brakes of the buggy, then hitch the diaper bag with the blue cartoon elephant head on it over her shoulder, a study in competence. I breathed in and out, waiting for the urge to run after them to pass as they set off down the driveway and into the empty road. Finally, deliberately, I turned away from the window and went back to my desk.

The silence of the house thickened about me, and there was only the computer and Ben Lodging's odd experiment of a story, the sample of which I read and reread with no sense that twenty minutes had turned into an hour, then two, until the morning was gone.

Chapter Nine

The big man showed his badge in one hand and the photograph in the other.

"Edward Flanders," he said. "FBI. Do you think you've seen this woman? Maybe working here as an orderly. Maybe just in the patient waiting room. She could be a volunteer."

He was in the labor-and-delivery department at Saint Luke's Hospital of Kansas City, Missouri.

"What's her name?" asked the OB-GYN nurse. She was middle-aged, heavy, and pink, her blonde hair dark at the roots. Her name badge read *Shelly*.

"She goes by different names," said Flanders.

Shelly's eyes got wide and interested.

"Is she dangerous?" she said.

"I can't discuss that," said Flanders. "Does she look familiar to you?"

Shelly stared hard at the picture, then shook her head, reluctant to let the drama go.

"No. I'm sorry."

"And you've been here how long?"

"Five years. Nearly six."

"OK," said Flanders, pocketing the picture. "Thanks, anyway. Can you point me to the Neonatal Intensive Care Unit?"

"Through those doors down there, then along the corridor to the end and turn left. You'll see the signs."

It was almost certainly a waste of time, but he would check it out, anyway. Hospitals were pretty compartmentalized these days, so it was just possible that someone working in one department would be unknown to those in another. Not likely, but possible.

He couldn't get beyond the duty nurse at the NICU's reception desk, but his badge cut through some of her professional gatekeeper demeanor, and she took a long look at the picture. She shook her head, but as Flanders was thanking her for her time, another nurse, black and coat-hanger thin, came in and picked up a clipboard.

"Hey, Marcie," said the first, whose name was Corinne. "You seen her?"

Marcie made a skeptical face, brows knitted like a cartoon character, then looked up, the puzzlement clearing like the sun breaking through clouds.

"Yeah," she said. "I've seen her. Not here. At Mercy. I transferred. She was an orderly in peds." She pronounced it *peeds*. "Pediatrics."

"When?"

"Not sure. I think she finished before I came here. So . . . five months ago, maybe."

"Do you remember her name?"

The nurse shook her head slowly.

"It wasn't, by chance, Nadine, was it?" asked Flanders.

Another head shake. Then the woman raised an index finger in triumph.

"Charlene!" she said. "That was it. I remember now. She seemed so nice. She's not in trouble, is she?"

Charlene? thought Flanders, amused. *Good one.*

"I'm afraid I'm not at liberty to say," said Flanders.

"But she seemed so nice," said Marcie again.

"Guess you can never tell with people, huh?" said the other.

Flanders nodded at that.

"You may be right there," he said.

He gave them a broad smile of gratitude. It was impossible not to feel flattered by their awed glee at being close to something that felt like television. "You've been very helpful, ladies. Thank you."

Chapter Ten

A part of her was still Nadine, of course, but she no longer thought of herself that way. She was Oaklynn Durst. It wasn't a role as much as it was an identity with which she had bonded at what she thought of as a deep-tissue level, a formative place where the granular specifics of personal experience had twined them into the very muscle and bone of her body. It had to be that way, or all the work—the research into child care, the careful attention with which she had studied the real Oaklynn and her friends (some nannies; others, mothers)—would feel merely like a coat she put on to go outside. That would never do. Eventually, she would be caught without it, lulled into complacency by a break in the weather. Think of it as an act, and one day she would forget she was being watched, judged according to the experience and personality of someone she wasn't. So she relegated Nadine to passive memory, a person she had once known who no longer had any relevance to her life, and she embraced being Oaklynn Durst even in her most private moments.

Long ago, when she had been someone quite different, Nadine had read about method acting, about Stanislavski, Strasberg, Adler, Meisner, and their various approaches to inhabiting roles so completely that as performers, they married their own experiences to the given circumstances of their parts so that they seemed to truly *be* the characters. The lines might be scripted, but the emotional realities that fired them as they came from the actors were real; the thoughts, the feelings behind them always true and clear. It was the only way to act, she had decided, however much people warned that you might lose yourself in the performance; that only mattered if you planned to come offstage.

Oaklynn didn't.

Nadine was gone—dead or living in Japan with her husband; it really didn't matter. The person here, nannying for a literary agent and her banker husband in Charlotte, North Carolina, *was* Oaklynn Durst. If you believed it, the audience would believe it, and as those theater types agreed, where there was no deception, there could be no false moments onstage.

Oaklynn walked the streets with the Klein family's two-seater buggy, Grace sleeping fitfully, Veronica peering about her and commenting on everything she saw. For her, the stage now extended forever in all directions. She was inside the play now. It encircled her, defined her, until fiction became fact. For Oaklynn Durst, nanny, there was no dressing room, no offstage of any kind.

They walked up Tanglewood Lane to Harris Road, and Oaklynn marveled at the rising heat and the unwelcome humidity that, she remembered from long ago, was typical of summer in the South. After Salt Lake City, she found the vivid greens of the manicured lawns a little surreal, but the massive, looming trees were what truly unnerved her. She hadn't seen anything like them in a good while. She thought they were oaks or elms, though she wasn't sure. Some of them were surely older than any of the buildings, and they towered over the neighborhood, crowding the skyline with a dense canopy of leaves. In some cases, their limbs reached right across the road, casting deep shadows on the asphalt. They seemed to be brooding, watching, in spite of the brightness of the day, and though the cool of the shade was a welcome break, Oaklynn found herself relieved when she stepped out into the direct sunlight again.

She had been studying the area on Google Maps for weeks and had, after breakfast, outlined her route to Anna, who had approved, impressed and a little overwhelmed, as she should be. As they made the slow climb up Tanglewood, Oaklynn saw what she took to be two other nannies, an older black woman and a Latina, both pushing their white children in strollers. It made her think briefly, unpleasantly, of Carl, who would have had something to say about that. She gritted her teeth, repressed the urge to spit, and swallowed the unpleasantness. Carl was part of Nadine, and Nadine was gone, taking her grim little secrets with her.

She was Oaklynn now. She smiled and nodded at the other nannies, making a mental note that one day in a week or two, she might exchange pleasantries with them, get to know them a little, but she wasn't ready for that yet and so said nothing. When the black woman seemed to hesitate outside a big stone-fronted house on the corner of Harris and Tanglewood, Oaklynn paused to fuss with Grace's sippy cup till the woman went inside and closed the door. From there, Oaklynn picked up the pace all the way down to the corner of Providence and right to the only traffic signal she had seen so far. As they approached the next corner, Veronica, who had been craning to look back and down at the sidewalk, looked up.

"You have witchy shoes," she said.

Oaklynn considered her battered black boots with the silver buckles. "You think so?"

"I have a book with a witch called Griselda, and she has shoes *exactly* like yours."

"Guess I'm a witch, then."

"You have a broomstick?" asked Veronica, grinning slyly, playing but knowing she was being rude.

"Of course," said Oaklynn. "How do you think I got here from Utah?"

Veronica smiled uncertainly.

"Are you really a witch?" she asked.

"A good witch. I use my magic to protect you."

"That's OK, then. And you keep the bad witches away?"

"That's my job."

"Doggy!" shouted Grace, joyously pointing across the road to where a twentysomething girl was walking a yellow Lab on a long red leash, one of those retractable things with the big handle that spooled out like a tape measure.

This was as far from the house as they would get, the only area where they left behind the quiet neighborhood streets and saw anything like real traffic: two lanes in each direction. It was almost lunchtime, and the cars were moving quickly and steadily. The woman on the other side of the road saw them looking and waved at them. Oaklynn took one hand off the buggy and splayed her fingers in greeting, smiling as the girl—she might have been college age—called out, "He's so strong!"

The dog was pulling her along, stopping to sniff, then bounding a little farther.

Not full grown, thought Oaklynn. *Still at least part puppy.*

"Hi, doggy!" called Veronica.

The dog turned to face them, pulling again, and the girl laughed.

And then he was in the road, running toward them.

The impact was staggeringly sudden and loud. There was a squeal of tires and a blown horn as a second car narrowly avoided the first. And then the woman was just standing there and screaming.

The cars stopped, and people spilled out. Oaklynn hesitated, caught between wanting to flee and feeling the tug of responsibility that needed to be answered. The dog had been trying to reach them, after all.

"What happened?" cried Veronica, her tone wild, desperate. "Where's the doggy?"

Oaklynn dithered for a second, staring across the road. The girl was still screaming incoherently, standing several yards from where the dog lay bleeding.

The road was still, and it was easy to steer the buggy through the halted traffic and up the curb on the other side. Oaklynn pushed it up onto someone's lawn and locked the wheels a safe distance from the site of the accident. She told Veronica to wait and crossed hurriedly to the hysterical dog walker.

Two people were already with her, and a third was kneeling over the Labrador, which was alive and panting but otherwise still. The blood around its head was as red as paint. Another woman had pulled her car over and was clambering out, looking dazed and horrified. A portion of the fender had been knocked clean away.

A solid hit, then. Not good.

"I'm so sorry," said Oaklynn, meaning it, stunned and horrified by how quickly it had happened.

"She's not my dog," said the woman, her desolation increasing. "I was walking her for a friend."

It was the first coherent thing she'd said since the accident, and it added new layers of trauma to the moment. Her grief and shock were at least partly an anticipation of her friend's feelings. One of the women put an arm around her shoulders, and she turned into the embrace, sobbing. The other woman was already working with a man to get the injured dog onto a blanket and into her car, while yet another was comforting the driver, who was crying as she tried to call the police.

"It's not your fault," she heard someone say to her, just as someone else said the same thing to the dog walker.

Actually, Oaklynn thought, it was both of their faults. The dog walker had not had the animal under control, letting out the retractable leash and allowing it to get way out into the street. A long way. The car that had hit the dog had been in the middle lane, which meant the animal was almost twenty feet from the dog walker at the point of impact. That also meant that the driver had ample time to see it run out but had not reacted. There was no rubber on the road near the crash site, so the car hadn't braked till after the collision, though there was no curve in the road that might have hidden the dog up to the last second. Oaklynn considered the phone in the driver's trembling hand and wondered where it had been the moment before she had hit the Labrador.

Oaklynn felt no outrage. She even felt a sort of sympathy for them. It was an awful thing to be responsible for that garish red wetness on the road, the lolling tongue, the stillness of the dog as it became incapable of its own distress. Instead, she felt like she was playing Tetris, rotating the puzzle pieces to see where they would fit so that the full picture of what happened came into coherent focus. She watched the two women as the bystanders consoled them, embracing them, speaking in low, soothing terms, as if it had all been an utterly random act like a lightning strike, what the real Oaklynn might have called an act of God.

She turned to focus on the dog, and she felt her eyes swim with tears of genuine grief and horror. When she looked back at the driver and the dog walker, now the center of a tight huddle of benevolent empathy, she felt a rush of outrage, sharp and bitter as iron in her mouth.

Not your fault? Nonsense. This was human error: one person who didn't have control of the animal she was supposed to be looking after, and another who, even if not actually texting at the time of the collision, was clearly not fully alert and focused on her driving. But instead of being called out for their negligence, they were being hugged, calmed, their errors ignored and erased in the hurry to make them feel better.

It wasn't right.

A tall woman in business slacks who had been tending to the Labrador and whose perfectly white blouse was spotted with red on one cuff leaned into the dog walker, holding her with such tenderness that it was hard to believe that they had not laid eyes on each other till only a minute earlier. For her part, the dog walker—in spite of her anguish—seemed to glow with gratitude, as if her body were leeching something out of the businesswoman's body. Something reviving, nurturing. Something like love.

Oaklynn marveled, though it would be truer to say that the person who was watching with such fascinated hunger, such strange and unknowable yearning verging on jealousy, was actually Nadine. She turned slowly to the buggy, and her eyes fell on Veronica. It made no sense, but for just a moment, Nadine saw not Veronica, her new nearly four-year-old charge, but a different girl entirely.

Maddie.

The ages weren't even close to right, so it had to be something of the desperation in Veronica's face that had triggered the bittersweet memory, the need for comfort, for hope. Veronica was pretending not to know what had happened, wanted Nadine—*Oaklynn*—to tell her all was or would be well, just as Maddie once had. It wouldn't be, of course, not now. It certainly had not been then.

Because of you, said the voice in her head. *Because of what you are and what you aren't.*

Seeming to sense some conflicted emotion in her, Veronica's eyes tightened, wary and suddenly close to tears. For a moment, Nadine just looked back at her, eyes shielded against the sun. Then she smiled abruptly with just her mouth.

"Time to go home," she said.

Chapter Eleven

ANNA

"Oh my God!" I exclaimed, folding Oaklynn into my arms in a sudden, desperate impulse. "It must have been awful for you."

Even as I did so, my eyes slid over her shoulder to where Veronica was watching us, puzzled but not distraught. I pulled back to look into Oaklynn's teary eyes, but she read the question on my lips before I could ask it.

"They didn't see," she said, her voice low. "Veronica knows something happened, but I made sure she didn't see. It was very upsetting."

"I'm sure it was," I said, pulling her to me again and squeezing her with greater warmth. "Did the dog . . . ?"

I couldn't finish the sentence, and Oaklynn could only shrug, her face contorted with renewed anguish inches from mine. She was clinging to me, her breasts heaving against me with each ragged breath.

"I don't know," she said. "A lady in an SUV said she would take her to the closest vet, but I couldn't stay to help, what with the girls and all."

How she had kept the girls from the worst of the accident I wasn't sure, but I felt a rush of gratitude that was so fierce, it was almost overwhelming. "Thank you," I said.

"I wish I knew if she was OK, but I don't know how to find out. I didn't know what to do. It was just horrible."

I squeezed her tighter still, then felt her resolve stiffen and released her.

Oaklynn swallowed down a sob, then pulled away, wiped her eyes, and composed herself, her face in her hands. When her fingers parted, her countenance was almost clear, and a version of her signature smile was in place again as she turned to the girls. Veronica was watching her shrewdly, but something of the wary uncertainty in her face dissolved as Oaklynn started chivvying her out of her shoes and up to the playroom. It was impossible not to be impressed by her dedication, her refusal to let the trauma of what had happened get to the kids.

"Head on up," she said. "I need to change Grace. Then I'll be right there."

"Miss Oaklynn, can we do the Leapfrog? I'm getting really good at it."

"You are at that, Veronica," she said, still managing to smile. "I'll tell you what: why don't you practice for a few minutes, and then you can show me what you can do?"

Satisfied, Veronica beamed and headed up the stairs, Oaklynn watching her carefully all the way. Even so, I had to fight an impulse to go up after her. Josh and I usually held her hand as she went up and down the stairs, and we kept the gate at the top closed. Veronica knew as much, and there was a furtive glee in the way she avoided my eyes as she made her way up and then turned in triumph once she reached the top.

"Made it!" she announced. "See, Mommy? I told you I could do it by myself."

Oaklynn turned to me, suddenly anxious.

"You don't normally let her go by herself?" she asked.

"Not usually," I said, soft-pedaling it because of what Oaklynn had been through.

"Oh cripes!" said Oaklynn, something of her former distress flickering back into her eyes. "Sorry."

"It's fine," I said. "So long as she's careful and you keep an eye on her."

"Of course," said Oaklynn. "And she is almost four. It's good for her to have a little independence."

I felt a prickle of defensiveness.

"Sure," I said. "It's just a long way to fall is all."

Oaklynn opened her mouth to say something, and for a split second, her eyes were blank, appraising and quite unfamiliar. Then the smile was back, and she was nodding.

"Absolutely," she said, tapping the side of her head playfully. "I'll make a note."

I hesitated, feeling awkward at overruling her, knowing that Josh said I worried too much, that I was overprotective. It was important that we didn't get off on the wrong foot so early in our relationship, and the woman had already had a lousy morning.

"You know," I said, "I'm sure you're right. Just . . . you know."

"I do," said Oaklynn. "I know how strange this must be for you. How hard. But don't worry. I'll watch the girls as if they were my own."

I nodded fervently, feeling something like pity for her now as I looked at her, her eyes red from weeping, the ridiculous hat and baggy dress adding ten years and fifty pounds.

"Listen," I said, "Veronica will be fine by herself for a few minutes. I'll check on her while you change Grace. Then we'll call around to the local vets and see what we can find out about the dog."

"Really?" said Oaklynn, her face buckling into something that oscillated between pleasure and sorrow. "You don't mind?"

"Of course not," I replied. "While you're living with us, you're family."

Chapter Twelve

Anna had been busy in her office for most of the afternoon, and by the time she started calling the local vets, they were already closed. She listened while Anna left voice mails with requests for any information on vehicular accidents involving dogs in the Wendover Road area, and she smiled bravely when Anna promised they would check in again tomorrow. It wasn't the closure Oaklynn wanted, but the sense of them working together, the look Anna kept giving her—earnest and pitying and desperate to help—was almost as good.

Alone in the basement after everyone had gone to bed, Oaklynn replayed the day as she sat in her rocker, Mr. Quietly purring loudly in her lap. She stroked him absently, feeling his warmth through her dress. The bedroom was dark, the blinds on the windows down and the lights—including the reading lamp by her armchair—off, so that the gloom was thick. The only thing she could see was the thin pallor of the white molding where the ceiling met the wall. But Oaklyn wasn't seeing with her real eyes. She was replaying the day in her head: the dog, the conversation with Anna afterward, and the tender warmth of her embrace, nurturing and calming as warm milk. Alone in the darkness, she could almost feel it again.

Almost.

"While you're living with us," Anna had said, "you're family."

Oaklynn drew a breath at the thought, an almost gasp of longing, of satisfaction, of hunger for more.

Chapter Thirteen

Josh turned his key in the front door, but it didn't open when he twisted the handle. He blundered into it and stepped back, irritated.

"Oh cripes!" Oaklynn called from inside. "Sorry. One second."

He waited for a few seconds, listening to the fumbling, then tried the door again. This time it opened, but only a few inches before it stuck against something soft but immovable.

"Jiminy Christmas," said Oaklynn again. "Nearly there."

More movement, and then the door opened fully. It was immediately clear what had caused the blockage. The hall was full of mismatched bags and cardboard cartons spewing canned food, boxes of pasta, bulk-bound stacks of underarm deodorant, and three massive shrink-wrapped packages of toilet paper, some of which had gotten wedged up against the foot of the stairs. Each package contained thirty-six rolls. Josh slid sideways, toeing some of the boxes out of the way and casting an inquiring look around as he did so.

"Hi," said Oaklynn brightly. Anna was behind her, looking simultaneously amused and baffled. Her eyes met Josh's, and she suppressed a smirk.

"Oaklynn went to BJ's," said Anna, daring him to laugh.

"I see that," he replied. "And are we expecting visitors? A major sports franchise, perhaps? And, you know, a dysentery outbreak?"

Oaklynn gave him a blank look, her smile unwavering.

"You have to buy in bulk to get the best deals," she said cheerfully.

"Right," said Josh. "Great. And now we're covered until . . . I don't know. What year is it?"

"Thanks so much, Oaklynn," said Anna pointedly. "This is great. I'm always running out of aluminum foil."

She had just picked up a box containing what looked to be a dozen rolls.

"You won't now," said Josh.

Anna gave him a murderous look, but she was also clearly struggling not to laugh.

"I'll start stocking the pantry," said Oaklynn, bustling out, loaded down but apparently oblivious.

"Let me know if we need, you know, another house . . . ," said Josh.

Anna slapped his arm. He winced, then turned on her and pantomimed, "What the hell?"

"Shh," said Anna. "She was taking initiative."

"Are you sure she's not on commission at BJ's?"

Anna gave him another look but couldn't hide her own grin.

"I'll just get the next load from the car," said Oaklynn.

"There's more?" said Josh.

"Oh yes," said Oaklynn cheerfully. "This is just the first load."

"Right," said Josh. "I'll give you a hand."

"No, no," she said, waving him off. "You've had a hard day at work. I know a man needs to relax when he gets home."

Anna's grin developed an eye roll.

"It's fine," said Josh. "I'm happy to help out."

Oaklynn turned abruptly to face him, and her smile now was fixed. Though it was wide, it did not reach her eyes.

"No," she said firmly. "This is my job. Kindly let me perform it unaided."

Thrown as much by the peculiar wording as he was by her manner, Josh hesitated, then mumbled his "If you're sure" agreements. As she bustled officiously out, he gave Anna a searching look.

"Are we expecting a hard winter?" he said. "Or some kind of thermonuclear holocaust?"

"She's just trying to help."

"On our nickel!" he said, watching Oaklynn humping boxes out of the back of the car.

"It will all get used."

"Just in time for Gracie's sweet sixteenth."

She shushed him again, and he gave her a sidelong look.

"It doesn't bother you?" he said. "You don't think she's overstepping?"

Anna shrugged and smiled that thoughtful, sympathetic smile he knew so well.

"I think she wants to do her bit," she said.

"She already does . . ."

"She wants to be more than just an employee," said Anna.

Josh frowned at that.

"But that's what she is, Anna. You know that, right? We pay her, and she works for us."

Anna blushed, then met his eyes and smiled.

"I know," she said.

"Yeah?" he said.

She turned and gave him a hard look.

"Yeah," she echoed.

The front door opened, and Oaklynn came in, loaded down under a stack of boxes, the contents of which included a sealed six-pack of green olives.

"You got a couple of gallons of gin to go with these?" Josh quipped.

Anna's glance held no shared mirth now.

"Good with cheese," said Oaklynn, oblivious.

"Which is arriving on a flatbed truck?" said Josh.

"Gosh, you're such a tease!" said Oaklynn, unoffended. "Isn't he a tease?"

"He is," said Anna, her gaze on him level and fixed.

Chapter Fourteen

Edward Flanders parked outside Children's Mercy hospital in Kansas City and shaped his beard in the rearview mirror. It needed trimming. Maybe tonight. It would make a change from the motel's cable TV offerings.

He showed his badge in the entry foyer and got a nod to the pediatrics wing from the officious-looking woman at the front desk. He took the elevator to the third floor. The staff recognized the woman in his photograph right away.

"Charlene!" said a young man with immaculately close-cropped hair and an earring with a shiny blue stone. "Aw, I miss her."

"Me, too!" said his colleague, a broad-shouldered black woman who might have been sitting in that chair all her adult life. "Where is she now?"

"Well, that's what I'm trying to determine, ma'am," said Flanders.

"She's missing?" said the guy, like a startled parakeet.

"She left Mercy in March?" said Flanders.

"That's right," said the woman. "Beginning of the month."

"And did she say where she was headed?"

"West," said the guy, like he was answering a question on a TV game show and was about to win a prize. "She said she'd never been out west and wanted to see what it was like."

"Anything more specific?" said Flanders, taking out his notebook and pen.

The male nurse made a sour face and shook his head.

"Did she say why she was leaving?" Flanders tried. "Trouble at work or something?"

They both fought to contradict that.

"Nothing like that. She was our best orderly. Everyone loved her."

"Then why did she leave?"

"She seemed restless, you know?" said the black woman. Angela, according to her name tag. "Never quite settled. Always looking over her shoulder. I saw her with some of the battered women, you know, the abuse victims, and I thought there was kind of a connection there. You know? Like she understood. I asked her about it, and she sort of shrugged it off, said it was all in the past, but if you ask me, it wasn't that far in the past, and she wasn't over it. When she stopped coming in, I figured it was something like that. That she'd decided to move on . . . or maybe go back to the guy, you know? Sometimes they do that."

"Or maybe she was trying to make it harder for him to find her?" said her colleague, giving her a significant look.

"You know," Angela said, "you might be right at that. Maybe so. She said something once about how you never really know men, like she had learned the hard way. Somebody in her past who had turned out to be, you know, bad. Something like that."

"Oh my God!" said the male nurse, slapping his hands to his forehead in a theatrical *How dumb am I?* way. "One time we saw some news coverage of some rally, and she said she knew a guy who turned out to be a *Nazi*! You know, a white-supremacist type! Klansman or something. For real. Said she didn't even suspect it till she was living with him. Had books and hidden tattoos and all kinds of scary stuff. Can you believe that?"

"No!" said Angela.

"Swear to God."

"Well," she replied, folding her arms defiantly, "if this was something to do with *that guy*, I hope she got well away."

They exchanged significant looks.

"And other than *west*," said Flanders, "you've no idea where she might have gone?"

"You should talk to HR," said the guy, boiling over with excitement again. "She must have filed termination paperwork. They may have a forwarding address for her or a new place of employment."

"I'll look in on my way out," said Flanders. "Thanks. Though she may not have known where she was heading yet." He considered the notes he had made on his clipboard and chewed his pen thoughtfully.

"You know," said Angela, "I have a cousin out in Utah. I told Charlene once. Showed her some pictures. I didn't think much of it, but a week or so later, she started asking me about it."

"About your cousin?" asked the other nurse, who was now at least as invested in the case as Flanders.

"About Utah. What it was like out there. Weather. Cost of living. Stuff like that."

"Really?" said the male nurse, making a face. *"Utah?"*

"Anywhere in particular?" said Flanders.

"My cousin's in Salt Lake City. I think we talked about that, but I don't really remember."

"Any particular job she expressed interest in?"

The black woman shook her head and shrugged.

"Sorry," she said.

"It's no problem," said Flanders. "You've been most helpful."

"Whatever it is she's doing, I bet it involves kids," said Angela. "She loved kids. Loved being around them. I'll bet that's what she's doing."

The male nurse nodded enthusiastically, but there was something else in his face, a hesitance that Flanders was used to seeing when people were on the verge of confiding something they weren't entirely happy about. He eyed the young man, leaning in just a fraction so that his bulk seemed to fill the space between them.

"Anything else you think might be helpful?" he asked genially.

The male nurse frowned and gave a half glance at his colleague, as if wishing he didn't have to say what was on his mind in front of her.

"Well, it probably doesn't matter," he said. "And I don't have any good reason for thinking it . . ."

"Yeah?"

"Well, that thing about the Nazi boyfriend . . ."

The nurse's voice faltered, but Flanders said nothing, waiting him out.

"I don't really know or anything," said the nurse, "not really, but I kind of thought she had made it up."

The other nurse looked like a parody of shock, her mouth falling into a wide O and staying there.

"How do you mean?" asked Flanders.

"Well, you know Charlene," said the other man, addressing his colleague as much as Flanders, his tone confiding and a little defensive. "She liked drama. And sometimes she kind of . . . what's the word? *Embroidered* stories, you know? Like her life wasn't that interesting, and she wanted to seem more fun, more exciting, you know?"

"Sure," said Flanders, nodding.

"So yeah," said the male nurse, more sure of himself now. "When she told me about the Nazi boyfriend, I was like, *huh?* Charlene? I mean, she didn't seem the type."

"What's the type?" asked his colleague, a fraction cooler than she had been.

The male nurse flushed.

"The type to have a boyfriend," he clarified.

"But you don't really know either way," said the other nurse.

"No," he said, backpedaling but still trying to save face. "It was just a feeling."

"What is this about, anyway?" said the other nurse, returning her gaze to Flanders. Her colleague's remark had clearly annoyed her.

"I'm sorry, ma'am. I really can't say. We have some questions about some incidents in her past, that's all."

"Some incidents?" said the woman.

"I appreciate your help," said Flanders. "Both of you."

~

Flanders left the hospital and went to a McDonald's drive-through, where he got a Double Quarter Pounder with cheese, large fries, and a Coke that was too big for the cupholder. He sat in the parking lot, munching away, staring at nothing.

He scowled at the map propped on the steering wheel. She had taken a bus from Saint Louis to Kansas City and set up shop here for a time, then moved on without warning or a clear reason. She'd not been close to anyone, hadn't shared her plans or dreams with any friends, but then, he wouldn't expect her to. Nadine—*Charlene*, as she had been here—was a perpetual outsider. She could fool people for a time, but it always showed through in the end. She could be anywhere now, living under a new name in a big, open state . . .

But then, maybe she hadn't stayed in Missouri at all. If she'd taken a Greyhound this far, maybe she'd kept going west, staying on Interstate 70 all the way through Kansas and into Colorado and Utah. The black nurse's story wasn't really a lead at all, but it was better than nothing.

Utah.

The name of the place in connection to Nadine rang a distant bell. And what had that nurse said?

"She loved kids. Loved being around them. I'll bet that's what she's doing."

He thought so, too. Pulling out his phone, he tried a few random searches involving the name of the state and anything to do with children: *Utah pediatrics. Utah child welfare. Utah childhood disease. Utah child care.*

And there it was. A few more refinements to the search, a *Newsweek* article, and half a dozen agency websites later, he felt a swelling sense of optimism. Flanders finished his burger as he joined the dots and weighed the strength of the lead. Utah, it seemed, was the center of a billion-dollar nanny industry. Charlene/Nadine could get herself hired, switch her identity using a few simple tricks with which she had proved herself familiar, and go anywhere in the country. A new life, a new start . . .

"Oh, Nadine, you clever little psychopath," Edward Flanders said to the picture as he turned the engine over. "You do keep me on my toes."

Chapter Fifteen

ANNA

I had reread the sample from Ben Lodging's *Hell Is Empty*, making sure it was as strong as I had thought it was before I requested the whole manuscript, or as much as his idiosyncratic writing style permitted. Sometimes a little time away from a manuscript reveals the stylistic flaws and plot holes that your enthusiasm masked on the initial read, but in this case, my first impression still felt right. The story and its central character were both taut and strange, recognizably human and specific but also oddly, unsettlingly remote, as if you were watching a scientist conducting an intriguing experiment that may or may not result in someone's death. It was impossible to say how it would end, but I felt that special pull of the well-crafted mystery that makes the reader desperate to know what happens.

It was, I decided with a thrill of excitement, more than enough.

Dear Mr. Lodging, I typed. *I have read the synopsis and sample of your novel,* Hell Is Empty, *with interest and would like to see the rest of the manuscript, or at least (given your intrigueingly unorthodox writing process) as much of it as you can send at this time. Please email it to me as an attachment, and I will respond as soon as possible—no more than two weeks. During this time, I would like you to consider the submission exclusive to me. If I haven't responded in that time, you should feel free to send the book out more widely.*

Sincerely yours, et cetera.

I reread it, fixed a typo—I had misspelled *intriguingly*—and hit "Send." The sense of satisfaction in doing so was immense, and not for the first time, I reminded myself that I wouldn't have been able to work like this without Oaklynn.

Around here, it's common to hear people say how blessed they are. Must be a southern thing, I guess. I generally smile and say nothing, though Josh and I will often exchange the closest thing to an eye roll that we dare under the circumstances. I've never understood the concept of a God who looks down and chooses to bless some but not others, and though I know it's unfair of me to judge what may be little more than a figure of speech, the phrase always seems to me just a little sanctimonious. So you can imagine just how amazed I was to hear myself say it later that day when, pleased with my morning's work, I rewarded myself with a quick visit to Mary Beth's and a chat over a glass of Chablis. Mary Beth stared at me, her sharp face not bothering to conceal her disbelief, but I couldn't take it back. I didn't even want to.

Because that was how those first September weeks felt. Through no great achievement of my own, I had stumbled into a life with Oaklynn, and it felt like a blessing. She was all we could possibly have hoped for and more: unflappable, nurturing, generous, and always, *always* ready and willing. Her capacity to supply whatever I needed whenever I needed it bordered on the uncanny. I could work, cook, clean, and look after the girls as and when I wanted, always knowing that she was there to step in with at least as much care and attention as I could muster at any moment. Grace and Veronica adored her, but rather than this making me feel insecure, guilty, or jealous, I felt a curious sense of magnanimity, as if I had learned from Oaklynn to be kinder and more loving. Nor was my contentedness confined to our professional relationship. For all our differences in background and outlook, I genuinely liked her and found myself spending more and more time in her company. We discovered odd coincidences in our lives and tastes that brought us closer still, until we had an almost sisterly bond, something that—as only children—neither of us had experienced before. We liked the same music, the same kids' shows, the same thin-sliced turkey pastrami. Contrary to my—slightly patronizing—assumptions about her background, she turned out to be bright with surprisingly educated tastes, which she had, apparently, discovered largely on her own. Having grown up in a not-very-bookish household, I could relate, though it made our discovery that we shared a passion for Dickens all the more extraordinary. Late in the month, we stumbled into several long late-evening conversations about our shared frustration and outrage at the odious Mr. Skimpole in *Bleak House*. It should have seemed bizarre but felt oddly natural, as if such a curious alignment in personality came with the territory. As I said, I felt blessed.

Josh was, in his usual way, quietly amazed. I think a part of him had feared the whole situation would unravel after a few weeks, but the faultless way in which Oaklynn had slotted into our lives, moved into their very center, was undeniable. Sometimes when we were alone, he would shake his head in wonder at the way she had anticipated our needs—ensuring that the girls were properly looked after so that we could have an unrequested date night on our anniversary, say, or using her free time to shop for the picture book Veronica had been eyeing at the little independent store on Park Road.

"Amazing," he muttered almost to himself. He was dressing in the mirror, tying the lavender-and-silver tie I had bought him for last Christmas. He was wearing his blue suit with the tan shoes he'd bought at JoS. A. Bank early in the summer and looked, as he always did when heading out to the office, like something out of *GQ*, sharp but somehow both edgy and casual. "All of it," he added absently. "Amazing. I wouldn't have thought it possible."

"Right?" I said. "I can't believe our luck."

"She gave me a tip for your Christmas present today," he said musingly, tightening the Windsor knot and sliding it into place. "A good one. She processes everything you say, everything you seem to notice. That should be weird, but it's not because it's just so *her*, you know? She just wants us to be happy."

"I know," I said. "This is going to sound ridiculous, but apart from all the work stuff her being here lets me do, I think she is actually making me a better person!"

"Impossible," he replied, grinning.

"I mean it."

"She's making you happier. Maybe that's the same thing."

"Maybe it is," I said. "But I do feel a bit different. I mean, take Mary Beth, for instance. I told her how good things were with Oaklynn, with work, and she seems sort of baffled and a bit resentful, like she thinks I've pushed her away or something. Which I really haven't. Anyway, by the time I'd been there a half hour, her snide remarks were getting on my nerves. I know it's just her sense of humor . . ."

"Her bitchiness, you mean," said Josh.

"Well, she can be pretty caustic, and I don't want her tearing Oaklynn down, you know? Even if it's just to me."

"Makes sense."

"Anyway, yes, I do think I'm happier with Oaklynn here. What about you?"

He hesitated, then turned from the mirror to face me.

"What about me?" he said. He sounded casual, almost flippant but deliberately so, and it was impossible not to think he was being very slightly guarded.

"Are you happy with Oaklynn?" I said.

"Sure. Of course. Why wouldn't I be?"

"I don't know," I said. "You seem a little . . . I don't know. Quiet." I was careful not to say *distant*, but that was what I meant. "Like, I don't know . . . like you feel a bit left out."

"What? No!" he said, and it sounded so completely natural—even amused—that I thought I had misjudged the previous moment. "I mean, it's great that you guys have bonded."

"Yeah?" I said, trying not to sound too attentive. "And things at work are OK?"

"Fine," he said, smiling. "Busy is all."

The hesitation before he had spoken was so slight that anyone in the world but me would have missed it.

I didn't.

I watched him pull out of the drive ten minutes later after insisting on kissing the girls. He was a good father. A perfect husband. I had always thought so.

"You got lucky there," said Oaklynn, sidling up to me in the kitchen. I turned suddenly, sure I was blushing at being caught watching him, thinking about him. Oaklynn had a way of looking at you and seeming to know what was going through your head. It was one of her many gifts, but the only one that sometimes made me feel self-conscious.

"I did," I said. "Don't think I don't know it." I grinned, shook my head as if to clear it, and concluded, "Coffee. I need coffee."

"I'll make it."

"You don't even drink coffee. I'm not having you make something you won't share."

"There's some lemonade in the fridge," she answered. "I'll have some of that."

Oaklynn made the world's best lemonade. She added orange zest and got the sweet-and-sour balance just right.

"Hmm," I mused. "Then coffee can wait. I'll join you."

We had upped her wages by $150 a week because of the cooking and other extras she had volunteered that went way beyond the letter of her contract. She had said it wasn't necessary, but it hadn't seemed fair, and we began by offering her twice as much. She had argued us down, if you can believe that, and accepted the extra gratefully but with a touch of something else I didn't understand that almost seemed like disappointment. Later, I wondered if we had insulted her by insisting on paying her more, as if we were deliberately reminding her that she worked for the family rather than being a member of it. I made a note to get her something nice for the holidays. I didn't know what that would be, but I still had a couple of months to find out. The idea pleased me.

"You are such a sweet couple," she said out of the blue, still gazing vaguely down the street where Josh had driven away, one hand on the fridge door. "I said you were lucky to snag Josh, but you weren't." She turned to face me but kept her eyes down. Her cheeks were pinker than usual, and she looked embarrassed and awkward, like she was confessing a crush. "You guys are perfect together. You match each other so well. You're so smart and elegant. That hair . . ."

She looked up and grinned. She was always going on about how much she liked my hair, which is, unsurprisingly, straight and black, worn just longer than shoulder length. I've always thought it pretty ordinary, but Oaklynn had a way of making me feel like a swan.

"What about you?" I asked, catching something of her embarrassment. "No man in your life waiting for you to move in with him and make him lemonade?"

"Hardly," she said. She still smiled, but she opened the fridge and got the pitcher out as if a spell had broken.

"How come?" I said.

She shot me a knowing look that, for a split second, flickered down at herself, her funny "witchy shoes" (Veronica's words), her oversize body in its frumpy floral dress, and shrugged. For that tiny moment, she looked sad and lost and then, almost as quickly, wry and self-knowing so that the following smile had a tang of sourness to it.

"You'd be quite the catch yourself," I said deliberately.

"I'm the kind of catch that breaks the line and tears the nets," she murmured, flashing me another smile, this one mischievous as she set a pair of glass tumblers on the counter and splashed some lemonade into each. A few weeks ago, the joke would have surprised me, not because of its deprecation but because of its wit. I knew her better now, knew there was a cleverness below the down-home "Oh cripes!" Mormon would-be housewife. I laughed and shook my head as she added, "The men who like me . . . Well, there was only ever one, to be honest, and he turned out not to be very nice. Not nice at all. Believe me, I'm better by myself."

"But you are so warm and loving!" I exclaimed. "So good with people, with kids. People can see that. One day . . ."

She held up a single finger and for a moment said nothing, so that I could hear the girls running around upstairs, hear Veronica's big-sister voice as she instructed Grace on the proper way to play. I wanted to say more to Oaklynn, but we had stumbled into honesty, and I knew that trying to finish the sentence I had begun with romantic platitudes would violate that. For a long moment, we seemed to just look at each other, and then she smiled again, unreadably but maybe—*maybe*—gratefully, and chinked my glass with hers.

Chapter Sixteen

That night, Oaklynn/Nadine sat in the basement with Mr. Quietly sleeping in her lap as she scrolled through Anna's Facebook page. It was amazing how much you could learn about someone from social media if you went back far enough, the picture of a person's life and opinions you could build out of its fragments and offhand remarks. One of the first things she'd learned way back in the first week of September was Anna's fascination with Charles Dickens, and not a moment too soon: it had taken Oaklynn the rest of the summer just to get through a few of the novels. But long though they were, the books had already proved useful, even if she felt that this simulation of closeness to another person was a risk that could easily unravel. Nadine wasn't good at intimacy of any kind. She knew that. She wanted to be better at it and thought that if she practiced it, faked it, it might come more naturally, but doing so always felt like she was venturing out onto ice. The impulse to say she had been an only child had felt especially risky, a long step out onto the frozen lake, waiting for the telltale groan underfoot, the spreading cracks that presaged disaster as the lie collapsed.

What would you have said about that, Mom? she wondered, her mouth buckling into a hard, mirthless smile. *Nothing good.*

Today's conversation with Anna about men and settling down had been a still more dangerous step out onto the ice, but for the opposite reason: not because what she was saying was a lie, but because it was true. Another few moments, and she knew the ice would have split beneath her, all her carefully constructed Oaklynness crashing, splashing through to a muddy death, the closeness unsustainable in the face of all the old terror and hurt. As Oaklynn vanished through the frozen pond, Nadine would have somehow been left standing, exposed for all she was, like some monstrous cicada crawling slick and foul out of its shell. Thinking back on the moment now, she felt awash with confused emotions, angry at herself for letting her guard down, touched that her pretty young employer seemed to care so much about her well-being, and caught in old and bitter memories.

Carl.

If Anna knew even the smallest part of Nadine's past, their little chat would have been an altogether different beast.

That was, however, water under the bridge. Or the ice. She smiled wryly to herself, but before she could stop it, the metaphor shifted again. Not water under the bridge, but blood. It was more fitting, even if she didn't want to think about it. And instead of the icy lake she had been picturing only moments before, she now thought of the creek at the bottom of the garden only yards from where she sat, in the house with Anna and Josh and Veronica and Grace, seeing it in her mind not as a brown and sluggish worm but a raging, foaming torrent of vivid crimson. She could almost smell its coppery, rank sweetness, and though she tried to push the image away, it wouldn't completely leave her. She spent an hour tapping away at her computer keyboard merely to banish the idea, but when she finally went to bed, she dreamed of it all the same, the blood creek rising higher and higher till it lapped at the ankles of Grace and Veronica, who stood barefoot on its bank, lost and afraid.

Chapter Seventeen

ANNA

The moment I logged on, I saw Ben Lodging's email in the block of bold-typed new messages, but I waded through the other six before opening it, like a child deliberately putting off dessert so that it would taste the sweeter. It was simple and to the point:

Dear Ms. Klein, it read.

> I am delighted that you are enjoying the book.
> I am attaching the rest of what I have written so
> far (some 200 pages). I continue to wonder what
> Mr. Carried will do at the end of the book, how
> many—if any—bodies will litter the final pages,
> and whether his will be among them. I really do
> not know, and can but wait and see. In any case,
> I hope you enjoy this substantial addition to what
> you already have, and I look forward to hearing
> from you. The first chapters are currently out with
> a couple of other agents, so I'm not in a position

to make the submission exclusive to you right now, but I will keep you informed on any movement with the other readers.

Very best wishes, Ben Lodging

I couldn't help but smile to myself at the tone of the message and its continuing pretense of ignorance as to how the book would end. Could he seriously not know? Or was he waiting for a professional insider like me to nudge him one way or the other, to tell him what the market wanted most? Either way, it was a curious strategy, and I reminded myself not to commit to the writer as a client until I had a good sense of his ability to deliver a finished and marketable product. Agents—reputable ones, at least—are paid exclusively on commissions from sales, so you don't want to sign clients unless you are pretty sure that one day—after a lot of time and energy finding the right house—you can actually sell their work. Lodging could tease me for a while, and his method would indeed make for good interview material if the book ever got sold, but I wasn't signing him up till I saw the final chapter and a coherent buildup to those two magical words: *The End.*

The nonexclusivity of my dealings with him meant that I needed to be ready with a hard offer soon, though. I didn't want to miss the opportunity because some other agent had beaten me to it. So I dived in to what he had sent with a little deliberate caution, forcing myself to withhold judgment. The prose didn't have a strong sense of personality, but it was lucid and engaging, and since the book was written in first person, that very lack of a distinctive voice produced an intriguingly odd sense of clinical detachment on the part of the main character. The narrator—the accountant, Joseph Carried—seemed to view the world through a telescope, as if even the coworkers and neighbors around whom his life revolved were miles away. It was a curious effect, but I found it compelling all the same, laced as it was with both ironic humor and an edge of something dangerous. Carried read like one of those experiments in artificial intelligence, a computer masquerading as a human being, faking his way through life but seeing those around him as both irrelevant to his existence and—this was the scary part—not obviously worth anything. When his mind wandered to the possibility of murder, it was no more than a kind of thought experiment. One passage in particular stood out. It took place when Carried was watering plants in a window box on the balcony of his fourth-floor apartment.

I looked down past the plastic watering can and saw the shapeless jacketed shoulders and scarfed, gray head of the woman called Mrs. Winterburn, a retired schoolteacher. I watched her movements as she put out her garbage, the effort and inefficiency. I had heard that she used to teach French. The end result of which was what? Mostly disinterest and frustration, I suspected, her students seeing her merely as an obstacle to their contentment, while the good students, the successful ones, emerged as what? Smaller versions of her, I supposed. Did she think in French as she clumsily manhandled her garbage into the street? Did she think her life well spent, years of inculcating a foreign language into kids who could barely use their own and resented her for the effort? Was that what life was for? I could, I thought, considering one of the ceramic flowerpots, end it for her now. It was a dense terracotta pot, full of dirt clumped together around the bulbous roots of three or four hyacinths and overlaid with teardrop ivy. It was a heavy pot. Dropped from this height, it would surely have the velocity to split her skull. It would need to be a clean hit, but if I timed it just right, it would splash her French-speaking brains across the sidewalk. She'd be dead before she hit the ground probably.

"Hi, Mrs. Winterburn!" I called. Not au revoir. Not today.

She looked up, peered for a second, then smiled, waved, and called back something pleasant but unintelligible, though I assumed it was English, not French. I rested one hand on the hyacinth pot and waved back with the other.

I didn't kill her. Not today. Tomorrow? Perhaps. Her, or someone else.

The confidence of the writing and the queasy feeling of the moment left me unsettled and wanting more, torn between the need to know what would happen next and the desire to see the self-assured and disconnected Mr. Carried brought to justice before he could unleash whatever mayhem with which he seemed to be toying. I shuddered and read on, watching the accountant sighting down the barrel of his life at the people who, cheerfully ignorant of who and what he was, drifted in and out of range. It was alarming in a strange, almost comic way, but I couldn't stop reading, and my instinct said that this might be not just a marketable book but a big book, the kind that gets trumpeted in all the industry publications. The kind that brings Hollywood sniffing around before it's even in print. The kind buzzing through every book club and cocktail party within days of release . . . It was a guilty pleasure, perhaps, but a well-drawn one, and it dodged the *American Psycho* stigma by steering clear of grisly and gratuitous violence, being positively Hitchcockian in its building of suspense. If it was merely a potboiler, it was an extremely well-constructed pot, and you couldn't look away as the temperature rose.

Hooked, I abandoned my previous reservations, stopped reading, and typed the email all writers love to get:

Dear Mr. Lodging,

I'm thoroughly enjoying *Hell Is Empty* and would like to set up a time to discuss representing this and your other work at your earliest convenience. Shoot me some possible times we can talk in the next couple of days, if possible, or early next week by phone or video conference.

Best,
Anna Klein
Literary Agent

I hit "Send," then glanced over the material once more, feeling pleased with myself. It was only a few minutes later when I found myself wondering about the mind that could create so dispassionate a killer—or would-be killer. Being his agent meant we would have a relationship, probably one that lasted years. What if he was like his protagonist: odd, distant, socially difficult, and more than a little worrying? All agents had tales of unstable clients, writers who expected the moon and turned their fury on their agents when the deals didn't come or the books didn't sell. There was no place in my life for nurturing anyone who might be unbalanced, even dangerous.

Way to overreact, I told myself. *You just reached out to what might be your first new client in three years, and you are already looking for ways to derail the process.*

I sighed noisily and shook my head at my own nervous stupidity, glad that I couldn't unsend the message to Ben Lodging. This might be just the book I needed to relaunch my career. I had to learn to stop second-guessing myself, particularly when the roadblocks I started throwing up came from baseless worry and paranoia.

I heard feet on the stairs. I bit my lip, my chest and arms tightening so that my hands hovered over the keyboard like suspended spiders. I had another submission to read and wanted to be left alone.

"Anna?" said Oaklynn, tapping discreetly at the office door I had left ajar and leaning halfway around the jamb, as if not being entirely present made the interruption somehow less.

"What's up?" I asked, my tone just a little crisper than usual.

"Did Grace eat OK this morning?"

I frowned at her, my irritation increasing slightly. We had agreed that I would continue to give Grace her first feeding each day. It made me feel involved.

"Yes," I said. "Fine. Why?"

"Well, she spit most of it up about a half hour after, and now she won't eat at all."

I rotated the chair to face her properly, my annoyance turning slowly into concern.

"That's not like her," I said. Grace's fussiness had tailed off after she'd reached six months, and since then she had been eating heartily. "Let me have a try." I got up and crossed the room toward her. "What did you give her?"

"A bottle, then the sweet potatoes and chicken," said Oaklynn, backing off, her face earnest and careful. "Then the pureed peaches."

"Which wouldn't she take?"

"Neither."

I quickened my step out into the hall and down the stairs, Oaklynn almost jogging to keep up so that I felt her weight on the hardwood steps. The bassinet was set up in the living room. As I entered, Veronica looked up from a scattering of felt-pen drawings that half covered the floor. Grace was crying, not bawling, but a low, cycling whine of distress. I couldn't believe I hadn't noticed it. I snatched her up, immediately feeling how hot and sweaty she felt.

"She feels feverish," I gasped, lifting her onto my shoulder, the warm, soft skin of her head against my neck. "I don't understand. She seemed fine at breakfast."

"I'll take her temperature," said Oaklynn. She rummaged in a translucent plastic storage bin on the floor by the bassinet and came up with a digital thermometer. It beeped once, and Oaklynn stood behind me, guiding it into Grace's ear. My daughter mewed with distress again, but Oaklynn made soothing noises, and she went quiet again till the thermometer chirped again.

"Well?" I asked.

"One hundred four," said Oaklynn.

"Christ!" I exclaimed. "OK," I added, forcing myself to slow down and breathe. "OK. Where's the phone?"

I was forever losing the handset because it always worked, unlike the one in the bedroom, so I used it all over the house.

"We should go to the emergency room," said Oaklynn with grim certainty. "You can call your pediatrician, but that's what they'll tell you to do."

"Yes," I said, starting to pace, agitating Grace up and down in what was supposed to be a calming rhythm. She was still making vague, animal noises of misery. "OK. It's OK, Grace. It's going to be OK. All right, sweetheart? Mommy's here."

But I didn't sound OK. I could hear my own panic rising. Veronica had stopped what she was doing and was starting to watch me. She looked unnerved, frightened.

"What's wrong with Gracie, Mommy?" she asked.

"She's just not feeling so good, honey," I said.

"She's sick?"

"I think she might be," I said, trying to smile but conscious that my face was stiff and anxious.

"Like the doggy?" asked Veronica, her face pale, her gaze level.

"What?" I asked, momentarily completely lost, then filled with sudden horror as I realized what she meant. "No! She's fine. She will be fine. Babies get temperatures all the time. We just have to get her looked at."

Veronica looked scared.

"Mommy?" she said, her own voice rising as she caught my panic.

"She'll be fine," proclaimed Oaklynn, as if nothing could be more obvious. "Right as rain. Baby Grace has a bit of a fever is all. We'll get that seen to right quick; you just see if we don't."

Again, the smile: full, composed, and confident.

"I'll drive," she continued. "Unless you'd rather I stayed home with Veronica?"

I hesitated. Grace had been colicky, but it had never led to the emergency room, and I had always been just a little unnerved by hospitals. Oaklynn checked the thermometer again, looking coolheaded and professional, just like a nurse.

"We'll all go," I said.

"To the pospital?" Veronica ventured, her unease swelling.

"Absolutely to the hospital," Oaklynn breezed, as if this had all been planned as a special treat. "Why don't you grab Lamby and a nice book, and we'll get ready to go?"

Oaklynn's manner and the mention of the stuffed toy worked on Veronica like music, and though she was still serious, she went out of the room with a sense of purpose I had not been able to find.

"I can drive," I tried.

"If you like," said Oaklynn. "But you might be better in the back with the girls. Keep an eye on them. Keep them happy."

I blinked and nodded, sensing that Veronica had returned, or had never really left, and was hovering in the doorway, watching.

"Yes," I said, managing a smile for my eldest.

"Grab that diaper bag, will you?"

I did, sleepwalking through the action and those that followed as we went out and buckled the children into their car seats. I couldn't take my eyes off Grace for more than a few seconds, which was, of course, no state to drive in. Oaklynn, by contrast, moved with easy efficiency, taking charge, and I was glad to let her lead, albeit distractedly and always a step behind.

"The emergency room is at the corner of Queens and Fourth," I supplied.

"I have it in my phone," said Oaklynn, checking the kids once more before setting the Camry rolling softly backward and angling around to face the main road. There were no other cars on the quiet street, and I was reminded of just how isolated the house could feel. I was barely aware of where we were, my attention staying on Grace except to give Veronica an encouraging smile and assure her all would be well, but I sensed my surroundings as if I were inside a dream where even ordinary things had a strangeness to them and the merest indefinable hint of menace.

Grace was still making those odd, discomforted noises, and though they seemed to be slackening off, I found the change more disturbing than encouraging.

"She's going quiet," I said. "You think that's better or worse?"

I should know, I thought, feeling stupid and incompetent.

"Nearly there," said Oaklynn softly. She never took her eyes off the road.

We followed the signs down to Presbyterian Medical Center, Oaklynn barely glancing at her phone as if she intuitively knew the way or was drawn there by some inner force. The more anxious I became, the more she had become steely and focused, the arrow in flight to the bull's-eye. I was impressed and grateful, but I felt unnerved by my sense of Grace's suddenly obvious fragility, so that the journey continued to have a fuzzy, dreamlike quality. I muttered vague encouragements I didn't quite believe as the world slipped by the car too slowly.

"How much farther?" I muttered. "She's stopped moaning. What do you think that means?"

"Pulling in now," said Oaklynn. "I'll let you out here and find a place to park. You go on in with Grace, and I'll be along with Veronica in a moment."

My panic spiked, but I wrestled it down and nodded.

"OK," I said. I hated the idea of going in alone, not knowing exactly what to say or where to go, but Oaklynn seemed to read my thoughts.

"There will be signs. The staff will ask you questions . . ."

"Right," I said. "Come quickly, though, yes? You know as much about her usual routine as I do, and there may be something you noticed even if you didn't realize it . . ."

"Go on in, Anna," said Oaklynn patiently. We were idling outside the main doors. A cop had already noticed us. Another moment and he'd come over and ask us to move. "I'll be right there." I hesitated for just a second, and she turned to me, smiling. "You'll be fine, Anna. You're her mom. I'll be with you in just a moment, I promise. Go."

And I did. Veronica sat very still, her eyes wide as she watched me climb out, and then I was gathering Grace into my arms and walking away. She felt cooler now and had gone quiet, sleepy, but I took no comfort from that. Not yet. Once through the automatic doors, I hesitated and turned back to the Camry, but it was already pulling away, and I had no choice but to handle things alone.

And, again, I did. It wasn't hard. The staff—as Oaklynn had said—took charge, asked questions, and I, apart from an anxious disorientation and niggling sense of shame, contributed what I could while nurses buzzed around Grace, who, startled by all the activity, had begun to cry again. It was a normal, healthy crying this time, not the animal whining of before, the droning distress that had seemed so unlike her. Before she had sounded feral, like one of the neighborhood coyotes in the darkness of the woods, but now she was my daughter again, and some of that unsettling dreamy quality of the last twenty minutes or so melted away. Even so, I stood there feeling useless, still unfocused and a little jittery, so that when Oaklynn appeared holding Veronica's hand, I clung to them both.

"How are we doing?" asked Oaklynn, addressing not just me but also the attendant nurses. There were two of them, both in pale green scrubs, both in their midthirties, one white and fleshy, the other black and pencil thin.

"Temperature is still a tiny bit high," said the black nurse whose name badge said *Alysha*, "but that might just be the excitement of coming here."

"Excitement?" I said blankly.

"There's no party like an ER party," said Alysha. She said it deadpan but flashed a little grin at the end to show she was joking.

"It was one hundred four when we left," said Oaklynn.

"One oh four?" said the other nurse, Jackie.

Oaklynn gave me a questioning look.

"She just said it was high," said Jackie.

"Feverish," I inserted, knowing my voice was unnaturally shrill and brittle. "I said feverish."

"It was one oh four," said Oaklynn.

"It's not now," said Alysha, shaking her head. "And she was throwing up?"

"Yes," I pushed in. "I told you."

The nurses hesitated just long enough to make it clear they wanted Oaklynn's confirmation.

"Had breakfast at seven. Threw it up twenty minutes later and hasn't eaten since," said Oaklynn.

"How's she acting?" asked Jackie. "She seem herself?"

"Well, I don't really know her moods that well yet," Oaklynn began. The nurses frowned, puzzled.

"I'm her mother," I said stiffly. "She's the nanny."

"I know," said Alysha, giving me an odd look.

Of course I was the mother. Grace had my coloring, my eyes. That big, pale Oaklynn wasn't a blood relative was almost insultingly obvious.

"Sorry," I said, not sure to which of them I was apologizing but feeling flustered and foolish.

"No problem," said Alysha. "So can you say if Grace seems to be behaving normally?"

Having ensured the question came to me rather than Oaklynn, I suddenly realized I didn't know how to answer it.

"Well, she was making odd noises," I said. "Like she was . . . distressed. Uncomfortable. And she was really hot."

"Which would explain the distress," said Jackie, half to herself. "Well, she seems OK now, but at her age, we don't want to take any chances. We should check her over properly. Have a seat, and the doctor will be out in a few minutes."

I did as I was told, holding Grace tightly to me, while Veronica looked on, stroking her baby sister's hand.

"It will be fine," said Oaklynn. "She's better already."

I nodded mutely, but when Oaklynn just kept smiling with understanding, with compassion, I found a kind of explanation for my defensiveness.

"I haven't been to the hospital since she was born," I said. "Checkups at the doctor's office, sure, but never a hospital. Nothing for Veronica either. They freak me out. Hospitals, I mean. Something about the smell or . . . I don't know. I don't really smell it here. It's just in my head, I guess. An association. A fear. Infection, maybe. They say you can catch all kinds of resistant bugs in hospitals. But that's not it either," I confessed, puzzling my neurotic reaction through, trying to make sense of it, while Oaklynn held my hand and nodded without judgment.

"You love your daughter," she said, smiling with such tenderness, such total comprehension, that my eyes filled with tears. All I could do was nod, holding my baby tight to my breast. "That's how it's supposed to be," she went on. "You love her, and you were frightened for her. That's all there was to it. You did fine. Everything will be OK."

"Thanks to you," I managed, caught between a self-deprecating laugh and a sob that made a surly-looking young couple two chairs down turn and stare at me. "I'm not sure what I would have done without you."

"You would have been fine. You're making too much of it."

"Well, you were a big help."

"Good," said Oaklynn, beaming. "That's my job."

The doctor, when he arrived, looked barely old enough to be qualified, but he seemed efficient, and though he spoke with practiced ease and fluency, he didn't seem cocky. He was white and slim, with heavy black-framed glasses that looked somehow ironic, as if they were part of a costume he was wearing for a joke. He busied himself with his stethoscope, consulted Grace's chart, and put the back of his hand to her forehead. She was sleeping now and looked both healthy and angelic, so that a part of me felt ridiculous for having brought her in at all.

"When was her last wet diaper?" he asked.

I blinked stupidly, blushed, and looked at Oaklynn.

"I changed her at eight," she said. "Nothing since then."

"And it was just wet or dirty, too?" asked the doctor, pulling his gaze from me to her.

"Both. No blood or anything, and it looked normal."

I hadn't thought to ask about that.

"Good," he said.

"What do you think it is?" I said. It was a stupid question, but I needed to feel involved in the conversation.

"Could be a number of things," he replied, "but she seems fine now. I'm going to send you home with some Pedialyte and have you watch her. If she isn't back to normal before she goes to bed tonight, you should take her to see her pediatrician in the morning. Of course, if anything gets worse, you bring her back here."

"Thank you, Doctor," said Oaklynn. "I hope we haven't wasted your time."

"Not at all," he replied, smiling at her warmly. "You did the right thing. Baby Grace is very lucky to have you."

He turned to include me in that last remark, but he did it as an afterthought. In other circumstances, I might have been indignant, but as it was, I just felt weary and irrelevant.

"He was a very nice doctor," said Veronica as we signed out and dealt with insurance cards and copays. "I think I might be a doctor when I grow up."

"Really?" said Oaklynn. "That's a wonderful idea. But you'll have to work very hard."

"I know," she said.

"You're all set," said the receptionist. "Have a good day."

"Thanks," I said, feeling better about it all now that it seemed to be over. As we headed out, I took Veronica's hand.

"I thought you wanted to write books when you grew up," I said, trying to sound cheery, even playful.

"That was when I was little," Veronica replied, rolling her eyes dramatically at Oaklynn and taking her hand as we approached the double doors to the outside world. In spite of everything, I felt a prickle of annoyance that my daughter was so enthralled by my sweet and capable nanny, even as I knew the thought was unworthy of me.

Chapter Eighteen

Edward Flanders had called every nanny agency based in Utah he could find, but no one using Nadine's name showed up in their records. That wasn't a surprise, but it meant that he was looking for a needle in a haystack. A needle that might not actually be there. He tried Charlene and other known aliases, but Nadine, for all her many faults, wasn't that stupid. He revisited his list, which featured names like Helpers West, All About Nannies, Family Connection, and Nanny on the Net, and jotted down the addresses of the biggest agencies, figuring he'd have his best shot in person.

He drew blanks on the first four, getting a combination of blank looks in response to his picture and party-line blather about privacy and the need for warrants to see internal records. But at the fifth, an agency called Nurture, he saw a look of panic flash through the receptionist's face as she considered the photo and knew he was onto something.

"If you'll just wait a moment, I'll see if the manager is available," said the receptionist, whose badge identified her simply as Rachel. She was white and wholesome-looking.

"You processed her paperwork?" he said, smiling, his voice low, almost soothing.

"I'm not sure," said Rachel, flushing, her eyes moving uneasily to his badge.

He nodded at the lie and looked to the door. The receptionist's hand had gone to the phone, but she hadn't picked up the receiver. For a moment, she just looked at it like it might sting her.

"Would you rather we took care of this just between the two of us?" he said kindly. "I'm not looking to get you into trouble here, and I'm sure your manager . . . ?"

"Mrs. Hennessy."

She said the name in a breathy whisper that dripped with dread. She fidgeted with a stapler on the desk, put it down self-consciously, and then clenched her fist to hide the nervous flutter in her fingers.

Little Rachel here, Flanders concluded, was a serial screwup. He could use that.

"I'm sure Mrs. Hennessy is busy and all."

"Yes, sir," said Rachel, meek and wide-eyed.

"You recognize the picture?"

"I couldn't be sure," she said, trying to push back from what she'd already given away.

Flanders smiled sympathetically.

"But you think so," he said. "It's OK. You're not in trouble."

She returned his smile reflexively, but it was uneven, and her eyes wouldn't hold his.

"So," he said. "Rachel, yeah? Have another look at the picture, Rachel. Take your time. It's very important that I find this woman. And like I said, you're not in trouble. But if you had some dealings with the person in the picture and don't tell me . . ." He let the sentence hang and made a sympathetic face. The look said that he would feel bad about what might happen if she didn't come clean now, but it would be out of his hands.

"I think . . . ," said Rachel, cautious and apprehensive, her voice lowered, her eyes flicking to the office door in case Mrs. Hennessy might suddenly appear.

"You think you recognize her?" he said, still going easy, playing the ally.

She nodded once, minutely, like a frightened rabbit.

"OK," he said, rewarding her with a broad, encouraging smile. "That's great, Rachel. Really helpful. Think you can pull up her file?"

The receptionist took a long, unsteady breath and found a wobbly smile of her own.

"It was a reactivation. About five months ago. I remember it because she'd changed between pictures, but it had been a long time, and pictures can sometimes make you look really different, right?"

"Right," said Flanders, still soothing. He had her on the hook and was starting to draw her in. "Sometimes when my girlfriend takes my picture, I'm like, 'Who's that guy?'"

"Right? Anyway, I remembered. It will just take me a few moments to sort through the reactivations. Is she in trouble?"

The tremble in her voice belied the question. Rachel wasn't asking if the girl in the picture was in trouble, or at least was only asking if it meant trouble for herself.

"She might be," said Flanders, "but if you can help me find her, I'll do what I can to keep you out of it. Sound like a deal?"

Rachel bobbed her rabbit head again and returned her eyes to the computer screen on which she was sorting nanny profiles by date of activation. She hesitated over one file, then shook her head and moved on. A moment later, she had it.

"Oaklynn Durst," she said.

Flanders very deliberately showed no emotion, though it wasn't easy.

"And does Miss Durst live locally?" he asked at length.

"She did, but she is on assignment now."

"On assignment?"

"Resident with a family. In Charlotte, North Carolina."

This time, he couldn't quite suppress the flicker of his lips into a thin but satisfied smile. Rachel, thinking it was directed at her, smiled back and breathed a sigh of relief: *off the hook*.

"That's great, Rachel," said Flanders, his cool, professional self again. "Very helpful indeed. Can I get that name and address from you, please?"

Chapter Nineteen

ANNA

By the time we had left the hospital, Grace showed no sign of the sickness that had led us to the ER in the first place, and none of her previous symptoms reappeared over the next twenty-four hours. I called my pediatrician's office and spoke to one of the nurses, who had access to the hospital's electronic medical records, and was told that beyond being alert for any recurring signs of fever or gastro discomfort, there was really nothing to do. Kids got sick, she said, and they got better. Their bodies were remarkable at shrugging off the kinds of infections that would level an adult, and while it would be nice to know exactly what had happened in this instance, no news was good news. I was due to take her in for a checkup in a couple of weeks. Assuming there were no developments in the meantime, we'd review then.

In other circumstances, I might have been dissatisfied with this assessment, but in truth, I was so relieved that Grace's illness had blown over so completely that I was positively elated. I told Oaklynn, who smiled and said she was so glad, then got on with preparing the girls' lunch. With a weight lifted from my shoulders, I went up to the office to work.

$$\backsim$$

I checked my email an hour later and saw Ben Lodging's response. It was and was not what I had expected. It read:

> Dear Ms. Klein.
>
> I'm so happy to hear this, though that phrase is, perhaps, unfortunately ironic. I am almost completely deaf, so phones and videoconferencing don't really work for me. Sorry! Please don't take this as a lack of enthusiasm about your very exciting interest in me and my work. Could we continue to "talk" by email? Or by some kind of instant messenger? I have Facebook and Twitter accounts that we could use to communicate directly. Sorry for the inconvenience. Again, please don't read anything more than my disability into my request. I am very excited about the possibility of signing with you.
>
> Best wishes,
> Ben Lodging

I read it twice. I had never had a disabled client before, and I immediately began to worry if it would make working together more difficult or whether acquisition editors might be less willing to enter into a relationship with someone they couldn't easily communicate with in person. In my gut, I felt sure all matters related to producing and editing the book could be done in writing, but it seemed I would have to rethink the possibility of TV and radio interviews.

Perhaps not, though. A sign language interpreter might scare off some interviewers or slow proceedings down, but maybe that, too, could be a kind of asset, a way of differentiating Ben from the hundreds—thousands—of mystery and thriller writers competing for a place in the limelight. Was that a cynical exploitation of the man's disability? Probably, though deaf authors must surely have faced enough discrimination that making their condition work for them rather than against them for once didn't seem too bad.

But I was getting ahead of myself. There would be a lot of talk—well, *type*—before we were strategizing TV and radio interviews, something most writers never got near.

He will, though, I thought. *I can feel it. He's special.*

I typed my email response immediately, laying out my boilerplate questions about his work, his sense of what he would like to write next, and where he saw himself in five years as a writer. They wouldn't catch the spontaneity I got in a phone call—that sense of whether the writer was in it for the long haul or was just angling for a big payout—but I felt like I had a sense of the man already. It might be wishful thinking, but I had a good feeling about him, however quirky he might be. In a crowded marketplace, quirk was good. It made you different, and difference made you visible. Combine that with a facility for language and structure—the nuts and bolts of storytelling—and there was real potential. Ben Lodging might be just the author I had been looking for to break my way back into the business.

I said as much to Josh.

"What?" he said, looking up from his computer, his face tight and hollowed out by the bluish light of the screen.

"I said I think he might be the real deal," I said.

"That's great, Anna," he said, his eyes returning to his work.

"Yes," I said pointedly, "it is."

I waited until my tone registered, and he looked up again.

"Sorry," he said. "Yes, you're right. We should do something to celebrate."

I backtracked.

"Well, it's hardly anything to celebrate yet," I said.

"Not signing him," said Josh. "Feeling like you are back at work for real. Grace is healthy. Oaklynn is helping out, and you are back in the saddle. Sounds worthy of a celebration to me."

"OK," I conceded. "Like what?"

"I don't know. Have some friends over, maybe. Drinks? Dinner?"

"Friends?"

"Yeah. Kurt and Mary Beth, the Wards. Whoever you want."

I considered this, warming to the idea.

"It would give me a chance to properly introduce them to Oaklynn," I said. "I feel like I've been keeping her away from our friends a bit."

"Why?"

"I don't know," I said. "I mean, I really like her, but she is a little . . . different."

"Eccentric," Josh supplied.

"That, too," I conceded.

"Are you embarrassed to have her meet your friends?" he said, raising an eyebrow.

"No!" I said. "Maybe. A little."

"Are you afraid she won't measure up to them, or the other way around?" he asked.

I thought about that for a second: dog-obsessed Tammy Ward and her babysitter-fancying husband, Tommy; bland, acquisitive Kurt Wilson and his acid-tongued wife, Mary Beth.

"You know," I said, mildly surprised by the idea, "I'm really not sure."

"It will be fine," said Josh. "Mary Beth can be a bit sharp, but she's fun."

"Fun?"

He hesitated.

"Yeah," he said, shrugging. "Basically sweet, right?"

Fun and now sweet? That made her sound like the kind of guest determined to have her friends sing karaoke or drink cocktails with salacious names because she knew in her heart how much they'd love it. A night with Mary Beth was more like playing catch with a live grenade. She could be hysterically funny, often when she was being mean, but *fun? Sweet?* They were nice words, cautious words, words like *cute*, which you used when you meant *hot*, words you used to dodge other things.

But what things?

I watched Josh as he studied his computer screen again, trying to decide if he was avoiding my gaze.

Chapter Twenty

Oaklynn put her laptop down and flexed her wrists. Outside the light of the screen, the basement room felt dark and oddly unlived in, even though Oaklynn was the person who lived in it. Except not really, because Oaklynn wasn't real, and Nadine had been wiped away, and the person sitting here in her stupid felt hat and her witchy shoes was a kind of no one: a job performed for other people who needed help, who needed eyes on their children, though if they knew . . .

The hospital had been hard. Glorious in its way, of course, but also hard. Each moment was a memory, sharp and clear and weighted like smells from childhood. Sour smells of blood and decay and death barely masked by disinfectant. It was impossible not to see Maddie there, just in the corner of her eye as she glanced at the curtained beds, wondering vaguely which patients would live and which would not.

Everyone dies, the doctor had told her long ago, when he had brought the news she had known was coming. She had watched his face for an unspoken accusation as he said Maddie's name, and she had lain there, tense and watchful, feeling the guilt radiate off her like heat from an oven door. He would see it. He would demand to know what she had done or not done. He would call the police.

But none of that had happened, though a part of her thought it still might, that they might still be tailing her, pursuing the scent of her culpability across the miles, the years . . .

Everyone dies, he had said, as if that was a comfort. The question was only when.

Oaklynn looked at her laptop screen, her eyes sliding over the numbered boxes on the calendar in the corner, the minutes ticking over on the clock at the top, and thought it again.

The question was only when.

Chapter Twenty-One

ANNA

I read more of *Hell Is Empty*, a deliciously creepy scene in which Carried, the sociopathic accountant, returns some misdelivered mail to the single mother who lives next door, all the while fingering the handle of a bread knife he has strapped to his thigh, easily accessible from a hole in his trouser pocket. It was electrically unnerving, and I read with one hand clamped to my mouth, conscious that my heart was racing as I considered the looming but unwritten ending.

Will he or won't he?

It was quite a tightrope act. The book world had moved steadily toward action-driven thrillers and the kinds of mysteries where there's a body within the first chapter if not on page one, but Lodging was managing to do the impossible, keeping my attention while—page after anxious page—nothing happened. Would flying in the face of industry wisdom be a problem when I came to sell it? Perhaps. But only until people read it. This was a book that would sell not as an outline and a sample but as a complete manuscript, where every sentence would work to prove the strength of the premise.

I was still thinking about this when Ben Lodging's meticulously detailed answers to my questions arrived by email. They were all I could hope for and more: specific, ambitious, and dedicated. This was not a one-book author but a focused writer with a career I could build. Within a half hour, I had formally offered him representation. Ten minutes after that, I got his delighted acceptance. I called Ramkins and Deale and spoke to Jim Ramkins, letting him know I was sending a letter of agreement over to Ben Lodging and outlining the project. Jim was, as ever, enthusiastic and hands-off, careful not to try and sway my judgment either way, and twenty minutes later, the deal was done. Ben Lodging had representation, and I had my first new client in over three years.

It was still not really worthy of a celebration, but it felt like an achievement, and I was glad we had agreed to host the dinner party. As the evening got closer, however, I became more and more convinced that it had been a bad idea. I think Josh thought so, too, but he clearly wanted to assert some kind of normalcy, a return to some version of our pre-Oaklynn life, and after my minor meltdown over Grace's ER visit, he was keen to get me out of what he referred to as "Mommy mode." That was ironic, really, since the incident had resurrected some of my insecurities about the kind of mother I was when compared to Oaklynn. Beyond her coolheaded efficiency at the hospital, Oaklynn seemed to know just what to do and say to keep Grace and Veronica happy, while being utterly unfazed by our assorted minor dramas.

Mommy mode, my ass.

Neurotic-and-inadequate mode might be closer to the truth.

Either way, the dinner party was supposed to be a break of sorts, though it wasn't entirely clear from what. With still more irony, I was acutely conscious that I wouldn't have been able to manage it at all without Oaklynn's help.

Help was an understatement. As Josh and I had been talking idly about what to serve a few nights prior, I had remarked that what we really wanted was something like the meal she had served to us the night she'd arrived.

"I could do that, if you like," she volunteered. "It's easy to adjust for more people. I made it several times for my previous families. You could handle dessert and appetizers, Josh can look after drinks, and I'll do the main course."

And that was that. We told her it was too much to ask of her, and I know we both felt the awkwardness of having the meal prepared by someone who wouldn't then eat with us, like she was a servant, but when we invited her to join us, she said that she'd rather dine with Grace and Veronica.

"I mean, you guys are great," she confided, "but I don't think I'm ready for your high-finance friends. I would feel out of place."

Being a servant . . .

"I'll say hi," she added, as if sensing that part of the point of the party was to put her on display, "but I'm happier with the girls, if that's OK with you."

I said that was fine, but I still worried about her shouldering the bulk of the cooking. Josh shrugged it off.

"She's happy to do it," he said. "She likes being useful."

"You don't think it's humiliating?"

"She's getting paid for it! It's her job!"

"Not really," I said. "She's supposed to be a nanny. We added extra duties, including cooking and other housework that she's getting a stipend for, but we never said anything about entertaining our friends."

"It's all the same to her, and at this point, you'll hurt her feelings if you say no. She'll think you don't think her cooking is good enough for our fancy East Coast executive friends."

"She wouldn't think that!" I replied. "She knows we love her food."

"I just don't see why you want to blow off something that she clearly wants to do."

He had a point, but it still didn't sit right with me.

"Maybe we should pay her a bonus," I said. Josh turned to me, frowning. "It's only fair. A hundred bucks or so."

"For one meal?" Josh said. "We could just have the party catered."

"Not for a hundred bucks we couldn't," I said. "What's the big deal? Is it the money? We're rolling in money, Josh. Hadn't you noticed? Our bank balance has barely taken a hit since she moved in, and I'll be pulling in more soon."

"We don't know when that will be," he said.

It was true, but I couldn't help but be annoyed by the remark, as if I wasn't doing my part for the family.

"I will soon," I said carefully. "And you make more than enough. I can't believe you are haggling over a hundred bucks."

His face tightened, and for a second, I remembered how cagey he had been about work lately, but he just shrugged and looked away.

"OK," he said. "But make her understand this is a one-off, OK? I'm glad she's here and all, and I'm happy to make sure she's properly compensated, but we're not a bottomless well."

"Look at this place, Josh! We have money. I don't see why we have to . . ."

"It's the principle of the thing. I don't like being taken advantage of."

"We're *offering* her a bonus. No one is taking advantage . . ."

"I just don't want her to think that she just has to show courtesy, and I'll get my wallet out!" He caught my look and backtracked. "*Our* wallet," he corrected.

Josh could be . . . *careful* when it came to money. It was probably why he was good at making it and investing it for other people.

"It's a hundred bucks, Josh."

"I know. I said it was fine."

"Grudgingly."

"It's fine."

"Yeah?"

"Yeah," he said. "Let it go."

I took him at his word, and the following day, I presented Oaklynn with our proposal. She cried with gratitude, which made me feel, paradoxically, like a heel. But the next night, she helped us prepare the best dinner we had offered our friends in the almost four years since we had lived on Settle Road.

And yet.

I'd hidden it as best I could, and I wasn't about to unload any of it on Josh, whom I had had to convince to try the nanny idea in the first place. But I'd be lying if, when it actually came down to it, with Oaklynn working her magic in the kitchen and me reduced to assistant, I said I didn't feel just a teeny bit overshadowed. I wondered again, as I had that first night Oaklynn arrived, if I had inadvertently made myself irrelevant. I had given up my family to someone better suited to running it. A stranger, no less, but one who would be beloved by all but my most cynical friends. With that thought came the memory of the semicircular shadows of the dogwood leaves, and the sliver of sun peeking out behind the moon . . .

Eclipsed.

Chapter Twenty-Two

At seven, Mary Beth dragged Kurt from whatever idiocy he was watching on TV and made him put on a jacket. They called on Tommy and Tammy on their way over, their maddening dog yipping around them as they dithered, eventually getting their shit together, and left. She gossiped excitedly with Tammy about the Mormon nanny whom they had glimpsed in the street for weeks but who was going to be properly unveiled tonight as they headed over to the Kleins' for what promised to be an eventful evening. They brought chardonnay, suitably chilled, which Mary Beth presented to Anna at the door and said, "Get your Mary Poppins to uncork that."

The nanny, vast and nervous but smiling like some fifties housewife in a soap commercial, was at the foot of the stairs with Anna's eldest kid, and surely within earshot. Anna blushed guiltily, as if the remark had been hers, but the nanny didn't respond. Mary Beth mouthed a theatrical apology but followed it up with a mischievous grin. And if the nanny couldn't take a Mary Poppins joke, to hell with her. At least she hadn't called her Mammy. Not that the nanny was black or anything. That would have made an already strange situation even weirder.

People got so sensitive about race these days, always dragging the issue up again just as it was finally over. You never knew when someone would get all offended about something that was only a joke. Anna was usually cool, but Mary Beth—who liked to tell people that she didn't see race at all—had learned to be careful around her and never mentioned her Asian Americanness, or whatever the hell you were supposed to call it. The important thing was that the wine got uncorked fast, and whether it was the Mormon weight lifter who did it or someone else entirely didn't much matter. Just bring on the vino.

In fact, the nanny just nodded her hellos, smiling as wide as Utah itself, and offered each guest just two fingers to shake. It was so deeply odd. Who shakes hands like that? It was like being offered the end of a rope. Mary Beth gaped from her to Tammy, and everyone smirked, and then the nanny went upstairs to hang with the rug rats. She'd be down later, she promised, as if that were a special treat for everyone. There was a momentary hush as everyone watched her go, got their drinks, and moved into the Kleins' spacious kitchen, where the whispering started.

"Well?" Mary Beth demanded.

"Well, what?" asked Anna.

"What's she like?" said Mary Beth, as if Anna was being stupid on purpose.

"Really nice," said Anna.

"Nice?" said Mary Beth, making a face. "I hate her already."

"Capable, professional . . . ," Anna began.

"Great with the kids," said Josh.

"Oh, so long as she's great with the kids," said Mary Beth, rolling her eyes but managing a playful smirk at Josh at the end. Josh smiled, meeting her eyes so frankly that when Anna glanced at him, he looked caught out and turned quickly away.

"She was a rock when we had to go to the ER," Anna said with just a hint of defiance.

"That's right," said Josh loyally, rallying, and drawing another amused eye roll from Mary Beth.

"When did you go to the ER?" asked Tammy.

"Couple of days ago," said Anna. "Grace spiked a fever and was throwing up . . ."

"But she's living in your house," Mary Beth inserted. "Isn't that weird?"

"We have a babysitter all the time," said Tammy. "You get used to it."

Mary Beth shot Tammy's husband a knowing look but managed not to say that some people got more used to it than others. Tommy was gazing stupidly around the house, as if he was appraising for resale, and didn't seem to notice.

It was a nice enough house, older than the others on the street and less ostentatious, but it had been remodeled before the Kleins moved in, and it still had something clunkily eighties about it. Four years on and some of the rooms still had their gaudy brass light fixtures, and the upstairs bathroom looked like something out of *Pretty in Pink*. Anna and Josh had put more work into the kids' rooms than their own, and according to Tammy, they had really gone to town with the nanny's quarters, even installing a gorgeous new shower studded with metallic glass tile. You could almost forget that the nanny was actually being paid.

"Oh my God!" Mary Beth exclaimed in mock horror. "You have a cat!"

The brownish thing was skulking around the baseboards by the fridge. Then—as if sensing everyone turning to stare at it—it slunk away, its body low to the stone slab floor.

"What the hell?" Mary Beth persisted. "A *cat*?"

"It's Oaklynn's," said Josh noncommittally. "Bit of a surprise, to be honest, but he's OK."

"She brought a cat without telling you?" Mary Beth said, her jaw dropping and eyes widening as if the nanny had brought an elephant.

"Oh, I don't *think* so! Why didn't you tell her to get it out of your house?"

"Well, the girls like it," said Anna, her head on one side as if that was a real point in the creature's favor.

"Of course the *girls* like it," said Mary Beth, pausing in her outrage long enough to sip her wine. "They're kids. They're practically animals themselves. And they sure as hell aren't paying for the furniture the beast shreds and pees on."

"It's fine," said Anna. She looked embarrassed, though whether that was because she felt she'd been exposed as weak or because she was afraid the nanny might overhear, Mary Beth couldn't say.

"Wouldn't be fine in my house," Mary Beth said, shooting Kurt a warning look in case he had been secretly planning to bring home a cat himself.

"I'm allergic," said Tammy.

Of course she was.

In fact, Mary Beth thought, Tammy looked as if her husband had brought home several cats, and she'd eaten them. Still, better than the other kinds of pussy Tommy was chasing. She snorted at the joke, even though she hadn't actually said it, and drank some more, privately storing the line away to share with Anna later. Or Josh. She liked amusing Josh, especially if it was with something that might make him blush. He was cute when he blushed.

The guys had already spun off into their own group. They were still in the same room and were only a couple of feet from the women, but they had turned in on themselves, and Kurt was pontificating about the Panthers' weakness at the goddamned wide-receiver position. He'd probably pulled that line from ESPN the night before. It was all he watched on TV. Josh was nodding along, sage but bored, while Tommy watched Anna moving around the kitchen, pretending to listen to what she was saying while he was actually checking out her ass.

He was such a lowlife. Kind of cute in an annoying man-child kind of way, but definitely a total skeeze. It was hard to believe his wife couldn't tell just by looking at him: the tight jeans, the shiny shirt with one too many buttons undone, the nonchalant flip of his moussed black hair, and the constant smirk that almost covered the vacancy in his eyes. Almost. He looked like a man pretending to have a personality. Kurt, himself not the brightest bulb in the light fitting, called him *Midnight Cowboy*, after the Dustin Hoffman and Jon Voight movie. Mary Beth thought that was funny, though she hadn't actually seen the film.

There were olives in bowls, a decent (store-bought) spinach-and-artichoke dip, and bruschetta hot from the oven, which was a good sign. Mary Beth had been worried that Anna would go full-on Asian for the dinner: bits of fucking tofu and some Chinky bean-sprout shit or something, but this looked better. Already on her second glass of wine, she decided she was going to have a good time, something that might have worried Kurt if he'd known. She hadn't had a proper blowout for a long time, and when Mary Beth really partied, people got crushed in the wreckage. Or they used to, back in the day. She smiled secretly at the memory, laughed loudly at something Anna had just said, and topped off her glass. Maybe this nanny malarkey was a good thing, after all: weird as all hell, of course, but if it gave Anna more free time and made her fun again, she'd take it. Because Anna *had* been fun, briefly, before she had popped out the first kid. She'd been pregnant and increasingly anxious about that, sure, but she had also been smart and funny and *so* New York, and it was like the wind of a real city had blown in with her . . .

For a little while. Before the rug rats. Before the nanny.

Speak of the devil. The nanny—*Oaklynn*, and what the hell kind of name was *that*?—had just reappeared. She was smiling and nodding but looked out of her element and—the word was unavoidable—bashful. Mary Beth introduced herself, watching the woman's response shrewdly, and pressed a glass on her, though she insisted on filling it with cranberry juice.

"You need a splash of vodka in there," Mary Beth confided, and the nanny giggled, her hand coming up to her mouth like a Catholic schoolgirl hearing a dirty joke.

Christ.

"I hear you made the main course," said Mary Beth, throwing her a bone.

Another smiling nod, as if to actually say the words would be outrageously prideful, then said, "Tuscan chicken. I sure hope y'all like it."

"Oh my God," said Mary Beth, "where *did* they find you?"

Anna swooped in then, pretending it was a real question, and started talking about the rigorous selection process used by the company—Nature or Nurture, Mary Beth didn't catch which. She also didn't care, but she saw the way Anna slipped a protective arm around Oaklynn's broad waist and felt a prickle of annoyance. Anna was playing straight man, or doing damage control. Something. She clearly didn't want Mary Beth's brand of humor—brassy as the upstairs bathroom—souring her relationship with her precious nanny.

Dinner, Mary Beth had to admit, was pretty damn good. She said as much, and Oaklynn colored as if she'd just been given very specific directions for some illegal sex act. There was a place at the table set for Oaklynn, but she contrived never to sit in it for more than a few minutes at a time, spending most of her time checking on the kids and bringing out food. It was bizarre, as if she felt more comfortable with the holy innocents upstairs with their stuffed animals and crayons than she did with the grown-ups. At first, since Oaklynn clearly had nothing to say, Mary Beth assumed she was just embarrassed, out of her element, and a bit intimidated by the adult company, but after a while, she started to wonder if the nanny's attitude was actually an embarrassment for *them*, that her constant leaving the table was a judgment verging on distaste. They weren't just too sophisticated for her down-home, wide-ass nanny self; they were morally repugnant.

Mary Beth didn't care. Why should she? But the idea annoyed her nonetheless, and as she poured herself another glass of wine, she eyed Oaklynn, who was chewing in bovine vacancy, and slopped some of it on the table.

"Easy there, Mary Beth," said Kurt, leaning over to blot the spill with his napkin. "Maybe you've had enough."

"Maybe I shouldn't have to pour my own damn wine, Kurt," she snapped back.

"More chicken?" suggested Oaklynn sweetly.

Mary Beth shot her a look, then bit her tongue and shook her head minutely.

"More wine, I think," she said, turning her gaze on Kurt and holding it like an outstretched spear. Kurt shrugged with little more than his eyebrows, his eyes half closing, then finding Josh and rolling in a "You know how it is" kind of way. Except that Josh didn't know how it was. Not really. Because while Anna had her idiosyncrasies and had lately become a bit of a prissy stick in the proverbial mud, she was never the kind of pain in the ass that Mary Beth had perfected, the sort that made people keep track of just how much booze she was downing and shrink away in case they got hit by the shrapnel when she finally blew. Some people might have been embarrassed by such wariness around her, but Mary Beth—who was used to it—took a certain perverse pride in being the loose cannon, the rabble-rouser. Hell, at least she was honest. And then, as if deking one of Kurt's favorite cornerbacks, she smiled amiably at Oaklynn and said, "You really are a chef. This is delicious. Anna and Josh are lucky to have you."

Oaklynn looked momentarily stunned, then anxious, as she hunted for an irony that wasn't obviously there, and the room pushed through its puzzlement and, eventually, relaxed. When Mary Beth caught Josh's eye, she shot him a wink. It was satisfyingly like flicking a bobblehead toy that had finally come to rest. She caught Anna watching and gave her a smile as sweet as a bucket of southern iced tea. Anna returned it, but only after a momentary hesitation.

"You guys have a good time on Tuesday?" asked Tommy. From anyone else, the question would have been a deliberate shift of direction to steer away from the previous awkwardness, but Tommy Ward was so reliably clueless about what was going on around him that you couldn't be sure.

Josh gave him a puzzled look.

"Tuesday?" he said.

"That golf thing at Quail Hollow," Tommy said.

Josh started to shake his head, still baffled, but Kurt cut in.

"Tuesday, right, Josh?" he nudged. "Yeah, it was a good time. Kind of cold for the full eighteen holes, but yeah. A good time and drinks after. Sorry you missed it."

Mary Beth's gaze hardened, flicking from Josh to Kurt and back.

"Right!" said Josh. "I was . . . I thought you meant *last* Tuesday."

It was a lie. Mary Beth would have spotted it at a thousand yards. Josh Klein was lying, and so was Kurt, but for whose benefit? Tommy's? And if they were, what were they trying to hide? She watched her husband, the more accomplished storyteller of the two, ease into talk of fairways and wind speeds while Josh sat staring at him, his smile fixed and, she thought, anxious. All of Mary Beth's previous alcoholic fuzziness burned off in an instant, and she became still and focused. Kurt kept his attention on Tommy, avoiding her eyes, and Josh sat silent beside him, nodding along as if the conversation were the most gripping thing he had ever heard. She could almost smell his panic.

It couldn't be about Tommy Ward. Not really. So who was being lied to? Her? Mary Beth watched her husband, the way he refused to look at her, and she was almost sure. Kurt was lying, and Josh was covering for him, and while it was Tommy who had triggered the whole performance, he was no more than an innocent bystander. So what had her husband been up to on Tuesday that might involve Josh and that they didn't want her to know about?

Mary Beth glanced around the room to see who else had noticed this little sideshow, but Anna was talking to Tammy about choosing kindergartens for the rug rats, and both seemed oblivious. Oaklynn was part of that conversation, too, albeit passively, but Mary Beth could have sworn she had seen the nanny watching the men for a second. There had been something in her eyes quite different from anything she had seen in her before, something thoughtful that was almost . . .

Calculation.

And that, Mary Beth thought, was very interesting indeed.

Chapter Twenty-Three

ANNA

The party went well, I thought. Mary Beth got a little salty early on—always a danger—but seemed to settle down over dinner. Part of what makes her fun, of course, is her sharpness. Her self-consciously slightly wicked persona that makes her both flirty and playfully cruel can be difficult to navigate, but it's not really who she is. She's quite sweet, really. Sometimes I wish she wasn't quite so attentive to Josh, but she doesn't mean anything by it. Not really.

And Josh? What does he mean when she shoots him one of those half-mocking sexy pouts of hers, and he looks at her for just a half second too long . . . ?

Nothing. He doesn't mean anything by it. They are just friends.

Almost certainly.

I shook the thoughts away, determined not to lapse into new paranoias.

I had spent a lot of the evening chatting to Tammy, which meant that I had to do most of the heavy lifting, but things livened up once we had adjourned to the living room again. By then, the kids were asleep, and Oaklynn had said her good nights and moved downstairs, instantly becoming the main topic of conversation again. I had been steeling myself to have to defend why we had her but found I didn't really need to. Mary Beth was enjoying a certain sense of superiority. The guys barely seemed to have noticed her, except that she had cooked—and everyone had nothing but praise for her food—and Tammy was, I think, frankly jealous. I felt a little bad for her, to be honest, because she saw how useful Oaklynn was, how easily she had already fit in, and how careful she was not to get in the way of the family. And I'd be lying if I didn't say that Tammy also liked the fact that Oaklynn's looks weren't going to make her a target for the guys. However much Mary Beth said Tammy was clueless about her husband's roving eye—other body parts, too, she thought, but I didn't know that for sure—I had my doubts. She seemed sad. Not despairing or weepy, just slightly broken. Worn down, perhaps. She only became slightly animated when she was talking about her kids or—and this was harder for me to fathom—her terrier, Angus. Whatever was going on between Tommy and the leggy babysitter, Tammy knew, and I doubted she was watching it happen for the first time.

Oaklynn had managed to do most of the dishes before she vanished into her basement apartment, so there was no real work to do when everyone left a little after midnight. I was tempted to have a whiskey and sit awhile, but Josh was quieter than usual and said he wanted to go to bed.

"What was that business about playing golf on Tuesday?" I asked.

He looked momentarily startled, then shrugged, crumpling as he breathed out.

"Tommy had asked Kurt to do something with him, and Kurt didn't want to," Josh said. "Used me as an excuse."

He sounded annoyed—bitter even—which was unlike him.

"What was he really doing?" I asked.

"No idea," said Josh.

"You think he's having an affair?"

I'm not sure why the idea came to me. All that speculation about Tommy, probably.

Josh shook his head.

"I don't think so," he said. "He said he wanted to get Mary Beth a surprise birthday present. Maybe it was about that."

"Why would he lie about that to Tommy?"

Another shrug, and now the irritation with Kurt was spreading toward me like spilled oil.

"Who knows? Kurt and Tommy have a weird relationship. Very macho. Competitive."

"I don't see why that—"

"I don't either, Anna," said Josh crisply.

I gave him a look.

"Sorry," he added. "I'm just tired. Can we . . . ?"

He nodded toward the bed.

"Sure," I said. "Was the party a bad idea? I thought you wanted . . . ?"

"I did. I'm just . . . beat. Work."

"Anything particular?" I asked. As I had noted before, he seemed more than tired. He seemed troubled, tense. "Something you want to talk about?"

"No," he said. "Thanks. It's just the usual shit. It's no wonder people burn out on this job."

"I guess that's why you make the big bucks," I said, smiling and giving him an affectionate peck on the cheek.

"I guess," he said, not looking at me.

Instantly, all the well-being the party had given me seemed to siphon off, and unbidden, that image of Mary Beth winking discreetly at my husband across the table floated up in my head. I tried again.

"Is there something we need to discuss, Josh?" I said.

"No," he said. He seemed to think about it for a moment, then just shook his head wearily and said again, "No."

It wasn't the answer I wanted, but I let it go because while he had said, "No," what it felt like was "Not yet."

My stomach flexed and knotted, but I just nodded and left him alone, wondering vaguely how the success of the evening could have so quickly soured. Nothing had happened. Nothing had been said. Was I missing something that was obvious to everyone else?

I stayed up for another hour, finishing tidying up, looking for jobs that would keep me from going to bed, then poured myself the Scotch I had denied myself earlier. I even considered getting the laptop out and doing some work, but I'd had a couple of glasses of wine as well as the whiskey, so that wasn't feasible. When I did finally go upstairs, I hesitated at the bedroom door, something I don't think I had ever done before, listening to the sound of Josh snoring softly. Though I had wanted to talk, I found I was relieved to hear it, and got ready for bed as quietly as I could so as not to wake him.

⚯

"Anna, I'm sorry to get you up so early, but Grace is sick again."

Oaklynn had been tapping at the bedroom door. She looked anxious, upset. Josh had already gone to work, but I had not slept well and had opted to have a few more minutes before taking a shower. I rubbed my eyes, heart sinking, stomach turning.

"The same as before?" I managed, fumbling for a robe to pull over my panties and T-shirt.

"Same high fever. Her diaper has some blood in it."

Fuck.

I blundered down the stairs, Oaklynn in my wake, her hands slapping at the banister rail as she chuffed heavily after me. I think I was cursing as I went, but she said nothing, still purposeful and controlled, despite her worry. Later, I would reflect that her obvious distress was especially alarming. She had been with us less than two months, but I had grown used to her solid dependability; seeing it shaken like this filled me with dread.

Grace was exactly as before, hot and uncomfortable, moaning.

"She threw up in the night," said Oaklynn. "I tried to give her a bottle, but she wasn't interested."

"I guess . . . we go back to the ER?" I said, holding my baby, feeling the unnatural warmth of her against my face. "We could call the pediatrician and see if he can squeeze us in, but the hospital said to bring her back if the symptoms returned."

"Then we should do that."

I hesitated.

"She seemed so much better," I said, flushing, feeling like I had screwed up. "She has been fine. I don't understand it."

"Still," said Oaklynn, "we should probably go . . ."

"I know. Get the diaper bag together. I'll drive."

"It's no trouble . . . ," Oaklynn began, but I cut her off.

"For me either," I said. "She's my child. I'll drive."

I was being defensive because I felt guilty for not having been more vigilant. I knew that but couldn't stop it from coming out. Oaklynn just nodded and set to getting Grace's things together, calling for Veronica. I considered telling her not to bother, that I could manage with Grace by myself, that Oaklynn should stay home with Veronica, but I didn't, because even though I wanted to say it, a part of me was afraid she'd agree. I wanted to be Mommy, but I had come to depend on Oaklynn, and I knew that having her with me would steady my nerves and protect me from the accusatory looks of the nurses.

Here she is again, the incompetent mother, the repeat offender, the type who doesn't know the names of her kids' friends, her teachers, because she's too wrapped up in her own life, the goddamned dinner parties for which she doesn't even cook . . .

So I drove and did my best to look like I was in charge and informed, though even as I did so, I found myself resenting Oaklynn for being in the back with the kids, sponging Grace's forehead and whispering encouragingly to Veronica, who sat beside her, infected by our panic.

Poor Oaklynn. Talk about a no-win situation . . .

I was relieved to see different nurses on duty this time. The doctor was also different, an Indian woman with a New Jersey accent who was kind and attentive as she went through the notes from our last visit.

"I should have taken her to see our pediatrician," I said, like I was confessing to a priest, as if saying it would somehow make sure my daughter was treated properly and not discounted as not worth the effort. "I called, but in the end, I just talked to the nurse because she seemed to have recovered. I'm sorry," I added stupidly.

The doctor waved the apology away but said they would need to do some blood work "to rule some things out."

"Blood work?" I said.

Oaklynn took my hand.

"Is that really necessary? I mean, she's already distressed."

"I know," said the doctor. "But this is the best way to see what's going on. Her temperature is down again, but two fevers in a few days means something isn't quite right. You didn't bring her last diaper with you, did you?"

I shook my head, my eyes swimming again, and the doctor's smile slipped a little.

"We need a urine sample," she said. "If she's not wet now, we may have to have you wait a while. I'd prefer not to cath her if I can avoid it."

I blinked, almost numb, then nodded quickly.

Stupid.

I should have seen this coming. If I'd spent more time with Grace instead of fretting about the stupid dinner party and squabbling with Josh, I would have spotted something, some sign that she wasn't quite right. Then maybe I could have spared her whatever had to happen now.

Grace looked so small and frail, smaller and frailer still as the nurse prepped her to have her blood drawn. I wasn't ready for it and felt tricked or betrayed, as if my confession about not actually seeing the pediatrician should have been enough to barter Grace out of further misery. Which was ridiculous. Obviously.

The nurse poked and prodded Grace, studying her forearm, but looked unhappy.

"Everything OK?" I asked.

"Not really used to kids this young," muttered the nurse, as if this was more than should be expected of her. "Hold on."

I watched, aghast, as she left. There was a TV on in the corner playing some infomercially thing about diabetes. I gave Oaklynn a desperate look.

"It's OK," she said. "She's just taking precautions. Doesn't want to stick little Gracie more than necessary."

I didn't know what to say to this, and in the same instant, the nurse returned, leading Alysha, the black nurse from our last ER visit. Her eyes met mine, and I saw the fractional hesitation, the appraising consideration before the formal smile snapped on.

"Let me take a look here," she said. "Can you hold her for me?"

It wasn't clear whom she was addressing, and when I hesitated, Oaklynn picked Grace up and held her while the nurse rubbed her arm, then bound it with a rubber ligature. Grace cried as the needle went in, more in surprise than pain, and Veronica buried her face in Oaklynn's skirts, one hand toying with the silver buckle on her shoes.

"It's OK, honeybun," Oaklynn cooed to each of them in turn. "All part of getting her well again. Good news," she added, smiling up at the nurse. "I think we have a wet diaper."

"You're so good with her," said Alysha to Oaklynn, not looking at me. "It's hard when they are this small. You don't understand what's happening, do you, babe?" She smiled into Grace's face. Grace had already stopped crying.

"Who's my brave girl?" said Oaklynn.

"Can I have her, please?" I said, extending my arms.

Alysha watched the handoff critically, as if I might drop her, then said that I should make an appointment to see my pediatrician.

"Leave the diaper with us, please. We'll send the blood and urine tests over to your physician as soon as we have the results."

Chapter Twenty-Four

ANNA

Grace's tests all came back normal, which should have made me happy but only served to inflate my anxiety.

"What would cause her symptoms that wouldn't show up on the tests?" I asked the nurse over the phone.

Nothing they could pinpoint at this stage, I was told. I should continue to monitor her—as if I might not—and update the doctor with any changes or persistent symptoms. I told Oaklynn, and she made a pouty, sad face and hugged me and promised to keep a "super-close eye" on Grace, so that I felt bad and hugged her back, as if she might be more upset than I was. We were sitting on the lower back deck, watching Veronica playing with Mr. Quietly in the yard below. The cat had a way of sitting very still, jaws apart and eyes fixed—usually on a bird or a squirrel—making these odd chittering noises in his throat. Veronica thought it hilarious. I found it faintly demonic. Somehow it suggested a distance between us so that I felt lost, a bad mother who was losing her relationship with her older daughter and couldn't keep her younger one healthy.

"What am I doing wrong?" I said, as much to myself as to Oaklynn.

"Nothing. It's just one of those things. We'll stay on top of it, and it will blow over. I promise."

I had been momentarily sure she was going to say something about God or how everything happened for a reason, or some other damn thing that would make me pull my hair out. I was so grateful that she didn't that I hugged her and whispered, "Thank you" into her soap-scented hair.

I had been facing her as I spoke, so it was only out of the corner of my eye that I caught something streaking across the backyard. I turned to look properly, my heart in my mouth, and the dreaded word—*coyote*—in my mind. In the same instant, Veronica squealed with alarm and shouted, "No!" just as I realized that the blur I had half seen was not a coyote at all but Tammy Ward's mangy terrier, Angus, which had escaped and was chasing Oaklynn's cat.

I started for the stairs, but Oaklynn was faster, barreling down into the yard and shouting at the errant dog as Mr. Quietly bolted, yowling into some undergrowth by the fence. Veronica blundered after him, and I actually screamed as I leaped down the last few steps in pursuit.

"Veronica, stop!" I yelled, as she got alarmingly close to the thin strands of wire that separated her from the steep and slippery bank of the creek. There was such force in my voice, such horror, that Veronica froze as if she were about to be electrified or bitten by a snake. Her face was a mask of horror and fear, tears in her eyes, confused distraction in every part of her. I swept toward her and caught her up.

"I'm sorry, Mommy!" she babbled over and over, tears rolling down her cheeks.

"It's OK, honey," I said, startled by the way my panic had infected her. "You didn't do anything wrong."

"Get out of here!" Oaklynn commanded the terrier, but it sprang for the bush where the cat was nestled, hackles raised, mouth open and spitting. Oaklynn stormed over, snatching at the dog's collar and pulling it back, and as it strained to get free, it snarled and yipped at Mr. Quietly with undisguised malice. If we hadn't been there, I think it would have killed him.

I joined Oaklynn, grasping the dog's collar and holding it in place so she could reach for Mr. Quietly. For a moment, her eyes—usually so placid—were fierce, raging. She caught the cat up in her arms protectively and made for the house, Mr. Quietly shrinking into her bosom but watching the terrier with baleful yellow eyes.

"Oh my goodness," Oaklynn cooed as she mounted the steps, her previous anger entirely gone. "You *are* frightened, aren't you, my love?"

"Is he OK?" I called after her.

"I think so," said Oaklynn, managing to smile.

"I'll speak to Tammy," I said. "The dog shouldn't be out. If someone reports her, she'll be in trouble."

Oaklynn nodded but didn't respond, and a moment later, she disappeared inside, closing the door behind her.

"Is Mr. Quietly OK?" asked Veronica, genuinely concerned.

"Yes, I think so," I said. "I'm sorry I yelled. I just don't like you getting so close to the water."

"Are there snakes in the water?"

Veronica had a particular horror of snakes.

"There could be," I said. I had never seen one there, though we sometimes got small copperheads in the garden, and it was too late in the year now. She took my hand, shrinking into my legs.

"Let's go inside," she said. "It's getting cold."

This was true, but I saw the evasion for what it was and marveled at how quickly we learned to hide things, even from ourselves.

Josh flipped the plain brown flaps of the huge Amazon box and peered inside.

"What the hell?" he said.

Oaklynn pursed her lips but managed to smile.

"Language," said Anna.

Josh gave her a blank look, remembered Oaklynn, and said, "Oh. Sorry."

"It's not a problem," said Oaklynn, in a way that wasn't quite convincing.

Josh's attention had already returned to the contents of the cardboard box. Inside was another box, glossy with photographs featuring lots of camo and a bold, comic-book-type font proclaiming the words *Barnett Jackal.*

"You bought a *crossbow?*" he said. "When did you buy a crossbow? *Why* did you buy a crossbow?"

"I was worried about the coyotes," said Anna. "Oaklynn said it was a good idea. Better than a shotgun or something."

"I thought . . . ," Josh began, then redirected. "What about the girls?"

"What about them?" said Oaklynn. Anna seemed to have receded into the background.

"You don't want them getting their hands on this," said Josh. He kind of wished Oaklynn would go away. He wanted to talk to his wife, if only because the purchase seemed so . . . odd. Out of character.

"It's quite safe," said Oaklynn. "This thing has a hundred-and-fifty-pound draw. Without the rope-cocking mechanism, even you might struggle to load it."

"And with it?" said Josh, considering the separate blister pack containing a length of rope with a plastic handle on each end.

"You'll be fine," said Oaklynn. "But Anna probably couldn't do it. No chance the girls could."

"Still," said Josh, considering the box warily. It had a kind of undeniable appeal, but the gift—if that was what it was—bothered him, like he was being invited to enjoy something he had always thought illicit and dangerous, something that might be morally suspect. His wife was fiercely antigun and had been known to blame most of the evils of the world on the NRA. This was different, of course, but still . . . It felt strange, slightly dreamlike in its unexpected perversity. If Anna had bought him porn for Christmas, he thought wildly, it would feel like this. He considered her, deliberately looking past Oaklynn.

"You really think we need to worry about the coyotes?" he said. "We haven't heard them in weeks."

"It's just a safety precaution," she said. "I thought you'd think it was fun."

That didn't seem quite true, and suddenly, he thought he understood. Anna had been miserable after they had taken Grace to the hospital again, convinced she'd blown some key parenting thing. But Grace had made another complete recovery, and none of the hospital's tests had shown anything wrong. It had been some weird anomaly, and maybe not even the same one that had made her sick the previous time. Anna couldn't fix that, couldn't ensure her children would always be healthy or that her role as Mommy would always be flawless. So she had fastened onto a different threat, one she could see or at least hear, one that she could keep from the door with this lethal little trinket. She couldn't keep bacteria and viruses from harming the kids, but she could sure as hell keep the coyotes at bay.

"You sure about this, Anna?"

"Of course," said Anna, with a casualness she almost certainly didn't feel. "You'll have to learn how to use it properly, safely, but yes."

"And where am I going to do that?" he asked.

"I can show you," said Oaklynn. "Set up a target in the yard now, if you like."

So they did. The "target" was just the Amazon box with a couple of circles drawn on with Magic Marker, stuffed with rags, and set against a willow oak by the creek. If he missed, which Josh thought pretty likely, the arrow would lose itself in the overgrown bank. Because the land sloped so drastically, he'd have to miss very high indeed for the arrow to fly any distance beyond the little belt of water, and there was no danger of hitting anything living beyond leaves and branches. But first, the crossbow had to be assembled, the bow part fixed to the stock, and the cables waxed with something that looked almost exactly like lip balm. The bow had a built-in quiver holding three arrows with screw-in metal heads. They felt purposeful. Josh had thought the whole thing would feel like a toy, but it was big and heavy, and he could sense its raw power long before he fired it.

Oaklynn walked him through each step in that methodical farm-hand way of hers, pragmatic and polite in equal measure, then showed him how to thread the rope around the groove in the stock and attach its hooks to the drawstring on either side of the stock. She had been right about the force required to cock the thing, and for an awful moment, Josh feared he wouldn't be able to manage it, standing with his foot in the stirrup at the end of the bow to hold it down while he drew directly up with both hands. The green drawstring moved slowly in its pulleys, and he had to haul much harder than he had expected, but at last, it latched into place.

"Safety's there," said Oaklynn, glancing up from the instructions. "Goes on automatically when the bow is drawn. Arrow has to go in with the white flights down, or it won't fire."

Anna was cradling Grace, whom she had barely put down since they'd returned from the hospital. Veronica was watching warily, half-hidden behind Oaklynn, not saying anything.

"The sights are set to show three green dots," said Oaklynn. "The middle one should be set at thirty yards, so the top one is twenty, and the bottom is forty."

"Shouldn't it be the other way around?" asked Anna. She was looking less sure about this idea now that the thing was ready to fire.

"Sighting on the higher dot means you are lowering the business end of the bow," said Oaklynn.

"OK," said Josh. "Well, here goes nothing."

He knelt down, the stock of the crossbow against his shoulder, peering into the scope with one eye, squeezing the other closed.

"Safety," he said, feeling for it, then pressing the button gingerly, half expecting the bow to go off. "This feels really dangerous," he added, almost to himself.

"OK," he said again, then aimed at the target box and squeezed the trigger.

It was quieter than he had expected, little more than a snap, and there was no kick like what he associated with a firearm, but the arrow smashed through the target, out the other side, and deep into the tree. He wasn't surprised when he approached the target to consider the damage. Though he had initially assumed the crossbow would deliver a hit like an air rifle, he had felt the power of the thing as he shot it. An air rifle might break the skin of a coyote, but he doubted it would seriously slow it down. The crossbow would skewer it where it stood.

"Holy shit," he said. "Did you see that?"

He couldn't suppress a giddy thrill.

"Yeah," said Anna, less certain in her enthusiasm.

"I'm going to have another go," he said. "Or do you want to try?"

Anna shook her head, regarding the crossbow as if it were an unfriendly dog or, ironically, a coyote.

"Go on," said Oaklynn. "Have a go."

Anna hesitated, then sucked in a little breath and said, "OK."

She handed Grace to Oaklynn, and Josh handed the bow to her. They watched as she put it end down and stepped into the stirrup as he had done, lacing the cocking rope into place and trying to pull it up vertically. She could move the taut green bowstring only a few inches, nowhere near enough to latch it in firing position. She abandoned the effort, blushing with exertion but not embarrassment.

"Never mind," she said, handing it back to him.

"I'll load it, and you can shoot it," said Josh.

"No," she said, certain now. "I don't want to. You go ahead."

She was glad when he took it from her, he could see from her face, the way she snatched her hands away from it as soon as the bow's weight was in his hands. It revolted her just a little. That annoyed him because he was enjoying himself and didn't want to feel bad about it, so he loaded and fired again, whooping as the arrow stuck in the rim of the circle they had drawn onto the target. He shot her a look then and knew she wanted to stop, wanted to get back in the house. She kept her hands clasped tight in front of her waist, and her eyes kept straying over the creek to the strip of woods on the far bank, as if a pack of wild animals was about to come spewing out, yapping and snarling.

"Here, Oaklynn," he said, punishing Anna very slightly for spoiling the moment. "Why don't you take a turn?"

She blushed in response and did that thing of hers where she looked down and sort of shrugged, as if she wanted to disappear, but then she held her big hands out to take it from him. Josh grinned as she took it, avoiding Anna's eyes. He watched Oaklynn as she assessed the mechanism, her hands strong and efficient as she positioned it on the ground. She drew the cocking rope up to her chin with both hands, expanding through the shoulder and pinking in the face, shedding her matronly, lace-cuffed femininity, becoming bearlike with raw, unexpected power. Josh found the transformation a little unnerving, along with her private smile as the weapon latched, and she sighted through the scope, ready to fire.

Chapter Twenty-Five

ANNA

It was a true fall day, crisp and cool. The dogwood in the front was bronze, and the maples were the kind of true, hot red that always surprises, year after year, while one of the trees in Mary Beth's yard was a pure golden yellow. Leaves were falling into drifts on the ground, and the sky was a clear and cloudless blue. It was the kind of day that made moving to Charlotte seem so obviously right, a bucolic escape from the gray rat race of New York. The girls wanted to be outside, but Veronica had grown obsessed with a playlist Oaklynn had made to her demands, so we had her iPod and a pair of tinny little speakers outside with us.

I should be working, I thought, but I couldn't walk away.

I had been surprised by Oaklynn's eclectic musical taste, partly because I was pretty out of touch myself since I listened to the radio so rarely. In college, I had been a real music fan, listening obsessively, learning all the lyrics, and regularly attending concerts. But something happened when I got married, and I found that I was listening only to what I already knew. After a while, new music sounded strange, not repellent but somehow not for me.

"The first mark of age," said Josh shrewdly when I said so.

For all her Mormon background, though, Oaklynn's tastes were more contemporary, and as I got used to them, I found myself liking what I heard. Veronica did, too, and as the time passed—Oaklynn had been with us about two months by now—the music became another bond between them that had me on the outside looking in. I didn't resent that, but I'd be lying if I said I wasn't at all envious, and I kicked myself for not sharing my own musical past with my daughter more deliberately. I tried, playing her samples from my CD collection, but it all sounded dated compared to Oaklynn's offerings.

So yes, maybe I did resent it a little.

But then I got to watch Veronica singing along, the words garbled but fresh in her mouth, as if she were making them up on the spot, singing out her very soul as if this and only this could speak to who she was to the world. How could I resent that?

She had a particular favorite, an Imagine Dragons song called "Demons," which began quiet and reflective but rose to a rousing anthemic chorus. She loved it so much that it took several listens for me to notice the strangeness of her joy against the brooding overtones of trauma and despair in the words. Keep your distance, suggested the chorus. The singer had a darkness inside, and in that darkness were the demons of the title, shadows of past events, buried deep but never erased.

I glanced up, looking to share a knowing smile with Oaklynn, as Veronica belted out the words she couldn't possibly understand, and was shocked to see Oaklynn looking distant and numb, her face pale, her eyes shining, as if looking through the music to something bleak and cold that only she could see. I stared, taken aback, and then the song ended, and she was Oaklynn again.

Grace turned one four days later. She was, of course, pretty much oblivious to the fact, but Veronica wanted to do something to mark the occasion and, if I was honest, so did I. It felt important, necessary, even if it was mostly just an opportunity to take photographs we would be able to look over as she grew older, more conscious of her past. I thought about that as I picked up a cake from Harris Teeter and some sparkly candles, reflecting on how quickly the time had passed since Veronica's first birthday and how much she had changed. I chose a bunch of bright pink helium balloons with a swelling sense of panic and found myself driving too fast on the way home, as if afraid I would miss some landmark event in my baby's life. By the time I got home, I was ridiculously misty-eyed at how fast the girls were growing up and had to fight off images of them as adults, married and living far away . . .

I lugged the bags of treats from the car, the balloons trailing and bobbing in the breeze, bumping against each other as I struggled to get through the door.

"'Loons!" exclaimed Veronica when she saw them, using one of the babyisms she wasn't yet ready to give up.

"That's right, Vronny," I said in a stage whisper, setting a bag down so I could put a finger on her lips. "But be quiet. We don't want to spoil the surprise for Gracie."

"Gracie's 'loons?" said Veronica, a little put out.

"For her birthday. But you can share."

Veronica considered this, then grinned and nodded solemnly.

"Secret," she said. "I'm good at secrets."

"You are good at secrets," I agreed, arranging my purchases on the kitchen counter.

"Like, Oaklynn's cake," she said, giving me a meaningful look.

I started to agree, then peered at her, perplexed.

"Oaklynn's cake?" I repeated.

157

"For Gracie!" hissed Veronica as if it were obvious. "Her birthday cake."

"I just bought . . . Did Miss Oaklynn already buy a birthday cake for Gracie?"

"*Made*," said Veronica, very impressed. "She made a cake, and it's glorious!"

That was the word she saved for very special things. *Glorious*.

I blinked.

"She made her a cake? Where is it?"

"In the fridge," she replied as if this, too, should be obvious. "She was working on it all morning. It's glorious."

I wasn't listening. I moved quickly to the fridge and opened it. There, on the lowest shelf, was a masterpiece of pink-and-white frosting with *Happy Birthday, Grace!* feathered across the top in fluid cursive lettering. It looked professional.

"She made this?"

Veronica nodded, but her previous beaming smile—half delight, half triumph at knowing about so wonderful a thing—had faltered, and she looked uncertain.

"Did Oaklynn not do right making the cake, Mommy?"

"No," I said, feeling suddenly frustrated and stupid at the same time, knowing my cheeks were nearly as pink as the frosting. "I just wish she'd said something. Then I wouldn't have bothered to . . . I mean, it's just that . . ."

"You don't think Gracie will like Miss Oaklynn's cake?"

I stared at the thing in the fridge, then very deliberately closed the door, catching the way the interior light winked out just before the door sucked shut.

"No," I said, turning and managing to smile. "I'm sure she'll love it."

And, of course, she did. So did Josh. The store-bought cake went largely unnoticed, and most of it had to be thrown away two days later.

Forgetting the effects of the warmth and humidity of the South, I had left it out overnight and came down to find the cake spotted with black mold and with the beginnings of a gray-green fur on one side. I put the trash out quickly so that no one would notice, though I don't know whom I was trying to protect. No one said anything about it until later that week when Veronica asked if there was cake, and I said there was none left and we shouldn't have cake every day.

She slumped, crestfallen, into her chair and said as if to herself, "Mommy makes the most glorious cakes."

I gave her a sharp look.

"Mommy does?" I said.

"I mean Oaklynn," said Veronica guilelessly, with no sense that she had made a mistake. "My other mommy."

For a moment, I stared at her with my mouth open, speechless. Then I took a plate quickly to the sink and held it under the faucet while the water ran for almost a minute until I was ready to go back to the table.

─

Josh had a drinks meeting. In the old days, that had meant strip clubs for the all-male out-of-towners—with some minimal show of reluctance from the Charlotte boys—but I was assured that the so-called banking culture had evolved at last. Now, drinks meetings were as likely to take place at one of the city's up-and-coming craft breweries. I still didn't get invited, and Josh would blunder in late, stinking of beer and having to keep getting up to pee. I had long since stopped waiting up for him to arrive, bleary and exhausted if not actually drunk.

I was lying awake in bed, trying not to think about Veronica's earlier remark—*my other mommy*—focusing instead on how to build a fledgling client list, feeling that same mixture of happy anticipation and guilty dread that had so characterized my life of late, when I suddenly froze. I had heard something, something that had seemed to come from mere inches above my head. I lay still, eyes wide in the gloom, listening hard.

It came again, a sharp scratching noise—small but seeming to reverberate through the room. I sat up, rigid, and for a second, nothing happened. Then it came again, a scraping, gnawing sound.

Mr. Quietly?

Oaklynn kept him in the basement with her at night. Even without the coyotes beyond the creek and Tammy's damn terrier running free, she hadn't wanted the cat to be out after dark.

Sitting up had changed my sense of the sound. It seemed to be coming less from the wall behind the bed and more from the ceiling above me. I pressed my ear to the wall nevertheless and felt rather than heard the rumble of the sound again, accompanied this time by the whisper of animal feet.

Too big for a mouse, surely.

The bed felt huge, vacant without Josh. I got up silently, folding back the covers, and treading lightly over the carpet to the hall door. I opened it, muffling the snap of the latch as best I could and snapped on the light, flooding the upper hall and the foyer downstairs with a hard radiance that made me feel conspicuous, vulnerable. There was no sign of Mr. Quietly scratching at the wall, and I hadn't really expected there to be. I briefly considered the ceiling hatch up to the attic but dismissed the idea. The flooring up there was incomplete, and even with a flashlight, I didn't trust myself to not put a foot wrong and come crashing through the ceiling.

That was another of those little dodges, like when Veronica had pretended she had come in from the garden because of the cold rather than the possibility of snakes down by the creek. I didn't want to go up there in the dark by myself, and I certainly didn't want to come face-to-face with whatever was scurrying around above the bedroom. It wouldn't be anything dangerous. That wasn't the issue. I wasn't sure what the issue was, but I felt revolted by the idea of an animal in the house, gnawing on the wallboard, pissing on the rafters. What if it was a rat that had gotten inside via a drainpipe? I'd heard of such things in New York. What if it burrowed through the Sheetrock and dropped down from the ceiling onto our bed in the middle of the night? Or onto the girls . . .

Jesus. The thought of its matted fur and beady eyes, its twining, fibrous tail and hard little claws skittering across my sleeping face . . .

I moved quickly along the hall to Veronica's room, opened the door—still listening for the sound of movement in the walls—and peered inside. She was sleeping soundly with Lamby and other assorted toys, softly lit by the Winnie-the-Pooh night-light under the window. Her face, so often clouded with thought when she was awake, looked clear, open, like a cherub in a painting, so that for a moment, I forgot the animal in the attic and stood staring at her.

At last, I closed the door and went across the hall to Grace's room, thinking that I could change her and make sure her fever had gone. I tried the door with the same caution and stepped into its baby-scented sweetness. My eyes went straight to the crib, registering something strange, and as my steps grew longer, less careful, I felt the shrill note of panic rising in my throat.

And then I saw the rocker, where Oaklynn sat, shrouded in blankets, a dark, shapeless mound cradling Grace, who was sound asleep. She seemed malevolent, toad-like in the gloom, and for a split second I wanted to scream at her, demand who she was and what she was doing in my house.

A demon in the dark.

I managed a kind of control but couldn't keep back the confused indignation that was the tail end of my momentary terror.

"What are you doing up here?" I demanded.

"Wanted to make sure she was OK," whispered Oaklynn. "Hope you don't mind. She's so sweet when she's asleep. Heck, she's sweet all the time. Kind of recharges my batteries, you know?"

She sounded like her old self, smiling, nurturing, and as my eyes adjusted to the light and I made sense of her shape, the malevolence I had imagined melted away. I felt stupid, neurotic. Still, I couldn't just leave. Grace was mine, after all.

My other mommy . . .

"Why don't you go to bed?" I managed. "I'll sit with her."

There was a fractional, unreadable silence. Then Oaklynn said simply, "Sure."

"You didn't hear anything, did you? In the ceiling? Like, an animal, maybe?"

"No," she replied, handing Grace to me, using the crook of her arm to make sure her head didn't loll too much. "I checked her temperature and her diapers. Everything seems normal."

"Right," I said, mad at myself for not asking. I had been thinking about it. I just hadn't said it. "Great. Hopefully it—whatever it was—is over. And buy some mousetraps next time you're at the store, will you? I don't want things nesting up there for the winter and then chewing through the wiring or something."

"We could try mothballs," said Oaklynn. "Place a few in the attic. The smell is supposed to ward off rodents."

She gave me a bland smile.

"OK," I said, keeping my voice low so as not to wake Grace. "You are a treasury of good ideas."

I meant it sincerely, but I was tired and still a little rattled by finding her there, so it sounded just a little drier than I had meant it, as if I were being patronizing or even sarcastic.

She was out of the chair and making for the door, but for a moment, she froze in the act, stopping only inches away. In the low light, I had the impression that her eyes were narrow and her face was set. For a second, neither of us moved, and I held my breath, holding Grace close in a way that was instinctively protective. I was suddenly acutely aware of how large Oaklynn was, how strong, and I felt the hair on the back of my neck rise. I pulled back a fraction, but Oaklynn did not move. I could smell the soapy aroma of her hair, feel the warmth of her breath. And then she was moving again.

"Night," she said.

She made it to the door before I could whisper "Night" in return, the word sticking in my throat. When she stepped out and closed the door softly behind her, I stayed where I was for a long moment, conscious that my heart was racing.

Chapter Twenty-Six

Anna was in bed when Josh got home, which was as he had expected. She was awake, though. *Maybe*, he thought, *this is as good a time as any.* It felt easier in the dark.

"Sorry to be late," he said, fumbling his suit jacket onto a hanger.

"It's OK. I knew you would be."

She didn't sound sleepy. He hesitated, sitting on the foot of the bed and pulling his socks off.

"How are the girls?"

"Fine," said Anna, though her voice sounded a little stiff. "Grace is more herself, and Veronica is still talking about Oaklynn's cake."

"Great."

"I guess."

He hesitated and regrouped, knowing he'd missed something but not sure what.

"You knew I had to be out tonight," said Josh. "I told you last week."

"It's fine," said Anna.

"You don't really sound—"

"Really, Josh, it's OK."

She still sounded a little clipped, and he frowned into the gloom, knowing that his irritation was at least partly guilt. He considered getting into bed and saying nothing more, but he had to say it. It wasn't like he would be risking a tender moment.

"Hey, so I have to go to New York," he said without turning around. He heard her stir in the gloom.

"Again?" she said. "OK. When?"

"Thursday," said Josh.

"This week?"

"Yeah," Josh replied, trying to sound casual. More movement from the bed; then she was folding back the covers and clicking on her bedside lamp. The room was suddenly aglow, and feeling exposed, he fished his phone from his pocket to give his hands something to do. He glanced over his shoulder to find her sitting up, her hair spilling unevenly across her face. She pushed it aside, and he turned to his phone, saying, "Last-minute thing. Sorry."

"Two days' notice? That's crazy. What if I was traveling and we had child-care issues?"

"You're not," said Josh. "And we don't."

"But we could have."

"Let's focus on actual problems, not hypotheticals, OK, Anna?"

He hadn't intended the hardness in his voice, and it clearly caught her off guard. He half turned to face her but only glanced up from his phone for a second.

"What about Grace? I thought maybe this weekend we could give Oaklynn a day off, maybe drive down to Charleston, just the four of us . . ."

"I can't. I'm sorry. It's a last-minute thing. I let them know I was pissed about it, but apparently, it can't be moved."

She blew out a sigh and looked at her hands.

"I'm sorry," he said again, turning his attention back to his phone. *Coward*, he thought. *Liar.*

165

"It's OK," said Anna, backpedaling, watching him as he scrolled through his email, not really seeing any of it. "Is there one?"

"One what?"

"A nonhypothetical problem?"

"What?" he said, eyes still fixed on his phone. "No. Just, you know, meetings."

He felt her hesitation, her dissatisfaction, but he didn't know what to say to make them go away. In the end, he opted for minimizing the issue.

"At least you have Oaklynn," he said.

"Yeah," she said, without her usual enthusiasm.

"What?" he said, happy to change the subject, finally looking at her properly. "Did she do something to annoy you?"

Anna shook her head, but she was frowning.

"Not really," she said. "I had a slightly weird moment with her is all. She was sitting up in Grace's room after I'd gone to bed. I was . . . taken aback."

"That's it?"

"Yeah. It was nothing. Just . . . sometimes it seems like she's more important to the girls than I am."

"That's not true."

"Veronica called her *my other mommy*."

He had been prepared for something else, for suspicion and accusation, so this, he was ashamed to admit, was almost a relief. It made him kind. He came to her and settled on the edge of the bed, taking her hand in his.

"She doesn't mean it," he said. "Not really. Kids, you know. They just say things."

She nodded, but her face was set, and he thought there were tears in her eyes. He leaned in and hugged her.

"I'm OK," she said. Then, after a long pause, "Is this likely to happen more?"

"What?" he said again, knowing how wooden he sounded but unable to do anything about it.

"Sudden meetings in New York," she replied. "You usually have advance notice. Is this some new thing, something that is going to happen more now?"

He didn't know what to say to that but squeezed her into his shoulder encouragingly.

"For a little while," he said. "Maybe. Sorry." It was too much. Suddenly, he needed to be away from her. Her closeness, her warmth against him, made him feel guilty again, deceitful.

He got up quickly. He held up the phone like a TV lawyer presenting Exhibit A. "Something I have to handle," he said lightly. "Damn phone. No problem with the Wi-Fi, so I can't escape my fucking email, but there's zero cell service. I'll be back in a few. Gotta make a quick call. Work," he added stupidly, barely able to get the word out, his throat was so tight.

He moved to her side of the bed and kissed her lightly on the forehead, pretending not to see the dissatisfaction on her face. "Get some rest." He turned the light off so he wouldn't feel her eyes on him and fled from the room.

With the door closed behind him, he took a long breath.

His first direct lie to his wife. There had been evasions and half-truths before, as there were in all relationships, but this was the first straight-out, barefaced lie he could remember ever telling Anna, and it stung with particular bitterness because he knew it would be the first of many.

He went downstairs to the little book-lined office that was a feature of so many of the houses they had looked at when they'd first moved to Charlotte, as if every family had a lawyer who needed something suitably stuffy at home. They were all the same: heavy desks and dark wood bookcases with a few leather-bound volumes aesthetically spaced out to give a sense of seriousness, a framed diploma or two on the wall.

Most of the rooms had been open on one side and would therefore be continually full of the noise and distraction of the house, as if the purpose of the room was less about making a space for actual work than it was about signaling the prestige of the worker. Theirs at least had four walls and a door, though Josh had never really felt comfortable in it.

Now he sat in the buttoned leather office chair, the door safely closed behind him, picked up the phone on the desk, and dialed a number. Mary Beth Wilson answered on the second ring.

"It's me," said Josh, his voice low, his body hunched over the phone as if shielding it. "We need to talk about Thursday."

⌁

In the darkness of the basement, Oaklynn sat in the rocker she had moved from her bedroom suite to the foot of the stairs, where she could listen to the sounds of the house. Mr. Quietly pulsed softly in her lap. The children were asleep. She had baby monitors set up in both of their rooms. Though she had the receiver volume turned very low, her ears were sharp, and the little green lights rolled on when they so much as shifted in their slumber. She had considered putting another in Josh and Anna's room—under the bed, perhaps—but the risk of it being discovered was too great.

She had been doing nothing, thinking vaguely of times past, the tiny sliver of good weeks she had spent with Carl before he had shown her what he really was, who he was, before the bruises and the broken jaw, before she had fled. She rocked back and forth, trying to put the memories away again, when she heard the distinctive snap of the master bedroom door two floors up. It had been a careful, stealthy sound. She stopped rocking, listening to the bare feet on the hardwood hallway, then on the stairs down to the ground floor a dozen feet above her head.

Anna?

No. The steps were too heavy. Then came the distinctive creak of the office door.

Josh, then.

And what was he doing sneaking around at night only minutes after getting home?

Oaklynn got up silently, spilling Mr. Quietly out of her lap so that he grumbled softly and padded away. She moved quickly, surprisingly light on her feet for someone of her build, and eased into her darkened bedroom, closing the door carefully behind her. She picked up the house phone on her nightstand and thumbed it into life so a faint glow flickered over the blue walls.

She picked it up and pressed the phone to her ear, holding her breath.

"It's me," said Josh, his voice low. "We need to talk about Thursday."

Chapter Twenty-Seven

It had been a hell of a drive, thought Flanders, vaguely. Long but full of awesome scenery, something he noted almost grudgingly but that reminded him that the world had good things in it as well as bad. He mostly saw the bad, but out here on the road, he was reminded of some of the things he had once cared about. The last leg had taken him on I-40 right through Tennessee and then on I-26 through the wooded mountains of western North Carolina, near Asheville and Hendersonville, which was really pretty country, then through Shelby and Gastonia, which was less so. As he rolled into Charlotte proper, he stopped fiddling with the radio and checked the directions he had pulled up on his phone. A moment later, he pulled over at a Bojangles', where he ordered chicken thighs and biscuits while he considered his next move.

This had to be done carefully.

If Nadine saw him or got wind that someone—anyone—was watching her, she'd bolt and might be in the wind for weeks or longer. He couldn't risk that. He couldn't move till everything was lined up just perfectly, but neither could he delay too long. The timing had to be just right, or all his driving and poking around would be for nothing.

He tried the radio again and hummed along tunelessly while he ate his chicken. He was going to have to watch a while longer, he decided, but he was where he needed to be. The net he had been dragging behind him for weeks had found its prey, and it was tightening with each moment. Flanders considered his badge, wiping a smear of grease off the shield, and thought of Nadine, the things she had done.

He swallowed and stared off at nothing, his jaw set. She wouldn't get away this time.

Chapter Twenty-Eight

Anna

Josh was out of sorts for the next two days. The girls seemed to sense it in some oblique way and kept to themselves, as if sheltering from an approaching storm, while he drifted aimlessly around the house, sullen and broody. It was unlike him. Josh was the most even-keeled man I had ever met: famously, almost comically, unflappable. I remember once shortly after we had gotten married when he was broiling a sandwich in the toaster oven and, alerted by the acrid smell of burning, he turned and remarked, in a tone that was almost bored in its exasperation, "The oven's on fire." It was a deadpan remark, a little weary that the world was letting him down, and he followed it up—as I shrieked and ran around, freaked out by the honest-to-God flames leaping from the front and back of the appliance—by methodically dealing with the problem: disconnecting the power cord and smothering the tray and greasy particles with a damp towel. It was so him, and I had recounted the tale several times since whenever I wanted to convey exactly who Josh was, always to awe and laughter.

When he was angry, it was like lightning: here one moment and gone the next, utterly burned out so that it was hard to remember it had really flared at all. He didn't gnaw on feelings for days. He didn't hold grudges. He didn't stew. If he had something to say, he'd say it, and then it was done, and he would go back to moving through life like a sleek boat in a brisk but even current, smooth and steady, always closing on a destination only he could see.

So the relentless darkness of his mood, the sense that he was, for want of a better word, troubled, even anxious, alarmed me. I asked if he was OK, and he said he was, first changing the subject and then claiming he had work to do. This was worse. I was so used to being able to read him at a hundred paces that I didn't know how to handle this new evasive version of my husband.

Deceptive, you mean.

I'd be lying if I said otherwise. Yes, I thought he was hiding something. I just had no idea what and whether I should be concerned. When I pressed him the night before his trip, interrupting him as he packed his case with his slim-fitting suits and shiny silk ties, he just frowned and said, "It's just work stuff. Nothing to worry about. It will blow over."

"Are you in trouble?"

He shook his head dismissively, caught the stung look in my face, and tried to soften the look on his face, saying, "No. Don't worry. I just feel a bit . . . unprepared for this slew of meetings. I'll be OK, and when I get home, it should be fine."

He smiled as he said that last word, held my shoulders and kissed the top of my head so that I almost believed him.

"I could come with you," I said. "I need to go to New York soon. I'm sure I could get some editor lunches and evening drinks sessions together to make it worth my while. Then we could take in a show, maybe. Make a little holiday out of it. Oaklynn can handle the kids by herself for a couple of days."

I don't know why I said it. I almost certainly couldn't schedule any meaningful work for myself, and I didn't really like the idea of leaving the girls at home. But I said it, and I watched him, and I saw, just for a second, the merest flicker of panic before he recovered enough to shake his head sadly and tell me he would be too busy for us to do anything together. In other circumstances, I might have pressed him, but I was more than worried now. I felt like something of myself—something physical like my heart, lungs, or stomach—had been scooped out of me, and I was left hollow and incapable of functioning. At last, I managed a nod, and he returned to his packing so that he didn't see me finally leave the room with tears in my eyes.

They weren't tears of sadness, I don't think. I'm not some waif in a romance novel who collapses speechless and useless when men treat her badly. Nor were they tears of anger. Not yet. They were more like the tears you get when you chop onions or turn your face into a high wind: a physical response without a clear emotional register. My body was responding before my mind had been able to make sense of what was happening.

I didn't get up with him in the morning, which was unlike me. I lay in bed, pretending to sleep till I heard the front door lock behind him. Then I slid out of bed and went to the window, parting the blinds just enough to watch him put his case into the back of the car, trying to read his unselfconscious body language for something, anything. He looked like . . . Josh. Same as ever. Another business trip, another few days away that would probably be more fun than he let on, so I wouldn't feel jealous about having to stay home.

Only this and nothing more.

I almost grinned at the phrase, stupid and melodramatic as it was, but the thought of Poe's raven made me shudder in spite of myself, and I crawled back under the covers for another half hour before showering and facing the world. When I did shower, I stood there for a long moment after I had shut the water off, my hair dripping, watching the grout lines between the tiles become distinct as the water drained.

"You OK?" asked Oaklynn when I finally made it downstairs. "You look right down in the flipping dumps."

I gave her a look, but she was immune, and with the girls there having breakfast, I didn't want to get into a fight.

"Cripes, Anna," she said bracingly. "You are too strong a person to get down just because Hubby is out of town."

I almost laughed at the absurdity of her phrasing, almost told her to keep her nose out of my personal life, but she was giving me that wheat-field-wide Sunday schoolteacher smile, and I relented. And besides, she was right. I was too strong to let Josh's absence—and whatever it was truly about—ambush my day. I had work to do.

"You made pancakes?" I said. "I didn't think we had the stuff."

"I slipped out early," Oaklynn admitted. "We were low on milk, and I couldn't sleep, so I went to the store. Josh didn't say? He was leaving just as I got back."

"I haven't spoken to him since he left," I said, very slightly defensive. "Why would I?"

"No reason," said Oaklynn, shrinking back very slightly like a scolded dog. "Thought he might check in from the airport or something."

He usually does, I thought, feeling a twist in my stomach.

"You know what would be fun?" Oaklynn announced, deliberately changing the subject.

"What?" I said, humoring her, but still in a coffee-deprived state, which I knew might make me spiky if I didn't work at it.

"We'll go to the park, all of us together. Veronica loves the monkey bars and the slide and that big old train . . ."

"Yes!" said Veronica. "Please, Mommy, can we?"

"Train?" I said.

"The old steam loco by the soccer fields. You know! At Freedom Park."

"Oh," I said, pretending I knew what she meant. "Right." I had taken Veronica to parks before but never that one. It was so big. So full of people. "Won't it be really crowded?"

"Not at this time," Oaklynn said with a conspiratorial wink, like she was sharing secret insights. "Get there now and we'll have the place to ourselves for at least a half hour."

"I'm not sure," I said. "I really have to work."

"Bring it with you!" said Oaklynn. "I mean it, missy. I'm not leaving you at home to be a grumpy boots."

Veronica looked up and laughed.

"Grumpy boots," she echoed, delighted. "Witchy shoes and grumpy boots. Cripes!"

I met my daughter's gleeful face, the slight hint of mockery in her use of Oaklynn's favorite exclamation, and it was impossible to say no. Twenty minutes later, the car was loaded, and we were driving up past Queens University and across Kings Drive to East Boulevard. It was cold, though it would warm up some in the course of the morning, but the prospect of trying to use my laptop in the glare of the almost wintry sun was demoralizing. Still, I had a couple of new chapters of *Hell Is Empty* printed off in my backpack. I guessed I would read those, maybe in the shade of some great willow . . .

In fact, though the park did have trees and an artificial lake, the children's playground wasn't really near either. It was exposed and sun bleached, sitting beside the great rusting steam engine Oaklynn had mentioned, a network of metal walkways with climbing apparatus and slides with sand beneath, one of them a twirly plastic-tube thing. Veronica confided that she had worked up the courage to go down just a week ago but was going to do it again today if I would watch. The walkways around the edge of the playground radiated heat in the summer, but now they seemed dead, the grass on either side patchy and yellowing. I settled on a hard bench with my laptop, already convinced this had been a bad idea, while Veronica went whooping toward the swings, screaming for Oaklynn to push her "higher than a house." It struck me that this was a phrase they had used before, and I watched them, again feeling left out of the private rapport they had built over the last couple of months. Oaklynn set Grace in a sandbox in which some simple toys were fixed, and she amused herself lifting little scoops of sand, moving them from one side to the other, and dropping them with great concentration, committed to some project only she could understand.

The new chapters from Ben Lodging had been sitting among the slush-pile queries in my in-box when I'd checked my phone just before leaving the house. They had almost made me back out of Oaklynn's mini excursion. There was work I could do in the park, of course, but this was different. I wanted to savor it in private. I wanted, if I were honest, to keep it to myself.

A pretty odd attitude for an agent, I pointed out to myself as I opened the new file and began to read.

The new section was typical of Lodging—or of the accountant, Carried, around whom the book revolved: meticulously observed but unsettlingly dry and disconnected from the world around him. The first paragraph read as follows.

I took the bus home from work. Which is to say I took a series of buses to various parts of the downtown and into one of the western suburbs, getting off twice and walking around before taking an entirely different bus that took me to within 420 paces of my apartment building. There were faster ways home, of course, and sometimes I preferred the privacy of my own car, but from time to time, I liked to be among people with nothing to do but watch them. On this particular occasion, there were only nine people on the first bus, seven of whom were women: four of them black, one Latina, the others white. Most of them wore heavier coats than the weather seemed to demand. Perhaps they could not afford anything more suitable? Perhaps it was better to risk being too hot than too cold. Three of them were elderly, which is to say I thought them over sixty-five. It was strange to think that I had more money than any of them, but that was surely true, though I could not assume that that fact alone made them miserable.

But if it did, if they felt ignored, even abused, too busy making ends meet to wonder why they bothered doing so, would it not be a type of kindness to kill them? Not all of them, perhaps. Not at once. I could make the decision here and now as we all sat together as the bus rolled along Sharon Road, not talking to one another, but all moving in the same direction like fish in a shoal or starlings over a bright field of corn. I could decide to kill each of them in turn simply because we had shared this moment. I doubted any police profiler would ever figure that out!

The woman in front of me had her gray hair pulled back into tight bunches, so I could see the papery thinness of the skin on her scalp. I could lean forward and tap her with the hammer in my briefcase. One short blow. It would happen before anyone could stop me. Do it right and she wouldn't even cry out. There was no one sitting behind me, so it was just possible I could do it, get off the bus at the next stop, and no one would even notice.

That struck me as terrible. Not the killing itself, which might be doing her a favor, but the idea that life would go on as before in spite of her death. Her death would be hailed as a violation of nature, an abomination, but nature itself would do nothing. The world would turn as it always did. There would be no thunderclaps, no lightning bolts, no shouts of outrage and injustice from the cosmos.

Would other people mourn for her? Perhaps. She might have a husband. Children. But no one on the bus. When the story hit the news, they would gleefully tell their friends that they had been riding on the very same bus, but they would shed no tears for a woman they did not know. People only weep for themselves. So it would be ironic if I then targeted each of them individually. Get on the same bus tomorrow, follow one of them home, night after night.

That would be suicidal on my part, of course. The police wouldn't be so stupid as to fail to make a connection among the victims and the bus they all used. But then, that didn't much matter either. I wasn't so in love with my liberty or indeed my life that I much cared when it was taken away from me. There would be no thunderbolts for me either. The world would turn.

Bored with the idea, I got off at the next stop and sat on a park bench, watching the children play . . .

I closed my laptop with a little shudder, not wanting to read more. For all the casual existentialism of the thing that might make it respectable in a vague, literary sort of way, I didn't like the way Lodging's fiction had strayed into my own world. Not his fault, of course, but it bothered me to hear his detached, sociopathic thought processes penetrating my life so precisely. I knew that was the power of the book, of course, its frightening ordinariness, the way it made horror plausible, but his talk of parks and playing children was too near the bone. I closed my eyes for a second, trying to banish Lodging's calculating voice, then turned my attention back to Grace, who was playing in the sand with Oaklynn as before. I felt a sudden and ridiculous urge to snatch her into my arms and hold her but managed to push such hysteria away. Forcing myself to move slowly and to smile as I did so, I got up and went over to the sandbox so that my shadow made Oaklynn look up.

"Hi," said Oaklynn, shielding her eyes from the glare.

"I've come to play," I said, looking at Grace.

"You have work to do," said Oaklynn.

"It's OK," I said, meaning it (and nothing more). "You play with Vron."

Her other mommy.

Oaklynn gave me the briefest of looks, which might have been bafflement and might have just been because the sun was in her eyes. Then she hauled herself to her feet and stomped off to Veronica, calling to her as she walked. In spite of myself, I glanced quickly around the park to see who might be watching, like Ben Lodging's pathological accountant, his briefcase by his side.

But Oaklynn had been right. We had the place practically to ourselves. A dog walker strolled by, a maintenance woman in some kind of golf cart emptying trash cans, and another guy muffled against the chilly air cutting through on his way to . . . whatever, then no one. I watched my younger daughter and, eventually, stopped thinking about Ben Lodging and his blank-eyed maybe-killer.

"Want to see the train?" I said to Grace. Oaklynn had probably shown it to her a dozen times before, but this was my turn. I gathered her up, and we walked over to the great black-and-rust-spotted engine. We marveled at its massive wheels and the pistons that drove them, then climbed up into the cabin, though the firebox was welded shut and there wasn't much to see there. In truth, Grace was a bit young for it and soon wanted to go back to the sandbox.

After a quarter hour of Veronica shrieking with delight at the height of the swings, she graduated to the complex of railed walkways, playing some form of chase with Oaklynn. I felt almost sorry for my nanny, watching her lumbering around up there, the metal ringing under her heavy footsteps, watching her wheeze and sweat. In fact, and in spite of her exertion, Oaklynn seemed genuinely happy, so that I grew jealous again, not of her relationship with my daughter but of the way such simple things pleased her. I tried to brush the thought away as condescending, but it wouldn't go, instead taking root, tunneling into my flesh, my soul, like some ironically supercilious tick. The metaphor amused me for a second, but only a second. Oaklynn laughed and panted and lumbered after my screaming, gleeful daughter, while I— sitting in the sandbox—tried not to think about my work, my career, and what my husband might be doing in New York.

"Mommy!" yelled Veronica happily as she reached the upper platform of the twirly slide and waved frantically, scared and delighted by her own nerve. "I'm gonna go all the way down super fast! No touching the sides!"

"Watch your elbows, hon," said a wheezy Oaklynn, coming up behind her. "Don't want to get burned."

"Burned?" said Veronica quizzically, as if nothing could be more absurd. "I'm not going to get burned! See you at the bottom, Mommy!"

I waved back, beaming, watching her leave the stairs and crawl into the little cabin at the top, where her commentary became muffled and echoed.

I took a breath and brushed some of the sand from Grace's tiny hands before it could get in her eyes or mouth. I had to focus on what I had, on the good things, the truly wonderful things. I couldn't keep wishing things were different, waiting for happiness to arrive like some rare seasonal bird flying south for . . .

Veronica's scream ripped through the air.

She had been laughing and wailing in mock fright as Oaklynn chased her, but the new sound came from an entirely different place. It was a wail of shock and pain.

I leaped to my feet, expecting to see my elder daughter half sprawled on the lower part of the slide. But she hadn't fallen off, and for a moment, I was baffled and relieved, as if it had been nothing after all, just her girlish terror of the speed of the descent, which would turn into laughter and a need to do it all again.

I couldn't see her. She was inside the plastic tube slide, and though her keening yell had stalled for a second, it came back now, different.

Worse.

She fumbled around and finally appeared at the bottom, but the screaming had gone up in pitch and volume, a raw and terrible sound, half pain, half horror.

Even from here I could see the brilliant redness on the tiny hand that grabbed the rim of the tube as she tried to pull herself out. Then the red on her leg just above the ankle of her sneakers.

Oh God. Oh God. Oh God.

Veronica emerged, bawling, eyes doe-wide, her mouth frozen in an increasingly breathless *Oh*. I could see where the blood was running down the polished chute under her. Her favorite yellow leggings were puckered and scarred down the back of her left thigh, but it was her right hand that stopped me cold. I saw the horrible pallor of her skin and the dark red line where the wound opened across her palm. It snaked up and around her forearm in a long, winding gash.

Oaklynn was already with her, hugging her, screaming, to her breast so that blood smeared her clothes. There was a red handprint, small and perfectly printed on the side of the tube slide where Veronica had touched it. I stumbled in the sand as I ran to them, babbling, "What happened? Baby? What happened?"

"Owie," Veronica managed. "In the slide. It hurts, Mommy."

I stooped to take her hand, biting back the flinch, the impulse to look away. It was a deep cut. I folded Veronica and Oaklynn into my fierce and firm embrace, even as Oaklynn clamped a wadded handkerchief to my daughter's hand to stanch the blood flow, even as Grace began to wail in sympathy.

"I'll call an ambulance," said Oaklynn, handing Veronica to me.

The idea terrified me. So did the blood on my hands. I stood there, stunned, as Oaklynn pressed my hand over the handkerchief.

"Press down," she said. "Constant pressure."

It felt warm and wet, and I couldn't look directly at it. I turned away at last, but as I did so, my eyes saw that the rivulet of blood that ran down the inside of the tube began from higher up.

What the hell?

Suddenly, the brilliance of the sun, the way it made the crimson speckling the mulched ground strident and unavoidable was too much, and I pulled Veronica into the shade beneath the slide as Oaklynn snatched out her cell phone and dialed.

"Ambulance, please," she said. "Freedom Park. At the children's playground. Hurry, please. I have a little girl who is losing a lot of blood . . . A cut on her hand . . . I don't think so, no, but it's deep."

"Not what?" I mouthed.

"Not arterial," said Oaklynn.

Jesus, I thought. How could this be happening? A moment ago we had been playing and laughing, and now . . .

"We can walk to the parking lot and meet you there," said Oaklynn into the phone. "She's nearly four. My name is Oaklynn Durst. The little girl is Veronica Klein. Her mom is here, too . . . No, I'm just the nanny."

Veronica squirmed in my arms. Her face was clammy, white with shock. I turned, hugging her to me, as if trying to shut the rest of the world out, and as I did so, something caught my eye. It was small and bright and round with a cross-shaped slot.

Phillips-head.

The name came to me like something looming through fog, unexpected and unwanted.

It was positioned not in a seam of the slide, where the barrel-like sections joined together, but in the middle of the green molded plastic of the tube. I stared, processing what I was looking at, not quite believing it, hardly able to think above Veronica's desperate, panting sobs against my neck.

Someone had driven a screw through the underside of the chute. This thing that had happened to my daughter, this scarlet, screaming horror, had been done on purpose.

Chapter Twenty-Nine

Nurse Alysha Taylor did a double take as she took the child's hand and turned it in the light, dabbing at the dark, accumulated blood so that she could see the extent of the injury.

"She was in before," she remarked, eyeing the kid, who seemed to have cried herself out and was now limp and exhausted, looking dazed. "Not for herself. For her sister."

"Yeah?" said her colleague, giving her a raised eyebrow.

"Different kind of case," said Alysha, shrugging off the implied question but leaning over to whisper, "The mother's a piece of work. Nanny's good, though. Speak of the devil . . ."

The two women were hurrying up to them. The mother was trim, Asian; the nanny heavyset and anguished.

"How is it?" said the nanny.

"Just getting her cleaned up so we can see what's going on," said Alysha. "How you doing, honey? You hanging in there?"

The child nodded once but did not open her mouth, as if afraid of what might come out. She winced at every movement, which wasn't surprising. It was a nasty gash.

"This is gonna need suturing," Alysha announced in a cheery voice, "but I think we're gonna have to wait on that till the doctor has had a good look and made sure everything inside is all connected the way it's supposed to be. No good closing you up if we're gonna have to open it up again tomorrow, is there?"

The child shook her head, wide-eyed, but she looked scared, and her gaze slid back to the nanny.

"It's OK, Vronny," said the nanny. "Miss Alysha is gonna get you all fixed up good as new."

"Are you?" said the mom. "I mean, could there be any lasting—"

"OK," said Alysha, cheerily rolling over the woman. Some people! The child was already scared enough without Mom talking about *lasting damage* right there in front of her. "I'm gonna get you a sucker while we finish cleaning this up, and I want you to hold your hand up to your head, OK, like this, and keep your hand open. You think you can do that for me? Mom, why don't you come give me a hand with that sucker?"

She moved to the counter, where there was a clear plastic tub of lollipops and fished out a few.

"Give her a choice of flavors," said the nurse.

"And what about—"

"I'm going to have a specialist take a look to make sure there's no nerve or tendon damage," Alysha replied, heading off the rest of the question. "I think it looks good, mostly just skin and a little muscle puckering, but it was a sharp edge, and hands are complicated, so I don't want to take any chances. He's in surgery right now, so I'm gonna have you folks wait till he's free to take a look, and then—if he gives us the all clear—we'll stitch her up, and you'll be good to go."

"How long will that take?"

"Could be a few hours."

"*Hours?*"

"Like I said, I don't want to take any chances. We can stop the bleeding and make her comfortable. It might be good to give her a little peace and quiet while we dress the wound."

"Yes. Of course."

She sounded grudging, like she was forcing herself to go along with what she was being told against her better judgment. Alysha took in the woman's clothes, the designer purse, not to mention the attentive nanny.

Money, she thought. *Used to having everything just so.*

"We'll take her back, get her prepped for the surgeon to look her over, give her a tetanus shot . . ."

"A shot?" she replied, all aflutter.

"Yes, it's important. While we do that, you can talk to the police officer about the incident, then run home for a few things. With a bit of luck, by the time you get back, we'll be ready to discharge her anyway, OK?"

"OK."

"And you look after that nanny of yours. She looks about as upset as you."

More so, if the truth were told. The big woman looked distraught, ragged. The mom was too much on her tight-assed dignity to give so much away. Maybe she felt it inside, but Alysha liked to be able to see how people were feeling. The woman nodded, mute, and together they returned to her daughter and presented her with a selection of lollipops. The child chose with obvious pleasure. Mom probably didn't let the child have candy.

"OK, Mom, now you chat to Officer Randall here, and we'll get Miss Veronica taken care of."

Officer Randall was a tall, clean-shaven, and good-looking black man. Alysha had seen him around before and had remarked to her fellow nurses that he made her crave a little crime around the place. Young, too. Under thirty. Hell, if she were a decade younger . . . She gave the

186

nanny a knowing wink, but the woman didn't respond and gave her an odd, thoughtful look that made Alysha suddenly self-conscious.

───

Officer Paul Randall checked his watch and made a note on his pad. He was used to the hospital and even knew some of the staff, including the nurse who always gave him that grin when she saw him. She did it now, even as she shepherded the mother of the girl over to him.

"You are Anna Klein?" he said.

"That's right."

"Officer Paul Randall, Charlotte PD. You say there was a screw driven through the slide in Freedom Park?"

"One of the slides, yes. There are several."

"And you think it was placed deliberately rather than being part of the structure?"

"Yes."

"What time did the incident take place?"

"A little before nine this morning."

"Were there people around at the time, Ms. Klein?"

"No. We had the place pretty much to ourselves."

"And you didn't see anyone hanging around or watching the playground while you were there?"

"Like I said, the place was quiet. A few people walked through, but no one was playing there."

"Could the screw have been set while you were there?"

The mother started to shake her head, then frowned.

"I'm not sure. There was a woman who worked for the park, I think, in a uniform riding on one of those little electric carts, but I don't think she went near the slide. She was emptying trash cans. There was a guy with his dog, but I don't think he got near either."

"Anyone else?"

"One guy in a big coat who cut across the park. I guess he could have gone to the slides, but I was facing the swings at the time, so he would have been behind me. I'm sorry. I really don't know."

"You remember what this man looked like?"

Again, the head shake.

"He was all wrapped up. It was pretty cold when we first arrived. Big guy, I think."

"White? Black?"

"White, I think. I didn't see his face. I couldn't be sure."

"What about after the incident? Do you remember seeing bystanders, people attracted by the approach of the ambulance, maybe?"

"A couple, perhaps, but no one close. No one I could identify."

"Any of the people you saw earlier? The big guy or the dog walker, maybe?"

She shrugged wearily and shook her head.

"I guess I wasn't paying attention," she replied.

"I see. Well, we'll head over and make sure the slide is safe, see if anyone in the area saw anybody messing with the equipment. I don't think there's CCTV in that area, but we'll check."

"OK. Will you let me know?"

"Know what?"

"I don't know . . . If you make an arrest or something, I guess."

"Sure," he said, knowing it would never come to that. It would probably turn out to be a fault in the slide itself, and if a screw *had* been placed deliberately, it was probably just the kind of random malice you could never trace to a specific vandal. Probably some disgruntled teen lashing out at the world. Welcome to twenty-first-century America. They should probably be glad he hadn't staked the place out with a sniper rifle. "Absolutely," he said. "I have your contact info, and here's my card. If anything comes up, we'll let you know."

Chapter Thirty

Anna

"It's OK," said Oaklynn, putting her hand on mine, which was wrapped tight around the steering wheel. Our clothes were spotted with Veronica's blood. We were sitting on the edge of the hospital parking lot with the heat running, about to pull out into traffic. Except that I was suddenly frozen in my misery and shame and didn't trust myself to drive. "Anna," she said, forcing me to look at her, "it's really OK. There won't be any nerve damage. Just some blood loss. She'll be discharged in a few hours, and she'll be fine."

"We don't know that for sure yet," I said.

"She could move her fingers just fine. Even her ability to feel pain is actually a good sign. The nurse said so."

"There might be scarring."

I hated the whiny, fragile note in my voice, the way I seemed to be obsessed with something as superficial as a faint, pale line on my daughter's previously flawless hand and arm. But Oaklynn knew I was focusing on something minor because I couldn't bear the thought that my tiny child might have tendon damage in her hand that could affect the rest of her life.

"It wasn't your fault," she said. "If anything, it was mine."

"No!" I exclaimed, almost offended by the thought.

"It's true," said Oaklynn. "Veronica got to the slide ahead of me, and I didn't look it over before she went down and . . . I guess I was too slow, not thinking ahead properly. I should have called, told her to wait till . . ."

Her composure—rock solid till now—wavered slightly, a fractional quaver interrupting her like a car hitting a speed bump.

"No!" I said again, staring at her now, rocked by the glassy sheen in her eyes. "Oaklynn, this isn't on you. You couldn't have known someone would put a screw through the slide."

"It is," she said. She spoke with sad surety, and as she did so, she seemed to deflate, as if she had been steeling herself against the idea but had now given in. As she slumped forward, hanging her head, the tears brimming in her eyes ran down her face. She blinked as if annoyed by them and smeared them away with her sleeve.

"It's not your fault," I said. "We'll go home and get Grace set up, and then we'll take turns at going to sit with Veronica until they're done and we can bring her home. Take her some toys and books. She'll like that. Yes?"

Oaklynn nodded, mute, and I couldn't help feeling a little rush of pride that I was the one consoling her for once, taking charge and making plans. She wiped her eyes again and grunted with scorn and disgust.

"Look at me!" she muttered. "You'd think I was the one who got hurt. Poor Vron. OK." She drew herself up and sucked in a decisive breath. "I'm OK now. Let's go home."

So we did, and when we got back, I gathered some things for Veronica—Lamby, some *Magic Tree House* books, her Leapfrog electronic game pad, and her soft unicorn pillow—and put them in a pink rolling suitcase, then called Josh. This was my third attempt, and like the previous two attempts, it went to voice mail. I felt a prickle of irritation but left a message relaying what had happened and assuring him—more surely than I really felt—that everything was fine, that they were just keeping her in to have the surgeon give her the all clear and to make sure there was no infection.

I didn't say that their caution terrified me. I didn't say that I hadn't liked the way the doctor had looked at me as he muttered to one of the cops who had come to take down the accident report, or that I was afraid that I would be visited by some hard-faced woman from Social Services who would ask pointed questions about whether I thought I was giving the children the attention they required. I'm not sure why I didn't. I wanted to believe I was sparing him from probably needless worry, but I wondered if I was also punishing him a little for not picking up, for not being here, for . . . other possibilities I hadn't yet put into words for fear of making them real.

"I'm going to go to Mary Beth's," I called to Oaklynn. "Won't be long."

I was going to confide in my friend Mary Beth. I was going to share the anxieties and inadequacies I felt with someone who didn't work for me. I was going to say what I had barely allowed myself to think about my daughter's hand, use the poisonous phrases—*ligament damage, severed nerves, tendons*—words that tasted like battery acid in my mouth. I needed to speak to someone who would respond as an equal, not an employee, someone who would be just compassionate enough to say everything would be OK but would then shrug everything off and make a joke, probably a caustic one at someone else's expense. That was what I wanted. That was why I stepped back outside to the emptiness of Settle Road, the towering, oppressive trees yellowing and dropping their leaves in great straggling rifts where the asphalt dissolved alternately into lawns in front of the three completed houses and the high, tangled weeds of the vacant lots.

But though I rang and rang the doorbell, standing on what Mary Beth snarkily referred to as the "unwelcome mat" on the porch, no one came. I felt suddenly and unaccountably worse—bereft—so that I walked back slowly, inexplicably unsure what I would say to Oaklynn, as if possibilities I had hidden had suddenly coalesced into hard fact.

Josh is gone, and Mary Beth is gone. At the same time.

I told myself it was a coincidence, that it was meaningless, and that I had been imagining my husband's recent secretive manner. That Mary Beth was probably just out at the grocery store. I was just upset because of Veronica. Of course I was. Nothing else mattered. Nothing else meant anything.

Oaklynn was busying herself in the living room when I came back into the house, adding snacks in Tupperware to the bag I had been putting together for Veronica.

I should have thought to do that, I thought. It was a good thing, a helpful thing, but it made me feel guilty again.

"How's Mrs. Wilson?" said Oaklynn, smiling at me.

"She's good," I said reflexively, compounding the idiotic and unnecessary lie with something even more preposterous. "She wanted to know if we needed her to cook for us."

"Cook?" said Oaklynn blankly.

"A casserole or something," I said, feeling the blood rush to my face, wondering why I was doing this. "It's a southern thing. When people are sick or whatever, neighbors bring casseroles. I think she was joking."

Oaklynn watched me, as if picking up some weird tell in my manner, something that gave away the fact that I was talking nonsense, but seized on that last detail and rolled her eyes.

"She likes her jokes, that Mrs. Wilson," said Oaklynn, smiling again.

I agreed that she did. We shared an awkward laugh because we knew those jokes were often mean-spirited, and while I thought they were funny, Oaklynn—who was often the butt of them—surely didn't.

"She can be a little . . . acerbic," I confessed. It was supposed to be a kind of apology, but as soon as I said it, I realized I had made things worse with that last word that, judging by Oaklynn's clouded face, she didn't understand. "I mean, her sense of humor can be a bit, you know, *mean*. She doesn't intend it that way," I added quickly. "She's a good person. Just a bit . . ."

I wasn't sure how to end the sentence. Unconventional? Bored? Narcissistic?

"She seems real smart," said Oaklynn. "But . . ."

"What?" I said, trying to sound encouraging. Her hesitation had pricked my curiosity, and any conversation was better than the words swirling around my head like numbered balls in some hellish version of a TV lottery drawing: *tendons, ligaments, nerve damage* . . .

"Well, it's not for me to say."

"Go on. It's OK."

"Well, I think she isn't very happy, is all," said Oaklynn, as if confiding something embarrassing. "Like there's something missing from her life. A hole, you know? An absence she's looking to fill with all her . . . smart talk and what have you. But what do I know?"

I nodded, unsure of what to say, feeling defensive of my friend, instinctively guessing that what Oaklynn thought Mary Beth needed was God, or at least a different notion of family, of life. But then I had thought similar things about Mary Beth myself. For reasons I couldn't place, the thought worried me.

"I shouldn't have said that," said Oaklynn. "I'm sorry. She does seem like a good person."

A good person. Everyone is always a good person, no matter what they think. No matter what they do or don't do. Evil is for other people and for former ages.

The phrases came to me complete and clear, but for a second, I couldn't recall where they were from. Then it struck me. They were part of the protagonist's internal monologue in *Hell Is Empty*, Ben Lodging's troubling study in disaffection and potentially deadly alienation. Not for the first time, I felt like a tightrope walker who had just been nudged into wild imbalance.

"No," I said, dismissing her apology with a wave and a forced smile. "I think you may well be right. OK," I said, changing the subject. "So, you sure you'll be all right with Grace for a while if I sit with Veronica for a couple of hours?"

"Absolutely. I'll feed her and put her down for a nap, maybe read my book while she sleeps. You take your time. Vronny needs you."

Vronny. It was a name only I used. A secret name between my daughter and me.

I nodded.

"Great," I said.

Grace's voice came over the baby monitor, a soft but unhappy noise.

"She needs changing," said Oaklynn, grinning at me with something that was almost irony. "Fun, fun. See you later."

"Thanks," I said. "I really appreciate all your help. You keep me on the rails."

She waved the thought away with a noise like "pshaw," which also may or may not have been ironic, and leaned in for a slightly off-center hug. She squeezed me hard, and I felt both comforted and frail in her meaty embrace, and then she was leaning back so she could see my face.

"Give Vronny a hug from me," she said.

"Will do."

Another squall came from the baby monitor, and Oaklynn snatched up the blue diaper bag with the cartoon elephant head and waggled it like a clown.

"No rest for the wicked," she said, plucking a diaper, wipes, and powder from it, then zipping it shut and turning to go upstairs.

As she did so, I snatched up my car keys and considered the pink bag. Veronica was too old for diapers, but a change of underwear wasn't a bad idea. I knew for a fact that Oaklynn—ready for anything at all times—carried a spare set with her whenever she took the girls out. I unzipped the diaper bag and rummaged through it. I found the underwear easily, but as I did so, my fingertips hit something slim and hard. At first, I thought it was a pen, but it was too thin and cold, and one end was fat and shaped like a handle. I lifted it out, the cartoon elephant grinning happily at me from the side of the bag, and considered it.

It was a Phillips-head screwdriver.

Chapter Thirty-One

"You're overreacting," said Josh into the phone. "It doesn't mean anything. Oaklynn's just one of those Girl Scout types. *Be prepared*, and all that."

He was still in shock. He almost wished he could see the wound on Veronica's hand. Surely, being able to see it would be better than imagining it like this? His stomach knotted. But Anna's need to blame Oaklynn of all people was just crazy.

"It was the exact same kind of screwdriver, Josh!" said Anna. She was speaking in a frantic, desperate whisper. "You think that's a coincidence?"

"Yes! It's the most common type of screwdriver there is. Even you know the name of it," Josh shot back, rubbing a hand across his face. His daughter could lose part of the use of her hand, and Anna was talking about their fucking nanny's screwdriver . . . It was insane. He bit the thought back and spoke through gritted teeth. "What else did she have in the bag, Anna?"

"Spare clothes, diapers . . ."

"What else?"

"One of those utility-tool things, like a Swiss Army knife, a ball of string, some wire, a roll of tape . . ."

"See?" said Josh. "This is just her being anal Oaklynn. You can't believe she would want to hurt the kids. That's . . ."

"What? Crazy?" said Anna, her tone suddenly accusatory.

"I'm just saying it doesn't make sense," said Josh. "*Could* she even have done it? You said you arrived together, and you were with her the whole time at the playground. Did she have time to set the screw before Vron used the slide?"

There was a staticky silence. Then Anna's voice came back low and grudging.

"No," she said. "But she went to the store first thing. She could have gone to the park then and . . ."

"Anna."

"I'm just saying that . . ."

"What are you talking about?" said Josh, his composure finally cracking. "You think Oaklynn put a screw through the slide on purpose? To do serious injury to the child she looks after? *Oaklynn?* Listen to yourself, Anna! You know Oaklynn! Has she ever done anything that would make you think she'd hurt the girls?"

"Not exactly, but . . ."

"What does *not exactly* mean? Name one thing she has done."

"Sometimes I think . . ."

"What?"

"I don't know. I just feel like she's taking over and . . ."

"That's about you, Anna. Not her. It has nothing to do with this. You're projecting your own guilt and worry onto her."

"Guilt?"

"Yes, Anna," Josh snapped back. "You know it's true. You have been worrying that you aren't being a good mother because you wanted to go back to work and have the nanny look after—"

"I know that. This is different."

"I don't think it is." He took a calming breath, and there was a moment of silence. "Look, if you really aren't happy with Oaklynn, we'll deal with it. Let's just get through this, and we'll talk when I get home, OK?" She didn't reply, but he pressed on as if she had. "You need to get back to the hospital and be with our daughter. This other stuff is just . . . It doesn't matter."

"How can I leave Oaklynn with the girls again if . . . ?"

"Oh, for Christ's sake, Anna! If she had put the screw there before you went to the park, why would she keep the fucking screwdriver in the bag?"

"Maybe she forgot."

"No. Listen to me, Anna," he said, steeling himself, his eyes tight shut, his free hand clamped to his forehead. "You need to let this go and focus on Vron, OK? Talk to the doctor, and find out if there is any lasting damage. If there is, I'll come home early."

"I can handle it."

"Can you? Because right now, you aren't. Oaklynn is there to help. Use her and focus on Vron. OK? You can't make it unhappen by turning the accident into something out of one of your clients' mystery novels."

Another silence, and he thought he'd gone too far. Then . . .

"It wasn't an accident."

"What?"

"Someone did it on purpose."

"Yes, but not to hurt Vron," said Josh, conciliatory now. "Some sick sack of shit put it there to hurt whoever used the slide. It happened to be Veronica. It sucks, and I hate it for her and because you have to deal with this without me, but it wasn't aimed at her, Anna. You have to see that. You'll go nuts if you start not trusting Oaklynn. You have to focus on getting Vron well. Call me the moment you speak to the surgeon, OK?"

"You're busy," said Anna.

"It doesn't matter," said Josh, feeling another spike of anger. "Call me. Anytime. I have to know what's going on with Vron. OK?"

"OK." She hesitated, then added, "You didn't call from the airport."

"What?"

"Usually you call from the airport after you've gone through security and you're waiting at the gate. You usually check in. Today, you didn't."

"And?"

He thought he heard her sigh, though it might have just been the line.

"Nothing," she said. "I'll phone when I know what's going on."

"OK," he said. "And this other stuff about Oaklynn . . ."

"I know," she said. "Bye."

The line went dead. Josh hung up but didn't pocket the phone right away. For a moment, he stood where he was, gazing back to the hotel restaurant he had left when his cell had rung, where Mary Beth Wilson was sitting, toying with her salad. He frowned, thinking back to the moment he had been pulling out of the driveway only to meet Oaklynn coming in the opposite direction. He had been taken aback, having not even noticed Anna's car was gone. Oaklynn had waved and, as he was about to drive away, had wound done her window and said, "Have a great trip. Say hi to everyone for me."

He had nodded and smiled as she shut the window and pulled past, so that he had been on the road to the airport before he had processed the oddity of what she had said. Say hi to *whom* for her? As far as she knew, he was going to a meeting in New York with a bunch of financial managers she had never laid eyes on.

Unless . . .

Unless she had other ideas about what he was doing, though how she could have gotten them, he couldn't say.

The possibility had bothered him, so much so that he had considered calling the house to ask her what she had meant. Fortunately, he had come to his senses, realizing that any such conversation would have been a stupid overreaction that might raise any number of awkward questions. He had resolved to stay on Oaklynn's good side, to bring her a little memento of the Big Apple: show her she was like family to him. Just in case. He needed her to think of him as a friend, not just the husband of her employer.

Now, standing in the hotel lobby with his cell phone in his hand, he wondered dully if his determination to be nice to Oaklynn had influenced the way he had reacted to Anna's off-the-wall suspicions.

"Everything all right?" said Mary Beth, considering him shrewdly as he approached.

Josh blinked, unsure, then nodded.

"Not sure," he said.

Chapter Thirty-Two

ANNA

I hung up the phone and sat quite still for a moment. I had driven through the neighborhood to where I had pulled over to make the call in front of yet another partially constructed house as soon as I saw I was getting a usable signal. Now I drove back to the house, steeled myself as if I were about to step onto a stage, and got out.

At the back door, I had to steady my hand to make the keys work.

"Only me," I called as soon as I had the back door open.

Oaklynn appeared at the foot of the stairs with unusual speed, as if she had already seen the car.

"What's up?" she asked.

"I'm going to take Gracie with me," I said. "She's spooked by all this stuff with Veronica, so . . ."

Oaklynn's smile had a fixed, catlike quality.

"So . . . ?" she pressed.

It was unlike her.

"I just want to keep her with me," I said, feeling the blood rush to my face.

"She's practically asleep. Seems a shame to get her up now."

"Even so," I said, holding her eyes and smiling with an effort. For a moment that went on just a fraction of a second too long, she just looked back at me, and I was afraid she was going to say, "Even so . . . what?"

Then she shrugged and turned half away, saying, with none of her usual sweetness, "You're the boss."

Yes, I thought. *I am*, holding on to that simple truth as Oaklynn trudged pointedly through the laborious steps of getting Grace ready. I didn't need a reason to take my daughter with me.

"Why don't I come with?" Oaklynn suggested.

"No," I said, trying to make it sound like that would be too much to ask. "You stay home and have a break."

"I don't need a break," she said, the smile back now but taut and fragile as spun sugar.

"Sure you do," I said. "Everyone does. Put your feet up."

"I can drive, or hold Gracie while you go see Vronny . . ."

"It's fine, really," I said.

"It's no trouble."

"I want to do this by myself," I blurted. Immediately, there was a wariness in Oaklynn's eyes, a watchfulness. "I don't mean that you aren't welcome, or wouldn't be another time, but . . . Well, I just feel . . . you know, like I've been doing my own thing a lot lately. I need to feel, you know, more like *Mommy* again. You understand, right?"

"You want me to stay home," she said, her face blank, unreadable but quite unlike her usual self. I took an involuntary half step back.

"Just this once," I said.

Her eyes were fixed on mine, her fists clenched. I felt a powerful and irrational urge to run, to take my baby daughter and sprint for the car, but her gaze held me like a bug in amber. And then, without warning, the fixed, blank stare, the tension in her face and body that made her look poised to explode, all drained away, and she was her old charmingly innocent and sweet self again.

"I could cook," she suggested brightly.

"What?"

"While you are gone. I could make dinner. That would help, yeah? Golly, I don't know why I didn't think of it before!"

She grinned wide as ever, and I took a steadying breath, suddenly wondering if I was being paranoid and that all my vague doubts were just the projections of my own guilt, as Josh had implied. Either way, I wanted to be gone.

"That would be great!" I said, seizing on the notion as I would on anything that would end the conversation and get me and my daughter out of the house. "Perfect."

"Alrighty then," said Oaklynn, all smiles. "Let's see what I can rustle up."

<hr />

I drove back to the hospital in a daze, parking and rushing through to the ER in a harried state of distraction that drew the eyes of nurses and patients alike, as if I might have been a strangely well-dressed but clearly delusional homeless person or an opioid addict looking for a score. The only difference was that I had an infant asleep in my arms, though maybe that wasn't so unusual for homeless people and addicts either.

"Anna Klein," I said when the perky receptionist asked for my name. "My daughter Veronica got cut this morning . . ."

"Yes, I remember," she said, giving me a plaintive smile that didn't help quell my anxiety. Why did she remember me? Did she know something about Veronica's injury? Or had the staff been discussing me? My negligence?

"Have a seat, and we'll call you back as soon as we're ready," she concluded.

I dithered for a moment, then scanned the institutional chairs and chose one at least two seats away from the nearest person, avoiding the watchful gaze of a grandmotherly black woman in a thick coat and heavy winter boots and a stick-thin white woman who kept rubbing her hands together in a worryingly obsessive way. Her fingers looked almost raw. I fumbled with the rolling bag for something to do, wishing it wasn't a bright, cheery pink.

"You got a plane to catch, honey?" asked the grandmother lazily.

"What?" I said, starting in my seat as if poked.

"The bag," she said. "You got a plane to catch?"

For a second, her face was blank. Then the corner of her mouth twitched to show she was joking.

"Oh," I said. "It's my daughter's. She's . . . she likes it."

"Uh-huh," said the woman noncommittally. "They sure take their time around here. I been here forty-eight minutes now. You believe that? Forty-eight minutes. I don't even want to know what it will cost."

I nodded vaguely, not wanting to talk, but she didn't take the hint.

"How old is your daughter?" she asked, considering Grace, unsmiling.

"A year," I said.

"What's wrong with her?"

"Nothing. We're here to pick up her sister."

The woman nodded.

"She's cute," said the woman, finally breaking down and beaming.

"Thanks," I said, suddenly more grateful than made any sense, looking away quickly so the woman wouldn't see the tears in my eyes.

"You OK, hon?" she asked.

I nodded quickly, but the tears rolled down my face.

"Hey, there," she said, suddenly concerned, leaning over and taking my hand in hers. It was brown and gnarled with age, the skin fine and soft as paper. "Your little girl, the sick one, tell me about her."

"She cut herself on a slide," I said. "In the park. Her hand got cut."

"Uh-huh. But I mean, tell me about her. What's her name?"

"Veronica," I said, not sure why I was doing this.

"I thought it would be one of those Asian names," she said matter-of-factly. "Veronica. That's a nice, regular name. And what does she like to do?"

I blinked, swallowing down my indignation, then forced myself to tell her about the Leapfrog game pad that she liked to play because of the animal noises and the alphabet keys.

"She sounds smart," said the woman, whose name I still did not know. I nodded, then, like a child myself, and forgiving her previous insensitivity, I showed her Lamby and the other things I had brought from home. I knew the woman didn't really care and was just trying to get me to focus on a positive version of my daughter so that I wouldn't fixate on her injuries. She nodded and asked questions, her hand still clamped to mine, and I answered and nodded and finally smiled, though my cheeks were still wet with tears. They had been tears of anxiety and stress and fear—maybe some anger, too—but now they were mostly gratitude, and by the time I was called back to see Veronica, I turned to the woman I did not know and hugged her.

She nodded, consulted her watch, and, her face stiffening again, observed, "Fifty-four minutes. What do you think about that?"

It was a rhetorical question, and she followed it by shaking her head, then nodding toward the open door where the nurse was hovering, waiting for me.

"How is she?" I asked before I even reached her.

"The doctor will be by in a moment to talk to you . . ."

"But how is she? How is her hand?"

The nurse hesitated a moment, took in my bleary, red-rimmed eyes, and lowered her voice as she led me back toward a simple room surrounded by a plastic curtain such as might fit an overgrown shower stall.

"The doctor will explain everything, but she's going to be fine."

So saying, she parted the curtain, and there was Veronica, pale but sitting up in bed, her hand raised to shoulder height and dressed with a bandage from palm to elbow. Her eyes brightened as she saw me, and then I was wrapping her in my arms and squeezing her to my heart.

Chapter Thirty-Three

"She's really OK?" said Josh into his phone. "Oh, thank God."

"The doc wants to check on her in a couple of weeks," said Anna, "sooner if she develops any stiffness or pain in her fingers, but he sees no reason she should. She has full mobility of the hand," she added, clearly quoting. "I have new dressings to apply, but he said it was a very clean cut. They used those dissolving sutures so we don't have to come back to have stitches removed. I have an appointment in his office in two weeks."

"Thank God," Josh said again. There didn't seem to be anything else to say. He heard Anna's exhalation of relief. "Where are you now?"

"Still at the hospital. About to head home."

"And Oaklynn?"

"She's back at the house."

"With Grace?"

"No, I have Grace with me."

Josh frowned.

"Anna?"

"It's OK," she said, her usual self now. "I know I freaked, but it's fine."

"Really? Because if you can't trust Oaklynn around the kids, we need to talk seriously about sending her back to Utah . . ."

That was, he was aware, slightly underhanded. Anna's former nutso idea had faded, but in voicing the real possibility of sending Oaklynn back, he knew she would panic and run in the opposite direction. It was a low strategy, but he used it, anyway, because her freak-out had infected him, distracted him from the things he desperately needed to be focused on. He was, albeit subtly and only for a moment, punishing her.

"No," she said, quick, certain, and a little scared. "I was being crazy before. I see that. Oaklynn loves the girls. She wouldn't do anything to hurt them. I was just . . . I don't know."

"You were worried and stressed."

"And wanted someone to blame," said Anna.

He heard the self-condemnation in her voice and relented.

"Someone *was* to blame," he consoled. "It was a perfectly understandable response."

Well, mostly.

"How are things there?" Anna asked.

"Oh, you know," he said breezily. "Fine."

Again, mostly. Or rather, he qualified in his head. *Partly.*

"You have plans for the rest of the day?" he added, covering.

"Oaklynn was talking about going to BJ's."

"So I will come home to find you making a fort out of a hundred cans of beets."

"I hear they go well with Tuscan chicken," she said.

The joke pleased him, made him feel more like she really was herself again, and he felt bad for making that crack about sending Oaklynn back to Utah. That would never happen, he thought, his heart sinking. She would be in the house forever, or as long as Anna wanted to keep her. Whatever Oaklynn knew or thought she knew would be in her eyes every time she looked at him.

Have a great trip, she had said. *Say hi to everyone for me.*

"Let us know when you're getting in, and we'll make sure we have something nice on the table," said Anna.

"Great," he replied, refocusing. "I'll look forward to it. But I do have to go now. Meeting."

"Yes," she said. "Go do your thing."

He listened for a trace of irony, bitterness, or uncertainty, but hearing none felt like he had dodged a bullet. It was a miserable thought.

"Will do," he said, squeezing his eyes shut. "And thanks for calling. I'm so glad that everything is OK."

It wasn't, of course. Not for him. But Anna couldn't know that. Not yet. He just had to make sure she didn't find out from someone else first.

Chapter Thirty-Four

ANNA

I was feeing fine—good even—as I led Veronica back through the hospital, holding her unbandaged hand and cradling Grace in the sling around my neck as we came back through the reception area. That was when I saw Oaklynn. She was surrounded by staff—at least two nurses and a receptionist—and she looked like she had been crying. One of the nurses—the blonde one whose name I couldn't remember—had laced an arm around her shoulders consolingly. When she saw me, the nurse's face hardened, and she stood up.

"Hi," I said.

"I'm sorry," said Oaklynn, "I couldn't stay away. I felt so terrible . . ."

"She is *such* a treasure," said Nurse Alysha to me smilingly.

I nodded in agreement but knew I still looked confused.

"How did you get here?" I asked.

"I took a cab," she replied, to a chorus of sympathetic *Awws*. The blonde nurse squeezed her arm, as if to express how hard it must have been for her.

"I thought you were making dinner," I said.

It was a terrible thing to say, which I realized as soon as the words were out of my mouth, but I had only meant to ask why she had come, though I suppose she had already answered that.

She couldn't stay away.

In any case, the blonde nurse gave me a frosty stare and said, "She was worried about your daughter. She's obviously very close to the child. She's not just an employee."

I felt my head jerk back a fraction as if she had slapped me, and for a moment, I just gaped.

"I didn't mean . . . I know that . . . ," I faltered.

"I know," said Oaklynn hurriedly, giving me a teary smile to dull the edge of the daggers the nurses were looking at me.

"I shouldn't have asked you to stay home," I added, catching something of her overwrought emotional wobbliness. I suddenly felt very tired. "I was just feeling . . ."

"It's fine," said Oaklynn. "I totally get it. Really. Now, where's my brave girl?"

She dropped to her knees, and Veronica launched herself into Oaklynn's outstretched arms. Oaklynn's face shone with tears of happiness and relief. When it was done, Oaklynn squatted down on the floor with her hands on my daughter's shoulders, gazing at her till she giggled. As they hugged, the nurses eyed me coolly over her hunched shoulders.

See? they seemed to say. *Fancy excluding Oaklynn. The child loves her. But then, who wouldn't? She's such a treasure . . .*

I nodded and smiled and tried to look like I was part of the domestic tableau, and then I announced that we should go, and the nurses hugged Oaklynn again and said they hoped she felt better and how nice it had been to chat with her. I felt a prickle of anxiety at this. What had they been talking about? About the circumstances of the accident? About me?

As we drove home, I watched her out of the corner of my eye as I told her all the doctor had said—she would, after all, have to help change the dressing—and Oaklynn nodded, never taking her beaming eyes off Victoria's face all the way home.

"Dinner is almost ready," she said as we walked in the door.

"Oh," I said. "I assumed you hadn't had time."

"Did most of the work before I came back to the hospital," Oaklynn remarked.

"That's great," I said, processing the familiar aromas coming from the kitchen. "What are we having?"

Oaklynn gave me the smallest look of puzzlement, as if she had already explained this in great detail.

"Tuscan chicken," she remarked, as if that should be obvious.

"Like we had at the dinner party?" I said, momentarily baffled, though I managed not to jokingly suggest we serve it with canned beets.

"Yes," she said, pleased, then caught something in my face and hesitated. "That's OK, right? You like it?"

I nodded quickly.

"Of course!" I said, trying to sound enthusiastic. "I love it."

She watched me levelly so that I felt transparent, then said, in a cooler tone entirely, "Perhaps you would prefer something else?"

"No!" I protested. "Tuscan chicken. Awesome."

She held me in her steady, appraising eyes, then nodded, her trademark smile snapping into place.

"Great," she said. "Dinner in twenty minutes, or just as soon as I've gotten these little ladies taken care of." She stooped to take Grace's hand, then turned to Vronny. "You can't wash your hands with that on, so I'll be spoon-feeding you tonight like your baby sister."

"Yay!" said Veronica, as if this were a treat she had angled for in the past and been refused.

I watched them busying themselves with preparations for dinner as the scent of Tuscan chicken filled the kitchen, and for the briefest of moments, I felt like I had walked into someone else's house. It was an uncanny, dreamlike sensation, as if I were the stranger who didn't belong even though everything there—the faces, the furniture—all felt so familiar. Just a moment. It was, as Josh had said, a madness brewed from guilt and anxiety, and it passed almost as quickly as it had come, but for that one moment, it felt as bright and hot as a poker pulled from a fire.

The phone rang, and I answered it.

"Mrs. Klein? This is Officer Randall. From the hospital."

"Yes. Is there any news?"

"Not really, ma'am. I returned to the park and found what I think was the hole in the slide, but the screw was not there."

"Not there?"

"No, ma'am."

"Someone took it away then," I said. "That's weird, right? Maybe whoever did it thought you would be able to pull fingerprints or something, maybe."

"I guess that's possible."

He didn't sound convinced.

"So now what?"

"Well, I'd say go about your life. Keep your eyes open for anything suspicious, but try not to worry too much. There's no reason to think your daughter was targeted. This was just a random event. Best to treat it as such. I'll leave you my number in case you have questions or see anything, you know, out of the ordinary, but otherwise . . ."

Otherwise, it's as you were.

I wrote the number down, thanked him for the call, and went upstairs for a quick shower. The hospital air—sanitized but also somehow stale—seemed to linger in my hair and clothes, and I wanted to put it—all of it—behind me. It felt good, cleansing in more ways than one, and I emerged with a sense of closure and relief that I hadn't gotten from talking to the cop.

I was coming downstairs, toweling my hair dry, dressed in soft cotton and flannel, and listening to Veronica chattering away as Oaklynn fed her, when the doorbell rang. For a moment, I thought it might be Mary Beth. My heart leaped, and not only because I could use a little wine and gossip after today.

But it wasn't Mary Beth, and I felt her conspicuous and coincidental absence knocking me slightly out of my good mood. It was Tammy Ward. She was smiling in that slightly embarrassed way of hers, but it was clear there was something on her mind.

"Hi," she said. "I'm sorry to bother you, but I was wondering if you'd seen Angus?"

Her annoying terrier. I cast my mind back, shaking my head.

"Not for a day or so," I said. "He's missing?"

"He must have gotten through the fence when I let him out this morning." She made a childish what-are-you-gonna-do? gesture with both hands, waggling her head and framing a goofy smile that didn't quite reach her eyes. She was upset.

"How long has he been missing?"

"Almost twelve hours," she said, shedding some of the pretense and letting her concern shine through. "He's probably fine, but with those coyotes around . . ."

"Yeah, I haven't seen him," I said, trying to look and sound sad. I didn't really like the dog, and Josh and I had complained to each other a dozen times about the way it ran wild in the neighborhood, particularly after the incident with Mr. Quietly, but I still felt bad for her. Tammy's life was no picnic, and the dog—irritating though the rest of us thought it—was one of its bright spots. "I'm sorry," I said. "I'll keep an eye out. Have you called animal control or the local vets?"

Tammy suppressed a shudder of alarm.

"Not yet," she said, still smiling, though her eyes were welling up. "Someone reported him once before, so I'd rather not talk to the police unless we really need to. Tommy says not to worry, that he'll be back as soon as he gets hungry, but that's men for you. Never a care."

She managed another smile, and I tried to match it, though her husband's casualness and the way she accepted it both annoyed me.

"You want to come in, have a drink?" I asked.

"Thanks, but no," Tammy replied. "I want to walk around the neighborhood a bit. See if I see him. I have some of his favorite treats." She showed me a sad little plastic bag and attempted the smile again. "You have my cell number if you see him. Not that we can get much signal around here."

"Tell me about it," I agreed. The lousy cell reception down by the creek was one of our only true gripes about the neighborhood.

"OK." She took a step back. "Let me know if you see him. If it's OK, I'll leave a couple of these with you in case it takes me a moment to get over," she said, fishing a couple of mealy biscuits shaped like cartoon bones out of the bag and handing them to me. I took them between finger and thumb and held them away from my body.

"Have you tried Mary Beth?" I asked.

"She's out of town. Visiting family, she said. Kurt, too. I looked around their yard, but . . ." She shook her head.

Visiting family, I thought. I've never heard of Mary Beth choosing to visit family. If she had, why hadn't I been subjected to a lengthy diatribe on the subject beforehand?

More paranoia. Kurt was gone, too. Mary Beth had clearly taken a trip with her husband, not mine. I was being irrational. Combined with the earlier Oaklynn business, I was starting to wonder if maybe I was the crazy one.

"Right," I said, forcing myself back to the matter at hand. "Well, if I see it . . . I mean, *him*, I'll let you know."

Tammy nodded again but apparently didn't trust herself to speak. On impulse, I leaned forward and pulled her into a hug—amiable and encouraging (complete with back pats of the kind Josh might use) rather than truly intimate—then waved her on her way. She was wearing pink stretch pants and sneakers that made her feet look huge and childish, and as she toddled away, gazing about randomly for her lost dog, I felt a pang of pity for her and regret that I hadn't been able to do more. In the same instant, I remembered the accident up on Wendover that Oaklynn and the girls had witnessed, the dog that had been hit by the car. I had promised to keep calling the local vets to find out what had happened but hadn't done so. It had slipped my mind or—perhaps—I had screened it out, not wanting to upset the girls.

Too late now.

I wondered if Oaklynn had followed up with the vets by herself but felt sure she would have said something. She had been so upset. Strange that she would then forget about it . . .

I went back to Ben Lodging's latest chapters, put aside in the park and temporarily forgotten because of all the drama since. My head felt clearer now than it had, and I returned to the place I had left off, keen to see if the new material would make the book's outcome clearer. I felt a twinge of discomfort—a kind of emotional flashback—when I traced the story back to where Carried had gotten off the bus and was sitting in a park, watching children play, but I got over it and kept reading. It was fine for almost an entire paragraph, and then I read this sentence:

I watched the two little girls with the women, one the mother, I assumed, the other a friend or nanny, until the smallest of the girls left the sandbox where she had been playing to investigate the massive steam locomotive that sat between the parking lot and the sports fields.

I stared at the words, rereading the sentence over and over as my heart rate quickened.

How was this possible? Two girls, two women, and a park with an old steam train? This was more than coincidence. I put the laptop down with unsteady fingers and got quickly to my feet, pacing the study floor with a rising sense of agitation. I remembered being in the park, looking around for people watching us, one of whom had then turned the slide into a nasty little booby trap for my daughter. I put a hand to my heart and stared blankly out of the window as horror put the words in my head, clear as if I had just read them.

Ben Lodging is watching us.

Chapter Thirty-Five

ANNA

But Ben Lodging couldn't be watching me. It didn't make sense. He had sent that excerpt the night before we had gone to the park. I had been reading it while I sat there, moments before the slide incident. It wasn't an account of something the author had witnessed because it hadn't happened when he'd written it. I had never even been to that park when he sent it.

As to the similarity of the place, the park with an old steam train left as a historical curiosity, there must be countless such places dotted throughout the country. I did a Google Image search for *park steam engine* and pulled up dozens of pictures of trains quite different from the one in Freedom Park.

Coincidence, then.

It must be. As to the idea of two girls with two women, that, too, meant nothing. I stared at the picture of the train again, then reread the lines in Lodging's manuscript, thinking as I did so of what Josh had said about my turning the accident into something from one of my clients' mystery novels . . .

He was right. Of course, he was. I was being paranoid again, and while I had good reason to be, given the day I had experienced, there was no more to it than that. I forced myself to read the rest of the chapter and, finding nothing more that seemed directly relevant to my own situation, decided I was being stupid.

Suddenly, I felt exhausted and badly in need of a drink, though that would have to wait until after Oaklynn's famous Tuscan chicken. I was in no mood to be judged by my teetotaler nanny.

More paranoia, I thought irritably, and decided to pour myself a little glass of dry sherry just to make the point, though whether I was proving something to Oaklynn or myself, I wasn't sure.

Dinner managed to be both delicious and odd. The girls were already in bed by the time we sat down to eat, and the house felt curiously still and silent, magnifying every word and gesture Oaklynn and I exchanged. I asked her to put some music on, which lifted some of the pressure a little, though I quickly realized that what came over the little speakers was the playlist that included that Imagine Dragons song about the inner demons. If that came on, I'd have to excuse myself and go to the bathroom. After my previous rush of paranoid suspicion, I didn't think I could look at her while that played.

The song didn't come on, and as we ate, I began to relax again. The meal was an exact replica of the first time Oaklynn had cooked for us and was therefore a monument to both her skill and her eccentricity, but the meat was so tender and the flavors so perfectly balanced that I was able to see even the repetition as comforting rather than merely bizarre. Still, even having banished my previous doubts about Oaklynn, I'd be lying if I said I felt comfortable with her in the ways I had in those first weeks after her arrival. We were, I suppose, just too different, so that even the things I liked about her—her efficiency, her motherly devotion to the girls—made it harder to connect with her as someone I understood. And that was without the moments—rare but pointed—when her amiable niceness seemed to slip, and I felt like she was watching me the way a child watches an animal in a zoo, as something fascinating to them but foreign. I saw it in her eyes, a level watchfulness, sometimes puzzled, sometimes critical, always—at least for the second or so that it lasted—seeming to come from far away.

"This one is from before your time," she remarked, as a woman's voice started crooning over a showily meditative piano riff. "Bonnie Tyler."

I listened and started to shake my head, then caught myself.

"I've heard it," I said. I concentrated on the song as it unwound from the speakers. It was repetitive, labored in its anthemic, ballady glory but had, I supposed, a kind of emotional power. The lyrics were overwrought and the synthesizers just a bit too eighties for my taste, but I remembered the words of the title just before the singer got to them.

"Total Eclipse of the Heart," I said, jolted out of myself by the sense of something significant that I couldn't quite place.

Oaklynn gave me one of those strange looks, smiling, knowing but remote, like she was watching me through a telescope, seeing into my head, my past, the strange moment in August when the sun had been blotted out and I had made the decision to hire . . . her.

Eclipsed.

I sat there, my mouth half-open, not knowing what to say, thinking vaguely, distractedly, of screwdrivers and remembering how Veronica had once said Oaklynn was a witch in more than her shoes. As if on cue, she looked off and away to the window, paused in absent thought, and pronounced, "Gonna be weather."

There was. By the time Oaklynn was closing the dishwasher and turning it on, a storm had blown up from the southwest. Sometimes squalls like this parted around the city, but this one pushed through, bringing driving rain and sheet lightning that lit the swaying pecan tree behind the house like a strobe. The windows streamed as if there were a hose playing straight onto them, and I stood with my face pressed to the glass, trying to see through the darkness to the creek that was, I knew, rising fast. It had never breached since we had moved in, but I'd heard stories of the water creeping up what was now our backyard, the bottom ten feet of which was marked as being within the hundred-year floodplain. Like the coyotes, it reminded me of how unlike New York this place was, how close to a version of nature that was ancient, wild, and powerful.

"Poor Angus," Oaklynn observed. I had told her about the missing terrier over dinner. "If he's still out there, he's going to have a lousy night."

"Surely, the rain will make him go home," I said.

Neither of us said that he might have been killed on the roads—something we knew was a possibility from all-too-recent experience—let alone falling prey to the coyotes or the rapid waters of the swollen creek. The terrier hadn't been missing long, and it wasn't like he would get lost in unknown territory. He was always getting out. I considered calling Tammy to check in, but it was getting late, and I didn't want to upset her right before bed. I'd call in the morning. There was a good chance that Angus would have skulked home to get out of the rain by then, and it would all be over.

That turned out to be wishful thinking.

Morning came, and though the storm was gone, the ground was saturated and the creek flowing fast and brown just below the flood-mark. Tammy's dog had not returned, and though I called her twice and saw her padding disconsolately around the sodden neighborhood, I became increasingly sure that he never would.

The heavy rain had pushed the stormwater controls to their limits, and one of the drains that ran down Tanglewood Lane had been clogged with fallen leaves and other debris so that the road had turned into a steady brook where it met Brandon Circle. I went out with Oaklynn and the girls to survey the damage and get a little air. A crew from the city was already on-site. They had opened one of the manholes, and I was revolted to see forty or fifty fat brown cockroaches clinging to the underside of the cover. Veronica shrieked and hid her eyes, making the burly white guy who seemed to be in charge laugh. He had a beard and a hard hat and looked us over with something like amusement.

"Yeah, you don't wanna go down there, little girl," he said.

I didn't like the leering amusement in his tone and stepped between him and the girls, watching critically as he began feeding some kind of device on a cable into the manhole. As we walked past and up the street, it emitted a strange and resonating tone like a distant foghorn that seemed to vibrate through the ground. I turned back to look at him, but before I could say anything, he remarked simply, "Sonar. Helps us find the blockages."

"Wow," said Oaklynn. "Pretty cool, huh?"

"Yeah," I answered. "Pretty cool."

When we came back about twenty minutes later, they were still working on the sewer line, and the roadway was swimming in foul-smelling water. Tammy Ward was hovering on the periphery, watching with a handkerchief clamped to her nose. She was wearing pink sweats and stained sneakers and looked both pathetic and slightly ridiculous. She gave me a half-hearted wave as I passed but didn't say anything, and I hadn't the heart to ask if there was any sign of Angus. She was clearly waiting to hear that somewhere among the storm drain's blockage of silt and leaves and fertilizer runoff was the body of a small dog. I gave Oaklynn a look, but instead of seeing sympathy and concern in the nanny's face, I caught something hard and appraising.

I thought of her fury when little Angus had come tearing through our yard after Mr. Quietly. I thought of the crossbow with which she was so proficient, and once more, unbidden, the image of a Phillips-head screwdriver popped into my head. I took a deep breath, trying to shrug it off as my ever-increasing paranoia, but when I looked back at Oaklynn, I saw something else in her gaze—something like triumph.

Chapter Thirty-Six

Oaklynn sat in the dark basement with her laptop on her knee, typing, typing, typing, her face bluish in the glow of the screen and fierce in its frown of concentration. On the bed beside her chair, Mr. Quietly purred softly—his steady, knowing eyes on her. This was her usual nighttime activity. She had never slept much, and the habit—a single-minded hour or two at the computer before getting into bed—helped empty her mind before the attempt. Tonight she got under the duvet and lay still, but her writing had triggered memories she normally kept boxed and stacked away, and now she could not help but turn them over in her mind.

Her sister, Maddie, had been five years older than she, and Oaklynn's—which was to say Nadine's—earliest memories were of being with her in the hospital. She supposed her parents were there, too, but she remembered very little about her parents in the hospital, and their father might already have gone. It was a nice room, warm and surprisingly inviting, full of bright colors and things from home: toys, pictures, books. A kid's room, and not one for a short-term stay. Maddie had been there for months, enduring test after test and therapy after therapy, while Nadine sat by to keep her spirits up, holding her bruised, feverish fingers . . . teasing, playing, and Being Strong.

The nurses loved her, said she was a Trouper and a Good Sister. Even her mother smiled at her from time to time.

Acute lymphoblastic leukemia. They were the first long words Nadine had learned. Sometimes she felt she was born knowing them. They meant that her sister suffered pain and exhaustion all the time, even between bouts of chemo and radiation. They meant misery, confinement, fragility, and—eventually—death. Nadine learned this early.

And one day, she was offered the chance to take it all away.

Her mother came to her, squatted down beside her bed, and looked at her, smiling and excited. They were due to go to the hospital, and Nadine was unused to seeing this look of thrilled anticipation in her mother's watery-blue eyes. She sat up, sensing that something was coming, something that her mother had been thinking about for a long time. Later, much later, Nadine would wonder if she had been thinking of it before Nadine was even born—if it was *why* Nadine had been born.

All her sister's pain, all the misery and heartache of the failed treatments might be fixed at a stroke, and Nadine could be the person to do it. All she had to do, her mother explained, was give Maddie some of what was in her bones. Nadine had been confused by that because she hadn't known there was anything in her bones, but then she had caught that whisper of exhilaration from her mother, that hint of magic, that she, Nadine, was a kind of angel, using her special power to swoop in and save her sister, her family.

Nadine still remembered the feeling across three and a half decades, and the promise of it still thrilled her, even though she knew what had happened. Those hours as they prepared her for the transplant had been the pinnacle of her life, the way she had become the center of everything, borne upon a wave of hope and support, of love—and not just from her family. The doctors and nurses and staff in their scrubs and tennis shoes, stethoscopes, and blood-pressure cuffs swinging as they moved efficiently around—even they pulsed with whatever they had in place of love, that professional, walled-off space they kept in their heads and hearts for the good, selfless caregivers, the saviors of the sick and dying. She felt it like warmth coming off them. In those shining moments, Nadine was at the very center of all that mattered, and all it had taken was a willingness to sacrifice a little part of herself, a little pain and discomfort, a little time . . .

It was glorious, like walking a red carpet, like standing under hot lights in front of a cheering crowd, like receiving an award or a trophy and holding it up so that the world could scream with one voice, "Yes! This is what you deserve. This is who you are."

But it hadn't worked.

There had been complications from the transplant. As an adult, Nadine had spent countless hours studying precisely what had happened, learning the terms she needed to understand the reports, but none of it made any difference. Maddie was dead within the month, and her mother had never really looked at her surviving daughter again. She remembered coming to visit her mother as the woman lay dying in another hospital years later. By then, she was shrunken and stinking of sweat and the vodka that leeched out of her pores, lying on her side, her ratty gray hair in her face, her eyes on nothing. Nadine had sat beside her for three days before her mother spoke, and when she did, it was in a kind of fever dream in which she clutched at Nadine's fingers with a feeble, bony talon of a hand, only to open her eyes, their focus swimming, and say, "Oh. It's you."

Now Nadine—Oaklynn now—lay on the bed, listening to Mr. Quietly and the sibilant hiss of breathing on the baby monitors, and she repacked the memories into the little boxes of her mind, closing the lids and pushing them back into the dark. Then she stared at the ceiling, just visible through the gloom, and tried to think of nothing.

"Thank you for helping to look after things," said Josh, after the following day's dinner of Chinese takeout. "I know Anna was really grateful."

Oaklynn smiled her usual smile and said that she was just doing her job, but she watched him carefully, sensing something cautious and apologetic in his manner. He had been back from his trip only a few hours, so he wasn't apologizing for himself.

Anna, then. She must have said something since he got back, some whispered bedroom something that had made him think he had to cover for her. But what? That she hadn't wanted her at the hospital?

"How was your trip?" Oaklynn asked.

"Fine, fine," said Josh, reaching for his glass in the way he did when he was lying.

"Oh, that's good to hear," said Oaklynn, humoring him. "I know Anna was worried."

Josh hesitated, the wineglass halfway to his lips.

"She was worried?" he asked, trying to sound nonchalant. "About what?"

"She didn't say," said Oaklynn. "Not to me. She may have spoken to Tammy about it. She came over the other night."

Josh shifted uneasily.

"Tammy came over?"

"Yes."

"And they chatted about . . . what? My trip?"

Oaklynn could almost hear him sweating.

"I think so," she said. "I didn't really hear."

"But she sounded worried?"

"Probably just concerned about managing without you."

"But she had you to help out."

"Yes, but I'm just the nanny, not the husband," said Oaklynn, who had made guilelessness a very particular art form. "And with her friend being away, too . . ."

Josh was very still now.

"Her friend?"

"Mary Beth," said Oaklynn sweetly. "Kurt, too, of course."

She saw the moment in his face when he remembered her remark as he had headed off to the airport when she had told him to say hi to everyone, when she had planted the seed in his head. She wondered how long it had taken to sprout, that little insignificant idea, to take root and leap up into a sapling that, when the wind stirred its leaves, whispered, "She knows."

He blinked, thinking, then tried to sound perplexed, even indignant.

"You think Anna was worried because Mary Beth wasn't home?" The tone was almost defiant, but Oaklynn noticed the way he had lowered his voice so that Anna, who was putting the girls down upstairs, wouldn't overhear.

"I told her not to," said Oaklynn. "But . . ." She smiled, embarrassed, and looked at the table, saying nothing.

"What?" Josh pressed. He was agitated now. He had put the glass down but was fidgeting with it, his fingers flicking restlessly against the tabletop.

"I don't want to make trouble," said Oaklynn. "Particularly when it's unnecessary."

"What kind of trouble?"

"Oh, you know how people get the wrong end of things. These days it seems everyone thinks husbands and wives should know every detail of each other's lives. That doesn't seem healthy to me. And a husband has a right to his privacy, particularly if he's protecting his family. That's a man's job, right?"

"I'm not sure I follow," said Josh. He was getting red in the face now, though he was still trying to play confused.

"I mean," said Oaklynn, hunching down and dropping into a stage whisper, "the New York thing with the Wilsons."

Josh stared, his eyes widening just a fraction.

"How did you know . . . ?"

"Oh, you know how it is," said Oaklynn airily. "Servants are a bit like pieces of furniture. After a while, you get used to them and stop thinking they are people. So they hear things."

Josh bit his lip but recovered quickly enough to protest.

"You're not a servant!" he said, loud as he dared.

"Sure I am," said Oaklynn, unoffended. "And that's OK. I knew that when I came here. I work for you, and you pay me."

"You're part of the family!"

The untruth caught Oaklynn very slightly off-balance, and if Josh had been more attuned to such things, he might have noticed the wince in her smile, the pained quiver, the hesitation before she said, "Aww. That's very sweet of you, but you know what I mean."

She watched Josh let the point go as he committed to the question he had been hoping she would answer, unbidden.

"What did you hear?"

She smiled at that.

"Nothing I need to tell anyone else," said Oaklynn. "I know my place, and I'm not looking to sow discord."

"But if there's something on your mind, perhaps you could tell me, and then . . ."

She waved the thought away as if she was being kind, ignoring the way his agitation increased.

"I'm a very loyal person," she said. "You don't know that about me, but it's true. In this case, that means that you can trust me to keep whatever secrets you might have in the interest of the family."

"It's not a secret," said Josh. He couldn't let it slide. Not completely. He had to cover a little. "Not really."

Oaklynn nodded sympathetically, knowing she had already won.

"I know. But it's probably best if I kept things to myself, wouldn't you say?"

Josh wavered, looking for another way out, but she would not let him off the hook. He had to say it. Finally, he gave a couple of quick nods.

"Probably," he agreed. "Yes. Thanks."

She knew how that pained him, especially the last word.

"Then we're good," said Oaklynn. "No harm, no foul."

"OK," he said.

"Allies?" she said, smiling with playful innocence.

He bit his lip, but he had no choice.

"Allies," he said.

"Perfect. Now why don't you have another glass of your wine there, and I'll say my good nights to the girls. I'd like to do some reading before bed."

She left him then, though her smile shifted slightly as she got to the top of the stairs. She stood for a moment, listening to the sounds of the house and to Josh's stillness most of all.

Chapter Thirty-Seven

It was a nice house, Flanders thought. Not as flashy as some of the others in the neighborhood, but that wasn't such a bad thing. Some of the neighbors looked like they were trying too hard. He wondered what Nadine made of that.

He had seen her twice this morning. Once at the window when she opened the upstairs drapes, and once in the yard with the two Klein girls. Asian girls, he had been surprised to see. Or half, at least. They had their mother's features. He had seen her, too, on the phone through the kitchen window and then when she had driven off to do whatever she did for work or fun. Flanders had kept his distance, of course, using field glasses to keep an eye on things and making sure he stayed out of sight. He had to fight the urge to go in there then, not waste another second, but the moment had to be just right. Get it wrong and everything would be blown.

He reached blindly for his cell phone and called Noah, thumbing the call through with practiced fingers as he stared through the binoculars at the house in the trees. It rang eight times before Noah grunted.

"Gonna need that safe house ready," said Flanders.

"When?"

"Soon," said Flanders out of the side of his mouth. "Maybe tonight or tomorrow. Not much longer."

"'K," said Noah. "It's yours when you need it."

"And it's still quiet? No one likely to come snooping?"

"As the grave, brother man," said the other man. "As the grave."

Flanders smirked at that.

Brother man. Where did he get this shit?

"Good," said Flanders. "Keep your phone on."

"Everything OK?"

Flanders considered that.

"It will be," he said, and hung up.

Chapter Thirty-Eight

ANNA

I still had no final chapter from Ben Lodging and had written to him about it, raising the possibility of two alternate endings, one in which Carried killed someone, one in which he didn't. I wasn't really sure what to do next. Offer both endings to publishers and let them pick? That smacked of selling out. Suggest that we print both and let readers choose which one they liked best? Too gimmicky. Find a way to include both, perhaps presenting a killing and then revealing it merely to be a dark fantasy generated by Carried's fevered imagination, followed by the mundane reality where nothing happened but might one day?

I rather liked that last option, but I knew that this was a choice that would have to be made by the author, and I was afraid that if I leaned too hard on Lodging, he'd panic and bolt. I wasn't sure why, but for all his professionalism, I sensed something taut under the surface—a high-tension wire that sang with every touch. It wasn't fragility, exactly, more an awkwardness and sensitivity. More than once I wondered if the story of his deafness was no more than that: a story, a kind of dodge so that he wouldn't have to engage in person.

Perhaps I was reading too deeply into our correspondence, which was soon going between us several times a day, but I sensed that I was talking to someone cocooned, separate from the world. How else could he capture Carried's pathological isolation so perfectly? And in truth, my earlier paranoia about how closely parts of his book had come to my own life had left me cautious. It wasn't anxiety, precisely. I didn't really think he was watching me. In the cold light of day, I could see that for the craziness it was. It might have been for a few minutes on the day of Veronica's accident, but now it was mostly embarrassment that I had allowed myself to think such a thing. Still, I had to force myself to get in touch with him and raise the ideas that I had been kicking around for the book's ending.

Lodging responded almost immediately. He liked my idea of the false ending, the killing that was wiped out by the last chapter, so the reader was left with a pregnant sense of something that still might happen after the final pages. Even so, I warned him that publishers might balk at this as anticlimactic or too subtle for the genre.

"I guess we'll cross that bridge when we come to it," he said, which was, I thought, encouraging. It's important for authors to stand by the integrity of their visions, but sometimes they forget that their art is also a business, so it was nice to see a debut writer who wasn't digging in his heels or getting overly precious about the fate of his work.

I told him as much, and in a series of swift exchanges, we fell into something less like a business discussion and more like a chat, so that all my former paranoia and anxiety about him fell away. I found myself telling him about my career, my tastes in literature, and the pros and cons of being an agent from outside New York. I even mentioned the oddity of having Oaklynn living with us. He was a good audience, attentive, even fascinated to hear about the ins and outs of the business, and keen to learn. I even managed to put to bed the question that had been bothering me for a while.

"Have you ever been to Charlotte?" I asked. "That scene when Carried goes to the park with the train and watches the children felt weirdly familiar."

The delay in responding was just long enough to awaken my old anxieties again, so that they fluttered around my head mothlike, but the content of his message sent them back to sleep.

"No, I never have," he said. "But there's a place called Steamtown in Scranton. I think I must have been thinking of that."

That was all I needed. My previous anxieties evaporated and became ridiculous. We talked some more about story structure and what was hot in the market right now, but also about the literary life in general, how to make time for reading and writing when you have kids to look after, and—again—the difficulties of adjusting to having a strange woman living in your basement. Before I knew it, we had been chatting for almost two hours: nothing too confessional but friendlier and more intimate than I was used to being with clients.

That came as a shock. I told him I had to go, get some work done, and he said he'd be in touch. I signed off, conscious of an odd exhilaration at all these minor confidences flying between us, and went to the window to clear my head.

There was a car outside the house, an old-fashioned, olive-green thing that some part of my brain branded a muscle car. The windows were heavily tinted, but the engine was running, the brake lights on. I didn't recognize it, and since Settle Road was a cul-de-sac, we didn't get through traffic. As I looked out, it lurched into motion and sped away. I wasn't sure why, but it unsettled me.

I went downstairs and was peering out of the front window when Oaklynn came down from the girls' room.

"What?" she asked.

The street was usually quiet, so my looking at *anything* out there was unusual. But I felt a prickle of annoyance. Couldn't I look out of the window without having to report my findings to Oaklynn?

"Nothing," I said. "Someone must have gotten lost."

"I'm getting Vronny a drink," she said, moving to the fridge.

"OK. Just keep an eye on her. She spills when she's not paying attention."

"Sippy cup," said Oaklynn, holding it up.

"Even so," I said.

I didn't know why I was pushing back against her, but I could feel her watchfulness again, that sense that she was taking her time to do whatever she had to because she was monitoring me.

You're being paranoid.

Josh's voice in my head. I scowled, and the phone rang.

"I'll get it," said Oaklynn.

"It's OK," I said, crisper than I had meant to. I moved to the phone decisively so she could see I wasn't just being polite and snatched the receiver.

My house. My phone.

"Hello?" I said.

"Anna, it's Tammy."

She sounded emotional, but for a moment, I couldn't tell if she was happy or sad. An extreme of one or the other. I braced myself.

"Hi, Tammy. What's up? You OK?"

"It's Angus," she spluttered. "He came back! All wet and half-starved, but he came back! I just had to let you know because you were so worried."

My heart did a little jump, but it wasn't so much relief as panic, as if I had been caught. The dog was alive. It wasn't in the storm drain, skewered by a crossbow arrow.

"He came back!" I managed. "Oh, that is good news."

Oaklynn drifted into my field of view, her eyes locked on mine. I swallowed, trying to look normal, just a person talking to her friend on the phone.

"Angus," I mouthed to her. "He came back."

I tried to look pleased and slightly amused, like I was letting her know that things had worked out just as I had expected, and that Tammy's anxiety had been stupid and needless. Oaklynn smiled that expansive, beatific smile of hers, but it only moved her mouth. Her eyes stayed on mine, thoughtful and appraising. Knowing.

See? they said. *I didn't kill the dog, after all. Doesn't that make you feel better?*

"Well, that's a huge load off my mind," I said to Tammy, contriving to turn a little so that Oaklynn couldn't see my face.

I didn't feel better. I just felt transparent, and for reasons I couldn't pinpoint, that scared me.

Chapter Thirty-Nine

ANNA

It might have been the last day when it was still warm enough to sit outside. There had been a cold snap at the end of September, and though the weather had warmed up again afterward, the end of October had been positively wintry. Now it was November, and the trees were mostly bare. While it still got into the sixties during the day, and the sky was clear and blue, it cooled fast in the evening, the nights hovering just above freezing. Each day took longer to warm up, and the turkey vultures sat like scarecrows for most of the morning before taking to the air.

I had been surprised to receive Mary Beth's invitation. She rarely entertained—let alone hosting anything as casual as a cookout—and the emailed invitation had specified that the kids and even Oaklynn were welcome. A few weeks ago, I would have taken this simply as a concession designed to make sure the adults could do their own thing while the nanny handled the kids, but it was unusual enough to increase my anxiety. I hadn't seen Mary Beth since Josh's trip to New York. It was impossible not to wonder if she was engineering a situation in which we would meet but would not, could not, get into anything messy.

Not that I thought there was anything messy to get into. Not really. I just wondered occasionally—the thought of her being away when my husband was felt like a cold draft in the sun, like my thoughts about screwdrivers. Stupid, unearned, needless worries born of nothing more than a dark imagination and a sense of . . . what? That something bad was coming. Something I deserved.

When I mentioned the invitation to Josh, his face tightened with thought and surprise, but he just said, "Sounds good. But if it's no warmer than today, I'm not standing around freezing my ass off."

I didn't know what to think beyond the clear sense that I didn't want to go. I knew I would spend the whole party tense and uneasily vigilant, my attention moving from Josh to Mary Beth and Oaklynn and back, not sure what I was looking for, not sure which of them I could trust, or whether I was just being idiotically paranoid.

Again. Still. Whatever.

"At least Oaklynn can come along and look after the girls," said Josh.

I gave him a mildly surprised look.

"What?" he said.

"No *cripes* jokes?" I said, half teasing. "No snark about the crates of food she will take with her?"

"Of course not," he replied, flushing slightly. "She's great. Part of the family, right?"

The phrase sounded so odd in his mouth that I could only nod and smile.

When the day came—brighter and warmer than we had any reason to expect—I approached the Wilsons' house with a sense of foreboding, trying not to think that I would spend the afternoon watching the way Josh interacted with Mary Beth but knowing that I would, anyway.

As it turned out, I barely saw them speak to each other at all, though that, too, felt odd, loaded with unreadable significance. They seemed to actively avoid each other, always sitting apart, not meeting each other's eyes, talking to other people, though the group was small. A falling-out? Or an effort to hide something?

Or nothing at all, which I was seeing as something only because I was determined to . . .

In fact, the only person Mary Beth seemed interested in was Oaklynn.

"So you're a Mormon," said Mary Beth with customary frankness and a level, sardonic stare. "What's that all about?"

"LDS," said Oaklynn, clearly embarrassed by the eyes of the group turning onto her. "Yes. The Church of Latter-day Saints."

"Huh," said Mary Beth, her gaze still fixed and snakelike so that Oaklynn looked down. "But you didn't answer my question."

"What question was that?" said Oaklynn stiffly.

"The Mormon thing," Mary Beth pressed. "What's that all about?"

"It's the faith I was raised in," replied Oaklynn carefully, smiling, as if looking for a way out. I felt sure that, assuming she was capable of the feeling, she didn't like Mary Beth Wilson, and especially didn't like being cornered by her.

"We don't all stick with the faiths we were born into. I was raised Methodist," Mary Beth shot back with a raised eyebrow as she swilled the wine in her glass pointedly. "Anna was some kind of Japanese druid or some shit."

"Hardly," I replied, feeling embarrassed and needled. Mary Beth was one of those people who exploited other people's politeness, their desire to avoid conflict. "My parents were Buddhists, but they had some Shinto practices, too."

"Which you don't follow," said Mary Beth, as if closing a steel trap.

"Not as such," I said, soft-pedaling it. "We keep a little family shrine to our ancestors upstairs."

"But you don't really believe it all," Mary Beth pushed.

"Well, I'm not sure all of it is supposed to be literally true in the modern sense of—"

"In the sense that Oaklynn believes her—what would you call it—Moronism? I mean, Mormonism?"

Kurt chuckled. Josh frowned.

"Well, I know the church is true," said Oaklynn carefully, "for me. Other people have other ways to God."

"Like Anna's incense and dead relatives, you mean?"

"I think that's enough, Mary Beth," I said, irritated and confused. I had my own issues with Oaklynn and with religion generally, but I was suddenly tired of Mary Beth's love of drama and need to tear other people down. "We all have our different beliefs and traditions."

"But it's interesting, don't you think?" said Mary Beth, deliberately perky, like she was discussing the weather. "That your employee might think you are going to hell or whatever. You not being Christian and all. So she thinks you're damned, right, Oaklynn?"

Oaklynn flushed.

"I'm not much of a theologian," she said.

"But that's what you people do, right?" Mary Beth persisted. "Go around converting the world because if you don't, we'll all burn, right?"

"I should really check on the girls," said Oaklynn.

"They are right there," said Mary Beth, nodding across the immaculate lawn to where the neighborhood kids were all playing together.

"Thanks, Oaklynn," said Josh, "that would be great."

It was odd to see Josh going out of his way to look after her, and I wondered—with just a hint of pleasure—if he was deliberately trying to piss off Mary Beth. Oaklynn nodded, apparently relieved, and fled, though I was sure she caught Mary Beth's arch remark to Josh, "Well, aren't you the knight in shining armor?"

It was an odd remark, and my gaze lingered on each of them in turn, trying to decipher what had just passed between them. If anything.

"Miss Oaklynn! Miss Oaklynn!" called Veronica delightedly. "Chase us!"

"What?" said Mary Beth as soon as Oaklynn was out of earshot, meeting my look head-on and unflinchingly. "You people! Why do you have to tiptoe around her? She works for you! You pay her wages. She's not your little Mormon buddy who you have to look after. She's not anyone's *little* anything."

"OK," said Josh.

"Yeah," said Kurt. "You're starting to let your inner bitch show."

"Doubtless that's a huge surprise to everyone," said Mary Beth cheerfully. "Speaking of, are those damned burgers not done yet, Kurt? You've been cooking for, like, a year."

"Took me a while to get the coals going," said her husband. "Hot now, though."

"Finally," said Mary Beth, rolling her eyes. "Have you seen that guy who is always walking around the neighborhood with that huge white dog that looks like a goddamned dire wolf? Like, constantly. Does he work or what?"

"I think he's a professor or something at the university," said Tammy. "Lives up on Harris, I think. Dog seems nice. Angus doesn't usually like big dogs, but that one . . ."

She broke off, looking to where the terrier was yipping and chasing the kids around the yard contentedly. She looked desperately relieved, as if the safe return of the animal had been the kind of relief without which she couldn't have gone on. On impulse, I reached out and patted her hand. She gave me a startled, slightly teary look and smiled, embarrassed.

"I'm so silly," she said, wiping her eyes.

"Dogs and kids," said Mary Beth, shaking her head. "I don't get either."

"No shit," said Kurt. Mary Beth gave him a venomous look, and he shrugged, so that she made a little disgusted noise in her throat and rolled her eyes.

"How *is* the nanny thing working out?" she asked instead, keen for more gossip.

"Good," said Josh, turning deliberately to me, as if we were speaking with one voice, as a couple. "Yeah, Anna?"

"Yeah," I said, a tad less enthusiastically. "At least I'm getting some work done."

"The kids seem to like her," said Tammy, watching them.

"They love her," said Josh.

"What's not to love?" said Mary Beth dryly, speaking over the rim of her glass.

"Anna was worried that . . . ," Josh began. I shot him a shocked, fierce look, and he froze.

"What?" said Mary Beth, pouncing. "You think she's making moves on hubby or stealing your earrings or something?"

I shook my head dismissively, still staring at Josh.

What is he thinking?

"What, then?"

"It's nothing," said Josh, though he obviously felt obliged to explain. "But Gracie got sick a few times, and then there was that thing at the park."

"The slide," said Tammy. "That was awful."

"And you think Saint Oaklynn wasn't being super vigilant," Mary Beth said to me, clearly disappointed. "You thought she should have been sitting by their bedsides day and night—"

"No!" I said. "It was nothing. Forget it."

"Come on, Anna," said Mary Beth, scenting something fun in the air. "You can tell us. We're all friends here. Well, mostly."

She gave Josh a wicked grin, and I pressed my fingertips together.

"Go on, Anna," said Josh. "It's over now."

I stared at him, but with Mary Beth's eyes pinning me to my seat, I felt I had no choice if I wasn't going to make a scene.

"I just wondered if it wasn't a bit of a coincidence that they were suddenly spending so much time at the hospital," I conceded at last. Mary Beth and Tammy looked baffled. "I was just being overprotective. Paranoid."

"Wait," said Kurt. "You mean you thought she was *doing* it? She was hurting them *on purpose?*"

Tammy's mouth fell open. I shook my head and held up my hands, saying, "I said I was being paranoid," but it was too late.

"Oh my God, that is awesome!" said Mary Beth, gleeful. "The Mormon angel of death!"

"She doesn't think that now, do you, Anna?" said Josh.

I stared at him wide-eyed.

"What's that nutso condition people have who hurt kids to get attention?" said Tommy, the first time he'd spoken in a while.

"Munchausen's!" said Mary Beth. "Like the baron who used to make shit up."

"But isn't that people who just lie to get medical attention for themselves?" said Kurt. "It was on a *House* episode."

"Right," Mary Beth agreed. "People who do it through someone else have . . . Wait. Got it. Munchausen's *by proxy*! Pretty sure that's it. Oh, this is so cool. You have your own pet psycho!"

"Can we drop this?" I said, conscious of Oaklynn not so very far away playing with the kids.

"Watch out when you shower," said Kurt, making stabbing motions and shrill little chirping sounds with each thrust.

"You don't really think she's a loon, do you?" said Mary Beth. "Mormonism notwithstanding."

"No, I don't," said Anna. "And ease off on the religion thing. She's a good person."

"A second ago, you were thinking she was trying to waste your kids," said Mary Beth.

Josh winced at the phrase.

"I said I was being paranoid," said Anna. "Can we let it go?"

"I think she seems lovely," said Tammy.

"I'm astonished," said Mary Beth, giving her a withering look.

"I need a beer," said Kurt. "Anna's delusions are starting to get to me."

"Thanks," I said, shooting Josh a look that made him shrug and say, "What?" like he was some frat boy being called out for a stunt.

"The Munchausen Mormon," said Mary Beth wistfully, taking my hand and patting it with mock sympathy. "You have to admit, it's pretty cray-cray. You need to get out more. Still, I almost wish it were true," she added, considering Oaklynn as she lumbered around after Tammy's kids at the bottom of the yard. "It would at least make her interesting."

"I think things are plenty interesting around here without that," said Tammy sweetly.

"Yeah?" said Mary Beth, turning her piercing gaze on Tammy until she flushed. "You would. And you know what?" She took a sip of her wine. "You're not wrong."

I think Tammy felt the ripple of unease through the group, even if she didn't know what it meant. In the same instant, we heard the rumble of a car engine on the road out front, a deep, throaty sound quite unlike the whisper quietness of the neighborhood's usual hybrids and other state-of-the-art modern vehicles. It was a defiant snarl in the peaceful fall air, and I half turned toward it, thinking vaguely that I had heard the sound before. Even as I did so, I was conscious that I wasn't the only one to respond to the sound. Down near the creek, there among the laughing children, Oaklynn had stiffened and become very still, craning to hear.

Chapter Forty

ANNA

I sat on the couch with my laptop, clicked on Oaklynn's application folder, and scrolled through page after page of glowing references. I was being crazy. Josh had said as much. And, following his lead, so had my friends.

And yet . . .

I couldn't shake the image of the screwdriver in the diaper bag. And now, however mockingly Mary Beth had raised the idea, I had a few new magic words to fuel my anxiety.

Munchausen's by proxy. It was little more than nonsense: a meaningless term I would have ignored that morning but that now had an aura of menace and power in my head. I thought that I should probably pour myself a glass of wine and go to bed, allow myself to forget those words, let them turn again to nonsense . . .

But I couldn't.

I googled *Munchausen* and was surprised to see the *by proxy* part autofill in the search options. Was I the only person who had never heard of it? I clicked the first item in the list that came up and pulled up an overview on a medical site, bracing myself. It read:

Munchausen syndrome by proxy (MSBP) is a mental health condition in which someone in a caregiving role invents symptoms, causes injuries, or otherwise generates actual or simulated health problems in a child, elderly adult, or disabled person in their charge. The person suffering from the disorder seeks attention—particularly from health-care professionals—through the proxy victim as an end in itself rather than, for example, in pursuit of money or other material advantage. While the person with the syndrome may be genuinely ill, their actions are still considered a form of abuse.

I felt suddenly cold and sat very still.

The site began with warnings that my online browsing might be accessible to others, as if anyone looking at this page had good reason to think they were being watched by someone potentially dangerous. It went on to say that someone with this condition or disorder might lie about a child's symptoms or fabricate test results to make a child seem sick. The goal of the abuser was, it said, to receive sympathetic attention from other people, particularly health-care professionals. In some cases, the abusers would hurt or mistreat children in their care in order to receive this attention, and victims could suffer serious, even fatal, consequences as a result.

I stared. Then I read it all again, clicking on page after page to learn more, as if the next bullet point or text block would make clear what seemed inconceivable. The guilty parties were frequently—apparently—mothers, though anyone who functioned as a caregiver might have the disorder. The origins of the condition were unclear, though they often had roots in the abuser's own childhood, and there was no clear agreement as to whether MSBP (one site called it a "psychiatric factitious disorder imposed upon another") was a single condition or a collection of different conditions known by other names and only loosely connected by the motivation of the abuser.

Several sites listed traits common to people with Munchausen's by proxy. Such people often had medical skills or experience and seemed particularly at ease in hospitals and similar environments. They seemed to seek attention and attempted to get close to medical personnel. I thought of Oaklynn's manner in the ER, her combination of attentive efficiency and the way she garnered sympathetic support from the nurses and doctors, the way she had returned to the hospital even after I had told her to stay home, though it had taken a cab ride to bring her back. Most worryingly of all, the websites all said that people with MSBP seem devoted to the children in their care and do not see their behavior as harmful.

She's such a treasure . . .

I stared at the screen. Was this it, the explanation that proved me right, that said that everything Josh and the others had dismissed as delusion driven by guilt and inadequacy was in fact—?

"Everything all right?"

I jumped. Oaklynn was standing in the doorway.

"What?" I said, closing the laptop. "Oh. Yes. Sorry, you startled me."

Oaklynn gave me an odd look, that catlike watchfulness settling unreadably into her face.

"The girls are asleep," she said. "I'm going to turn in."

"Sure," I said with false brightness. "Great. Thanks. Sleep well."

Her hesitation was momentary, her gaze blank, but it chilled me, and I suddenly could not wait for her to leave any longer.

"I guess I'll head up, too," I said, getting quickly to my feet, the laptop clamped to my chest like a shield. I turned my back on her, muttering, "Night" as I headed for the stairs, forcing myself to walk, not run, albeit briskly, and not making eye contact with the nanny, who I knew was watching me all the way.

Chapter Forty-One

Nadine sat in the dark with her laptop and Mr. Quietly on the bed beside her, typing, typing, typing. Again, the screen lit her face from below so that she looked like a kid on Halloween trying to scare her friends. In the shadows, she looked squat and ghoulish and knew it. She had never been what you would call attractive, had never turned heads like her sister might have. The only man who had ever been interested in her was Carl, and God knew that hadn't been about attraction. Still, she had liked the attention for a time, looking past his many, many faults until his casual cruelties had become too much to bear, and the darkness inside him had finally revealed itself.

She wondered if beautiful people realized the way others saw them, the extra license they attracted, the resentment they earned, and wondered which they thought they deserved. Both? Neither? She pictured Anna and Josh, Mary Beth and Kurt, but the thought originated in what she had been writing, and she added it to the chapter, working the rumination into the character's head. *It works*, she thought, or at least it did to her, who shared her protagonist's confused and jaundiced view of the world. She wasn't sure what other people would make of it, but that was one of the reasons she had an agent, to help her see how ordinary readers would respond to the things that emerged from her head.

Emerged? Maybe that wasn't the word. Perhaps it was more like the things that her head *produced*, like a great clockwork engine, turning dispassionately over, cogs and springs ticking, adjusting and resetting, as words were stamped and minted on the screen. Or maybe it was less mechanical and more organic: the things that slithered from her brain, the words that uncoiled, pulsing on the screen like strange and amorphous sea creatures from deep, cold waters . . .

Well, we'll see, she thought.

She opened her email, attached the chapter, and wrote,

Dear Anna,

I've made some changes to this section. See what you think. I hope to have a final chapter to you soon. Good luck with all the nanny weirdness.

Best,
Ben Lodging

Chapter Forty-Two

ANNA

After the way he had made me feel stupid and belittled my concerns in front of our friends, then had professed not to understand why I was upset when we got home, I said nothing to Josh and spent the night on the floor of Veronica's room. I lay there, wondering why he seemed to be giving Oaklynn the benefit of the doubt, taking her side even when I thought she was endangering our children. It made no sense. Yes, he thought I overreacted to things, and he didn't always grasp the strength of my feelings, but this seemed out of character.

It worried me.

The next day, it rained, a cold and constant drizzle, so Oaklynn stayed in with the girls, and I sat in my study, trying to be inconspicuous, listening to the sound of their play. I was also stalling, trying to decide whether to risk making my calls on the home phone or not. Whatever else Oaklynn was, she was clever, and I did not want to tip my hand just yet. The bedroom was where I would get the most privacy, but the phone in there only worked about a quarter of the time, and I didn't want to change locations in the middle of my calls. At last, I made my excuses and said I was going to the Myers Park library. I didn't want to leave the house, leave the girls alone with her, but I had no choice.

I got into the car, my hands trembling. I had to be fast. I couldn't stay away along . . .

I drove to the library parking lot, where there was a decent wireless signal, parked, and made my calls, which I did with my laptop open on the passenger seat beside me. Jill Cavendish answered on the third ring. She sounded polite but a little stiff, as if expecting me to be a sales call for which she didn't have the time.

"Hi, Mrs. Cavendish?" I said. "This is Anna Klein. I spoke to you a few months ago before I hired Oaklynn Durst."

Mrs. Cavendish's manner changed immediately, as if a light inside her had been turned on, a light I could hear.

"Oh, Oaklynn! Of course. How is she?"

She sounded keen, solicitous, and very slightly pitying.

"She's well," I said. "She's working for me now."

"You must love her," she said.

"Yes," I said, feeling suddenly stupid. What was I doing? "She's wonderful."

"Isn't she? I'm so glad to hear she's doing well."

There it was again, that note of concern.

"Were you worried she wouldn't be?" I said, trying to sound casual.

"No, not really," said Jill Cavendish. "But you know. The world can be hard on good people. What was it you wanted to ask me about?"

I nearly lost my nerve, but I swallowed, watching an old woman in a camel-hair coat as she emerged from the library and peered at me while walking to her little beige car, as if I were doing something suspicious and might need reporting.

"I was just wondering if the kids had any issues with her . . . ?"

"Dot and Max just loved her."

"Sure. Yes. And they were always, you know, healthy when she was looking after them?"

"Healthy?"

My heart seemed to be pulsing in my throat.

"Right. They didn't get sick or hurt . . . ?"

"Hurt?" She sounded more than confused now, wary. "What is this about?"

"Nothing," I said airily. "So there were no medical issues with the kids?"

"Oaklynn was always wonderful with the kids when they were sick. As good as a trained nurse."

She sounded defensive, but I couldn't let the moment go.

"So the kids *did* get sick?"

"No more than usual. Minor stuff. Colds. Bumps and bruises."

"Nothing requiring visits to the hospital?"

"No more than usual, no."

"Usual? You mean checkups?"

"Well, Max has some issues requiring more frequent visits to the doctor than some kids, but she was always very attentive to his needs. The hospital staff thought she was an exemplary caregiver."

"What kind of issues?"

"He was very premature," she said, her voice clipped, brittle. "He has some breathing issues, some learning disabilities . . . I'm sorry, I don't see the relevance of any of this, and I have rather a lot to do today."

"Yes," I said. "I'm really sorry for disturbing you. You've been very helpful."

But she'd gone. I couldn't really blame her. And I had learned nothing. Given what I had read about Munchausen's by proxy, it was possible that Oaklynn had gotten some kind of fix from tending to a child with long-term health issues. Perhaps it had fed her need for medical attention, the sense of being an essential helper to little Max, but if Jill Cavendish had ever suspected her of somehow making the boy's symptoms worse for her own twisted ends, she had buried such suspicions completely. More likely, she'd never had them.

Again, I wondered what on earth I was doing. All this because I'd seen a screwdriver in Oaklynn's bag? I blew out a long sigh and resolved to finish things quickly.

I called Clara Hubert, who lived in Portland, mother of Janice and Arthur, almost hoping that she wouldn't answer. She did, and I went through the same idiotic obfuscation while I tossed my lure into the water and watched for ripples.

"Medical issues?" said Clara, who was positively bubbly despite the fact that it was ridiculously early on the West Coast. "No, nothing like that. Quite the contrary, actually."

"How so?"

"She was quite the hero in our house, Oaklynn."

"Really?" I said, already keen to get off the call. "Why was that?"

"One time there was a problem with the babysitter."

"A babysitter?"

"We gave Oaklynn one night off each week. Usually, it was easy to work around her schedule—mostly church stuff, you know, but this one time she had a Bible study meeting on the same night Mark and I had a gala-dinner thing connected to his work, which we just couldn't miss. So we got a local high school girl to babysit. A neighbor. I should have known better, but what are you going to do? We didn't have a lot of options. The girl meant well, but . . ."

"What happened?" I asked, my curiosity piqued.

"Oaklynn went out for the evening and left the babysitter in charge. When she came home, the babysitter was downstairs playing with Arthur, but there was no sign of Janice. Turns out, the girl had left her alone in the bath. Only one year old, and she'd left her unattended! Well, Oaklynn goes running upstairs and finds my daughter under the water. Not breathing. She gets her out, calls an ambulance, and performs mouth-to-mouth—you know, CPR, the whole bit. Basically brought her back from the dead. Straight up saved her life. That's what the doctors said."

"Wow," I said, straightening up in the car seat and staring ahead at the library walls, unseeing. "And when she went up to the bathroom, the babysitter was still downstairs?"

"Exactly," said Clara, as if this made things still more impressive. "Didn't think to come up until five minutes later. Found Oaklynn breathing life back into my drowned daughter's body right there on the tiles. Scared me to death, I can tell you. From that night on, we never had a babysitter but Oaklynn. Well, you wouldn't, would you?"

"No," I said. "You wouldn't."

Chapter Forty-Three

Josh knew that Anna had been waiting for him in the kitchen as soon as he walked in. He saw it in her eyes and the way she seemed to be listening out for Oaklynn downstairs.

Christ, he thought. *Not more of this. Not today.*

"I called her references," she said, after theatrically making sure they were alone.

"And?"

"Nothing certain, but one had a kid with health issues, and one said she saved her daughter from drowning in the bath. But here's the thing. No one else was there at the time. Oaklynn might just as well have held her under the water so that she could get credit for saving her."

"Anna," said Josh wearily.

"I'm serious, Josh."

"That's what worries me! This is nuts, Anna. Everyone thinks so. Oaklynn is the best thing that has happened to us in ages. You said it yourself."

"That was before."

"Nothing has changed."

"Tell that to the ER."

"It was an accident, Anna. You have no evidence to suggest it had anything to do with Oaklynn. None."

"I don't need any!" his wife shot back. "This isn't a court of law, Josh. This is my house. I don't need a reason to fire her if I'm not happy with her work."

"And are you? All this crazy stuff aside, are you happy with her work? Because if you aren't, you've never said so."

"Why do you always take her side?"

"What? I don't!"

"You do. Is it a pity thing? The need to look after the well-meaning Mormon? Mary Beth is right about you: you always have to play the white knight."

"What's that supposed to mean?"

"What it says, Josh. Maybe you could take my side for once. Stand up for me. But no. It's always, 'Oaklynn is so great. Such a treasure.' You know how fucking sick I am of hearing that?"

Anna's voice had gone up, and Josh reflexively put a finger to his lips. It was a mistake.

"You're afraid she'll hear?" said Anna, disbelieving. "You're afraid my anxieties about my children's lives might be embarrassing to her?"

"Our children's lives."

"What?"

"You said *my children*," said Josh. "Meaning yours. They are ours."

"Right," Anna snapped. "Because you are always around to help out with them."

"I work, Anna."

"So do I, Josh!"

"Which is why we need Oaklynn," he shot back in a stage whisper. "So unless you have real evidence . . ."

"You think I'm delusional," said Anna.

"No."

"Then what? Why do you keep taking her side? What does she have on you?"

The question seemed to catch Anna off guard as much as it did Josh, but she saw the weight of it land in his face. Her mouth fell open.

"Oh my God," she said. "She does. She knows something that you don't want me to find out!"

"She doesn't," said Josh, opting for bluster, but he couldn't hold her gaze and opened the fridge, ostensibly to get himself a beer.

"Oh my God," she said again. "What is it?"

"I told you: nothing."

"You're lying. I sensed it before, but I wasn't sure. Now . . . Josh? Look at me."

He turned reluctantly, closing the fridge and holding the beer bottle by the neck.

"What?" he said.

She looked at him then, read him like she used to, studying his face like it was a book she knew forward and backward. Her eyes narrowed slightly, as if trying to focus on some distant detail and then relaxed again, though she looked suddenly sad and tired.

"You're having an affair," she said. "I wondered. With Mary Beth."

Josh blinked, genuinely surprised.

"What?" he said. "No. Are you kidding? No. *Mary Beth?*"

Anna looked momentarily confused but not relieved.

"Then who?" she said.

"I'm not having an affair!"

"Then what is it?"

Josh looked down, his defenses buckling in the face of her determination and the grief she was just managing to keep back. He moved to the kitchen island without speaking, opened his beer, and took a long pull.

"Sit down," he said.

It was time. He didn't want it to be, and he wasn't ready, but it was time. Anna watched him, suddenly anxious, moving to the seat opposite him in what looked like a stunned haze. Her breathing was so shallow, she might have been holding it. She said nothing, but for all her former defiance, she suddenly looked young and hunted, almost meek.

He waited, took another long slug of beer, then laid both palms down on the counter between them, fingers splayed.

"So," he said at last, "I'm in some trouble at work."

Anna frowned, as if unable to process what he had said.

"What kind of trouble?" she asked.

"Kurt—I can't believe I did this," he began, adding the parenthetical almost to himself. "Kurt was diverting funds from some of his biggest clients. Small amounts at first. Investing them into undisclosed stocks, and then, when the stocks appreciated, keeping what he had made for himself and replacing the principal in his clients' accounts. He said it was a kind of bonus. The clients didn't lose any money, and they didn't know he had made anything off their money that hadn't been disclosed."

"What does this have to do with us?"

Not you, he noted with a lance of bitter pain. *Us.* He was telling her how much he had jeopardized their future, and she had immediately thrown her lot in with him, their previous row and the weeks of tension instantly forgotten.

"I saw the accounts," he said. "Realized what he was doing. I should have blown the whistle on him right away, but . . . well, it's Kurt. So I said nothing. Just told him to cut it out before someone noticed. But you know Kurt. He figures everything is sort of a game, and as long as he doesn't get caught . . ."

"So he kept doing it."

"I told him to quit. I really did. Not right away, but I did tell him. He offered me an in. A chance to make some money."

"Illegally."

"Right."

"Tell me you didn't."

"I didn't."

"But you took your time to decide and didn't speak to me about it."

"I was trying to keep you out of it," he said. Suddenly it all seemed so stupid and humiliating. "And there's more."

She waited, saying nothing, barely moving.

"The reason I hesitated before telling him no," he said. "I lost some money."

"Company money?"

"No," he said, swallowing. "Our money. The Wells Fargo savings. I made a bad investment."

"How much?"

"It was a tech stock. Made microprocessors. Looked like they were about to land a huge military deal . . ."

"How much?"

He bit his lip.

"Forty," he said.

"Thousand?"

"About that."

She almost smiled at that, a mirthless, stunned smile at her own idiocy. It stopped him in his tracks.

"Closer to fifty," he said, all pretense abandoned, shrinking in his chair. "I thought that maybe Kurt's thing would help me replace the money before anyone noticed."

"Me."

It was as if he had folded in on himself under the weight of that one syllable, but he held her eyes and nodded.

"Yes. I was trying to . . . I just thought you had so much going on and . . . I know I should have."

"So you waited. You didn't get in on the action, but you didn't report him to Vasquez or anyone while you decided if it was worth the risk."

"Right."

"And then he got caught."

Josh sighed.

"It might have been OK," he said, "but the Doherty file was being restructured. Their accountants noticed an anomaly. Just a small discrepancy in the accounts. But when they pulled on one thread, the whole thing unraveled. The file history showed that I had looked at the account, that I'd seen what Kurt had done. It would have been worse if I'd tried to delete my access history, but I wasn't trying to do anything criminal. I was, I guess, evasive. Tried to stay out of it. But the bank forced the issue, said I had to testify against him or face more serious charges myself. I agreed to tell them everything this morning."

"It might have been OK?"

"What?"

"You said it might have been OK till this Doherty file thing," said Anna. "How was it going to be OK, Josh? For how long? You think this was going to go unnoticed?"

"I guess not."

"And this all happened when?"

"I first became aware of it back in May. The company started poking around at the end of August."

He watched her doing the math in her head—the weeks and months that had gone by before he had told her anything. For a long, painful moment, she was rigidly silent, staring at him.

"Right," she said at last. She seemed quite calm, exasperated, for sure, but quiet, levelheaded, as if the worst of the matter had passed and she was now focused on solutions. "How much are we talking, Josh? What did Kurt make?"

"A couple hundred K."

"Jesus."

"I know. But I got none of it. Like I said, I didn't even try to hide the fact that I'd seen what he was doing. I mean, I guess I couldn't deny it, but still. My only real fault was not stepping forward."

"Your only fault? You blew fifty grand of our savings without discussing it with me, then kept it a secret from me for months, and you think not coming clean on Kurt's get-rich-quick bullshit was your only fault?"

"It was supposed to be a surprise."

She laughed at that, a wry, hard laugh frosted with a bitterness he had rarely heard from her.

"Well, I guess I got that, all right," she said.

He looked at the countertop.

"I'm sorry, Anna."

"What's going to happen?"

"Not sure. We'll both be disciplined. Penalized. Kurt more than me."

"Will you keep your jobs?"

"Don't know yet. There's an internal audit first. Then we talk to the companies involved and see what they want to do. If we're lucky, they'll be satisfied with remuneration and the promise it won't happen again."

"And if they aren't?"

"Then it goes to the SEC, and we'll lose our positions for sure. Kurt will never work in finance again. May face jail time. Me? I don't know, but I'm helping the investigation, so I may be OK."

"And how are you and Kurt?"

"We were fine until the barbecue, but I had to make a choice, and I made it today. I called Kurt first thing and told him I would be cooperating fully with the inquiry."

"So you're not fine now?"

"He understands that I covered for him as long as I could but that it had to happen eventually."

"And Mary Beth?"

He sighed and shook his head.

"She's less forgiving," said Anna, reading his look. "You should have told me. All of it. But God, Josh, fifty grand and you said *nothing?*"

"I know," he said. "I thought maybe we could fix it without anyone finding out. I didn't want to disappoint you or stress you out."

"You should have told me."

"You couldn't have done anything. I couldn't do anything."

"Even so."

"Yes," he said. "I know. It was just so . . . humiliating. I couldn't stand to tell you."

"I would have stood by you," she said. The sentiment was well-meaning, even tender, but her tone was full of cold fury.

"I know."

"Apparently not."

"It was just that the longer it went on, the harder it got. I kept waiting for you to look at the accounts. Almost wished you would. But I told Vasquez about the bad investment, and then Kurt and I were sworn not to discuss the matter while the firm went through its internal investigation to see exactly what laws had been broken and what they wanted to do about it."

"Did Mary Beth know?"

He nodded, mute. Ashamed.

"Kurt told her as soon as he got caught. She went with us to the company hearing in New York because he had diverted money into her account. That made her complicit."

"She must have loved that."

"No kidding. I think they'll split up when the dust settles."

This was a new surprise to Anna, greater than the details of the financial mess.

"Seriously?"

"You know what they're like," said Josh. "Barely able to keep from clawing each other's eyes out at the best of times. If Kurt is no longer bringing home the bacon . . ."

Anna nodded vaguely, suddenly sad again.

"I'm sorry," said Josh again. "I should have told you."

"Among other things."

He gritted his teeth and looked at the counter, but just said yes again.

"And Oaklynn knew?" said Anna, almost as if it was an after-thought, a memory of a previous conversation inserting itself into the present.

"At least some of it," said Josh. "I'm not sure how. She suggested she'd overheard something between me and Kurt or Mary Beth. Said she didn't want to make trouble."

"Is that right?" said Anna, frosty again.

"I don't think she meant anything by it."

"But you have been taking her side, consciously or otherwise, as if you were afraid to upset her."

"I really didn't mean . . ."

"Like I said, consciously or otherwise."

"Right. So now what?"

"With Oaklynn? Nothing, I guess. This isn't evidence of anything involving her. Neither is anything else, as you all keep reminding me."

He heard the stung sense of being ridiculed in the remark.

"It wasn't a conspiracy, you know, Anna. Like the three of us confiding or whatever. Pushing you away."

"No, I don't know that, Josh," said Anna. "It sounds like that's exactly what it was."

He opened his mouth to protest but knew it was fruitless and sagged. The beer bottle, untouched since he had begun his story, sweated, making rivulets on the countertop.

"I'm going to go to bed," she said.

"I'm really sorry, Anna."

"Yeah," she said. "I know."

Chapter Forty-Four

ANNA

I went to see Mary Beth the following day. I hadn't planned it, and a part of me thought it would be better to let things lie for a while, but I couldn't get any work done with the knowledge of this thing hanging over me, so I told Oaklynn I was stepping out and headed over to number 16. There was no immediate response to my bell ringing. I had started to turn away when the door was snatched open. Mary Beth stood in the door wearing pale green yoga sweats, her face drawn, her eyes hard.

"Yes?" she snapped.

I recoiled but managed to find the spirit in which I had left the house.

"Josh told me," I said. "I just wanted to check in. See how you guys were doing . . ."

"Gloat, you mean?" said Mary Beth.

I felt stung at the injustice of the remark but just shook my head.

"I wanted to know if I could help," I said.

"Too bad you didn't discuss that with your goody-goody husband a few weeks ago," she shot back.

"I'm sure Josh didn't mean . . ."

"Like I care what he *meant*. We're going to get screwed, and he'll get a slap on the wrist."

"Well, I don't understand all the details," I said, "but it doesn't seem like Josh did anything wrong exactly . . ."

"Oh, so Kurt's the villain, and Josh is the white knight again, huh?"

"What? No!"

"Yeah, well, that's about right, actually. Except that Kurt's more moron than villain, and Josh isn't so much the knight in shining armor than he is the idiot bystander who doesn't stick up for his friend."

"Kurt *stole* from people, Mary Beth," I said. This wasn't going the way I had planned it. "And Josh kept his secret."

"Well, no surprises that you'd take his side."

"He's my husband, and he's not the one at fault here. In fact, it was his friendship with Kurt that made him risk getting in trouble himself."

"By not turning his best buddy in to be disciplined and fired, you mean?"

"No! Well, yeah, I guess. Mary Beth, can we talk inside?"

"I should have known people like you wouldn't understand real loyalty. I bet if we'd been Asian, you'd have covered for us."

I stared at her, my mouth open, completely dumbfounded.

"What?" she shot back, radiating defiance as if she wanted to swing a clawed fist at me. "That too near the knuckle for you, Miss Nihon Princess?"

I shook my head, tears starting to my eyes.

"That's so not true," I managed.

"Yeah? You come down here with your superior New York bullshit and your psycho nanny, looking down your tiny nose at us like we're fucking Mayberry hicks, and you wonder why regular people don't trust you?"

"I never thought . . . ," I stammered.

"Well, you should. Except that you can't see beyond your precious family, can you? Like it's some big achievement to squeeze out a couple of kids. You think having a white servant makes you something? I swear, when that psycho bitch you keep chained up in your basement kills you all in your sleep, don't look to me for sympathy. You've made your bed, now you're going to lie in it."

And with that, she slammed the door.

⌐⌐

I retreated into my study, though I couldn't do anything productive. Mary Beth's words, her *malignance*—for want of a better word—had left me rattled and unsteady. I couldn't think. I certainly couldn't work. But I pretended to, hiding myself away and staring unseeing at the computer as my breathing steadied and my tears dried.

Was I surprised? Not entirely, I supposed, but that somehow made it worse, as if I had turned a blind eye to Mary Beth's meanness, her racism, desperately ignoring it because I had needed a friend who wouldn't invite me to her church or have me over to help her choose color swatches for her drapes . . .

She hadn't deceived me. I had done that all by myself. Now I felt alone, cut off from the sparsely populated neighborhood like I was living on a rock in the middle of a lake. Or an ocean. I had even farmed out my family, outsourced it to a stranger I didn't trust.

As if on cue, there was a knock at the study door.

"Come in," I said, wiping my eyes and turning.

"Do you mind if we go into the backyard?" said Oaklynn. "Vronny is bouncing off the walls. I know it's cold, but . . ."

"Sure," I said, not turning around so she wouldn't see my face.

"Gracie is asleep, and I don't want to wake her."

"It's fine," I said, managing not to yell. "I can keep an ear open for the monitor. Veronica could use some undivided attention for once."

"Are you sure? We won't be out more than a half hour or so. Vronny really wants to go on the swing."

"It's fine," I said again. "Go ahead."

I managed not to make it sound like I was telling her to leave me alone. Or I thought so, at least.

When she went downstairs, I listened to their preparations for going into the garden, the fussing with shoes and coats and gloves. When I heard them head down to the basement and the back door into the yard, I moved silently into Grace's room, where I could watch them unseen from the window. Grace was sleeping soundly, her little chest rising and falling with each breath. She had shown no signs of fever or vomiting since that second hospital visit. I sat beside the crib, listening to the distant, muted sound of girlish laughter in the yard. Veronica. I glanced down as she got onto the swing and then, as Oaklynn began to push her, glanced back to Grace, thinking about money and Josh and Mary Beth's unspeakable and unexpected malice. I was still trembling slightly. Outside, Veronica's scream of delight turned into something else. It was a high, shrill sound, almost a wail.

It went on a second too long.

And suddenly, I knew it wasn't laughter at all. It was a keening cry of pain that sent me spilling out of my chair and back to the window. The soft yellow curtains were still half-closed, but I yanked them apart, seizing the sash of the window and forcing it up.

Oaklynn was standing over Veronica, who was lying awkwardly on the ground beneath the swing set, her bandaged right hand clamped to her left forearm just below the elbow. One of the chains of the swing seemed longer than usual. Then I realized it looked that way because the seat was hanging straight down, disconnected from the chain hanging from the frame above.

I thrust my head out of the open window.

"What happened?" I shouted, though I already guessed.

"The chain broke," Oaklynn called back. She looked anguished, her face pink and shocked. Veronica had stopped screaming and had started to moan and rock back and forth, clutching her arm. "She landed on her elbow. There was nothing I could . . . The chain just snapped, and . . . I think her arm is broken."

It was. I went out into the yard and told Oaklynn to get Grace and a few things for Veronica. Once she was in the house, I examined the break in the chain, kneeling beside my injured daughter, who was now sitting up and keeping very still, cradling her broken arm against her chest. There was no rust on the chain where it should have hooked to the swing's seat. The broken end of the link was smooth—cut almost all the way through cleanly—and beside the cut, there was the rough burring made by what I took to be a hacksaw blade that hadn't yet found its groove.

I said nothing to Veronica, but I wasn't about to leave Grace alone with Oaklynn while I went to the hospital. We would all go to the hospital together. I think Oaklynn saw the pale fury in my face as we drove, but she said nothing, as if sensing something coming beyond the trauma of dealing with Veronica's injury. After we had checked in to the ER, I insisted on taking both girls back with me, despite the suggestions of the nurse that I should leave Grace with Oaklynn who—tellingly, guiltily—did not attempt to make a case for herself. I sat with them both until the X-rays were done and the arm—with its hairline fibula fracture—was braced and set.

My anger felt like the burning charcoal at Mary Beth's idiot cook-out: undramatic but searing hot. I needed no further evidence. I didn't care what Josh or Mary Beth or anyone else thought. I was sure, and that was almost a relief.

I returned to the waiting room to find Oaklynn teary and being hugged by the blonde nurse we had met before. The sight of her being comforted for what she had done to my child relit the furnace of the rage that had been smoldering within me. I marched over to her, seeing nothing else in the place, barely conscious of the way the staff stared at me with something like horror as they read my face.

"You're fired," I said. I managed to keep my voice down, though my hands were trembling. "I want you out of the house today. You can collect your belongings later. You should expect to hear from the police as well."

"I didn't do it!" she protested, tears pouring down her face. "I wouldn't. I love Veronica!"

"You're done, Oaklynn. We're done."

Chapter Forty-Five

Officer Paul Randall parked cruiser number 177 on the street, checking the GPS against his notes and peering at the numbers on the scattered houses. There were more vacant lots on Settle Road than there were houses, and though Randall had been patrolling these neighborhoods for three years now, he didn't think he had ever been down here before. Didn't know, in fact, that it even existed. It was tucked away between Brandon Circle and the creek—Sugar Creek, he thought, maybe Briar—a weird little wooded pocket only about three miles from the center of uptown. He got out of the car looking north for the skyscrapers—a new one going up every year, or so it seemed—that dotted the area around Trade and Tryon and made Charlotte feel like a real honest-to-God city, but there was nothing. Just trees.

He took the tablet computer from its stand in the vehicle and approached the front door of the house, moving between a Camry and a tree with silvery bark that he thought was probably a cherry. It was bare now, though some of the other deciduous trees in the Kleins' yard still held their leaves, mostly shades of brown, but with a couple of small maples that were red and glossy.

Deciduous, he thought, liking the word.

The front door was atop a half dozen stone steps, and there was more stonework around the door, though the sides of the house were finished in beige stucco. Randall considered the house as if it were about to give evidence, then rang the bell, stepping back from the window beside it so that the owner would get the full impression of his uniform. The residents of Myers Park weren't always fond of black men showing up at their doors. He put on his serious face and listened to the hurried footsteps inside.

Anna Klein was dressed in slim jeans and a hooded sweatshirt, the sleeves pushed up to the elbows. She was surely a rarity in this Waspy neighborhood and cute in a harried, high-maintenance way, though he was careful to keep both thoughts out of his face.

"Mrs. Klein?" he said, showing his badge unnecessarily. "I'm Officer Randall, Charlotte PD. We met in the hospital after the incident with the slide? I wonder if you had a moment to discuss the charges you made at the hospital earlier today against one"—he paused to check his notes—"Oaklynn Durst."

"Sure," she said. "Thanks. Come in."

She had no accent he could detect, though he'd reassess that after they chatted a bit. Randall was proud of his ability to pinpoint accents.

Anna Klein led him into a sitting room, where he took a place on a leather couch across a glass-topped coffee table from her after she ushered the elder daughter out, asking her to play upstairs for a while. The girl had been drawing clumsily with crayons, and she looked at him wonderingly, heading on up with obvious reluctance only when her mother's voice got taut as she repeated the request.

It wasn't just her voice that seemed tight, stretched to a breaking point. Mrs. Klein had her hair pulled back and kept rubbing her forehead as if in pain, and she sat stiffly, arms and legs braced like she was poised to rocket out of the chair. In spite of her casual clothes, she looked severe and stressed-out. Randall decided to take it easy.

"Nice neighborhood," he remarked. "You have a lovely home."

"Thanks," she said, not meeting his eyes.

"How's your daughter feeling?"

"Not too bad, considering."

She had no interest in small talk.

OK, then . . .

"So you reported your former housekeeper . . ."

"Nanny."

"Right," he said. Knowing no one who had either, he wasn't sure of the difference. "Oaklynn Durst."

"Yes."

"And you also fired her."

"Yes."

"And you think she willfully set out to hurt your daughter."

"Yes. Several times. Most recently, she cut through the link on the swing set. I'll show you."

"That would be great," said Randall. "But before we do that, why don't you tell me about this person? Oaklynn. Unusual name."

"She's from Utah," said Mrs. Klein, as if that meant something. "Mormon. They have unusual names sometimes."

"OK," said Randall. "I didn't know that."

She gave him a quick, hard look, as if what he'd said made him stupid.

"I have her file here," she said, the look melting away so that he thought he might have misread it. He didn't like interrogating good-looking women. It made him self-conscious. She opened a laptop on the chair beside her, clicked a couple of things, then turned it around and put it on the table, facing him.

"Her file?" said Randall, leaning forward to examine it.

"From when I hired her. I got her through an agency in Salt Lake City called Nurture. This is her profile."

Randall scrolled through it in silence.

"Can you email this to me?" he said.

"Sure."

He fished in his pocket for a card and pushed it across the table toward her, like he was dealing blackjack.

"And you have no idea where she might have gone now?"

"No. She had no friends or family in the area. But when we got back from the hospital this afternoon, all her stuff was gone. She must have packed very fast."

"Did she have a vehicle?"

"No. She had talked about getting one, but she used my car."

"And she'd been with you . . . ?"

"Since August."

"And in that time, you had reason to think she wanted to hurt your children?"

The question seemed to disarm her. For a second, her hard, businesslike exterior buckled, and she looked fragile and unsure of herself.

"I'm not sure what her motivation was," she said. "Most of the time, she seemed to really like the girls . . ."

"You have two?"

"Veronica, who you saw, and Grace. She just turned one."

"And the first incidents concerned Grace, yes?"

"That's right."

She told him of the hospital visits, the unexplained fevers, and the GI issues, and though he already had all that from the hospital report and the report she'd made to the duty cop there, he let her tell him all again, alert for nuance, for the emotional content of her story, and for any sign that she might be making it up. Spite against former employees was not unknown. Sometimes it was about wages the employer didn't feel like paying. Sometimes it was personal. Based on the pictures of this Oaklynn Durst, he doubted she posed much of a threat to the lithe Asian woman in front of him where the interests of her husband were concerned, but what the hell did he know? It took all sorts, and Randall had seen enough on the job to know that there was no rhyme or reason where sex was concerned. In fact, he suspected, it would be simpler than that. The precinct got daily calls from Myers Park—some old money, some new—reporting their Mexican cleaners for stealing earrings and going through purses. They screamed bloody murder right up to the time the missing shit was found, set down in the wrong drawer or locked away in a safe by the indignant homeowner who, more than half the time, still fired the cleaner.

So Randall listened and took notes with a bland, sympathetic look on his face, even as he weighed his own cautious doubts. When she was done outlining her own experience with the Durst woman, she started recounting incidents involving the nanny in her previous places of employment with other families.

"I'm sorry," he cut in. "You knew about these events before you hired her?"

"No. I just found out."

"How?"

"I called them."

"You called the families who had employed Ms. Durst before?"

"That's right."

"Why did you do that?"

"I was starting to feel like something was off with her. I wanted to know if there had been incidents with her previous employers."

"These people listed as her references?"

"Yes."

"And there were?"

"Yes. One involved a kid almost drowning in the bath."

"These people thought their children's lives were in danger from Ms. Durst, but they still wrote her letters of recommendation?"

She hesitated.

"They didn't realize she was responsible," she said.

"But you did. Even though you weren't there, and some of these events took place years ago."

He tried to sound neutral when he said it, but it was impossible not to sound skeptical.

"They couldn't see the pattern I was seeing," she said. She knew it sounded weak and looked away. "I know it sounds crazy. They still liked her. But that was Oaklynn. She made people like her, but she was hiding who she really was. The woman whose daughter nearly drowned thought Oaklynn was a hero who had saved her child. It just didn't occur to her that maybe Oaklynn engineered the event *in order* to play the hero. That's what she gets off on: gratitude, praise, everyone saying how wonderful she is. Especially nurses. Doctors. EMTs. Probably cops as well."

Randall considered this last, wondering if it was supposed to be an accusation, then nodded, still carefully nonjudgmental.

"That's very helpful," he said. "Thanks. Now, how about we take a look at that swing set?"

"Sure," she said, taking up the baby monitor that had been blinking on an end table by the couch. "Let me just tell Veronica that I'll be outside."

"You know," said Randall, glad of the opportunity, "I can find it myself. Let me go take a look, and I'll be right back."

"OK," she said, uncertain. "You can get out through the basement. I'll show you."

She led him down a stairwell that ran through the heart of the house to a complex of rooms.

"This was where Miss Durst lived?" he said.

"Yes."

"Mind if I take a look?"

"Go ahead."

She nodded to the left but made no move to come with him, folding her arms across her chest defensively. Randall went into the bedroom. It was blue, a guest suite left ready for its next visitor. The adjoining bathroom had little hand towels and a basket of untouched toiletries like some Wilmington guesthouse. The only thing even hinting at recent occupancy was a faint odor, part sweet and floral like perfume or soap, and another part fainter still, sour and animal.

"She had a pet?"

"A cat. Mr. Quietly."

Randall gave her a look.

"Sorry," she added. "I should have said."

"It's fine," he said. "And the cat went with her?"

"I assume so. We haven't seen it since she left. The door down to the backyard is through there. If you don't mind, I'm going to check on the girls."

He told her that was fine and picked his way through the gloomy sitting room with its flat-screen TV to where a screen door led out onto a cedar wood deck and a flight of a dozen steps down into the yard. It was a cold day, and he felt the wind bite as he stepped outside. The garden was lower than the street level at the front and sloped down to a fence and then the creek and the tangle of underbrush and trees on the far side. With his back to the house, Randall felt like he was in the woods.

The swing set was a fairly simple affair to the left side of the yard as he faced the brown, sluggish waters of the creek. There were two swings side by side attached by plastic-sheathed chain to a heavy timber crossbeam atop a pair of A-frame uprights. It abutted a little wooden tower with a ladder and a plastic slide. As a kid, Randall would have thought it pretty cool.

He looked it over, tugging on the chains, climbing up onto the tower to examine the housings at the top and the bolts that held them in place. He had just about finished when he heard footsteps on the deck and turned to find Anna Klein descending to meet him.

"You see the saw marks?" she said.

"Where?"

"Right where the seat is disconnected."

"I'm sorry, where is that?"

Randall stepped aside so she could see properly, her face clouding with confusion as she got closer. Both swings were perfectly fine. There was no sign of damage, and they looked perfectly usable, if a little stained with mildew.

"I don't understand," she said, rushing over and tugging experimentally at the chains. "This was broken right here. Cut away. The seat was hanging down."

"It seems OK now."

"It can't be. Someone has . . . I don't understand."

"Miss Klein, is it possible that Veronica simply fell off the swing?" said Randall, taking hold of the chains of the swing in question and, after yanking hard on them, settling into the saddle till it bore his entire weight. "That she just, you know, slipped out of the seat? Then maybe in the confusion, you thought there was something structurally wrong with . . ."

"No!" she shot back, her face suddenly contorted with outrage. "*No.* I saw it! It was *cut*. She did it on purpose. *She* did it!"

Chapter Forty-Six

ANNA

It made no sense. Oaklynn had barely had time to pack and get out before I had gotten home from the hospital. She couldn't also have repaired the swing.

Surely?

And even if she'd had time, why bother? She must have known it wouldn't change my sense of what had happened.

But it would change how many people believed you.

That gave me pause. She was covering her back, preparing for the inevitable investigation that would follow. It was her word against mine.

Not that it mattered much either way. She was gone. Vanished into thin air. But I doubted the cops would take anything I said about the woman seriously. By the time the police officer—Randall—had left my house, it was clear he wasn't going to push the issue. He thought I was a crazy person: just another entitled Myers Park housewife with too much time on her hands and a conviction that the world should revolve around her.

I called Nurture, not because I thought they could do anything or that they would have a current location for her, but because I needed to yell at someone who had no option but to listen. And I wanted them to know that they had sent me a psychopath and that their screening methods were garbage. So I laid out what had happened to a reception-ist called Britney, then to a manager called Alice, who spoke in calm, measured, and carefully sympathetic tones that said she understood all my concerns but promised nothing and took no responsibility for anything. For my part, speaking out of frustration and a mad desire to crack their professional placidity, I told her they should expect to hear from my lawyer.

I didn't have a lawyer, but they didn't know that. And maybe I'd get one just for this. Oaklynn was gone, but someone ought to pay for what had happened and for what *might* have happened had it been allowed to go on.

How far would the escalation have gone? Just how much would Oaklynn have risked to satisfy whatever sick urge she was feeding?

It was too terrible to think about.

~

Oaklynn's key still sat on the floor of the hall where it had fallen when she, presumably, had pushed it through the letter box. I didn't know if she had taken a cab or walked to the bus, dragging her suitcases after her, and I didn't know where she had gone. I also didn't care. She was gone, and that was all that mattered.

I picked up the key, telling Veronica I would get her a cup of juice as soon as I had gotten Grace changed, and stood for a moment, absorb-ing the silence of the house. Our house. Oaklynn was gone, and it was just us again. The experiment, if that was what it had been, was over.

"We could try another nanny," said Josh. He had left work early as soon as he got my call recounting what had happened.

"No," I said, flat and final. "I don't want another person in my house."

He watched me thoughtfully, and I knew he was wondering whether to say something about rethinking the matter when the dust had settled, when I wasn't quite so emotional, but he knew better than to say it. Even so, I give him a long look and waited till he nodded and looked sheepishly away. I didn't like playing for points with my husband the way some couples do, but it was going to be a while before he questioned my judgment about anything to do with the girls.

"What do you want for dinner?" I said. "I haven't had a chance to think about it."

"Of course," he said quickly. "As long as it's not Tuscan chicken, I don't care."

I bridled, then gave him a bleak smile.

"You sure you're going to be OK this week?" he said.

I shrugged and made a face, half-dismissive, half-baffled, then realized what he was talking about.

"You're away again?" I said. He winced at the exasperated annoyance in my tone, but I couldn't help it.

"From Wednesday," he said. "I told you last week, remember?"

"No," I snapped. "Yes. I guess. It slipped my mind what with—"

"I can cancel," he said.

"No. You can't."

He hung his head. He was in the doghouse as much at work as he was with me, and there was no point in pretending otherwise.

"Not really," he agreed.

"It's fine. I'll be fine. Give me a chance to be with the girls by ourselves. Calm down. Get used to this . . . new normal."

Life without Oaklynn. Nightmare though she had turned out to be, day-to-day functioning was going to be harder without her.

"What about your work?" asked Josh.

"Let me worry about my work," I said. Again, I saw the tightness in his face at my tone and relented. "Sorry. It's just going to be hard for a while, but talking about it won't make it any easier."

"Could have been worse."

"Yeah, Josh, it really could, but thinking about that doesn't make me feel any better either."

"OK."

"I'm just saying."

"I said OK," he replied. "How about we order pizza or something? I think we've earned an easy night."

"OK," I said.

But the night wasn't easy. A little before three in the morning, I woke to a familiar, haunting chorus that came cycling through my dreams of Oaklynn like some ancient alarm.

The wolf-voiced coyotes were back.

For a second, I was too stricken with dread, with an ominous sense of terrible things about to happen, and then I was tugging at Josh, dragging him out of unconsciousness so that he woke sputtering and irritated.

"What?" he demanded, but then he heard them, too, and his eyes widened.

He got up quickly, decisively, and went to the closet, emerging a moment later with something large and ungainly in his hands. It took me a second to realize that it was the crossbow. My mind was too full of the yipping howls that had broken out all around the house.

"My God, they sound so close!" Josh breathed, stepping into the bathroom so he could look down through the window into the back-yard. I resisted the urge to follow him, going instead into the hallway and down to the door of Vronny's room. I put my hand gently on the handle and listened.

Nothing at first, then another momentary round of yapping barks from the coyotes and a single looping howl that sounded much farther away. It rose like a ball thrown high and long, then fell as it tailed away into nothing.

I stood for a long time, eyes squeezed shut, listening for more, or for any signs of distress from the girls, but there was nothing. A minute or two later, Josh emerged from the bedroom in his shorts. He had put the crossbow down and looked like a bad actor who didn't know what to do with his hands.

"It's OK," he said. "They're gone."

For now, I thought, forcing myself to nod and smile while he gushed about how cool it was.

For now.

The next day was hard. Vronny kept finding new ways to ask if there was a way Oaklynn might come back, and the third time—when she suggested selling some of her less used toys, as if this might somehow compensate for the inconvenience—I snapped at her and told her Oaklynn had gone because she didn't really want to be here, an unworthy distortion I immediately regretted. Veronica gave me a wide-eyed stare, her face contorted as the tears built up.

"Miss Oaklynn didn't like it here?" she said.

"She loved it here, Vronny," I said, squatting down and getting hold of her shoulders so I could look her steadily in the eye. It was something I'd seen Oaklynn do countless times, and the gesture felt both labored and borrowed, so I dropped my eyes and talked to the carpet. "She loved you. But she had some problems she couldn't fix here. That's why she had to go."

"So when she's fixed her problems, she maybe could come back?"

I looked at her, feeling defeated, spineless.

"Maybe," I said. "If she gets everything taken care of. But for now, it's just us, OK? And I need you to help me with Gracie. Think you can do that?"

Veronica nodded solemnly, as if assigned a sacred trust, and I thanked her, feeling duplicitous. It was, I thought spitefully, part of Oaklynn's special talent that even in her absence and disgrace, she'd managed to make me feel like a bad mother.

And the truth was that I did need Vronny's help with Gracie. Over the last few months, I had lost track of all that Oaklynn had done routinely and unbidden, taking on chores and responsibilities far in excess of what she had technically been employed to do. When Vronny announced that we were out of her favorite cereal, I had—to my shame—to ask her what it was and promise to get more.

"And don't forget the strawberries," said Vronny.

"Strawberries?"

"Honey Nut Cheerios with strawberries, Mommy," she said, mock-scolding me, as if nothing could be more self-evident. "Cut up small and with no leaves on them."

"Right," I said. "Sure."

So we drove down to the Harris Teeter at Morrocroft Village, the one Oaklynn had said had the *best selection in the area*, a phrase Veronica pronounced like it was the word of an oracle. I had forgotten what a production shopping with two young children could be. The parking lot was just about full, and the oversize carts with the plastic bus seats and fake steering wheels were all gone.

"But we always ride in the store taxi," said Veronica, as if this were my fault.

"They are all gone, sweetie," I said. "Gracie will sit up in the basket. You'll have to walk."

"But why are they all gone?"

"I'm not sure, honey," I said.

Which was, depressingly, true. It was only once we were inside and I saw the russet-colored trimmings and turkey displays that I processed the obvious: we were only a week from Thanksgiving, a fact I had all but forgotten with everything else that had been going on.

The store was packed. It didn't have the frenzied quality that kicked in before hurricanes and ice storms, but it still felt overwhelming. Everyone but me seemed efficient, businesslike, moving swiftly and decisively down the aisles, stocking their carts, and moving on like people on a mission. I wandered, unsure where everything was, backtracking, getting lost, feeling stupid, incompetent. Gracie had to be changed midway through, and I agonized over leaving my half-full cart outside the bathroom, fearing a staff member would assume it had been abandoned and would set about restocking its contents, making me start over. Add to this Veronica's constant admonitions about which brands Oaklynn used to buy, and my nerves were already ragged. As I pored over the packages of ground beef scanning sell-by dates, I heard someone say, "Hey! You're Oaklynn's friend, right?"

I turned to find a great bear of a man bent over and talking to Veronica. He was perhaps forty, pale and craggy, with a bushy auburn beard and a mane of matching hair. He wore a red plaid shirt under a windbreaker and looked like a lumberjack or a construction worker. His cart was half-full: domestic beer, toilet paper, steak, and cornflakes.

"Hi," I said.

I spoke cautiously, questioningly, so that the word was just this side of "Can I help you?"

He looked up at me and smiled broadly, guilelessly, so that by the time he had straightened up and offered me a massive hand, I had already relaxed a little.

"I'm Martin," he said, his voice a low, throaty rumble. "Martin King."

"And you knew Oaklynn?"

"Yeah, a little. I used to see her when I took my nephews to the park. She works for you, right?"

"Not anymore," I said.

"She had some things she had to fix," Veronica volunteered. "She doesn't live with us now."

"I'm sorry to hear that," the man said.

"Me, too," said Veronica. "She was nice."

"Moved on, huh?" he said, turning to me. "She still in town or . . ."

"I really couldn't say," I said. "We're not in touch."

"That's too bad," he answered, putting his hands on his hips and looking strangely downcast. I wondered with a shock of realization if he had been romantically interested in her. "Tell you what, can I give you my number? So you can have her call me if she gets in touch. If she wants, of course."

I hesitated, feeling cornered.

"OK," I said, at last. "Though I don't think I'll hear from her."

"Just in case," he said, fishing a square of lined paper with a few groceries penciled on it from his pocket. He pulled a pen from inside his windbreaker and wrote his name and number in block capitals on the bottom of the sheet, then carefully tore the strip off and handed it to me. For a big man, his fingers were deft. He smiled again as he handed it to me, and thinking he looked bashful, exposed, I did my best to smile.

"You know," I said, "if you want to find her, you might try the local Mormon church. They may have more information about where she is now."

His eyes narrowed fractionally, and he seemed to smile, but his beard was so vast that at first I couldn't read the look.

"The church," he said.

"Yeah. The one down on Carmel Road. She was a regular."

"Uh-huh." He considered me, still smiling unreadably, so that I began to feel awkward. Then he leaned in close, as if he was going to hug me. I started to shrink away, but he took hold of my wrist with one powerful hand and held me in place. I couldn't pull back as he came so close that his rough beard brushed the side of my neck. I felt an impulse to run but was struck dumb with confusion and alarm. Slowly, deliberately, he whispered, "You really didn't know her at all, did you?"

For a second as he held me, I felt only numbness and dread, powerless in spite of the crowded store. Then, while I stood frozen to the spot, he leaned away again, still holding my wrist, reading the fear in my face, still smiling blandly. Then he let go.

"It was nice to meet you," he said. "You, too, little lady."

Veronica grinned at that, oblivious to my confused panic.

I stayed where I was, trembling, blinking back tears I didn't fully understand while he walked away from his half-full cart as if it belonged to someone else, rounded the corner, and vanished. I wasn't sure what had just happened.

Ben Lodging sent his last chapter, or rather what I hoped would actually turn out to be the *penultimate* chapter, the fake ending and not the real one. We had discussed an ending in which the broken, sociopathic protagonist of the novel appeared to act out one of his murderous fantasies. We would then, however, get an epilogue revealing the previous chapter's killing to be a kind of fantasy that hadn't actually happened, so that the book would end in uncertainty about what might yet occur. As I read the latest sample, I became desperate to know that such an epilogue was still to come, because in the pages I opened that evening on my laptop, Carried, the bland accountant, became a monster responsible for a bloodbath so appalling and indiscriminate that I could barely stand to read it.

He didn't select a single victim. He laid waste to the entire cast of the book, mixing savagery with something horribly close to playfulness so that the violence of the final paragraphs was made unspeakably hor-rific because it was so casual.

I finished reading in a breathless state of revulsion and immediately sent a new email asking for the next pages, the epilogue that would take back everything I had just read, unsaying the horrors of the final chap-ter. I was suddenly sure that if such pages did not come, I would not be able to represent Ben Lodging or his book. The darkness at their heart was too great, too disturbing. I couldn't live with myself for assisting in the birth of such a nightmarish creation.

For an hour, I sat at the computer waiting for a reply, but none came.

Chapter Forty-Seven

The night-light kept the room from slipping into total darkness, but there were still hollows and pockets where Veronica was careful not to look because she couldn't be sure what was there. Even her stuffed animals had to be specially placed before bedtime because she had a special terror of seeing eyes in the shadows where they shouldn't be. In the daytime, she liked nothing more than to picture her plush rabbits and bears coming to life and frolicking around the room with Lamby, freezing when a grown-up came up the stairs so that the secret would stay hers and hers alone, but at night, even that delicious flight of fancy made her uneasy. In daylight, it was fun, a magical delight, but in the dark, it was different, horrible. Mommy said there were no such things as monsters, but she'd seen one of the books in the shelves downstairs, one of the things Mommy had dismissed as "just a scary story for grown-ups." It was red, and there was a ragged hand on it, the fingers long and pale, ending in nails like bird claws. Veronica couldn't see what the hand was connected to, but that somehow made it worse, as if the body and face attached to it were too awful to be drawn.

Still, that didn't mean it wasn't there.

She thought of that whenever she lay in bed, studying the pools of darkness that formed in the corner by the closet, under the tiny desk by the door, and the rocking chair pushed back against the wall by the window: those shadowy holes that the cheery but pallid glow of the night-light couldn't reach. She stared now, wondering what had woken her, processing the shapeless mass of blackness in the rocker.

Wasn't it bigger than it had been when she went to sleep? Didn't it look heavier, somehow, thicker?

Normally, even when the shadow was deeper, she could see the pale sleigh-like runner at the bottom where it poked into the middle of the room and caught just a few inches of the light. Tonight, there was only darkness.

Veronica shifted, half rolling, squeezing her eyes closed and burying her face in Lamby's soft underbelly, but she couldn't stay like that for long. When she checked again a moment later, the darkness in the chair was still there, all the way to the bottom. In fact, now that she looked again, she thought the darkness at the foot of the rocking chair had a shape, strange and familiar at the same time, long and dark with the merest hint of shine that—with more of the night-light's glow upon them—may have amounted to a dull sparkle off silver buckles.

Witchy shoes.

Chapter Forty-Eight

Anna

Josh left first thing. I could tell he wasn't happy about leaving me alone with the kids, and it was also clear that he wasn't looking forward to what was going to happen in New York. He felt stupid, humiliated, feelings he had never been good at processing, and he was clearly dreading seeing Kurt and Mary Beth, who may or may not be at the meeting. I had caught the look on his face while he was packing the night before—that rubbery, dead look he sometimes got, but when I asked if he was OK, he just shrugged.

"Want to talk about it?" I asked.

"Nothing to talk about," he said. That wasn't precisely true, but Josh had always wielded words like tools. Some were easy in his grasp, so familiar that using them was second nature and gave him an air of easy confidence: saws and hammers that seemed molded to his grip. But that was only when the task at hand fit easily with his talents and experience. At other times, words became clumsy, unwieldy things, great crowbars that slipped when he leaned on them, or tiny screwdrivers too small to fit his big hands. Sometimes this slightly absurd and clumsy analogy made me laugh, like when I told him that listening to him explain his response to a movie was like watching an expert car mechanic trying to fix a toilet—none of his wrenches fit, and there was suddenly water everywhere. Now it just made me sad. Actually, it reminded me of Veronica drawing, trying to copy the puppies from a jigsaw puzzle and staring at her crayoned efforts with frustrated confusion and a profound disappointment that her bandaged fingers couldn't replicate what her imagination saw. I don't think I'd ever seen self-doubt in her before, a sudden and miserable certainty that she would never be good enough at this thing she so loved to do. It was like she had aged right there in front of me, and I felt the pain of it like a knife in my heart. I hugged her fiercely, my misery long outlasting hers so that she started to look bewildered by it. I felt that now with Josh, a surge of feeling I rarely felt for someone who always had seemed so at ease and in control. It was pity and compassion, and when I hugged him suddenly from behind, in spite of everything that had passed between us over the last few weeks, I felt sure he knew as much, though he did not, could not, say so.

We parted in better spirits than we had been lately, and his word-less smile as he left, a little wan and harried at what was awaiting him in New York, was one I shared. This was one more thing we had to get through, it said, but afterward, things would begin to get better.

I set about the girls' breakfast with a lighter heart, sure that though we had not hit the worst of what was to come, we would face it together and would find a way to move beyond it. I was thinking this when, without preamble of any kind, Veronica, who had been complaining about how the cast on her arm itched, looked up brightly from her cereal and remarked, "Oaklynn was in my room last night."

⌁

"She's making it up," said Josh, sitting at the gate before his flight. "She misses her, so she's making it up."

The call had disturbed a hard-achieved calm, and he couldn't help but be annoyed. Anna knew he had enough on his mind without this kind of nonsense.

"I don't think so," said Anna. "I think she believes it."

"That's nuts, Anna. You need to be tougher with her. There's a thin line between a vivid imagination and plain lying for attention."

"I really don't think that's it. She isn't making a big deal out of it. She seems, if anything, confused. Like, she thought Oaklynn was gone, but she's not and doesn't understand why we didn't say so."

"I don't know what to tell you, Anna. Show her the basement where all Oaklynn's stuff was. Show her the key she left behind. She's got to get used to the idea that Oaklynn is gone. I know she liked her and was used to her, but that part of our life is over, and she needs to get used to the idea. OK?"

"I guess. But she seems so sure. If you could hear her say it, if you were here . . ."

"But I'm not, Anna, and I'm about to board. You're gonna have to handle this. I'll talk to her when I get home, but—"

"Speak to her now. I'll give her the phone."

Josh closed his eyes, then opened them again and watched the line forming by the gate. He checked the boarding zone on his phone.

"OK," he said. "Put her on."

There was a muffled fumbling sound. Then Veronica's voice came on, bright and clear.

"Hi, Daddy."

"Hey, sweetie. You OK?"

"Yes. I'm having breakfast. Mommy is going to make fresh toast."

He smiled at the familiar mispronunciation.

"Wow," said Josh, feeling—in spite of everything—a pang of jealousy that he wasn't home with them. "I love French toast. Listen, honey, you know Oaklynn is gone, right? That she doesn't live with us anymore?"

"I know."

"OK. So why did you tell Mommy you saw her last night?"

"'Cause she was here."

"No, sweetie, she wasn't."

"She was in my room. In the rocking chair where she always used to sit."

"I think you must have been dreaming, Vronny. Oaklynn has moved away. I know that makes you sad, but things will be OK. And now you get to spend more time with me and Mommy."

"You're not here."

"No, but I will be. I have to take this trip, and then I'll be home again."

"And you won't go away so much?"

The question stung him, even as he felt the anxiety tightening in his throat that, with his job on the line, she might get more than her wish.

"I won't go away so much," he said, meaning it. "Promise."

"OK. Can I have my fresh toast now?"

"Sure thing, sweetie. And Vronny?"

"Yes, Daddy?"

"Don't talk so much about Oaklynn to Mommy, OK? It makes her sad."

"OK, Daddy."

"Love you, sweetie."

"Love you, Daddy."

And then she was gone. For a moment before Anna came on, cautious, wanting to know what he had told her, he heard the swirling white noise of the static between them, and it felt like the sound of distance, like the mile after mile of cloudy sky between Charlotte and New York he would soon be flying through, so that for a moment he felt unaccountably lost.

Chapter Forty-Nine

ANNA

I went through the house room by room with Vronny, trying to make a game of our search to show that Oaklynn was nowhere to be found. Veronica looked under beds and in closets, calling Oaklynn's name, and—at last—laughing at the idea that she was hidden away somewhere, and at herself for imagining she had seen her.

When the phone rang, I thought it would be Josh, but I knew from the slight hesitation when I answered, the chatter in the background, that it wasn't. A part of me had been dreading a call from Mary Beth, but I knew it wasn't her either. I was just about to hang up on what I assumed was a telemarketer when a deep male voice said, "Hi, Mrs. Klein? This is Officer Randall from the Charlotte Police Department."

Given the way our last conversation had ended, I was surprised to hear from him.

"Yes," I said. "Hi. Is there news about Oaklynn?"

"Not about her current whereabouts, no."

"Have other people come forward? Previous employers?"

"No, Mrs. Klein, but they wouldn't be relevant to your situation even if they did. That's why I'm calling."

"I don't understand."

"I made some preliminary inquiries as to Ms. Durst's possible whereabouts based on the information you gave me, treating the matter initially as a missing-persons case . . ."

"Missing persons?" I exclaimed, indignant.

"Hold on there, Mrs. Klein. My point is that in the course of some routine conversation with the placement agency and the Utah church headquarters that was listed under her contacts and references, we encountered an anomaly."

"What kind of anomaly? And why are Oaklynn's previous employers not relevant to my situation?"

"Because, Mrs. Klein, you never met Oaklynn Durst. The woman those previous employers hired never worked for you. That woman, the real Oaklynn Durst, is currently on a mission trip with her husband to Japan, a trip organized by the Church of Latter-day Saints."

I stood where I was, staring blindly into the middle distance, the phone mashed against my ear, saying nothing.

"Mrs. Klein?"

"I'm still here."

"So what I'm saying is that the woman you knew as Oaklynn Durst was an impostor. We don't know who she really is or what she was doing, but she seems to have committed a pretty thorough form of identity theft of the real Oaklynn Durst's particulars: bank details, the works. We are actively looking for her, and though there's no reason to think that she will come back to see you, if she does, you need to call us right away. You understand what I'm saying, Mrs. Klein? Until we know what this woman's motives are, she should be treated with extreme caution. If you see her, don't interact with her. Keep your distance, and call 911 immediately. You got that?"

I stayed home all day, never leaving the girls, barely taking my eyes off them except to look through the windows to the road, so that Vronny took to smoothing my hair and asking if I was all right. It was a relief to put them to bed, but even then, I found myself pacing the house, flattening my face to the windows and peering out into the dark.

When I eventually went to bed, I lay awake, listening to the low hum of the baby monitors and thinking how best to purge the house of the presence of the woman who had called herself Oaklynn Durst. It was important to me that we went into the holidays free from her, and that meant getting rid of any lingering sign of her time with us, however small. Vronny would resist, but that would pass. The girls were becoming thinking, hopeful children. That meant that they were—I was almost ashamed to admit it—interesting and fun in ways they had not been as babies. They were ready to appreciate joy and wonder, and, come hell or high water, I was going to give it to them.

We would get a Christmas tree. We would trim the house and make seasonal cookies, candy, peppermint bark, and whatever else we could salvage from Josh and my inadequate holiday traditions, neither of which had exactly embraced the holiday. We had both been parts of immigrant families who regarded the Christmas fuss with a kind of studied indifference, as if it was something for other people, a quaint and mystifying delusion. Well, not anymore. I was determined to make this a special time for all of us, a family time. We'd play festive music on the radio and watch *White Christmas* and *Elf*, or whatever the kid equivalent was. Maybe we'd even go to church. Perhaps there would be a kid-friendly version of *A Christmas Carol* we could watch or read together.

I hesitated over that one. Oaklynn—or whatever her real name was—had loved Dickens. Or claimed to. Maybe that, too, was a lie.

In any case, we would close ranks against the stupid and insidious world and—above all—against Oaklynn. She had to be banished, exorcised from the house like an evil spirit.

The ceiling above me creaked. Something had moved up there in the dark space of the roof. I listened, and it came again, a groan of pressure, not the gnawing and scratching I had heard before but a shift of weight on the unfinished timbers of the attic.

Too big for a squirrel. *A raccoon? A possum?*

My stomach squirmed, but I got up and padded to the bathroom. I pulled the little Maglite from the drawer by the sink and moved softly to the bedroom door. I didn't want to wake the girls, but I was struck by annoyance and determination, a strange certainty that the time for waiting around for other people to fix my problems was over. I needed to take the bull by the horns and push things into resolution.

I needed closure.

A portion of my life was ending. I had to wrap up all the old problems and embrace the future. I clicked the flashlight on, cycled through its odd flashing settings to a solid beam, and moved silently along the hardwood floor to the hatch up into the attic, reaching up on tiptoes to pull the rope that opened the panel with the fold-down stepladder. It squealed as it dropped into position, and I shuddered at the cold of the darkness above. It seemed to flow down through the rectangular opening like liquid.

I wasn't sure what I would do if I came face-to-face with a raccoon or—worse—a possum. Hopefully, the light would be enough to spook it, send it scurrying out the way it had come in. I wondered vaguely if I should have brought the crossbow, but I couldn't load the damn thing even if I could aim it, and it was too big and clumsy to use up there, anyway. I wasn't even sure where it was.

Just the flashlight, then. And yelling if necessary. Enough to scare the thing out.

Then tomorrow I would call animal control, find a company to come and set traps or whatever they did. I didn't want poison in the house and couldn't deal with the idea of Veronica seeing some cute woodland creature being carried out stiff and dead, but one way or another it—they?—had to go. The house, though it still felt huge after our New York apartment, was, paradoxically, not big enough for anything beyond the four of us.

So I made my way gingerly up the creaking ladder, the cold dark looming above me, and I poked my head up and in, clambering awkwardly up the final steps. I kept the flashlight's narrow beam low so that I could see where the floor was solid. I had taken a couple of steps back in the direction of the bedroom, where I had heard the noise, when something struck me as strange.

I froze, trying to place the feeling, unsure whether I had heard something. It certainly hadn't been something I'd seen, since my eyes were on the plywood-paneled flooring in front of me. I looked up, splashing the tight blue-white shaft of the Maglite's beam around and finding the long metal trunk of the heating and air system, its silvery ductwork spreading out like tentacles burrowing into the cotton-candy pinkness of the insulation. The place smelled of wood and dust and . . . something else I couldn't place that touched some primal nerve center in my head and made me afraid.

There was something here.

Not a raccoon or a possum.

I fiddled with the flashlight, trying to expand its narrow beam, and in the process, somehow set it to flashing again so that the attic seemed to strobe in and out of existence. Somehow, though, my eyes made sense of what I was seeing scratched onto the joists and roof timbers crisscrossing the space, the words written over and over in a variety of pens and pencils. I stared, aghast, as I read, and the words came out of me unbidden and aloud.

"Hell is empty."

I felt the presence behind me before I heard the answering voice and turned, the Maglite still flashing the world in and out.

Oaklynn was nestled toad-like in the dark, cradling the crossbow in her powerful hands as she spoke.

"And all the devils are here."

Chapter Fifty

ANNA

"Get out of my house."

My words hung in the chilly darkness of the attic, and I was amazed by how calm they sounded, how deliberate. I felt neither. The only light was still my uncannily, maddeningly blinking flashlight, fastened as it was on "Oaklynn's" blank, washed-out face, her steady, dead eyes. I wasn't sure if she could see the way I was trembling. A terror had gripped my heart, and all I could think of was the precise distance between where we stood and the rooms where my daughters slept.

It was not nearly enough.

Oaklynn spoke, but the flashing light confused me, and her voice was low.

"What?" I said. My voice quavered, but I found a little defiance through my fear.

"I can't," said Oaklynn. She looked down at the crossbow in her hands. It looked big, dangerous. "I can't leave. There's nowhere for me to go."

I stared at her, the cold of the attic seeping into my bones like dread.

"That's not my problem," I said.

She looked up at me again and smiled a hard, bitter smile. She looked like someone I had never seen before.

"Actually," she said, "it is."

I had no idea what she meant by that and barely heard it. She was between me and the hatch with the ladder, which was the only way down and out.

"I called the police," I said.

"I know. But that was hours ago. They aren't here now."

"I can bring them back. They know you aren't who you claim to be."

"Yes?" she half turned away, as if she had heard something somewhere else in the house. "OK. I'll go to prison. If I'm lucky."

"Still not my problem."

"No. You have a different problem."

"When you're gone," I said, my eyes on the crossbow, trying to decide if it was loaded, "I won't have a problem."

She looked down again then and made a long, slow noise that was half sigh and half groan. She shook her head.

"Yes," she said, "you will."

"I'm going down now," I said, trying to sound confident.

She shook her head again, more fervently this time, and she looked up. The flashing of the Maglite was driving me crazy, but I didn't dare try to reset it in case I turned it off. I couldn't be alone with her up here in the dark.

"Yes," I said. "Step away from the trapdoor."

She didn't move, and I knew it had been a stupid thing to say, revealing how little I had to threaten or bargain with. Oaklynn was close to twice my weight. She was solid and strong. I couldn't possibly fight her.

God, I thought, my heart hammering. *Let it not come to that.*

"So if you aren't my problem," I said, stalling, "what is?"

She stared at me as if I were stupid, and her face lit with a sudden mad fury that was terrifying to see.

"Him!" she said. "Who do you think?"

I shook my head dismissively, exasperated.

"I'm going down," I said again, trying to sound like I didn't care what she did. Down meant being closer to the girls, to the phone, to the street. If it came to it, we could run . . .

"Fine," she said. "But you're going to have to listen to me."

She stepped abruptly aside, clearing my way to the ladder, and dropped her eyes once more. She looked so unlike herself that I did not know what to do. She seemed surly but also defeated, caught, quite unlike the smiling, chipper Oaklynn who had lived with us.

"I know," she added, seemingly on impulse and with an effort, as if the words were hard to find, "that I'm not right." She kept staring down the square of light that was the hatch to the upstairs hallway. "In the head. I know I'm not quite right. I can't help it. It doesn't feel wrong to me. It's just how I am. Who I am." She added that with a bleak grin at her own expense, looking sad and sour at the same time.

"You shouldn't be around children," I said.

It was probably a stupid remark, but I couldn't help myself. It just spilled out on a wave of conviction.

She nodded vaguely, as if considering this seriously, then said, "I do love them, though."

My conviction hardened, turned into something colder, angrier.

"People don't hurt the things they love," I said.

She looked back at me then, still thoughtful, as if we were debating some abstract issue or idea.

"Don't they?" she said. "Perhaps in your world. In my world, love always comes with pain. With hurt."

"That doesn't justify anything," I shot back. "My children trusted you. I trusted you."

300

She nodded again.

"I'm sorry," she said. "I really am. I never meant them any harm. Or you. But now . . ."

"You never meant them harm!?" I said, my voice rising as indignation got the better of me. "What did you think was going to happen when you poisoned my baby daughter, or drove the screw through the slide Veronica was about to use? You broke her arm! You didn't mean to hurt her? I don't care what's in your head. I don't care what happened to you when you were little, or whatever the fuck you use to justify the monster you have become, but don't stand there in front of me and say you didn't mean it."

I was trembling more than ever now, but it was less fear than it was rage, and that felt good. I thought she might attack me then, or plead some twisted justification, but she frowned and shook her head.

"I didn't poison your baby. I would never . . ."

"You think I forgot the fevers, the hospital visits? You think I'm that big of an idiot?"

She just stood there, still shaking her head, her expression fixed like an automaton.

"She wasn't sick," she said at last. "The temperatures, the bloody diapers: none of it was real. I just . . . I wanted her to see the doctor. I lied. I admit that. But none of it was real. I made it up."

"Grace was feverish. I felt her."

"I put her on a hot water bottle for a few minutes. I would never have hurt her."

I glared at her but, for a moment, could think of nothing to say.

"And the screw?" I said at last. "The swing you sawed through so Veronica would fall."

"That wasn't me."

"It was in our yard!" I shouted. "Who else would do it?"

"Carl."

I stared.

"What?"

"Carl," she said again, her voice flat. It sounded like a litany, a repeated response in church. It unnerved me, even as I refused to believe her.

"Who the fuck is Carl?" I shot back, defiant rather than inquiring. "What are you talking about?"

"Carl. We were together once. Long ago. I left. But he keeps looking to take me back."

More insanity. More evasion.

"Whatever," I said again. "I'm going down."

Wordlessly, she thrust a hand out toward me, and I flinched away, half expecting a knife to come jabbing into my midriff. But it wasn't a knife. It was a sheet of paper, creased and ragged.

"What is this?" I said, taking it from her.

"He left it for me the day you fired me," she said. She sounded chastened, her voice barely more than a whisper. "Carl left it."

"You broke my daughter's arm," I said.

"No," she said. "That was him."

I shook my head in exasperation, but before I could say anything else, my eyes fell on the piece of paper. At last, I had the composure to click the switch on the Maglite till I got a solid and wide-angled beam. I turned it onto the paper and looked at it.

It was a photograph, slightly out of focus and printed in color on a home inkjet printer. It showed, I realized, the back of our house as seen from across the creek. The focus was the swing set and the pecan tree, and there were three figures in the garden: Veronica in her yellow sundress, no cast on her arm; Grace toddling in her wake; and Oaklynn standing beside the tree, smiling. The old Oaklynn. The lie.

I would have known my children anywhere, even though their eyes were obscured by a pair of angry X's scored so deeply in red ink that the paper had puckered and torn under the pen. Their bodies had been dotted with cartoon wounds that issued grotesque spouts of blood. Under the atrocity of a picture were words scrawled in the same red capitals:

FUCK WITH MY LOVE AND I'LL FUCK WITH WHAT YOU LOVE.

It curdled my guts, leaving me sick and outraged.

"What is this?" I spat, revolted, nausea and rage jockeying for place in my trembling voice.

"I told you," she said. "Carl."

"Bullshit!" I replied, incapable of real thought, wanting nothing more than to shut it all out, to get away.

"Look at it!" said Oaklynn. "I'm in the picture. Look where it was taken from. It's him. It's Carl. He's been watching, waiting. That's why I came back. I couldn't leave the girls alone. He'll go after them. You have to believe me. I know him."

"This is crazy," I said. "I don't believe any of it. You have to leave my house. Now."

And as I said it, a new voice joined the conversation coming up from the floor below.

"Mommy?" said Veronica, sounding bleary and confused by sleep. "Who are you talking to?"

The sound of her, so plaintive and vulnerable, transformed me, sweeping away all my other anxieties and sending me into surging motion. I strode toward Oaklynn, swallowing down my trepidation at her closeness, and clambered down into the hatchway. For a second, I had my back to her, hands and feet occupied as I tried to find the steps of the ladder, utterly at her dubious mercy, and then I was stumbling clumsily down, half falling down the bottom step and into the hall.

I sucked in a relieved breath, conscious that Oaklynn was not at my heels, then snatched Veronica into a hungry embrace. Her hair was tangled, flattened against her face, and she felt clammy to my touch.

I whispered her name, squeezing her to me, and then, rubbing her eyes and still sounding dazed with sleep, she said again, "Who are you talking to?"

"It's OK, honey," I said.

She peered at me, reading my confused emotions, and her face clouded with wary seriousness.

"Come with me, OK, honey?"

She nodded once, her eyes on mine.

I went to Grace's room, picked her up, and took her to the master bedroom. I put Gracie with Veronica on the bed, my half of which was still a little warm under the duvet.

"You know how to lock the door, Vronny?" I said. "With the little latch under the handle? Remember when we played hide-and-seek and you shut yourself in the bathroom?"

She nodded but said, "I'm not supposed to."

"It's OK tonight," I said. "I'm going to go, and you should lock the door after me, OK? Don't open it again for anyone but me, you hear?"

"OK. Mommy, what's happening?"

"No one but me," I said, ignoring the question. "Not even Miss Oaklynn."

"Miss Oaklynn isn't here, Mommy."

"Well, she may visit," I said, desperation making me stupid. "But even so. You don't open the door to her, OK? Just me. You stay here with your sister, OK? No matter what."

"OK. Mommy?"

"Yes, honey?"

"Are you scared?"

It was a strange question, one she had never asked me before, and I loved her for it. I also saw how absurd it would be to deny the truth.

"A little bit," I said. "But it will be OK. I promise. But you stay here, and keep quiet as mice, OK? Gracie, too."

"OK."

The idea that Oaklynn was outside the door, that she might have already slipped away or hidden in some other part of the house smoldered in my head. I had to know where she was, to make sure I was alert and ready, between her and my kids for all her stories of crazed ex-boyfriends. Still, I snatched up the phone, my eyes locked on the door she might use. I hadn't even started to hit the keys when I realized that there was no dial tone.

Damn. Stupid, useless phone.

We should have thrown the useless thing away months ago.

I clicked it and listened again. Still nothing. And the longer I stood here, the less I knew what Oaklynn was doing.

I wanted to scream in fear and frustration, but I pushed those feelings down, replaced the glitchy handset, and put on a cheery face for Veronica.

"I'm going to go now," I said, "but just for a little while. Lock the door after me, OK? And Veronica?"

"Yes, Mommy?"

"When I leave, call the police. The phone isn't working right now, but keep trying, OK?"

I whispered it into her ear while hugging her.

"You remember how?" I said, my voice unsteady.

"911," said Veronica, stunned.

"Tell them Oaklynn is here. Do it as soon as I leave."

I kissed her, straightened up quickly, fearing I had already taken too long, and left, listening for the snap of the pathetically ineffectual lock as soon as I closed the door behind me.

I turned, glancing down the hall toward the steps up to the attic, and found Oaklynn standing there, looking at me in that odd, detached way of hers, watching me absently, like a cow in a field, vacant and uninterested. She was still cradling the crossbow. I swallowed, then forced myself to take a step toward her.

"OK," I said. "Talk fast."

Chapter Fifty-One

Carl Jennings parked the olive-green Camaro outside a half-finished house on Chilton Place that skirted the country club's golf course and took a long duffel bag from the trunk. He was pretty sure no one saw him. The car might have stood out among the Beemers, Lexuses, and Range Rovers around Myers Park, but this was the third time he had parked here, and no one had raised the alarm. The great thing about neighborhoods with lots of construction was that the streets were always dotted with beat-up old vehicles belonging to the black and Mexican bricklayers, rough carpenters, and cement spreaders who did most of the real work. Carl had taken the precaution of scraping the Trump sticker off the rear bumper, just as he had covered the swastika tattoo on his arm when he had been posing as the FBI man, Edward Flanders, or—his favorite private joke—Martin (Luther) King, amiable neighborhood uncle, but he wasn't worried.

He was, in fact, exhilarated, and not just because of the 9mm in his waistband that, paired with the shotgun and the AR-15 in the duffel, were going to make for an interesting evening. The night was cold, crisp, and quiet, but he could almost smell the sense of excitement like the distant sounds of a fairground somehow growing closer. Carl grinned, feeling the weight of the duffel as he slung it over his shoulder with a muffled clink.

A fairground, smelling of oil and funnel cake, a place of sideshows and barkers and a big old wooden roller coaster . . .

The guns in the bag felt heavy with power and purpose. With destiny.

Oh yeah. The fair was coming to town. Or did he mean the circus? Either way.

He began walking down to Sharon Road, feeling the deepening chill of the creek air, lingering for a moment in the ground under a tree till he was sure there was no traffic, then crossing the road quickly where the little bridge spanned the creek. He grinned to himself at the thought of his alter ego the FBI agent called—after the weak dick neighbor on *The Simpsons*—Edward "Ned" Flanders.

Okely dokely, neighborino. Welcome to hell.

He walked down the embankment, ducking for a moment as a solitary vehicle rolled south, but its headlights never came near him. A moment later, he was in the thick, weedy scrub of the protected greenway on the north bank of Briar Creek and pushing east. To his left were woods, thick and black and still, the highest towers of the city skyline just occasionally visible in the distance. To his right was the steep bank down to the thin ribbon of water he would have to cross in a little while, then the equally steep and slippery clay bank on the other side and the backyards of Settle Road. The scattered houses were as dark and silent as the trees.

He pushed through the stiff, dead grass and strangling vines. The scent of winter was in the air, and vegetation that had been wall-thick only a few days ago had died back noticeably.

All the better. Nothing should delay the circus . . .

Hell, he might even get away afterward.

That didn't seem to matter so much, but he had never really seen the percentage in those guys who went out and killed the wives or bosses who had been giving them shit, only to turn the guns on themselves. Seemed to him that when you finally got what you'd been dreaming about, you'd want to enjoy the victory for a while. If the cops came, they might very well take him out, though he figured he'd get a couple of them first, and that was OK. But if he could wrap things up and just walk away, why the hell wouldn't he?

He was confident, almost swaggering, and he knew that was because he wore a cloak of righteousness. Nadine—whom he had spotted from his car as she'd sneaked back into the house after the Kleins had thought her gone—was his to do as he demanded, and the mixed-race brats and their Jap mother would be sacrificed in the name of white purity.

Multiple birds, one stone. He hadn't planned it that way, but it had a kind of symmetry. It was more than just punishing Nadine now. He was part of a movement putting the world back to how it used to be. How it would be again.

Something stirred in the bushes up ahead: a deer, maybe. Still, Carl's hand went to the nine and pulled it out. There was no talking his way out of sneaking around out here that would mean he could come back another night and finish things the way he'd planned it. If anyone was dumb enough to be walking around here at this time, he'd drop them. Simple as that. Maybe the sound of shots would draw attention, and maybe it wouldn't. There were all kinds of ways a city might make noise, and this was the kind of neighborhood where if there was anyone within earshot, they probably figured it was someone else's problem. *Anyway, it'll get plenty loud soon enough*, he thought, grinning to himself again. He sure as hell wasn't going to worry about waking the locals.

This night had been a long time coming.

Chapter Fifty-Two

"My name is Nadine," said the woman who had been calling herself Oaklynn. "I used the identity of a woman I worked for in Utah so that I could start over. For a little while. Thought I would get away from him for good this time. Stupid. He always finds me."

"Who is he?" said Anna.

"My ex. Carl Jennings."

"Big guy? Beard?"

Nadine's eyes widened with shock.

"You've seen him?"

"In the store a couple of days ago," said Anna. "Said he was looking for you. He seemed quite nice at first."

"Yes. He can do that. It never lasts."

"No," Anna agreed. "He scared me."

This is surreal, she thought. She was talking to this woman whom she had hated, whom she had been terrified of only moments before, as if they were on the same side. They weren't. Couldn't be. She forced herself to be wary. And besides, the longer they talked, the sooner the police would be here.

"And he hurt you?" she said.

Nadine nodded, speechless, then sighed and said, "Over and over. For years. And I ran, and he found me and hurt me again. I ran again. And again."

"Why didn't you report him?"

"I did. I have restraining orders and warrants scattered through the Southeast," she said. "But Carl has buddies in all kinds of places. He's a guy's guy, you know? Plausible. Nothing ever sticks to him. Whereas I'm just a liar, a head case . . ."

"You were a nurse?" said Anna, a guess she had been mulling for a while.

"For a couple of years," said Nadine, managing a smile.

"What happened?"

"What always happens? Carl. Between my bruises and him threatening to give me worse if I didn't bring him the pills he wanted . . ."

"You got fired."

Nadine nodded slowly.

"He preferred it when I didn't work," she said, voice and eyes both hollow.

"Why doesn't he leave you alone?" asked Anna. "What's the point in insisting on being with someone who doesn't want to be with you?"

Nadine gave her a look. It was both disbelieving and pitying.

"He thinks he loves me," she said, shrugging.

Love.

The two women looked at each other, and that most loaded of words hung between them, stuffed full of misconceptions willful and otherwise, a word that meant everything and nothing.

"Thinks he owns me," she added, as if refining the previous statement.

"And now?" said Anna.

"He won't leave without me, but he'll punish me either way."

"By hurting me, my children?"

"It's hard to know how his mind works, especially when he's mad, and he's mad now."

"But you think . . . ?"

"He has guns. He's planning to use them."

"Against us?"

"To spite me and . . ." She hesitated, as if suddenly embarrassed. Under the circumstances, it was bizarre.

"What?"

"He doesn't like people who aren't like him."

"People who . . . ? How do you mean?"

"White people," she whispered the words, ashamed of them. "He doesn't like people who aren't white. Or people who marry outside their race."

Anna just stared, but inside she curled up a little, like a beetle shrinking in on itself and turning its hard outer shell toward the world. A decade ago, even less, this would have seemed preposterous and convenient, the rampaging ex who was also a Nazi sympathizer. But now? She thought of the quiet neighborhood they had moved into, the friendly faces at the doors and windows. She had trusted them, assumed the smiles were real.

She thought of the attic, the words scrawled all over its timbers.

Hell is empty.

"You're Ben Lodging," she said, suddenly certain.

Nadine hesitated, recognizing the weight of the question and how she might answer it. She bit her lip, then nodded, eyes downcast.

"Yes," she said.

Anna considered her as if for the first time—the book's curious, watchful tone, and its awkward, damaged, and potentially dangerous protagonist spreading through her mind like a familiar tree caught in the strange and altering light of the eclipse.

Of course the woman in front of her had written the strange and unsettling novel. It seemed obvious now. It should have scared her, this further evidence that the nanny she had brought into her home was so deep and consummate a liar, Anna thought. But the logic of the thing, its symmetry, made so much sense that she processed the news as if it filled a hole in the plot, made it complete. More than that, it touched her with something like pity for the woman, as if the lie had revealed a larger and more profound truth about who she was, her separateness from the world and its people, the emptiness she carried around with her day after day as she gazed hungrily at the happiness of others. It was as if Oaklynn—Nadine—had stepped out into that odd eclipse light, revealing the demons in her shadow as they clawed and tore at her from inside.

"OK," Anna said.

That was all, but Nadine's eyes came up in astonished, disbelieving hope, and met hers.

"Let's go downstairs."

Nadine hesitated, but Anna simply stood at the top, waiting, nodded again, and started down, moving quickly in case the other woman might reach out and push her head over heels.

At the bottom, Nadine seemed to loiter, unsure what to do next, but Anna strode briskly past her and snatched up the phone from the cabinet, thumbing it on and hitting 911. *The police should be here by now.* Maybe Veronica had not been able to get through. Maybe she had but hadn't been taken seriously . . .

Anna listened for the dial tone.

Nothing.

Anna stared at it, feeling the orange glow of its keys against her face, then turned it off and on again. She pressed it to her ear, but there was only a distant, rattling static.

It wasn't just the bedroom handset. All the phones were dead.

Chapter Fifty-Three

The creek had been cold but barely ankle deep, and though he had stumbled and slid on the clay bank reaching the house, it had felt almost comically easy.

These stupid fucking rich liberals and their absurd sense of security.

Carl had inspected the house several times over the last few days. Seeing no outside lights or signs of an external siren box, he was as sure as he could be that there was no alarm system. Not that it would make that much difference. He wasn't intending to be inside for more than a few minutes. Just enough to say his piece and make his point. Three shots would do it, though he would savor each one. If he did indeed walk away tonight, make it back to the car before the place was swarming with black-and-whites, hightail it over the border into South Carolina and down to the coast, where he could lose himself in the tangle of Lowcountry mangroves and saltwater inlets around the cabin Noah had set up for him, he would want something to think back on. Three shots would do the job, but the AR-15 gave him some rather more dramatic options, as did the shotgun, which at close range could take a head off if you aimed it just right. Tonight he was going to show Nadine the kind of horrors from which she'd never recover.

Until a little while ago, she had been the sole target. The woman had walked out on him, lied to him once too often, and she would pay in blood. It was only when he saw the Klein family to which she was so stupidly attached that Carl had begun to wonder if the punishment might not cut that much sharper and deeper if the blood spilled wasn't hers. The thought had come to him like inspiration, a little flicker of black lightning that had stopped him in his tracks with its cruel brilliance like gunfire. He'd started small, terrorizing the Klein bitch and her kids and then vanishing the evidence away just to mess with their heads, but the time for little gestures was long past. The AR-15 cut a body into pieces if you hit it enough times in the right places. Think of that. Picture Nadine watching helplessly as he sliced and diced his way through the Jap bitch and her half-breed brood, then turned around to her as the blood ran and the hair stuck in red clumps to the walls, looked her in the face, and said, "Get in the car, Nadine."

Like a scene from a movie.

And now it would be a bigger statement than just him teaching Nadine a lesson. It would be a blow struck for the cause, a white light against the gathering brown fog of irreligion and modern liberalism. Show the world that blood matters, skin matters, and if the world won't listen, show them by spilling blood and flaying skin. Then maybe they'll pay attention.

Nazi. That's what they'd call him when he made the news. He preferred *white supremacist* because *Nazi* sounded German. Ideology aside, Carl was no great fan of Hitler and the rest of those old Krauts. America had fought and beaten them, and as he liked to tell Noah, Carl thought of himself as absolutely and defiantly American.

So he had crossed the creek like a knight on crusade in the land of infidels and stood in the unguarded backyard gazing up at the house, playing it all in his head like it was a tape of something that had already happened. Then the kid had appeared at the upstairs window, no more than a silhouetted head peering down over the window ledge, and that had broken the spell. He had gone to the box on the wall and snipped the phone line with the wire strippers in his back pocket, and then he had opened the duffel and chosen.

Here comes the circus, he thought now. *Clowns and acrobats and wild, wild animals.*

He racked the slide on the shotgun, enjoying the sharp and ominous sound of it in the still Charlotte night. Then Carl Jennings climbed the steps up to the basement door, whistling softly to himself.

Chapter Fifty-Four

Anna

I ran from room to room checking all the phones, deliberately not turn-ing the lights on, in case there was someone watching from outside, but they were all just as useless. I tried my cell phone but, as usual, got no signal. I turned on my laptop, but whatever was interfering with the landline was also disrupting the Wi-Fi. We were cut off.

I didn't say so to Oaklynn—Nadine, whatever—but she didn't need telling.

"You think it's him," I said. It wasn't a question.

"Yes."

I didn't know what to do. I looked at her, unsure whether I was feeling trust or merely desperation.

"We should get out of the house," she said.

"And go where?"

"It doesn't matter. Just . . . out. Away."

She said it with such certainty, though she seemed less scared than weary, as if she had been through all this before.

"I'll get the girls," I said, turning and heading up the stairs.

Veronica opened the door at the sound of my voice.

"The phone wouldn't work, Mommy," she said. "I tried and tried."

"I know. It's OK, honey."

"Is it the man?" she said.

I blinked.

"What?" I said.

"The person you were talking to," she said. "Is it the man with the beard?"

"The man with the beard?" I echoed blankly.

"I don't like him," she confided, her voice very low, her eyes haunted. "Why was he in our yard?"

For a second, I didn't understand what I was hearing and just stared at her.

"When was he in the yard, Vronny?"

It was Oaklynn, speaking urgently as she blundered up the stairs.

"Oaklynn!" exclaimed Veronica, confused. "Why are you here?" She turned quickly to me. "Is Miss Oaklynn coming back to live with us again, Mommy?"

"Answer Miss Oaklynn's question, Vronny," I said, all other concerns suddenly out of my head. "When did you see the man in the yard?"

"Just before," she said, looking suddenly chastened. "I went to the bathroom. I looked out through the window, and he was there in the yard. Just standing. Looking up at me. I'm sorry, Mommy. Did I do wrong?"

"Did he have anything in his hands?" I asked.

"Something long. I couldn't see."

"Oh God," said Oaklynn, her voice thin. "Oh God."

I spun to face her. She was chewing her finger ends, her eyes brimming. Her face, which I was used to seeing as a mask of efficiency and determination in moments of crisis, was white and terrified. I stared aghast as she clamped both hands over her mouth like a child, as if trying to muffle the proof of her despair.

"It's OK," I said, as much to her as to the girls, gathering Grace into my arms. "We'll get in the car. We'll get a cell phone signal as we go up the hill to Harris. We'll call the police."

Nadine nodded fervently, her tears spilling down her face as she fought to bite back the sob.

"Mommy?" said Veronica. She had been brave till now, confused and wary but brave. Now she had caught Nadine's fearful apprehension, and the line of her mouth had buckled. Her eyes were wide and wet.

I stooped to her, but whatever I was going to say died in my throat as we heard the blast of a firearm and, after the numb, hollow silence that followed, the crash of the basement door being kicked in.

Chapter Fifty-Five

It was dark in the basement, but Carl knew there was no one down there, and darkness didn't bother him. The shattered door quivered on its hinges as he pushed through it, not breaking stride as he crossed the fancy hardwood and went into the hall. He tried a couple of white shell doors—a bathroom and a blue bedroom, unslept in—and then he was at the foot of the stairs and coming up, switching from the shotgun to the AR-15 that had been slung across his back as he walked.

The stair treads were a golden oak, matching the banister rail supported on perfect white spindles.

A nice house. Sophisticated but still cozy.

Well, thought Carl as he cocked the semiautomatic rifle, *we'll see about that.*

⌇

Both women knew they couldn't get the children and make it down the stairs without meeting the gunman in the hall, so escaping in the car was out of the question. They also knew that the puny indoor locks would give way to a rough charge of the big man's shoulder, never mind the force of the arsenal he had surely brought with him. Veronica had picked up the flashlight and was clicking it on and off absently, her eyes on her mother. It wasn't producing a steady glow but the same intermittent flashing it had been doing before—three long blinks, then three short ones, then three long ones, over and over, unstopping. Anna was dimly aware of it, a needling annoyance on the edge of her consciousness as she tried to decide what to do. Nadine had sunk to the floor, hands still clasped over her mouth, defeated: a sacrificial lamb waiting for the slaughterer. The crossbow lay discarded at her feet.

"Can you load that?" Anna demanded.

Nadine looked up at her, blinking vaguely, as if Anna had spoken to her in another language.

"Load it!" Anna shouted.

The urgency in her voice acted on the other woman like a slap. She started, then looked at the crossbow as if she had never seen it before.

"Quickly!" yelled Anna. "Do it."

She could hear the man in the hallway downstairs. He was whistling. It sounded like "Born in the U.S.A."

Nadine got awkwardly to her feet, stood the crossbow up, and slid one shoe into its stirrup, fishing the rope-cocking device from a pocket. Anna watched her lace the cord around the butt and hook it to the drawstring.

"Hurry!" she said. The Maglite in Veronica's hands was still flashing—three long, three short, three long . . .

Morse code.

It was an SOS programmed into the flashlight! She snatched it from her daughter's hands and rounded the bed to the window at the front of the house, propping the Maglite up against the frame as best she could. She took her hand carefully away, and it stayed, blinking their cry for help.

Not that anyone would see it. The sleepy neighborhood that had seemed so idyllic suddenly felt remote and abandoned. No one would see. No one would come.

"Loaded," said Nadine.

She had fitted an arrow from the three-shot quiver. She looked wary, uncertain, as if the very act constituted a defiance that felt desperately bold, wrong, holding the weapon away from her body as if she was afraid of it. Anna just looked at her.

"OK," she said.

Chapter Fifty-Six

The woman had been on Officer Paul Randall's mind all day. He had sat in her house and listened to her talk about her psycho nanny, and he had only made notes for the look of the thing. When his sergeant had asked him if there was anything to the complaint, he had shaken his head and made some dismissive remark about Myers Park women with too much time on their hands. But then the call had come through about how the real Oaklynn Durst was out of the country, and it had all started to look very different. He had called to warn the Klein woman, but his failure to trust her instincts worried him, made him restless. He made a few more calls, and that was when things got weird.

Turns out, he wasn't the first law enforcement officer to be asking around after Oaklynn Durst lately. He spoke to Nurture, the placement agency, again, then to the church, and finally to the neighbors. They gave him the name of the Dursts' former housekeeper, one Nadine Clark, and of a bearded FBI agent who had shown up a few weeks ago, asking about them. Randall began hunting employment records for Nadine Clark—an identity that seemed to wink in and out of existence over the past decade as she moved from Georgia to Missouri and finally to Utah, employment records spanning day-care facilities, clinics, and hospitals, but always in short-term positions. He called their HR departments and got a checkered history of good work intersected with unreliability, absence, and the whisper of domestic abuse. When he managed to speak to people who had actually worked with her, he got more reports of the mystery FBI man who had been asking about her over the last few months, a big guy with a beard. One of them had a name and badge number.

Edward Flanders.

It was fake. The FBI had no record of such an agent or anyone in the organization past or present matching that name.

The guy had moved around hospitals, day-care facilities, nursing homes, and the like for months, never dealing with HR or anyone higher up in the organization who might run his credentials, relying on a smile and a chatty demeanor. He made everything look low-key, so almost no one followed up, and those who did, figured they'd gotten his details wrong. It was smart, but it was also indicative of someone playing a very long game, and that was worrying.

Then Randall had played a hunch. He went through Nadine Clark's file and pulled the ex against whom she had a restraining order: one Carl Jennings, an electrician by trade with a string of arrests for possession and domestic abuse, as well as various public-disturbance charges keyed to Nazi and other white-supremacist rallies.

White supremacist?

Maybe this wasn't what Randall had thought it was at all.

He called Mrs. Klein but got no reply and no answering service. He didn't have enough to merit drastic action, though he forwarded Jennings's details to the FBI, anyway. They might not think a manhunt worth the effort, but they'd want to follow up on the agent-imperson-ation charge. He checked his watch. Twenty minutes to one in the morning. Too late to drop by with nothing more than a warning. Still. He told Dispatch he was making a routine follow-up visit and got in his car. He was on Settle Road in twelve minutes. He'd just stop by. He wouldn't even leave the car. Just look, then sit for a while, till he was called elsewhere. Just in case.

The street was quiet, and the few houses were dark, save for the Klein house, where a light blinked in an upper window. *Some manic early Christmas decoration*, he thought, though it was more annoying than it was jolly, flashing away like that in a steady, regular pattern of long beats, then short, then long again . . .

Randall snatched his radio to his mouth, gave his call sign, and requested immediate assistance, thumbing on the cruiser's flashers as he did so. He gave the operator the address and said he would go in ahead.

"Negative," said the dispatcher. "Wait for backup."

"There isn't time," said Randall. "Get here fast."

And then he was out of the car and running to the front door.

Chapter Fifty-Seven

Carl felt like the big bad wolf from the fairy tale. He knew the little piggies were upstairs, hunkered down in the bedroom, sweating out their fear, squealing and helpless. It was almost funny.

Weird, he thought, how all the weeks of cold rage, the who-the-fuck-did-she-think-she-was rants delivered to no one as he drove half-way across America and back, could turn into this calm amusement now that push had come to hard shove. As Edward Flanders, FBI, he had gotten into the habit of being so careful, he didn't even admit what he was doing to himself. Now that he could be Carl again, it was like taking off a mask that had been hot and hard to breathe through. Now he felt free.

Free and clear.

Yes. He knew what he had to do. He could see it all like it had already happened.

He set his foot on the first step to the upper floor, the rifle held almost casually in front of him, and he wanted it all to slow down so that it wouldn't be over just yet. He looked around the place, knowing he would remember every detail, every picture on the walls, every arty knickknack and stick of furniture, taking step after careful step. That was why he had put the lights on. Partly, it was to make sure that those who knew the house better than he did didn't have an advantage as they moved around it, but mostly it was so it would all be burned into his memory forever in vivid detail.

What did the old movies say? *Filmed in fabulous Technicolor.*

Yeah. That was what he wanted.

So he took his time, savoring each step. Listening to the sounds of their frantic feet and sobbing in the room above him. He was only halfway up the stairs when the doorbell rang.

He turned.

There was a cop out there. Carl could see him in the long window by the door. A black guy at that. And beyond him, out in the dark street, was the strobing of blue lights.

It was impossible. How the fuck could they be here already?

For a second, Carl just stared. Then all his calm burned away, and there was only the old fury, the outrage that he might not get what he wanted. What he deserved.

He aimed the rifle at the door and opened fire.

Chapter Fifty-Eight

Officer Paul Randall saw the bearded man through the window a fraction of a second before the first shot shattered the wood of the door. He was there under the bright hallway lights, big as life and armed to the teeth. Randall saw the muzzle flash before the sound, before the door broke apart in a shower of fragments as the rifleman fired shot after shot through it.

Randall leaped sidewise, but there was no cover on the porch, and the front yard was small and open, all lawn, ground cover, a barren cherry tree, and a solitary dogwood. He hadn't been hit yet, but it was only a matter of time.

He dropped back, drawing his service weapon and squeezing off two quick shots at the doorframe, his heart pounding. He was massively outgunned.

The barrel of the rifle pushed through one of the smashed door panels, and for a second, Randall saw the face of the bearded man searching for him in the dark. Randall fired again, but the shot only gave away his position. There was another explosion of sound, and Randall felt the bullet rip the pistol from his shredded hand. He only realized that two fingers had been torn off at the knuckle when he looked.

He almost dropped but had just enough presence of mind to skulk back, doubled over, clutching his bleeding hand. The darkness of the street was his only hope. The car wouldn't protect him from a weapon like that whose rounds would go through the doors and out the other side, but if he sheltered behind the engine itself . . .

There was another burst of shots. Three, four, each less than a second apart, but unfocused, wild, like the shooter didn't care what he hit.

Randall pushed at his collar-mounted radio with his good hand as he loped away, knowing he was losing a lot of blood, feeling the shock and adrenaline threatening to overwhelm him.

"I'm hit," he managed. "Officer down. Repeat, officer . . ."

But then there was another burst of gunfire from the doorway, which made the windows of the police car explode, and he said no more.

Chapter Fifty-Nine

ANNA

The noise of the gun was deafening, hellish. Grace began to wail. Veronica's weeping was quieter but somehow worse. It had no performativity, no hope for comfort or attention. It was all dread and horror and hopelessness. We all felt it. I looked out the bedroom door and down to where the gunman stood at the foot of the stairs, aiming into the night. Then I felt Oaklynn—Nadine—push past me and raise the crossbow.

One shot. We had one shot.

I realized too late that he had seen us reflected in the window by the door, realized only as he turned, dropping to one knee and firing. I saw the flash of the gun through the acrid, smoky haze, and I shrank back even as Nadine cried out. The arrow slammed into the door behind him, piercing the wood almost to the flights. Then we were falling back into the bedroom, dragging the door pointlessly closed behind us, Nadine gasping in pain.

The bullet had caught her just below the elbow of her right arm. It wasn't a clean hole, as I would have expected, but a mess of chewed-up tissue. There was blood everywhere, and when I leaned in to see, I caught an alarming flash of ragged whiteness that I feared was bone.

The shooting downstairs had momentarily stopped, but it was replaced by the bearded man's voice, loud and flat.

"See what you made me do, Nadine?" he roared. "Know what I'm gonna do next?"

He paused, as if waiting for a reply, then added, quieter, "Yeah, you do. And you know what else? It's your fault. *Everything* that happens here tonight is on your head. Don't you ever forget that."

Nadine had collapsed into a kind of crouch again, childlike, her face haunted by more than pain. She gave me an appalled look that was full of something like entreaty.

"Veronica," I said, turning to my eldest daughter. "Take Gracie into the bathroom and get in the bath."

It wouldn't offer much protection as the bullets started flying around, but it might keep them alive for a moment, at least till he decided to target them directly.

Don't think about that.

"Nadine," I said, turning to her, "can you reload the crossbow?"

I knew the answer before she gave it. Her right arm was useless. I picked it up, anyway.

"In here," I said, pulling her up and after the girls into the bathroom. I closed the door and, again, put on the useless lock. We moved between the toilet and the twin sinks, and then I tried to pull the drawstring of the crossbow. It wouldn't move more than a few inches.

"Help," I said.

She seemed to think about it, to decide, then set her teeth and stamped down on the stirrup. I laced the cocking rope through and hooked it in place, as I had seen her do, while she held her ragged, dripping right arm away from her, as if afraid to look at it.

"I'm coming in now, Nadine," said the man at the bedroom door. He said it almost tenderly, but there was a bitterness underneath the tone that made my stomach tighten and my skin creep.

I nodded at Nadine, not daring to speak, and together we pulled, me with both hands, her with just her left. The drawstring moved six inches, nine, but wouldn't go all the way. I held it as long as I could but couldn't get it closer to the latching mechanism, and released it, panting, tears running down my face.

The bedroom door was shouldered open. It sounded like it was inches away. He burst in.

"Hiding under the bed, Nadine?" he speculated.

"Again," whispered Nadine.

I didn't think I could, but I tried. I felt his presence like a shadow, dark and eclipsing, squeezing me out of my life, swallowing up my children.

"Pull," I said.

The drawstring moved up, struggled, surged another inch, and latched. I snatched an arrow from the quiver and slammed it in place. I glanced at Nadine, but she had crumpled on the tiles. I fumbled for the safety catch, and in that instant two shots rang out. The bathroom door juddered and split. The door of the shower stall opposite exploded in a million shards of glass, stinging and slicing like grit and razors, and then he was in.

For a split second, his eyes flashed around the room, finding his target, and in that endless fraction of a moment, I lifted the heavy bow and fired.

Chapter Sixty

Nadine had been broken long before Carl's bullet shattered her arm. She knew that. She had thought herself beyond healing, beyond even the will to want it. She was broken and always would be.

Then there was the arrow, a shaft of carbon with rubbery flights sculpted like feathers and a hard steel tip. It hit him on the left side of his chest, sliding in under the stock of the rifle he was going to use to butcher the family who had taken her in, the family she had lied to over and over. She saw the surprise on his face, the indignation, and before the rage could come back into his eyes, she moved.

He wasn't dead. He was stunned and momentarily incapacitated, but he would be up again. He would always be up again.

He had slumped against the wall, his eyes wide. The arrow had gone deep, almost through, and for a moment, he looked at it, baffled, stupid, as if wondering how it had gotten there, outraged that these women had shot him. Nadine kicked him hard between the legs, kicked the rifle away from his clutching hands, and drew the pistol from his waistband.

She was conscious of Anna grabbing her screaming daughters and pushing past her, out into the bedroom and downstairs, but she could only see him and the gun in her hand as she pressed it to his neck.

She swallowed up his rage and made it hers. She was fury, justice, vengeance, death itself. The gun gave her power.

Nadine stood there for a long moment, feeling the pistol in her hand like a question mark, decisions fighting for attention in her head, the past—her past—lining up in front of her where she could see it, yelling at her, telling her what she was and what she was not.

And then there was Anna at her elbow, coming back for her, reaching out and putting her hand on the gun with pressure that was so gentle, it was almost a caress. They took the guns with them, Anna's arm around Nadine's broad shoulders, out and down to where the girls were waiting at the splintered front door, then out to where the wounded policeman was leaning across the hood of his car, waving them toward him with a ragged, bandaged hand, his handgun ready.

Even as she ran, Nadine twisted her face back toward the house where Carl lay sprawled but still breathing, still alive.

Chapter Sixty-One

The pain had knocked him down, but Carl Jennings was used to pain. It was hot and savage, but the arrow had not hit his heart, and though he knew he was bleeding heavily, he felt only a shortness of breath. He tried to get to his feet but found that the motion rolled him so that the arrow shaft brushed the ground, sending another bolt of agony through his chest.

It was going to have to come out.

He grasped it with both hands, braced himself, and pulled, roaring like a wounded lion. The crossbow bolt was slick with blood, but it moved. For a second, the surge of pain and nausea threatened to send him spinning into unconsciousness, but he fought for control, breathed, and dragged it free. The arrowhead was smooth and rounded, a target arrow rather than a hunting piece with the triangle razor-edged tip designed to stay in place.

Lucky for him. Not for them.

The arrow would leave a straight hole that might become infected and may have done other damage he couldn't see, but it wasn't like what a bullet would do. He was bleeding heavily, but he figured that if he could get out, he'd live.

Get out. Go back the way he came, through the backyard, and across the creek. If he could get back to the car before the police closed the roads, he was as good as free.

He could come back for Nadine another day. And the Kleins. It was the Jap bitch who had shot him, after all.

So he rolled to his knees, blood pattering onto the fancy tiled floor, and then he was up and staggering. There was no sign of life in the bedroom or in the hallway. At the foot of the stairs, the front door hung open. They'd gone.

Carl grasped the handrail and shambled down the stairs as fast as he dared. There was still only one car out front, its lights going, but he thought he could hear distant sirens. He didn't have long.

He made for the basement steps, conscious that his breathing was getting shallower as he forced his body to work. The pain on his left side wasn't constant but sharpened with each breath. For the first time since the evening had begun, Carl felt a spike of panic. This wasn't just blood loss and pain. The arrow had done something else.

He half fell down the last steps, leaving bloody handprints on the blue walls and misjudging his steps as his head seemed to fill with fog and anxiety. But the cops were at the front. He still had time.

He barreled out of the basement door and into the cold night. The sirens were louder now, closer, but the backyard was still, dark and empty. He made for the steps down from the deck, but his lungs felt tighter than ever, no matter how hard he gulped the frigid air. He couldn't get enough. He was panting, sucking in the night.

Something's wrong . . .

His feet fumbled on the steps, and this time he did go down, tumbling painfully into the grass at the bottom. It was harder to get up now. He couldn't stand tall but loped, apelike, doubled over, his breathing ragged, painful and uneven.

The lyrics from "Born in the U.S.A." cycled through his head. The chorus, at least. He only knew the chorus. But it worked like a battle cry and gave him focus, energy.

He rolled over the fence into the weeds, then slipped and fell down the slick bank into the creek. The landing was silty and wet, but it drove the air from his lungs anyway. The blackout that he sensed was hunting him almost had its way at last. Another agonizing gathering of his waning strength, another half crawl, this time through the chilly water to the other side, and then the rearing, stamping pain as he fought to haul himself up the north bank.

Carl Jennings's scattered mind fought to find something to hold on to, some sliver of hope. If he could get to the road, to the car, if he could sit and stem the bleeding, he could force himself to drive. He had to stay awake, to keep breathing.

But that was hard. His chest felt like something huge was straddling him, crushing him down into the weeds. Perhaps if he rested for a moment, got his breath back, he could make the final push to the car.

Dimly, he realized there was sound coming from the tall dry grass only yards from where he had collapsed, panting. It was the sound of movement, stealthy and careful.

Can't be the cops, he thought wildly. *Not yet. Not here.*

And in truth, it didn't sound like people. It certainly didn't smell like them. He was processing this vaguely, that strange animal musk, when the first wolfish head poked watchfully through the weeds, its hard eyes fixed on him. Then another and another, muzzles wet, jaws lolling. They were brown, bat-eared, and lean as foxes, but their eyes were steady and appraising. He could sense their hunger.

Carl tried to raise a hand to fend them off, but then the first coyote was tugging at the flesh of his leg, and as he tried to kick, sit up, and lash out, he succeeded only in rolling onto his back and exposing his throat, so that his dying cries were lost to the eerie chorus of their howling.

Chapter Sixty-Two

ANNA

Two months later

Mary Beth and Kurt moved out without speaking to us again. I guess there are some things you can't unsay. I tried not to care, and a part of me was genuinely glad not to have to face them after all that had passed between us, but it still made me sad. I didn't feel responsible, but it was impossible not to feel that something I had thought was basically good about our move to Charlotte had turned out to have been tarnished from the start.

Strange that I thought of it at all, really, given all the other things that had happened.

Carl Jennings's body was found in the early hours of the morning after the attack. Cause of death was cited as blood loss and severe damage to his airway inflicted by wild animals, pursuant to a tension pneumothorax, the lower lobe of his left lung having been perforated by an arrow fired from a crossbow and subsequently removed, aggravating the injury. This was relayed to me not by Officer Randall, who was now considered a witness as well as a victim, but by the homicide detective who led the case. His name was Neale. I listened and said nothing. I had already told him that it was me who'd fired the crossbow, though Nadine and I, in a curious moment of desperate solidarity, had loaded it together. There were no secrets to keep about what had happened that night, or in the months leading up to it.

Still, I had never killed a man before, and though Neale tried to suggest that I still hadn't, I knew differently.

Nadine was arrested for her various offenses, mostly connected to identity theft, though there might yet be charges emerging for wasting hospital time and resources. It seemed unlikely that her namesake—the real Oaklynn Durst—would press charges, given that Nadine hadn't actually stolen anything from her but her name. Nadine was also keeping no secrets, and the police seemed to think that she would get away with a suspended sentence, given the duress she had been under. As her personal history came out, it even seemed possible that she might not be prohibited from working in child services. I didn't know if they could mandate therapy, but she had voluntarily registered for a course of treatment, though whether she was curable was anyone's guess.

"They say that admitting you have a problem is the first step," she said with a wan smile when I went to visit her.

We sold her book at auction a month after the case hit the headlines. She is in the process of revising it, making the protagonist a woman and, at my suggestion, not an accountant but a nanny. Whether she'll see jail time or not is unclear, but if she does, she'll come out to a healthy nest egg and publishers lining up to see if she has more than one book in her. At first, I was wary of capitalizing on such a painful and personal experience, but as Josh observed, we'd already lived through the crap. If someone wanted to give us money as a result, who were we to argue? Actually, the acclaim I felt was coming for the book might do as much for Nadine as any therapist could. The more I talked to her, the more I saw how rarely she had ever been praised for anything other

than helping other people, being the giver of care. That she was about
to earn something for herself for once seemed long overdue.

This is not to say that we were suddenly bosom friends. I was still
wary of her, alert to the distance and calculation I had recognized in her
from the book's original incarnation, and though I felt sorry for her, I
worried that some kinds of damage could not be completely undone.
I believed her when she said she had come to love my daughters and
would never have hurt them, but she had, if nothing else, used them
to her own ends, and I wouldn't forget that in a hurry. If she stayed out
of prison, we would stay in touch, and she would be allowed to see the
girls—which they all wanted—but I would watch. I had been a half
second away from losing them. I would not take such a chance again.

As for me, I felt that I had emerged from the moon's shadow and
stepped back into my own life. I hugged my kids, loved my husband, did
my work, and felt, I suppose, a kind of happiness I had not experienced
before—a simple contentment that came from the way things were, not
from what might yet be. But if the events two months ago had taught me
anything, it's that I cannot know the hearts of people. The man in the grocery store who chats to my daughters might want people like me gone from
this country and is prepared to do his part to make that happen. They know
to hide their swastikas. Some of them don't even know they have them.

I do.

I've seen them. I cannot know their hearts, but I have learned the
kind of wary and watchful distance that is, at its core, untrusting and,
for all its defiance, fearful, and not just for my life or that of my family.
I fear for the people we have become, the country we live in, and the
future we are permitting to evolve. So I hold on to what I value all the
tighter, grip it closer to me, and in spite of all the fear, that is also an act
of defiance, faith, and even love. It is, I continue to believe as I sit down
with my daughters to read together, the one thing that might save us.

Acknowledgments

Thanks to Doctors Darin Kennedy and Phaenarete Osako; Janine Spendlove; Shellie Kingaby Hyser, Kerra Bolton, and Stacey Glick; as well as to Alicia Clancy and all at Lake Union.

About the Author

Andrew Hart is one of the pseudonyms of *New York Times* bestselling and award-winning author A.J. Hartley. His twenty novels straddle multiple genres for adults and younger readers, and they have been translated into dozens of languages worldwide. As Andrew James Hartley, he is also the Robinson Professor of Shakespeare Studies at the University of North Carolina, Charlotte. His website is www.ajhartley.net.